Anna and Christopher,

Yol Bolsun! (may there be a road)

# H. Jane Harrington

# Valoria's Honor

H. Jane Harrington

## Book Two of The Guardian Vambrace

Tumbleweed Crossing Publications®

Valoria's Honor

Copyright © 2011 by H. Jane Harrington

All rights reserved. No part of this book may be used or reproduced
in any manner whatsoever without written permission, except in the
case of brief quotations embodied in critical articles and reviews.
This is a work of fiction. All characters and events are products
of the author's overactive imagination. Any resemblance to actual
events or persons, living or dead, is purely coincidental,
and would be pretty darn hilarious.

---

ISBN-10: 1466373911

ISBN-13: 978-1466373914

---

Cover art and illustrations by H. Jane Harrington

www.guardianvambrace.com

Tumbleweed Crossing Publications®

For Andy and Haddie,
my own little Guardians

And to Terry,
for it all.

# Also by H. Jane Harrington

## <u>The Guardian Vambrace series</u>

Ithinar's Bloom
Valoria's Honor

As man is a fragile being, born of divinity but mortal still, the royal avatar of justice was consumed by the power of the Kion and his soul rent asunder. For no mere mortal can tame the fires of the Gods. And the Gods created for him an equalizer, to balance him.

Excerpt from
*The Book of Order,*
*King Loran Edition*

# Sanctuary

**\* \* \***

-1-
# Flight of the Guardian

*Don't be so focused on the rabbit hunkered before you that you overlook the wildcat crouching behind.* - Master Kozias

Brainy wordsmithies who fancied up scenes of the heroic chase had hit the target smack on. The escape was just like in those plays and stories—electrifying and wild, teased with the promise of glory. It painted the innards with a fiery animal yearning—a heart-stuttering thrill, like high-walking the edge of a cliff and looking down. It coated the tongue with the flavor of life and elation.

The wiry old sot Master Kozias had once said, "Many a snake has perished at the chompers of a desperate mouse." Kir Ithinar took heart in her master's drunken sermonizing. She wasn't accustomed to playing rodent, but her chompers could easily be turned tailways toward her pursuers. The trick was, finding the right place to stage her ambush.

And so, Kir ran.

It would have been easier if the ground weren't a muddy bog. It would have been easier if the ferns weren't tickling her legs as she tore through the moist brush. And it would have been easier if the path was anything more than a glorified deer trail.

But then, *easy* was as dry as dust. Kir welcomed a good challenge, and she was adept at finding the tactical advantage in any landscape. It was just such that towered before her, as though seeded there by the Seven Gods themselves for the just answer to Kir's asking. An oversized black gum tree, with branches that hung low over the trail, was exactly the kind of position she needed.

Kir planted her boot into the soft earth to mark a good eye-catcher, then sprang for the gum and shoved her toe into a knotty scar. Hoisting herself skyward, she scurried up the branches with feline silence. She had always been good at stealth. It was, in point of fact, the single tidbit of praise that Master Kozias had given during the entirety of her warrior training. That one shining moment, followed by a series of profanity-laced whacks for startling the ale onto his lap.

Finding a substantial branch to accommodate her weight, Kir inch-wormed on her belly along the leafy length until she was properly positioned over the trail.

Give them another five minutes or so and the trackers would be upon her. Or under her, more like. Technicalities, the Crown Prince had told her, could make or break diplomacy.

Kir cocked a lopsided grin at the thought. Unlike her sovereign, she found the most effective tool of negotiation to be of the shiny steel variety. "I got my own brand of diplomacy right here," she muttered under her breath, slowly drawing her Guardian sword from its dragon-embossed lumanere scabbard.

She remained still as a cat on the crouch, eyes scanning for any trace of movement through the moist landscape. Finally, a ripple tousled the fronds of a fern. A gleam of light flashed on a blade easing through the underbrush.

Kir's antsy fingers tightened around the hilt of her sword.

A mop of mussed blond corn silk bobbed and sky-blue eyes scanned the spoor. The tracker paused to examine Kir's intentional track in the soft loam, then eased onto the firmer soil of the open trail.

Studying the young man from her perch, Kir felt a tingling right down to the lining of her soul. She fought her breath to stillness and waited for the proper moment to strike. Her heart dance quickened pace with each careful stride of his foot.

When he was directly below, Kir thrust her Guardian sword downward. She whacked the pursuer sharply across his back with the flat of her blade. He stepped forward awkwardly, shoulders sagging in defeat.

"Gotcha," Kir chimed. She wrapped her legs around the limb and swung backward, hanging upside down with arms crossed in self-satisfaction.

"The object was for me to find *you*, Kiri," Vann scolded.

Kir held an inverted finger to his lips and shushed him. "You can't talk. You're dead."

Vann shook his head and his eyes creased with amusement. "I suppose this exercise has become a lesson in humility, rather than practice in tracking a target. You're certainly adept at breaking the rules of a game."

Kir flipped from her perch, landing softly before the Crown Prince. "When you're hunting a rodent, be sure you're not tracking a wildcat, instead, Stick. Real foes never play by rules."

"Hunter becomes the hunted? I wish I could do the same to High Priest Galvatine. I've been playing the role of rabbit to his Shadow Mages for almost fifteen years. If only I could show *them* what it's like to run for survival," Vann said through a sigh.

Kir sheathed her Guardian sword and leaned back against the tree. If only she could grant Vann that wish. On the run since the age of three, the prince had never known the security that most people took for granted. Galvatine had enlisted a terrorist group called the Keepers of Magic (or Shadow Mages, to the common), to hunt Vann like a dog, taking away any chance he might have had for a normal childhood. And all for some dusty old prophecy that named him the future Chaos Bringer. Kir didn't buy the claim for an eyeblink. Vann didn't harbor even a smidgen of evil in his pure soul, and there was no way he could ever be the force that would ultimately destroy Order.

Kir would relish the opportunity to introduce Galvatine to her Guardian sword, in payment for the years the shriveled wencher had stolen from Vann. But then, Kir fancied herself something of a new woman. She had given up the role of assassin when she met Vann and became his Guardian. She didn't want to revert back to her old hatred. Still, if given the chance, she wouldn't hesitate to put the point of her blade through Wrinkles' old belly.

"One day, Stick. Tides always turn. But right now, we have a game to finish, and so far, the rabbit's winning." Kir grinned cockily.

"Go on, Kiri. Catch your wildcats. I'll head back to camp," Vann said.

"By your lonesome?"

The Keepers believed Vann dead, thanks to a brilliant conjuring of Prophetic and Psychonic vision cast by Queen Palinora, but that didn't mean he would be completely safe on his own. They were on the outskirts of the wetlands, which presented a whole new variety of danger. From hazards like snakes and alligators, to the unnatural beasts called kaiyo, like kappas and malcravens.

"Fear not, Guardian Ithinar. I will continue to accompany His Majesty," a voice came from the trail behind Vann.

"Grand Master Ulivall," Kir greeted as he emerged from the brush.

Ulivall's shimmery golden chest was bare and he wore a loose article called a *pantling* from waist to thigh. Two circular blades hung from a pouch at his hip. Like most full-blooded Dimishuans, he had black hair and red irises. The man's well-muscled physique didn't lie about the measure of his might. After witnessing his prowess in their battle with the cloakers two days past, Kir could understand why Ulivall had been chosen as the leader of the Hilian forces.

"His Majesty performed well on this exercise. His eye for detail is quite impressive," Ulivall stated.

"He beat his own Guardians in this challenge, for dandy-sure. Though they're probably closing in. I'd best get a move-on before they catch up. Thanks for looking out for him, Grand Master," Kir thumped her fist to her chest in salute. She turned to Vann and grinned mischievously. "We'll be along shortly. I won't prolong their humiliation."

## -2-
## The Character of the Crown

*You never know where a man's principles will fall until you back him into a corner.* - Master Kozias

Vann stepped lightly in Ulivall's tread as they hiked for camp. Having just broken the edge of the marshy woods into a grassy field of rolling hills, they were to skirt the tree line for another league.

The royal party had been bivouacked on the edge of the

wetlands for two days, allowing for rest and recuperation following their desperate battle with the Keepers of Magic. The crossing of the Hilian border represented Vann's first diplomatic mission. Although he had not yet been recognized officially by the court, he stood to represent it nonetheless. The Hilians had been sheltering his mother for months, and Vann had a huge debt to repay for their kindness. He intended to earn their friendship, garner their support, and bridge the gap between their peoples. He was an accomplished stage actor. It shouldn't prove to be all that difficult for one of his experience.

Vann's adopted father, Inagor Arrelius, had kept him and his Guardians on their toes, utilizing the downtime for training exercises. Inagor was obviously enjoying the communion with others of his kind. As the sole Guardian to Vann's mother, Inagor had been fourteen years without peers. Guardianship involved a brotherhood and Inagor's situation, being a solitary Guardian, was rare.

Unlike his mother, who was perfectly content with one Guardian, Vann had acquired, through happenstance, three. In only a few months, Kir, Scilio and Malacar had become more like family than protectors.

As he walked, Vann began planning out a rough strategy for his Hilian approach. The first order of business was to form a friendship. Thus far, the Hilian delegates in the entourage had been polite, but distant. They were respectful of Vann's title, almost to a fault, which created a chasm that Vann desperately wanted to cross. There was no way to establish a bond across cultural lines if the chasm remained. Ulivall, as the leader of the Hilian military forces, would be a great place to start building a bridge.

"You seem young for so high a rank," Vann noted. The Hilian only appeared to be in his mid-thirties.

"I suppose I am, by the standards of your people," Ulivall replied simply.

"Might I ask how you came to be so phenomenal a warrior?"

"With practice."

Vann nodded absently. This man was almost as aloof and taciturn as Kir had been upon their first meeting in the Hatchel Forest. "Did you train with a Master Warrior?"

"I was on the receiving end of other mens' training," Ulivall replied. "Despite that, your father's army trained me well."

Vann blinked in surprise at such an unorthodox upbringing. The Dimishuans were a slave race; it was taught they had been gifts of the Gods; their very existence was wrapped around service to the Septaurian people, or Alakuwai, in their language. It was a belief woven into the very fabric of society and the seams of religion. He could not fathom the acceptance of a Dimishuan soldier in the Septaurian Army. Many masters did not even allow their slaves to read, let alone hold a weapon. "I mean no disrespect, but I've never heard of a Dimishuan serving as a soldier."

"Serving as a target is more accurate. I was forced to fight to win my life and daily bread, and so I did."

"They risked their valuable property just to train warriors?" Vann spoke without thinking.

"Valuable? Training dummies always wear a collar. Dimishuan, indentured servant, criminal—we all look the same in the eyes of the Crown. There is always a readily available supply of collars and necks to wear them. There is nothing of value in an expendable target."

Vann shuddered to his bones, despite the heat. "That's unconscionable. On behalf of the Crown—"

"Please do not speak for the Crown on this matter, Your Majesty," Ulivall interrupted. "You are in no real position to apologize for past grievances committed by kings and dead men."

Vann realized an opening in Ulivall's bitter statement. If he was to befriend the man, the time was now.

"You are correct. Therefore, I am looking to the future, rather than dwelling on the past. I hope your people understand that I am not my father. I extend an open hand to you. And never will it hold a blade."

Ulivall was silent for a moment. "But it may yet still hold key to a collar."

"Not all Alakuwai believe in collaring men. No matter their origins, debt or crime. When I sit in my father's chair, things will be different," Vann promised. "Please trust me in this."

Ulivall was silent for so long, Vann didn't think he was planning to speak again. Finally, he said, "Trust is not so easily dispensed. Words come easy to a man's lips that often die in the field of action."

"I would bargain my soul to the Gods for your trust. In days to come, I will bargain it to your people, instead."

"If you plan to bargain, be sure to do so in blood. Our people find the value of Alakuwai trade to be cheap."

"I know. I have a lot to prove. All I ask is the chance. My purpose in coming to your people is not merely to pay a visit, or to seek safe haven from the Keepers. I come to make peace, and ask to establish diplomatic relations."

"If you can find a way to bridge the gap between the Crown and those it has wronged, you may just be a crafter of the impossible. But I will watch with keen interest, anyway. Guardian Arrelius and Her Highness have my respect. Their prodigy may have hope, yet. If you can back your convictions with the heart of a dragon."

Ulivall's words were sincere and heartfelt. In Vann's eyes, the Dimishuans and Alakuwai did not seem that separate. The shades of their flesh may have been different, but the color of their blood and texture of their souls were exact. The trick was finding a way to convince both sides of that truth.

Ulivall's face was an emotionless mask, but the fire in his eyes reflected promise in Vann's abilities. Vann wondered if he could find confidence in the same.

He was about to speak, when a wisp of movement just over Ulivall's shoulder caught his attention.

Ulivall's eyes followed the alarmed trail Vann's had taken. He turned and his hands instinctively fell to the handguards of his circular weapons.

"Smoke," Vann breathed, tension suddenly knotting his stomach.

Ulivall was silent as his eyes scanned the smoke trailing over a nearby hill. "Would you come with me, Your Majesty?"

Vann followed the man quietly, mimicking his catlike footsteps. Ulivall came to a stop and crouched near the summit of the hill, then pointed through the tall grasses that crested the rise. "Look there. Tell me what you see."

Vann followed the direction of Ulivall's arm and surveyed the terrain, immediately spying the encampment below. It took only a glance for him to realize that this was no military operation. It was too haphazard and unguarded. There was no recognizable structure or layout to the tents. Vann listed his observations to Ulivall, who nodded affirmation. "What else?"

After a scrutinizing examination, Vann noticed several poles sticking upright from the ground at the center of the encampment. A network of chains spider-webbed between them, and a long Blazer Whip, a device often used for punishment or torture, hung from a nail on the nearest post.

Vann shot a heated look of query at Ulivall. "This is a slaver's camp."

"Correct. They patrol the perimeter of the wetlands for the unwary. While they cannot penetrate our defenses, they lie in wait. We have lost many messengers and traders to them, not to mention the diplomats who have attempted to establish ties with the Crown."

"What happens to those they capture?"

"They are sold into bondage. On occasion, a slave owner might make a contract for the retrieval of a runaway."

"When your diplomats have attempted to reach High Empyrea, can they not rely on large numbers of your armed warriors? Surely your men can take on such a ragtag band as this." Vann motioned to the camp.

"Imagine your father's position. If you received a military report regarding a large band of armed 'barbarians' in procession to your doorstep, what would you do?"

Vann considered, then he grimaced. "I see your point."

"Let us away. We should not linger here. They are stupid, but dangerous nonetheless."

Vann eased backward and slipped quietly toward the tree line.

Ulivall's pace had been leisurely, but it was now purposeful.

When they arrived at camp, Vann was shocked to find the Guardians already there. Inagor and Malacar were kicked back over their coffee cups, engaged in light conversation. Scilio was sprawled upon the ground with his head in Lili's lap, staring at the sky, and quite probably at the attendant's buxom chest. Kir, sitting beside Palinora, was polishing her shortsword with the hem of Scilio's posh white cloak, which she wore proudly.

Vann studied his Guardians fondly, noting with some mirth how amazingly dissimilar three warriors could be, physically and otherwise.

Denian Malacar, a warrior class soldier and former Captain in the Royal Army, was a bear of a man. Large, coffee-skinned, square-jawed and muscular. His dark hair was cropped short in military fashion, and his brown eyes were commanding and alert. He cut a striking figure. Vann was rather surprised that he had shown little interest in women, for he surely would have no trouble attracting them. His demeanor was cool and confident, and he was the epitomical Guardian.

While Malacar was quiet and reserved, Toma Scilio was exuberant and gregarious. The traveling bard, or "Bardian," as he had taken to calling himself (a fusion of his chosen profession and his accidental Guardianship), was a natural Creative. The youngest of twelve in a noble family, Scilio was somewhat ostentatious and foppish, preferring a luxurious style with his well-tailored clothes and pristine white cloak. He was an accomplished womanizer; there was no doubt that women loved him. Where Malacar's features were bold and thick, Scilio's face was long and slender, and his violet eyes shone brilliantly with winsome spirit. He was wirier than Malacar, and he bore his tawny-brown hair in a high ponytail, as was the latest trend amongst the noble class. Scilio's jovial personality complimented Vann's well; they had become instant friends.

And then, there was Kir.

Vann's first introduction to Kir had been at sword-point and his early impressions had been colored by her admitted dark intentions toward the Crown. She had been brooding and sarcastic, sad yet stoic, living in the shadow of a tragic past that tormented her constantly.

But that was then, and she had been blossoming ever since. Even through her forced masculine behaviors, Kir was all woman, and Vann had been noticing that more lately. She had once hidden her features beneath a dirty hat and ragged clothes, but in the extremely feminine and revealing crimson Hilian outfit she was now sporting, no one could mistake her beauty. Her ice-blue eyes were captivating. She was slender and athletic, and though petite, there was strength in her bearing. She wore her chestnut hair in a ponytail bound at the nape of her neck and, while Vann would never confess such, he loved those scant moments she let it cascade down her broad shoulders.

Kir and Vann seemed to be creatures of an opposite compass bearing, but there was a connection between them that Vann could not deny. Their souls resonated with magnetic harmony, and they were drawing each other away from their extremes to a common middle.

Vann chuckled at the sight of his Guardians. "I see you three fared no better than I."

Scilio sat up gruffly. "Majesty! The iniquitous harpy left me hanging in her snare for ten minutes! And she absconded with my cloak."

Kir raised her polished weapon to examine the sheen. "Be thankful I didn't want your trousers, you pompous coxcomb."

"Now those, I would have happily surrendered," Scilio said suavely, with a bobbing of his eyebrows, to which Kir responded with rolling eyes.

Having no formal Weapons training, Scilio was probably not difficult to ensnare. Malacar and Inagor, however, were exemplary members of the warrior class. That Kir had tagged them so quickly was impressive.

"She got you, too?" Vann asked his adopted father.

Inagor laughed heartily, raising his cup to Kir in salute. "I like her. She cheats."

She smiled mischievously and acknowledged him with a graceful nod.

"Yes. She cheats," Malacar huffed. "Dishonorable, as usual."

"There's no honor in losing honorably. And anyway, what's wrong with the hunted becoming the hunter?" Kir asked smugly.

"I've never seen a rabbit eat a wildcat," Malacar answered with a mild grin. He turned to Vann. "What took you so long, Majesty? I was growing concerned."

"We were sidetracked," Vann answered as his smile dissolved. He nodded to Ulivall, who commenced briefing the others regarding the slavers' camp.

Kir rose, thrusting her shortsword into her belt. The feral look of battle-lust appeared in her eyes as she stared distantly in the direction Ulivall had indicated. Her hand rested on her sword and her thumb rubbed the hilt in a circular pattern. She was considering a course of action.

Vann frowned and slipped to her side. "I know what you're thinking, Kiri."

"I can take them, Vann," Kir assured him confidently. "And I'd be back in time for supper."

"I know you could, and I appreciate the sentiment, but the last thing we need is to engage in another battle. Judgment will be issued upon them eventually, whether by our hands or the Gods'."

"Better by our hands," Kir pressed.

Ulivall sidled up and grasped Kir shoulder firmly, as though the pressure in his grip could staunch the fire in her veins. "No matter how many bands you dispatch, more will come to replace them. Better to concentrate on protecting your Guarded, don't you agree?"

Vann smiled, recognizing the leader in Ulivall. He had been told that the Hili forces were an unorganized band of boys with butter knives when Ulivall had arrived fifteen years ago. His military experiences were instrumental in developing their disciplined organization. The Grand Master had probably been faced with the overzealous passion of many young warriors in his ranks and he knew just how to bring Kir down to earth. By reminding her of the Guardian's duty. Namely, protecting Vann.

Kir sighed in defeat. "I suppose. But that doesn't mean I have to like it. They're too close for my comfort."

"Fear not. I will send a detachment to deal with them swiftly. Their operation is lucrative, but as they will discover, it is also very risky."

As Ulivall departed to issue his orders, Lili detached Scilio's head from her lap and rose. "I will see about the midday meal."

Scilio remained on the ground, staring at the sky dejectedly. "Yes. Women always depart in my hour of need. This makes twice in one day..."

Kir sauntered to Scilio's side and unceremoniously dropped the cloak in his face. "You can have this back, priggish popinjay. Too uppity to fit me."

"Churlish termagant," Scilio mumbled, pulling himself apeak and inspecting the cloak affectionately.

Vann grinned at the antics and sat down beside his mother, replaying the conversation with Ulivall in his mind. He intended to negotiate with the Hilians for a political alliance, and he had initially been concerned that they would not treat with the race which had enslaved them, and a representative of the Crown that had enabled it.

If Vann could find a way to prove himself, he could surely win their allegiance. Now, all he had to do was find a dragon's heart.

**-3-**
## By Longboat to Hilihar

*Never curse your surroundings. There are*
*tactical advantages in any landscape.* - Master Kozias

"I'm surprised," Vann commented from his seat in the royal longboat, which was about three times larger than the standard ones on the waters, and heaps more flashy. He leaned across the open space and handed Kir a piece of jerked meat.

"'Bout what?" She gnawed her molars on the sharply seasoned slice.

"The swamps aren't as 'swampy' as I expected."

Kir was quiet for a moment, contemplating the lack of murk. The Hili wetlands were not what she had pictured, either. Some of the cypress were massive, sporting trunks that were wider than Kir was tall. Spidery moss hung from the alien foliage around them and slimy stumps rose from the waters amidst the submerged tree trunks, but it was not at all foggy or dark as she had expected. Vines hung from the branches, many of them long enough to disappear into the depths. Fingers of sun filtered through the treetops and tickled splotches of light on the viridian waters. But for the sloshing at the base of the boat and the occasional squawking of a water bird, there was little sound in the wilds around them.

"Not everywhere in Hili is as domesticated, Majesty," Malacar said. "The waterway we travel is a direct course to the lake. It is heavily used and well-tended, but some of the outlying swamps are quite dismal and dangerous. That's one pivotal reason the Dimishuans settled here. The swamps create a perimeter of ideal natural defenses. Kaiyo abound. And there are extraordinary Wards and other Defensive magics in place. Hili has enjoyed relative peace because no one is foolish enough to attack. We'll be safe enough, now that we've crossed the Hili border, but when we depart for High Empyrea we should be alert. That will be the most dangerous leg of your journey."

"But Galvatine believes me dead," Vann said. "Or do you believe our ruse short-lived?"

"Eventually, they'll figure out that you're still kickin', Stick. Probably sooner than later. From here on out, we have to assume they know," Kir remarked.

Malacar agreed. "Perhaps the Hilians will offer us an entourage. When you negotiate for their support, you must include a request for assistance in our journey to the capitol."

"Any way you reckon it, the cloakers will take no more chances. When they realize they've been hornswoggled, they'll send another army," Kir cautioned.

Scilio's purple eyes popped over the edge of his journal for the first time. "More? Ah well. The more trouble we face, the more heroic material I have for my gems of the muse. I only wish my inspirations were more easily accessible at the moment. These swampy wastelands are dampening my spirit." He returned attention to the journal, scribbling half-heartedly.

"How many mages are there?" Vann asked. He held a piece of meat toward Scilio. The Bardian accepted it without ungluing nose from prose.

"I'm not sure anyone knows that information, Majesty. The Keepers of Magic are just men. They live regular lives and hold down normal jobs. From what I understand, they come when summoned, but no one knows how many there actually are, or how their shadow-hopping is accomplished. They do seem to materialize out of thin air," Malacar replied.

Scilio glanced up and raised a finger to garner attention. "Not that I can provide any useful additions to this conversation, Vann, but what are these dried strips you're so generously distributing? The texture is rather peculiar." Scilio wrinkled his nose for effect as he sniffed the meat.

"I didn't ask. Lili offered me the pouch before we left dry land."

Scilio turned toward the man named Junan, who was busy at the oar behind him. He held his jerky up and asked, "What is this?"

Junan bowed low to the bard over his oar for a good long minute.

Scilio pointed to the bowing man and bobbed his eyebrows to Kir like he'd won the naked-wench lottery. His expression screamed *I told you so!*

Kir crinkled a gnarly face back at him. Scilio had been gloating in the Hilians' infatuation for days, and Kir was beginning to notice their overzealous respect. She could not describe it as outright hero-worship, but their attitudes were unmistakably fawning where he was concerned. They had even given him the nickname of Shunatar (but no one seemed willing to give the weight of explanation to the word). Kir had pretended ignorance. If his head got any bigger, it was likely to explode.

Junan erected himself and gestured to the meat in Scilio's hand. "Hin-kanan."

"Alakuwai-speak...?"

Junan, obviously a Hili native and limited in knowledge of the Alakuwai language, furrowed his brow in thought. He looked upwards toward the overhanging tree limbs and pointed to random branches. "Hin-kanan," he replied again.

Scilio jumbled his pretty face to confusion.

Kir followed his gaze, but she was as clueless as the next one.

"The trees? Moss?" Malacar tried.

Junan shook his head and thought hard for a moment. He dropped his shoulders and hunched over his paddle. His mouth curled into an "o" and he began heeing and hooing a squirrely song.

"A monkey?" The corner of Vann's mouth turned up in a puerile grin that painted a hint of boyish youth across his face.

Junan nodded. "Yes, mon-kee."

Scilio's complexion turned Hili-water green and Kir snickered at his displeasure.

"Monkey jerky?" Scilio asked, holding his piece away like it was a putrefied lizard.

Malacar snatched it and popped it into his mouth. "Much obliged."

The bottomless bear could eat more gruel than a passel of starving pigs.

"Really, Vann. I do so adore the attention lavished by our Hilian friends, but I'm afraid if we don't arrive in High Empyrea soon, I may succumb to emaciation," Scilio griped. He dropped his eyeballs back to the comfort of his journal.

"Lili tells me there will be a feast to welcome our arrival in Hilihar. I'm sure you'll find something there to suit you," Vann said.

"Considering the eclectic selection of meals we've sampled already, the thought of a *feast* prepared by our Hilian hosts does not reassure my delicate palate," Scilio replied.

Kir cast her gaze to the surroundings and she scanned for potential enemies. Her eyes fell on the royal longboat in the lead and everything seemed to be quiet. Queen Palinora and Guardian Arrelius were seated in the middle of the boat, with Ulivall and Lili before them and another Hilian paddling at the stern.

Kir pushed away at a passing vine that brushed her arm and turned to view the longboat bringing up the rear, which carried the boy healer Bertrand, and the handful of Hilian delegates that had come to greet them.

Time and silence settled around them for a piece while the party gave themselves to their thoughts.

When Kir turned her eyes back to Vann, his features had drawn like a belt pouch.

"What's ruckin' your plunket, Stick?"

Vann barely stirred. He usually lopped a grin at her creative vernacular. "Come again?" he asked dourly.

"You're fretting. In the brace-the-world-on-your-shoulders kinda way."

Vann shrugged. "Not really. I was just thinking."

Kir bobbed her head, unconvinced. Vann rarely squinched his brow to his ponderings. He was very good at hiding his worries, and only rarely had Kir glimpsed the uncertainty hidden by his actor's smile.

Recent revelations were turning the gears in Vann's head to grinding speed. Only days past, he had learned that someone had marked his Creative magics during his six-month sojourn in Findelore. The tracking mark had allowed the Keepers to locate and intercept him whenever he accessed his Creatives through a brush or graphite. Such a revelation was surely difficult to stomach, because it meant someone Vann trusted had sold him out to the priesthood that wanted his head on a pike. Whoever it was must have been powerful, since such Prophetic magic was rare and difficult to harness. It was no wonder Vann was lost in his head. He was certainly trying to put together pieces of a puzzle that didn't yet seem to match up.

Vann stared beyond the watery road. The verdant tinge

reflected from the waters turned his blue eyes to green, but the sparkle that usually illuminated his face his wasn't sparkly. He absently leaned forward to avoid a vine that brushed by his head.

Kir took the opportunity to knock on his corn silk melon as it entered her arm's reach. It was a playful gesture, but laced with gentle concern. He recoiled and cocked his head.

"Nope. Not as hollow as I reckoned," Kir jested mildly. "What's tumbling around in there? Seriously, Vann. If you don't batten down that worry now, it will sneak up and whack you later."

He plastered a forced smile across his too-perfect lips. "I'm fine."

"No doubt," Malacar agreed. "But you do seem troubled. As your Guardians, we are in a unique position to counsel and guide, whenever you feel the need requires. Burden us, Majesty. That's why we exist."

Vann's mouth didn't utter a thank-you, but his eyes did. It was like the permission to unload his soul had been granted. "Back in Arjo, I held a scrap of parchment in my hand that once was the Chaos Bringer prophecy. The prose-bound warning that I would be the downfall of the world. The scroll was destroyed, but three words remained, before the scrap crumbled to dust in my hand. It said, 'by the Betrayer.' I was just wondering if that part of the prophecy has already been initiated. Maybe the person who marked me set the prophecy in motion when he cast the mark. I can't imagine who it might have been. I had many acquaintances in Findelore, mostly in the theater. Might any one of them have been a mage in disguise all along?"

Kir hadn't noticed that Scilio had set his journal in his lap and was chewing his brain on Vann's ruminations.

"Prophecy can be difficult to interpret, even when considered in its entirety. Three little words can change the meaning of the world, so I dare admonish you to caution in vexations of prophecy," Scilio warned. "At what point the chain of events is interdicted doesn't matter, as long as it is. We Guardians stand in the way to obstruct your prophetic fate, just as we do in the face of an enemy."

"I always thought *I* was the only person in the world who made a lifestyle of challenging the word of the Gods," Vann quipped lightly.

"We can't allow you to hoard the fun for yourself," Scilio chimed.

"I am ecstatic and relieved to have trusted friends at my side, believe me," Vann said. "But this whole business about a betrayer... I always entertained a romantic notion of winning over any foe with kindness and friendship. The possibility that someone betrayed me while knowing me...it's just disheartening. I believed myself a better judge of character than my track record is proving."

"You can't expect everyone to jump on your rig with a keg and a smile," Kir said. "Even your closest relations can turn their backs and abandon you in a heartbeat. Experience was my bitter tutor to such."

Vann studied her. "You tried to tell me that back in Southport. Not to trust anyone."

Kir put on a face of agreement. Vann dished out trust as readily as thunderhead dished out rain. Over-trusting was a weakness, but he couldn't go through life cowering behind a rock for fear of betrayal, either. Finding balance between wariness and trust would be an essential lesson for him.

"I just wanted you to face reality. You're high-walking the edge of a dangerous cliff. Just gotta be mindful of every and anyone, okay?"

Vann inhaled resolutely. "At least I know I can trust my Guardians."

Kir swallowed a hard lump of nothing and stared at Vann with warning. "I wouldn't suggest you get all cozy in that idea. There's obviously a flaw in the magic. How else could a Guardian have killed Tarnavarian? The Guardian Bonding supposedly prevents Guardians from bringing harm to their Guarded, yet your brother was done in by his own. You should be wary, even with us. Placing your life in our hands is unavoidable to an extent, but don't let your guard down. Ever."

"You truly believe, after all we've been through, that any one of us could betray the other? That you could turn on me?" There was pain in Vann's voice. "That I could abandon you?"

"No way of knowing how a boat will sail 'til she's caught in an ill wind, Stick, but the conditions can be primed and ripe for a betraying gale," Kir responded firmly, against the nagging protest at such a harsh inkling. For a brief moment, Mirhana's image flashed in her mind. Her best friend had died on a field of Kir's shame, and the guilt was always teasing the backdrop of her awareness. She willed the thought away.

"I never intend to betray you. I swear on Nomah's sword and honor, I don't. But who knows what warped web High Priest Galvatine can snare us in? Hallucinations and illusions are sticky. Your mother has demonstrated that to our certainty already. If Wrinkles can use his Prophetics and Psychonics to turn enemy of friend, we may not realize until it's too late. Don't rely on the Guardian magic to protect you. If someone close is ever manipulated somehow, your life may depend on a quick decision, so aim swift and true for the kill. Even if it's one of us."

The boaters sulled up under knit brows and frowns. Scilio and Malacar looked none to happy with the suggestion of what was possible at the tips of their blades, but neither argued.

Vann's eyes examined the longboat deck for flaws. They finally worked their way up to Kir. Her conviction wavered under his penetrating gaze. She threw her eyeballs past his shoulder to avoid the visual scolding.

"Ask no such abomination of me, Guardians," Vann said resolutely. He had that authoritative Princey-quality in his tone. "I will never draw my blade against you in malice, no matter the circumstance. If I value my life over yours, I am no better than Tarnavarian."

Kir suddenly whipped her shortsword from the scabbard and popped to her feet like a cardamom seed on a sizzle pan. She crouched low for balance and drew precise aim at Vann's temple.

Vann sucked in a belly of staggered air and the Guardians' tense hands fell to their weapons. Kir paused with narrowed eyes fixed on Vann, as a cat targeting prey.

## -4-
## The Burden of Shadows

*If at first you don't succeed, give up and go wenching.*
*It'll all work out tomorrow.* - Master Kozias

Grand Master Wardion slammed his fist on the magic-imbued message scroll and watched Galvatine's elegant script shatter and vanish. His blood was boiling, and not only for the High Priest's insults. The Keepers of Magic had lost over seventy mages in the assassination attempt on the princeling near the Hili border. Seven more lay within the imminent clutches of the Soul Collectors. And yet, those devoted souls had died for nothing.

Vannisarian lived.

*Clever boy*, Wardion thought bitterly when he had received Xavien's report.

That a weasel like Sandavall Xavien enjoyed slinking around in the shadows was a burr in Wardion's side. Xavien was a rogue and seemed to be chasing after his own petty agenda, rather than entirely committing to the Holy Cause. In any other Keeper, such behavior would not be tolerated. Xavien's abilities were the sole reason Wardion had allowed him to remain in the order, and alive. It was better to keep potential problems happy and within arm's reach. No other Keeper could shadow-hop more than twice in a week without risking depletion of the deadly kind. No other Keeper could shadow-hop to places he had never been or could not visualize. And no other Keeper could hop across large distances. Xavien was too dangerous to ignore, too intelligent to risk assassinating, and too valuable to do either. His talents were well-suited to espionage, so Wardion would play it safe for now and tolerate Xavien's personality quarks. He didn't want an enemy in Sandavall Xavien.

Because they were so limited in their shadow-hopping capabilities, Wardion relied on local units of mages to handle local affairs. Massing an army was a huge and time-consuming undertaking. This was the first time so many Keepers had been mustered to one island, and Wardion dearly hoped it would be the last. They were trained for individual actions, not large-scale battle. Facing down the Hilian army had proven just how inept they were as a military unit. It was a problem they were addressing, as evidenced by the clanging sounds of training just outside Wardion's tent. They would coax the men to battle-readiness before the next campaign, and this time, they would not fail. Their cloaks would provide their ace-in-the-hole. If only his Keepers could move as often and as far as Xavien. An army that could come on call would be unstoppable.

Wardion put the finishing touches on the report and signed it off. All he needed was Keeper Xavien's signature to close the file. This case was just another example of how Xavien's skulking about had been advantageous. Without his espionage, Wardion might not have known that the princeling had survived their brilliant ambush until it was too late.

Wardion was not entirely sure how Vannisarian's party had pulled off such an elaborate and realistic ploy. But they were royalty, after all, and as such, had access to a higher level of magics than those of lower breeding.

The only saving grace was that Hili was far from Empyrea. The Prince might be behind safe borders now, but eventually, a mouse always leaves its hole. The Keepers had time, and with time came opportunity.

Galvatine did not share Wardion's optimistic outlook, and he had completely lost his patience with the Keepers. He had commanded Wardion to employ Soreina of the Web. An interesting choice.

Soreina was well-known in the underworld as the most capable assassin in Septauria. Rumor had it that even the King had employed her services on occasion. That Galvatine had decided to use her was indicative of his desperation. Soreina was allegedly a user of the Forbidden magics, and that fact should have meant a death sentence, not a job offer. Even the King's own assassin group, the Night Wind, were wary of her.

It was no surprise that the most feared fangs in the kingdom belonged to a wench. There were several women that Wardion knew, his own wife included, that had a touch of black widow in their veins. Soreina's seductive allure was almost inescapable and she used it to her full advantage. Gods help the man who fell into *her* snare.

Wardion's footsteps thumped angrily against the dust as he stormed toward his tent flap. He paused briefly to pay respects to the Gods at the altar in his tent. It was a large object to lug half-way across the isles, but if it gained him favor in the eyes of the Gods, it was worth the hassle. Wardion placed a small offering to Nomah and issued a prayer. He would need every blessing the God of the Offensives could bestow.

Finding Soreina in the wilds of northern Arcadia would be difficult, but not impossible. Contracting with her, however, could prove to be deadly.

He only hoped that he could stay out of reach of the witch's mandibles.

-5-
## A Reflection of Dragons

*The dragon is valued for its fierceness and power, but
don't besmirch the mouse. The mouse that gnaws holes in
the hull of a ship has killed it as surely as the
dragon that smashes it. -* Master Kozias

"Kiri?" Vann's voice didn't quiver, but it was overloaded with alarm.

"Stone-still," she hissed.

She struck spit-quick and sure at Vann's ear before a lash could bat or question utter. The razor edge of her shortsword perfectly divorced a viper from its arrowed head, just as it opened its grinner to smile at Vann's cheek. The viney serpent slid right into the boat. It whacked tail to Scilio's face as the body commenced flopping and jerking its protestation at being dead. Scilio slapped at the air with his journal and kicked the snake away from his space. He traded constricted glances with Vann and Malacar, then all six peepers parked on Kir expectantly.

Kir sat down like nothing and dipped her sword overboard to wash off the gunk. She flicked the excess from the blade, making sure to land most of the spray on Scilio, then dried it on the leg of her flowing pant-skirt.

"Well now," Scilio said, playing with strained mirth as he slicked back his prissified mane, "that was certainly an adventure into the macabre."

The tension seemed to evaporate and the men passed around relieved breaths.

Malacar tested a chuckle. "You had me going there, Kir. I was beginning to think you were trying to illustrate your argument."

"Yes, the timing was rather ironic," Scilio agreed.

"Then, why didn't you draw your weapons? If you thought I was about to attack him—"

"Because they trust you, Kiri," Vann interrupted. "And I trust you. I didn't really think that you would have—how did you know that was a snake, anyway? It looks like a vine." He nudged Twitchy tentatively with his foot.

"'Cause none of the other vines stuck their tongues at me," Kir laughed.

Junan pointed to the snake and displayed a wide smile of impression. "Ut-saka. Good eats." He licked his lips for effect.

"Ut-saka? Oh Gods," Scilio closed his eyes and clutched his stomach like it was about to abandon ship. "Hence our delicacies graduate from horrible to horror."

"Guardian Malacar? We heard a ruckus..." Inagor called over his boat's edge.

Malacar scooped up Twitchy's tail and hauled it aloft for Inagor's scrutiny. "Guardian Ithinar was procuring our supper," he hollered back.

"I should ride in your boat," Inagor responded, his voice smiling. "Your journey sounds abundantly more lively than ours."

"Yes, Guardian Ithinar is providing us an abundance of entertainment," Scilio projected distastefully. "I would gladly trade places, Guardian Arrelius. When a woman entertains me, I'd prefer it to be bereft of melancholy sentiments and beheadings. I'm sure your feminine companions would be much more agreeable to my refined tastes."

"I love you, too, Ponytail," Kir muttered darkly, crossing her arms.

Inagor's laughter boomed. "I would happily swap, but dare not abandon my post to the Queen. Be patient, good man!"

Scilio sighed dramatically. "I must endure. For our treasured Prince we Guardians toil."

"Keep up the sweet talk, Ponytail," Kir grumbled. "I'll remember your heartfelt adorations the next time you beg me to take your watch shift for your wenching."


The water forest gave way to Hili Lake, which opened before them like a blooming bud. The longboats glided by a handful of smaller towns on the edges of the inland sea, and after a handful of hours, the outskirts of the capitol were in sight.

Hilihar was unlike anything Kir could have imagined. The large city buoyed on a lake with the barest minimum in magics wobbled her jaw into a gawk. Some of the houses stood on stilt legs, while others floated. Most were simple bamboo and wood structures with thatched roofs. Some of the beamier, well-heeled dwellings were surrounded by dirt or rocks at their bases, faking the illusion of solid ground. Malacar had explained that the dirt was actually packed on planks of wood.

The floating strips of land astounded Kir even more than the float-abodes. Each strip was about ten feet wide and hundreds of feet long, providing ample room to grow produce. As they passed by rows and rows, Kir had to force herself not to stare at the Hilians working their crop as though there weren't a whole sea lapping around them. A goat stepped through the beaded curtain that doored one shanty and bleated an offended obscenity at the passing longboats.

"Farming on a lake. 'Bout as kooky as a collar on a king," she mumbled to no one in particular.

The twinkle of wonderment in her features was hard to mask, so she didn't bother trying. Everyone was equally enthralled, except Malacar, who'd seen it before.

The deeper into the city, the grander the architecture. The

buildings became increasingly polished and less rustic. They still held a natural feel about them, but it was obvious that the structures in the central districts were not homes. Most likely meant for public or governmental use. They were handsome, walled in river stones and connected by long roofed bridge-like walkways.

Bertrand's longboat veered down a separate course and Malacar waved a parting hand to the healer's oarsman, who returned the gesture. She didn't say it, but Kir was half-relieved to be rid of the kid. There was something about Betrand that muddied up her calm.

The boats rounded an avenue and were assaulted with a magnificent spectacle of rainbow and ostentation. The structure looming before them was as out of place in Hilihar as a bull in a chicken pen. It was elaborate and proud, holding its dragonmast head aloft with an elegant confidence that Kir likened to a prancing priest come preaching time. Not a square-inch was untouched by a carver's hand, and even from a distance, the detail was evident and breathtaking. There was an almost-glow about the body, such that the nooks and crannies forbade shadow, but it wasn't of the eye-squinting type of brilliance. Billowing streamers of ephemeral fabric undulated in a wind that wasn't. There was an essence of movement about the thing, although it was moored fast against a dock. The behemoth seemed to know that it was magnificent, and it wanted to share that knowledge with everyone who had eyes.

"That's the Kion ship," Malacar reported.

"That's a *ship*?" Vann asked. His eyes were big as flapfritters.

"It's used for festivals and such. Can't say I know enough to enlighten you about it."

It looked more like a temple in the Citadel than a seaworthy vessel. Kir tried to compare the size of the Kion to Scilio's ego, but she couldn't harness her sarcasm for the magnitude of the ornate craft that tripped her boggles up.

The longboats sidled up to the wooden pier that hugged the Kion's tail. Palinora's boat emptied first, then Ulivall made his way to Vann's and offered a hand.

"Can you tell me about this artistic feat of wonderment?" Vann asked as he grasped it and stepped onto the planks. Kir jumped up after him, trailed by her brother Guardians.

Ulivall cleared his throat coarsely. "I'm not much for speechifying. It's our dragon. See the head?"

Lili's cheeks puffed and she touched Ulivall's bicep lightly. "He is better with blades than words. Allow me, Grand Master," she tittered.

Ulivall seemed relieved to be relieved.

"This is the revered Kion—dragon, in your tongue. Our people celebrate the dragons of the Gods."

"I've always loved the dragon myths, too." Vann's eyes twinkled.

"Do not confuse myth with legend, Majesty. Dragons were once as real as you and I."

Kir snuffed her amusement but kept her tongue from wagging. Seemed the Hilians clung to a few good bedtime stories.

"The dragon was the hand of the Gods," Lili continued, leading them up the gangplank as she talked. "Gifted to the world for its protection from the Forbiddens. Surely, as royalty you know all about the dragons."

The corners of Vann's eyes creased uneasily. "I know something of them, but not authoritatively." His cautious wording was likely a strategic means of keeping his knowledge guarded so as not to appear ignorant.

"The dragons are the beginning and the end. They breathed their fires for the Gods to raze the first world, and their flame breathed life into the new world upon its birth," Lili explained. She gestured to a mural on the bulkhead that looked to be a winding serpentine dragon hugging the land and conducting business at the end of its snout. "They are the greatest of all beings, only second to the Gods themselves. In days of old, Kings held power over the dragons to protect Order. The day has long since passed that their glory is needed here. But our people revere them as an ancient and formidable harbinger of justice and peace. Did you know that the Guardians were once known as *Kion-Eska*, or Dragon Guard?"

They all *huh'd* their impression with that bit of interesting trivia.

Kir was surprised that the Hilians were so devout in beliefs wrapped in the shrouded history of the Gods. The priests taught that the Dimishuan people were gifts from the Gods, only meant as a tool for mankind to survive. She had assumed they would have shunned any religious sentiments that supported a belief in their own bondage.

"Are the Hilians close to the Gods? That is, do your people worship them as ours do?" Scilio asked.

Lili nodded gracefully and cast her cascading black silk trusses over her shoulder. "We do, and we know the truths that the priests will not speak. The Dimishuans were the first ones. Our ancestors inhabited the old world before it was destroyed. Our skin was not always painted in hues of gold, and we looked no different than any Alakuwai. In the aftermath of apocalypse, the shame and fire tainted our skin to the golden shimmer you can see in the dim. The Dimishuan language is, itself, the first. The tongue of the Gods. They have told us this."

Kir choked back a guffaw. She chomped on her lip to hold her expression steady. The Hilians talked to the Gods? She could only imagine the look on Galvatine's face if confronted with such blasphemy. The priests alone communed with the Gods, and even then, only through Prophetic magic in special Holy chambers. The Gods issued their word through prophecies, which were used to warn for change, to better the world. The claim that the divine messages could reach this backwoods part of the world was just ridiculous, even for a self-proclaimed and proud blasphemer like her.

"What function does the Kion serve to your people?" Scilio asked, pulling Kir from her contrary thoughts.

"The Kion holds a treasured spiritual role, as the flagship of our faith. It is a symbolic icon during the dragon festivals, when it sails across Hili Lake to collect offerings to the Gods. Dancers stand upon the decks and treat viewers to performances as it passes them by," Lili said, then turned to Vann. "The Kion will serve as your residence for the duration of your stay in Hili, Majesty. Her Highness has been residing onboard these past months. Our humble city has no residence suitable for royalty, and the Kion is as close to luxury as we can offer on these waters."

"Make no mistake," Palinora said, "I'd have taken a common Hilian dwelling in a heartbeat. The Circle would not hear of it."

"We may not cherish the Crown, but we cannot deny the blood of the Gods," Ulivall cut in. "The Kion is our representation of the Divine Hand. As such, we thought it suitable for the descendants of our makers. It would not be seemly otherwise."

"So, it's not usually a guest residence?"

"No," Lili said. "The inner chambers were converted to living quarters when milady graced us with her presence. This situation is unprecedented. We've never had royalty sail among us before. The only guests we get are messengers."

"Messengers? Do you not communicate with magic-imbued messenger scrolls? It seems more efficient than sending runners out on foot," Vann commented.

"Communiques sent by magical means can be intercepted, and sometimes manipulated. Therefore, messages are usually hand-scribed and sent by swamp eagle, or delivered in person. We cannot trust the information otherwise," Ulivall replied.

"Swamp eagles?"

"They are native to Aquiline, and prized among noble falconers. Our austringers breed and train them with Natural magic. They serve as message runners between here and Havenlen, where our friends in the Underground are headquartered."

Kir bobbed her head in understanding, although it seemed difficult to wage a silent war without a means of instant communication, like that a magic-imbued messenger scroll would provide. She wondered as to the story behind the sorta-war that she'd heard talk of on the trip. There wasn't much to know, beyond the fact that the Hilians were working together with a secret organization in Havenlen, this so-called Underground. She assumed they were recruiting abolitionists and acting against the priests in subtle ways. Kir wondered how effective such an underground war could be against the overt power of the Crown and Priesthood.

The group turned toward the stern for their next lesson in

Hilian art and dragonology. Kir fell back to examine an elaborate canvas banner that adorned the outer bulkhead. The long, winding body of a dragon encompassed most of the banner, but Kir's eye hung up on the tiny figure of a man that was almost lost in the enormity of the scene. The figure, brandishing a large broadsword before him, looked to be faced off with the dragon in a death-match. A glimmer of sparkle on his wrist suggested a lumanere vambrace. She wondered why an ancient Guardian would be fighting a dragon, especially if they were both on the same side of the Gods. Feeling a kinship with the fictional figure, Kir silently cheered his impossible task and hoped Snakey had tasted lots of Guardian steel.

She moved to the next banner. It shimmered and danced, and Kir was drawn in by the splays of color in the purple silken draperies. Before her eyes, the patterns began to shift and move, delighting her to pause. A collection of woven butterflies suddenly sprang to life, fluttering their gossamer wings on the canvas of fabric that trapped them. Kir drank in the picture of peace and tranquility that she so rarely had opportunity to taste.

"War is not underground," Bertrand's voice pierced her ear.

So much for that pleasant little delusion...

# -6-
## Unexpected Encounters

*Visitors are the reason we carry swords.* - Master Kozias

Kir might have jumped out of her skin, were it not glued to her bones. The boy healer had been standing smack behind her, but she had not sensed him there. She turned, biting back complaint at the peace lost and disquiet found.

Bertrand was, surprisingly, without his usual entourage of clingy attendants. Despite the sticky heat, Kir suddenly froze over like a high-mountain lake in blizzards. The child sucked the very warmth from the air around her.

Though Bertrand was only twelve years old, he was a Supreme Master Healer, the highest level of magic user. This made him singular in his own right. But he made Kir's skin crawl. She was certain he could see into her murky soul with his bloody gaze.

If that was not enough to make Kir shudder, he talked and behaved funny. She heard-tell that Bertrand would not look a person in the eye unless he was in the midst of a Healing. She took issue with that observation, because he had stared her down on several occasions. His mind seemed to exist in another state of being, and he constantly rocked on his heels, fingering his precious shell necklace.

The one time she'd traded words with the boy, he'd spun a tangled mess of befuddlement that left Kir with more questions than answers. She had tried her best to stay away from the kid on their journey, and mostly succeeded. Until now.

"War will wage bitterly in the open. Soon," Bertrand continued.

"Huh?" Kir stumbled on her tongue. "War is coming? Probably right about that..."

Bertrand shook his head. "No. Not here. Not here," he said, motioning to the ship and the waters off the deck. He pointed a finger at her heart. "In there lies the battlefield."

"Sure. War. In here," Kir said, slapping her own chest. "I gotcha."

Her teeth chattered madly, despite all her efforts to control it. She clenched her muscles firmly, unable to shake the shakes. A frigid grip tried to ice her feet to the deck. She wasn't about to let Bertrand rope her in his mind-grasp again, but the chill turned her sluggish in finding a path out. When she heard Lili's voice lilt somewhere on the deck above, it tipped her awareness that the royal entourage had left her behind. That one thought broke the bind.

"Guardian duty calls," Kir said on the fly. She turned on her heel and raced away until she found a staircase leading to the upper decks. She sprang upward, taking three steps at a time. Atop the flight, she threw her body against the wall and peeked around the corner to make positive sure Bertrand did not follow.

"Hello the wench!"

Kir's heart tumbled and capsized at the purposefully piercing voice in her ear. She instinctively slammed her hand against the mural-covered bulkhead to release the mounting tension. "Damnation, Ponytail! You just took two years off my hide!" She examined her palm and grimaced at the large paint chips that stuck to it. "And two layers off the pretty picture..."

She pasted them back with spit and pressure, hoping nobody would notice.

Scilio cackled heartily at her unease. He was too much big-brother for his own good. "Vann sent me to retrieve you. I never thought I'd enjoy it so immensely."

Kir exhaled a shaky breath and rubbed her bare arms vigorously, trying to coax them back to warmth.

"Are you ill?" Scilio asked, eyeballing her with sudden awareness. "You're not one to shudder under my jesting, no matter how ill-conceived."

"I'm fine," she grumbled.

"Are you sure? How could you possibly find a shiver in this sweltering, cling-all humidity?" He tested a hand on her shoulder. "Begads, Kir! You are absolutely frigid."

She slapped his hand away. "It's nothing. Let's go."

"I should summon Bertrand..."

"Don't bring him near me, Toma," Kir pleaded, against her nature. "It's all *his* fault."

"What do you mean?"

"I ran into him on the lower deck and it started me to chattering. He saps the warmth from a room. Haven't you noticed that?"

"In all candor, I've spent little time with him. He always seems lost in thought, staring at the floor or lining up shells, so I haven't endeavored to approach him. Besides, Lili has kept me rather... preoccupied," Scilio replied with a glimmer of a smirk.

"There's something odd about him. The things he says. The way he looks at me. It's like he can read every thought in my head, even when I'm guarding myself against him. Quite honestly, he scares the wenchin furies outta me," Kir admitted.

Scilio removed his cloak and threw it around her shoulders, rubbing her arms for friction.

"No need to go all gentlemanly. I'll live."

"This place is too hot for a cloak," Scilio replied sincerely. "Besides, we can't have you quivering like a Berndian belly-dancer now, can we?" He stopped at the thought and cast a quirky grin her way.

"Don't even think it, Ponytail. You best control your letchy mind where I'm concerned. Lest I wipe more than just that grin off'a your person," Kir warned with a smile in the words.

When the tremors had fled, she removed the cloak and returned it with muttered gratitude.

"Consider it recompense for my earlier behavior in the boat," Scilio said. It was rare to hear an apology in his tone. "You are not so terrible a companion as I depicted."

"Yes I am," Kir retorted devilishly. She bumped her shoulder against his playfully. "I'm cruel and heartless when it comes to your comfort. Suggestifying to eat that dead snake turned you seven shades of putrid. Let me borrow your journal and I'll draw a picture of your face."

"Eleven cordial, mature blood siblings, yet I am forever Bonded to the likes of *you*." Scilio ushered Kir toward the royal party, all the while throwing concerned glances her way.


*The Keeper tried to cast a Wisp, but Vann had a Shield, flimsy though it were, in place quickly. Frustrated, the opponent charged in, using his superior size to corner Vann against the skiff. Vann parried, but brute strength was forcing the edge to his throat.*

Kir remembered this. It was a sleep-memory. This happened on the road to Northport. It had been Vann's first victory at bladepoint. She briefly toyed with the idea of rousing herself from the dream, then chastised the over-protectiveness of her own mind. This recollection wasn't dangerous; it had a happy ending. If you reckoned *happy* described the memory of Vann's first experience gutting a man. But

Vann had prevailed and would not lie dead in this dream. And so:
happy.

*Kir moved to act. Before she took a step, Vann dropped to his
knees, allowing the cloaker's blade to shoot overhead, where it lodged
deep in the hull of the skiff. He thrust upwards, securing his victory.
The assassin stiffened, then collapsed at his feet.*

*Vann stared blankly at the corpse for a moment. He rose on
shaky legs and turned.*

*"What took you so long?" he asked weakly, yet his tone
betrayed a hint of pride.*

*The image morphed and Kir was standing on a battlefield,
strewn with corpses. "What took you so long?" echoed in the chasm of
her mind.*

*Her blade was in her hand, dripping blood from the tip. It
slashed at the man before her, but he blocked her strikes. Kir knew
him. His hat and features were familiar, although she could not
identify him. His skill with his twin blades surpassed that of any
warrior she had ever faced. He could read her every move.*

*Kir wanted this fight; she had lived for it since the moment
she'd met him. The thrill of combat, the promise of defeating her
opponent, the blood lust: all overtook Kir's sense of time and place.
She fleetingly remembered Vann—she should be protecting him. But
he could fight; she had taught him, after all. He could protect himself
for a piece longer.*

*The battle raged. The blood splattered. And Kir's heart soared.*

*When she finally slid her blade deep into the opponent's chest,
she acknowledged him with a salute. A worthy adversary.*

*Then, she remembered Vann.*

*He was several meters away, fighting his own worthy
opponent. But Vann was not a warrior, and this opponent was not a
prince. A blade flashed and Vann fell to his knees, cursing her with his
eyes. Then, he pitched forward.*

*Kir tried to run to him, tried to scream. The terror stole her
voice away. The strength in her trembling legs dissolved and she
crawled through the blood and the dirt, over corpses and ownerless
limbs. She reached Vann's side, pulling him to her chest. He stared
into space, unblinking. A flash of light, and Kir's Guardian vambrace
melted away.*

*Vann's body seemed to evaporate into nothingness, but his
severed head remained in her hands, staring. Piercing with emptiness.
"You killed me," Vann's lips mouthed in silent accusation. Just as
Mirhana's had in her imagination...*

*Vann's voice echoed in her mind, looped in eternal repetition.
"What took you so long?"*

*"This is just a dream... just a dream," Kir muttered, squeezing
her eyes closed. She jerked Vann's image to the forefront of her
awareness. The picture of him wearing a genuine smile and sparkles*

*in his blue eyes. It was her only defense against the demons of the night. She willed herself awake.*

Kir jerked on the bench of the Kion, panting in the darkness. She caught her breath and steadied herself, angry for having allowed the dream sequence to continue. She should have called upon Vann's image—her Princey Charm—immediately to dispel the dream, but the memory of his victory at the skiff had seemed so innocent. She had not expected it to turn sinister.

For months, Kir had been plagued by terrible nightmares just like the recent one, and they had been getting worse. With Vann's help in Arshenholm, she had finally figured out how to erect a bulwark against them. By simply thinking about him, she could prevent the realistic terror from invading her head every night. She had no inkling how the Princey Charm worked. But it did, and that was all she needed to know.

"Guardian Ithinar? Are you unwell?" a familiar voice spoke.

Kir blinked and allowed her eyes to adjust to the light of the twin moons glistening on the waters just off the deck.

"I'm fine, Guardian Arrelius. Just a wicked nightmare," Kir answered. Her fingers clutched her shortsword tensely. The sheathe was cold, familiar and comforting.

"One can hardly be untouched by the darkness when one has seen such as you have," Inagor said mildly.

Kir stretched her arms and shook away the fatigue. She realized with some irritation that she had been on watch. "Did I doze off? I reckon I did if I was dreaming. Apologies. I've never fallen asleep on duty before."

"Don't worry. I was awake. No need for two night watchmen while we're in Hili, anyway."

"Still, you should have whacked me to waking." She wrestled with annoyance at her own carelessness.

"No harm done. I was patrolling the forward deck when I found something of interest on the railing. I believe it might be addressed to you."

Inagor sat on the bench beside Kir and offered a small box the size of her palm. It was wrapped in red twine and the lid was decorated with the blossom of a flower. Red splotches across delicate white petals announced its variety clearly.

Kir's jaw clenched.

"The flower. It is ithinar, correct? It appears you have an admirer on board. Any idea who it might be from?" Inagor beamed. His tone of voice indicated that he might have a suspect in mind, though it was unlikely to be the same one that sprang to Kir's.

His eyes sparkled, but Kir couldn't read whether he was radiating pride or amusement.

She accepted the gift and studied it silently. It seemed harmless enough, though she was not about to open it in the presence of another. There was no telling what might lie inside and was not about to take chances.

An ithinar-entwined gift had been left before, from a strange cigar-smoking man with twin swords. Kir had seen him on several occasions during their journey across Mercaria and Aquiline. His identity escaped her, but he knew exactly who she was. The shovel he'd decorated for her benefit made that fact plain as yellow on a butterbean. It was a tribute to the spade that had landed her in a heap of trouble when she'd introduced it to Prince Tarnavarian's head on the eve of their engagement.

Vann and the Guardians were not aware of the elusive mystery man. Malacar had dismissed the man's existence as a dream once before, and any more insisting on Kir's part might land her in a loon farm. There was no cause to worry them needlessly, as he didn't appear to be interested in Vann.

"I haven't the foggiest," Kir shrugged, feigning disinterest. "Probably one of Ponytail's monkeyshines."

"I'll leave you some solitude. If it turns out to be from someone other than Guardian Scilio, perhaps you'll want a private moment with whomever the sender might be."

"I can assure you I will."

"Take all night in. The Hilians patrol their waters. We're safe enough here. I'll stand the watch until Ulivall sends someone to relieve me," Inagor said.

Kir nodded appreciation and bid him good night. He rose and made his way down the aft deck.

When Inagor's shadow had vanished around a corner and his footfalls faded to a whisper, Kir turned her attention back to the box. She sniffed the flower tentatively. Rather than a floral fragrance, she could only detect a hint of sweet tobacco. Cigar smoke.

An admirer indeed.

## -7-
## Laid Up

*Many a battle has been lost on the underestimation of a pawn's value.* - Master Kozias

Soventine threw a plaster bust of some obscure, long-dead nobleman across the room and watched it shatter against the closing door. His sole regret was missing the retreating Master Healer's head. He cursed his failing body, his idiot healing staff and whomever the decorator of this ghastly room might have been. Perhaps he should pass a mandate outlawing the use of burnt-orange paint in bedrooms.

Settling onto his pillow, Soventine rubbed his eyes wearily.

What should have been an easy trip by air ferry from High Empyrea to northern Aquiline had utterly depleted him of his energy and health. He had ignored the warnings of his Master Healers and undertaken the journey to collect Vannisarian, as it appeared that no one else could be trusted to carry out such a simple, yet vital task. But he had barely finished the first leg before becoming so ill that he could hardly even function.

Thankfully, being the King allowed one privileges that were not afforded those of lesser status, and his retainers had quickly secured lodging in the estate of Earl and Lady Kester. At least he would be comfortable until he was well enough to resume his journey.

Soventine opened one eye to see Gensing, his trustworthy chamberlain, slip into the room.

"Oh dear. You've ruined another priceless heirloom, sire," Gensing said wryly, stepping over the fragments of plaster.

"Guard your tongue, man. I'm in no mood," Soventine barked. "They should be thanking me for removing such a hideous visage from a sleeping chamber. It's amazing anyone could find peace and slumber here with that monstrosity staring at them. Its eyes followed you, I swear it."

Gensing handed Soventine a cup. "I am truly relieved to see you feeling better, Majesty. This herbal tea should help you relax. Compliments of Lady Kester. She insisted on paying her respects, but the woman is annoyingly garrulous. I informed the sentries to keep her away, lest she entice you to a comatose state."

Soventine felt his tension easing away and he allowed a tight-lipped smile.

"I've been told by the Master Healers of your prescription..."

"Two months," Soventine groaned. "How can I rule if I am bound by silken sheets and orange walls for two months?"

"It is your health, sire," Gensing reminded him. "If you push yourself too much, there will be no moonless night in your future."

"If I do not bring Vannisarian home, there will be none, anyway," Soventine said. "No, I must summon him to me."

Gensing produced a messenger scroll from his belt. "I'm a step ahead of you," He readied the quill for Soventine's order. "But, if I may, a message will be difficult to deliver beyond the wetland borders."

"Not by magic. Bring Horse Master Copellian to me. He can personally deliver my summons to the princeling."

"But sire," Gensing said carefully, "The slave will not return. After all, you would be returning a once free man to his home..."

"Pawns can only move forward, Gensing. His loss is inconsequential. What is one mere slave, compared to eternity?"

"Of course." Gensing scribbled the order across his scroll. "How many soldiers will accompany him?"

"Two," Soventine began, and quickly continued as Gensing's

head shot up in incredulity. "I want my Night Wind tasked with this. Send Trual and Jurian."

"Would not a company of regular army be better suited for this, sire?"

"No. A group moves slowly and obviously. I may as well announce their journey to the bloody Keepers. Two Night Wind can handle this task better than a hundred soldiers."

"Of course," Gensing nodded.

"And make it quick. They must leave within the hour," Soventine added.

"Very good." Gensing rose and made for the door. His toe accidentally kicked a shard of plaster across the room. "Oh yes, and I will have the Kesters recompensed for their monstrosity, sire. But do take care not to destroy anything else. I don't know if your coffers can withstand your strident taste in art."

## -8-
## Gifts of Hilihar

*We face all enemies with honor. Except those we can't beat. Those, we stab in the back when they're not looking.* - Master Kozias

Kir removed the twine gingerly and set the flower aside. Gods only knew what lay inside the box. After a brief breath and bracing, she plucked up and opened it.

Her heart fluttered with memory and fluster. A single silver hair comb inlaid with lumanere sat in the bottom. The detailed swirls and decorations had been masterfully etched into the plating by one of Empyrea's greatest silversmiths.

There was no mistaking what it was, but she picked it up and rubbed her thumb over the smooth opalescent faceplate, then flipped it over just to be sure. The initials *KAK* were engraved into the back.

It had been hers. One of a twin set. Tarnavarian's engagement gift.

Although she had been unable to catch the slinky shadow man, he had not lifted a hostile hand to the royal party. What stuck in Kir's craw was Slinky's apparent delight in tormenting her. She couldn't fathom how he had come by one of her old possessions.

The jolting realization smacked her mind and she matched it with a chastising palm to her forehead. The man in her nightmare was none other than the slippery cigar-puffer. She had faced him in the dream battle. His hat and twin swords—*he* had been the adversary! She rolled her eyes that it hadn't smacked her a lot sooner.

"If you wanna face me, let's get it on. I only fancy games when my opponent will play to my face," Kir said boldly into the night, careful not to project her voice too much. She dared not wake anyone or alert

Inagor.

She was answered only with silence and the cry of a night hawk overhead.

Kir held her breath. She felt like a child waiting for a glimpse of a kortenfairy out a twilight windowpane. No matter how long it took, she'd hang onto that ledge of belief that in the next breath, her wait would be over. That glimpse never came. When she finally convinced herself that he wasn't ready to dance, she sighed in disappointment and tucked the hope away for later.

The comb and ithinar blossom were dropped into her pouch as she started for Vann's stateroom. They would make their grand entrance into Hilihar society in the morning. A good round of shut-eye would rest her for the busy day ahead.

Kir slipped into the gilded chamber she shared with the men. The Guardians had been offered individual quarters, but they had all opted to room with Vann with the excuse of security and the reality of companionship. They had been sharing a tent for so long, the thought of being separated, even in slumber, felt unnatural. Even though the stateroom was small, it was well roomy enough for three cots to line the wall near the hatch.

Kir gave the chamber the once-over. Vann was resting soundly in his plush bed and her sweeping gaze hung up on him. Her feet wanted to move for the cots, but her eyeballs wouldn't budge.

Something about him just kept entangling her, even when she tried to sort the knots. Beyond his strikingly handsome features, the pureness of his soul was captivating. Vann approached each day as a gift, even as each day brought him closer to his cursed destiny. It was a remarkable quality, to light a smile in the face of darkness. He had lit up the crannies in Kir's own darkness, and illuminated a shadowed well of foreign feelings in the pit of her awareness. She couldn't wrap her mind around the strange emotions he was rubbing raw. It wasn't simply admiration—it was deeper and more complex than that.

Staring at him in peaceful repose, Kir's heart filled with the warmest sensation she had ever known. It was like a need that could never fully be sated. She was standing in the middle of a stream, yet she was dying of thirst...

"Kir?" Malacar's voice roused her.

"Did I wake you?" Kir asked self-consciously.

"No. Is it my turn for watch?"

"Inagor says there's no need for two sentries on duty here. We're relieved for the night," Kir hushed-talked, eying the lonely cot beside Malacar's. "Where's Ponytail?"

"Lili has him occupied at the moment. I think she's tutoring him on more than just Hilian culture. Don't expect his return until daybreak."

Kir plopped on her mattress and tugged off her boots. "Good

for him. 'Bout time."

"Good? I thought you'd grumble complaint."

"It's long overdue. Celibacy and Scilio don't make a merry mix." Kir tried to sound annoyed, but she knew the giggles soaked through her voice. "Can't turn a tide from its true and natural course."

Malacar chortled softly, then settled into his pillow. "Pleasant dreams, Kir."

Dreams. If only such things *were* pleasant.

When his eyes were closed, Kir pulled off her halter and slipped into the wispy silken nightdress Lili had provided. It was soft and soothing, but she made a mental note to awaken before the men. She dared not get caught wearing such girly foofaraw. She had a reputation to maintain that didn't include luxurizing. Even though the gown *was* on the blushing side of heavenly. Kir had to appear strong and sturdy and confident. A warrior. Warriors did not outfit themselves in silks and lace. It just wasn't fitting.

After convincing herself that she was still in possession of a leathery warrior's heart, Kir slid between the sheets and her mind returned to the mystery man. It would do no good to fret on him. He would sign her dance card soon enough.

Before she drifted off, Kir pulled the Princey Charm to the forefront of her mind to barrier the nightmares. The stranger might have found a way onto the boat, but Kir would be damned if she would allow him back into her dreams.


The Kion floated slowly through the streets of Hilihar. Kir felt like she was in a parade. Six smaller boats escorted them in stately ceremony, all decorated with shimmering banners in Vann's chosen royal colors of sky blue and silver. The waterway was well-marked by a row of Hilians who leaned over longboat edge to drum the water in rhythmic cadence as the Kion passed them by.

They were on the path of delivery to the Circle for the official presentation of the Crown Prince. This was Vann's chance to negotiate for the support and allegiance of the Hilian people. Kir was happy that the Hilians would finally have a voice in the Empyrean court, and she knew Vann would argue for them when he reached High Empyrea. Such a deliberate association would make his reign no easier, but she wholeheartedly believed that he was in the right. The Hilians were just as much a part of the country as the Alakuwai, and they deserved to be recognized officially as an autonomous body.

Thousands of Hilians lined the waterway in their longboats, hoping for a glimpse of the prince. They cheered and waved to Vann and Palinora, who stood at the beakhead, on a rostrum above the ornately carved dragon's head.

Vann's arrival was announced in the native language, and while Kir did not speak it, a few familiar words popped from the backdrop of the muddle. Three years ago, Mirhana had taught her some Dimishuan phrases in anticipation of their arrival in Hili. Kir could not speak the language, but she understood enough to be dangerous, if nothing else.

The Guardians stood at attention behind Palinora and Vann in a ceremonial queue. They had dressed themselves as immaculately as possible, given the limited wardrobe available. Their polished Guardian swords occupied places of honor at their hips, situated on their belts at exactly the same degree. It was rather ridiculous to position your sword at such an inconvenient angle for drawing, but Kir begrudged an understanding of the necessity of formality. They were not dressed alike, but at least their swords were uniform.

Malacar and Inagor wore leather cuirasses and formal capes, reminiscent of the standard army dress cape of the day. Scilio was outfitted in his usual prissy shirt, black pants and white cloak that looked as misplaced in summer as a malcraven in an aviary. Kir wore a Hilian red halter top and flowing pant-skirt, and her hair was pulled back into an elaborate twisting ponytail, compliments of Queen Palinora. As Kir had no jewelry or accessories, save the silver comb, she had taken the ithinar blooms left by the mystery man and woven them into the cleavage of the hair-twist for decoration. Of the four, Kir looked the least like a Guardian, but at least she was presentable.

Vann was spectacularly outfitted in the dress robes of a ruler. The long and flowing formal royal garments had always seemed knee-slapping sissified to Kir, but she couldn't argue with eons of tradition. Wearing the robes, Vann looked regal and powerful, almost a different person than the kid she had found hiding in the brush all those months ago. But when he threw a glance sideways, his eyes showcased the same innocent sparkle Kir had come to cherish. The wrappings might have changed his appearance, but underneath he was still Vann.

The Kion drew upon a wondrous rotunda in the center of the city and sidled up to the pier slowly. The structure was beautiful and gargantuan. The tiled roof was shaped with angles that curved upward like a smile. The outer walls were plastered with pieces of opalescent shells and beads in ornate mosaic patterns. As with the Kion, banners of fabrics hung from the beams. The attention to form and fancy detail was a stark contrast to the simple and unpretentious homes of the typical Hili resident.

As the Kion made its approach, Ulivall directed Vann and Palinora to the gangplank. They descended to a pier that connected by covered bridge to the large structure.

"The Grand Hall," Ulivall presented with a sweeping hand. "Our political center and home to the Circle, our governing body."

The party disembarked and were ushered into the building. Ulivall led them down a hallway toward a set of heavy double doors.

"Remember Vann," Palinora reminded him softly. "Speak little, say much."

Vann nodded curtly, his muscles clenched to stone in apprehension.

"And for Alokien's sake," Inagor added, "loosen up."

After a deep breath, Vann nodded to Ulivall. "Proceed, Grand Master."

### -9-
# The Circle

*Remember that negotiation is another form of war. It may not be bloody, but it can most certainly be deadly.* - Master Kozias

"This is the Inner Chamber of the Circle. All of our current counselors speak your tongue, Majesty," Ulivall told Vann.

Two sentries opened the doors to a large, circular room. Twenty-one Hilians were seated cross-legged around a raised pedestal of obsidian glass, which supported a roaring fire in its center. They each wore matching pendants around their necks.

"I present His Majesty, Vannisarian Ellesainia, Crown Prince of Septauria, and Her Royal Highness, Palinora Ellesainia de Craimwauld, Queen of Septauria," Ulivall boomed.

As Vann stepped through the frame, the members of the assembly tipped forward and touched their foreheads to the floor in reverence. Vann raised his hand and bid them rise.

"I bring greetings and an offer of friendship to the people of Hili," Vann said, projecting all the pomp of his status.

One of the members raised a welcoming hand. "I am Counsel Elder Trenen. Please, Majesties, join our circle and share our words."

Trenen beckoned Vann and Palinora to an empty place at the circle, which sported a lady's prop for Palinora's use. Vann took his mother's hands to offer stability as she lowered herself into the squat wooden chair, which was specially designed for women of noble status, to prevent crumpling of their multi-layered skirts.

When Palinora's dress was arranged and she was comfortable, Vann was offered a similar seat. He politely refused, choosing to rest on the floor as the counselors did, rather than sit regally above the throng as he would be expected to do in Empyrea. He was attempting to "be the people," as Kir had always instructed.

The Guardians remained standing in their formal queue, ever vigilant behind their charges. Their prior casual informality had been packed away for the officiality in the occasion.

"Welcome to Hili, Prince Vannisarian. To Queen Palinora, we bid you greetings upon your safe return," Trenen said. He held up an ornately carved wooden chalice, as though offering it to the heavens. "That I will be true," he announced, taking a sip from the rim.

The Elder passed the chalice to the counselor sitting to his right. The man accepted the cup and introduced himself before repeating the phrase that Trenen had spoken. When he had sipped from the cup, he then passed it on. The chalice made its way around the circle of counselors, each of whom made a brief introduction before pledging their veracity. Finally, the chalice found itself in Palinora's hands. When the Queen had completed the ritual, she handed the chalice to Vann, who did likewise.

Kir choked back protest. To drink an unidentified liquid in the company of strangers was reckless. Even if they were supposedly safe in Hilihar, it still took everything Kir had to keep from slapping the foreign cup away from Vann's lips. When he had finished drinking and displayed no immediate ill effects, Kir berated herself for being overprotective.

"Now, we may begin our talks," Elder Trenen announced.

"Your Honors, I come to initiate rapprochement. I bear an offering of peace between the Alakuwai of Septauria and the Dimishuans of Hili," Vann began. "And to prove my friendship, I offer your people a voice in the court, in exchange for your political allegiance."

One counselor, a younger man seated on the far side of the circle, stretched his hand outward. The flame contained on the obsidian pedestal seemed to leap toward the man, as though it were a solid mass. It congealed before the counselor and collected into a fiery ball floating just above his outstretched palm.

"Your Majesty, allow me to be frank," the counselor said. His keen eyes glowed with a passion that Kir had only seen in the heat of combat, and she wondered if this room was his battlefield. "Long have our people wished to be heard and heeded. But a voice is just that. Only *action* begets progress."

When the counselor had finished speaking, the ball of fire sped back toward the pedestal, where it resumed its original brilliance.

Another counselor raised her hand and the flame, once again, sped away from its platform. As it congealed into a ball above the woman's open palm, Kir realized that the flame was some sort of indicator to mark the next in line to speak. How clever, to have devised such a method of turn-taking!

"Counselor Ferinar makes a valid point. What good a voice, if no heart with which to back it?" the woman asked. The flame returned to its place quickly.

"I understand your apprehension," Vann said sincerely when the Speaking Flame hovered before him. "I have every intention of addressing the King in regards to your plight. My heartfelt desire is the ultimate abolition of slavery, but please understand that I am a newcomer to the Crown and the court. Until I am King, my authority only reaches so far. I hope that your people can offer me your support until that time, based on my word of trust."

"Can you guarantee that you will abolish slavery upon your Ascension?" one counselor asked.

Vann hesitated. It was clear that he was trying to determine just how far he could stretch a promise. "I am afraid I cannot make such a claim. Not at this time. When I am established in the court and better understand the workings of the Crown, perhaps then I may be able to devise a way to legally abolish the practice."

"Your Majesty," Ferinar reached quickly for another turn. "You offer us vague *perhapses* and future *maybes*. While your people hold ours in bonds. How can you claim to be friend when you suffer this outrage under your very nose?"

Kir could detect the anger in the man's voice. It was a bitterness that was well familiar to her tongue.

"If only injustices were so easily cast aside, Counselor Ferinar," Vann said. "It is complicated."

"You are the Crown Prince. Uncomplicate it."

"All I can promise is that I will try," Vann offered. Kir could hear the strain in his voice. Things were not going as well as he had likely hoped.

Elder Trenen held his hand out and awaited the fire ball. "Your Majesty, what absolute assurance *can* you make us?"

Vann considered for a moment before speaking. "Since the dawning of the new world, Septauria has built a kingdom on the foundation of a magic-based class system. The priests have long taught that the Dimishuan people were gifts from the Gods, as evidenced by their lack of magics. Clearly, those teachings are false. I cannot wipe away eons of tradition in the class structure with a causal wave of my hand, but I can demonstrate the fallacy in what we have always been taught. Magic is power in the eyes of the world. You are not without magic. You are not powerless. Therefore, you should not be placed at the bottom of Septaurian society. This is the best argument I can make in favor of your emancipation. I need your help to demonstrate your capabilities before the court.

"By your leave, a delegation will accompany me upon my journey to High Empyrea. We will negotiate with the King and his court immediately upon our arrival. We'll start with a petition for legal recognition of Hili as an independent territory, and a bill of emancipation. Your case will be argued with my unyielding support. Additionally, I will ensure safe passage for any future ambassadors. No longer will you fear being captured and returned to bondage while on official delegation. That I can promise you."

Elder Trenen nodded approval. "That, Your Majesty, is a start."

Mixed murmurs of disapproval and endorsement rippled around the circle. Kir could not quite make out which were more dominant.

"As Counsel Elder, I submit that a vote shall be held regarding your treaty. Our political allegiance in exchange for your voice. We will confer in private to deliberate and issue a vote. I will announce our decision tomorrow night at the welcoming feast," Trenen said.

Vann inclined his head politely. "I await your decision. Thank you for the opportunity to speak."

"Grand Master," Trenen addressed Ulivall. "Please see His Majesty's party to their next destination, then return to the Circle. We will reconvene at that time."

After respects and dismissals were paid, the royal party exited the chamber swiftly, following Ulivall back down the bridge toward the Kion. When they had boarded and Vann had removed his robes in favor of his casual attire, the group returned to the parlor. Lili announced that their next stop would be an official visit with Master Prophet Farning.

Kir knew that Vann was anxious to meet the man, who had become something of a celebrity among the Hilians for his contributions to their freedom. Farning had been granted asylum in Hili after being exiled from the Citadel and he was able to remove slave collars with his Prophetic magic.

"Is Farning's residence nearby?" Vann asked Lili.

"He is afforded a domicile near the Grand Hall, but he has requested that you meet with him this afternoon at a public location."

"In public?" Vann seemed surprised, and Kir couldn't help but echo the sentiment. It was unusual for official royal jibber-jabber to happen outside a controlled residence or meeting hall.

"Yes. He prefers to conduct his affairs while lounging in the local bathhouse. You will meet with him this afternoon. Please make yourselves comfortable in the parlor. Your meal will be served momentarily," Lili reported. She retreated down a passage toward the kitchens, directing busy staff as she went.

Vann sank onto a cushioned bench. His slumping shoulders mirrored his spirit. Kir was about to prod him with a question, when Malacar beat her to it.

"What troubles you, Majesty?"

Vann sighed heavily. "My first official negotiations and I utterly failed."

"Not true, Vann. The Circle is divided, but you are not defeated. Remember, dear one. These are an oppressed people. You must expect them to harbor ill feelings and skepticism toward their oppressors," Palinora soothed.

"I just don't know if I am able to do this job, mother. I have no experience in diplomacy, and I feel entirely out of my league." Vann shook his head despondently. "There were things I wanted to speak. Promises I wanted to make. But something held me back. I could not bring myself to voice assurances that I was not absolutely positive I could back up. I felt extremely limited as to what I could say."

"If I may interject?" Ulivall spoke up from his post at the door.

"That was likely due to the Veracity Potion you consumed."

"Veracity Potion? The chalice's contents," Vann blew out an exasperated breath. "I thought it was just a ritual pledge."

"The Circle always begins meetings in such a way. It allows the counselors to feel more assured as to the speaker's honesty."

"It's a good idea," Vann agreed sheepishly. "I only wish I had realized. Perhaps I would have chosen my words differently or—"

"You did fine, Vann. Trust me. Negotiation will be more comfortable with time, I promise you."

"The Queen speaks truth, Your Majesty," Ulivall said. "She is still under the Veracity Potion's effects, same as you."

Vann threw his mother a wary glance, then looked back to Ulivall. "How long does said potion last?"

"The effects should wear off within the hour."

Vann nodded, seemingly appeased.

The Kion floated down the Hiliharian waterways slowly, and while the talk in the parlor turned to lighter subjects, Vann remained silent. He was probably replaying the negotiations in his head, trying to determine where he had gone wrong or what he might have said that would have snared the counselors' instant loyalty.

Lili joined the party after a few minutes and announced the meal. She indicated a table that was packed with an array of light refreshments, both Alakuwai and Hilian in origin.

Malacar, Ulivall and Inagor, delighted with the variety of food, retreated to a corner with their loaded plates. They seemed to be heavily engaged in old combat stories, from what Kir could make out.

Scilio, Palinora and Lili began discussing the finer points of Hilian décor over their own meals. Lili led them around the parlor room, pointing out particular shift-paintings and tapestries.

Vann and Kir, alone, remained at the seating area. They sat in silence for a few minutes before Kir slipped away to the table and loaded a plate with a selection of bite-sized foods. She returned and offered the plate to Vann as she sat beside him on the bench.

He thanked her half-heartedly and poked at the munchies with a finger. He seemed like he'd lost his way inside his own thoughts.

"What do you think of this place, Stick?" Kir asked, trying to distract him from his insecurity.

"It definitely sports a character all its own, doesn't it?"

Kir agreed with a head bob. "I think I like it. Hilihar has a kind of elegance that's primal and unpretentious. It doesn't need jewels, lumanere and gold to showcase its natural beauty."

"Like you," Vann said boldly, meeting her eyes.

The sun rose in Kir's cheeks and she turned her head away. Her hand absently covered the thin scar that trailed down her neck. "Please don't tease me."

"I wasn't jesting, Kiri. I mean it. You look beautiful in Hilian attire," Vann insisted. "It becomes you."

Kir didn't feel beautiful. She was skinny as a bean pole post picking time and her skin was about as tanned and stropped as a stretch-hide. Even her manner, given to willfulness and candor, wasn't suited to delicate and desired ladyness. Such an observation on purported beauty was certainly false cajolery. Yet, it seemed as though Vann had offered it sincerely. He was still under the Veracity Potion's effects. The statement made her heart flutter. It had been ages since anyone had thought her comely.

"Well don't get used to it, Stick. I gotta find some clothes that cover a little more of my flesh before we get to Empyrea."

"Of what style were you thinking?" Vann inquired.

Kir knew what he was asking. "You mean, am I planning to dress like a man again? I have to, don't I? I've never seen a Guardian in a frock."

They shared a casual chuckle at the thought. The tension that had tightened Vann's shoulders seemed to evaporate to nothingness.

"I'll take more care in my choice of wardrobe, though," Kir added. "I'm a member of the royal entourage now and we're not hiding from the world anymore. Reckon I gotta endeavor to look like a Guardian. No more scruffy hats for me."

"Fantastic! Hats hide your eyes. They're too pretty to douse in shadow," Vann said.

"These things?" Kir blinked a few times. "They're not even mine. The color, I mean."

"Not yours?"

"Nope. Bought and paid for by my father. He wanted to impress yours, and he figured blue eyes were a better royal match than browns. A few potions and a lot of lorans later, my amber bogs turned icy skies."

"It's not the color that captures me. It's the depth and passion behind them that I love. I feel like if I were to fall into them, I'd never want to climb back out." He seemed surprised at his own admission, but he made no apology for it.

It had been a long road from the place where men paid compliment to Kir's anything, and she almost couldn't remember how to react to niceties. If they kept talking pretty, they might find themselves surfacing admissions they'd regret later. She nudged his arm lightly. "Well, fall into that plate, Stick. You'll never be able to climb outta anything if we don't get some meat on those bones."

Vann seemed thankful that she had diverted the topic away from awkward compliments. He bit into a flat biscuit topped with a sweet paste and a dusted with fine sugary powder. His eyes jumped to saucers in delight. "Taste this, Kiri. It's delicious!"

He offered her the remainder of the morsel and she leaned forward to accept it, allowing him to place it on her tongue. The delicate layers of flaky sweetness melted as the paste dissolved into a light and delectable whip. Kir closed her eyes and savored the pastry.

"You're right. It's a humdinger," she agreed euphorically.

Vann leaned toward her, rifling through his hip pocket. "You've got some sugar on you." He produced a handkerchief and brushed the white powder from her chin. His hand lingered a moment longer and he offered his dazzling smile.

Kir returned it gratefully, then motioned to the food remaining on Vann's plate. "Anything else worth trying?"

Vann slid sideways on the bench until their shoulders touched. He held the plate between them. "Let's find out."

A gradual change in the atmosphere of the parlor caught Kir's attention and her senses were suddenly alert. The light conversation that had hummed in the background had been slowly diminishing and was now gone, replaced by a tentative silence that hung on the air.

Kir turned her head to scan the room and realized with some agitation that every eye was parked on her and Vann. There was an odd level of amusement expressed in their features that Kir could not get a read on.

"Something wrong?" she asked to nobody in particular.

The quietude was abruptly replaced by a flurry of forced conversation, somehow louder and more contrived than it had been before.

"What's that all about?" Kir whispered.

"I haven't a clue," Vann replied, studying the two parties out of the corner of his eye.

Kir stayed mindful of the Guardians and their respective social cliques. As she and Vann continued a light discourse and exchanged opinions on the sampler foods, every now and again Kir would catch the Queen smiling at her in feigned innocence or Scilio's eyes wandering their way. Even Malacar, his features stoic but relaxed, would throw them an occasional inquisitive glance.

Kir shuddered at the strange behaviors. And it struck her as odd: even though their faces no longer projected amusement, she could see their eyes laughing.

# Revelations

* * *

## -10-
# Bathhouse Scenery

*Heat is a natural cure-all. It opens the pores, opens the blood vessels,*
*opens the mind, and opens the eyes. - Master Kozias*

"Master Prophet Farning awaits," Ulivall gestured toward a door marked with a vertical reed.

When Malacar pushed it open, misty steam scampered along the decking at their feet.

The men entered the bathhouse in turn, with Kir lagging behind. She stepped inside the humid room and tailed the party a few steps before skidding to a halt as she took in the environment. The large room did house an indoor public bath, just as Ulivall had described, but he had failed to mention that this particular bath was reserved for the male population. Unlike the public baths in Cornia, the occupants of this bathhouse liked sweating in the nekkid.

As man in his all and glories walked by, Kir felt her cheeks explore seven hues of crimson.

"The disrobing facilities are this way," Ulivall instructed, leading the party toward a hut on the far side of the room.

Kir shuffled sternway toward the door. She wasn't sure whether Ulivall had forgotten her presence or just chosen to ignore it, but the prospect of sitting sunny-side up beside her brother Guardians shuddered her bones with mortification.

A brief, unbidden fantasy of Vann stepping into the rocky pool, caressed by rolling billows of steamy humidity, played across the theater of Kir's mind. She shooed the perversion away as swiftly as it registered.

*It's the heat making me loopy*, she thought, unconvinced at her own explanation, but clinging to it dearly for justification anyway.

Her feet shuffled backward, each step bringing her closer to the escape. Her efforts to slip out unnoticed were in vain.

"Guardian Ithinar? Aren't you joining us?" Inagor asked.

The entire royal party turned about on their heels, as if cued to the question. Their eyes bored expectant holes into her face.

"Uh—well—you go on ahead. Queen—the umm—the Queen needs a gargantuan...a Guardian," Kir stammered.

"Come bathe with us, Guardian Ithinar. Don't you want to meet Farning?" Vann urged.

"You can send him my warmest regards." She inched backward purposefully.

The men stood there. They stood there, simply staring. And smiling. And staring. And smiling some more.

Guarded hilarity was painted all over their faces and Kir suddenly realized that they had lured her into the malcraven's den for just such a reaction. She had fallen victim to their joke. What would they have done had she been brazen enough to join them? If only she were that bold!

Her retreat was cut off as her stern smacked against a hull of chiseled muscle and rigging. Her neck craned on a path of horror to the aft view.

"Teneka na," the stranger said simply, in pardon.

Snickers and muffled laughter rippled from behind as Kir muttered a fleeting, "'Scuse me!" and fled toward the door. She thrust herself into the cooler air and cursed as the door clapped shut.

"Perverted blackguards," she murmured under her breath.

Much to Kir's dismay, Lili rounded the corner.

"Guardian Ithinar? Are you looking for the women's bath?"

"I was just seeing His Majesty safely inside," Kir managed through a clenched jaw.

Lili cocked her head suspiciously. "Did they lure you in there? I overheard them discussing such an evil plot just before the Kion docked."

"Wenchin furies, Lili, but you should have warned me!" Kir cried.

"I'm sorry. I was sworn to secrecy. Toma—pardon me— Guardian Scilio wanted to see how red he could make your face. And I believe lorans were wagered on the form of your reaction."

"Ponytail was the instigator, huh? I shoulda known," Kir said, rolling her eyes. The prior embarrassment, still evident on her cheeks, was replaced with the strong desire to exact revenge. Her mind raced, toying with ways to repay the Bardian. "He should have thought about the other men in the room. I'm sure they were much more flustered than I was."

Lili placed a reassuring hand on Kir's arm. "The Dimishuan people do not share the same level of modesty as the Alakuwai. I am positive the occupants were not distressed by your presence. If you care to relax in a more comfortable environment, the women's bath is down this hall. The Queen is waiting for you."

Kir nodded gratefully and followed Lili down the hallway. The women's bathhouse door was marked with a horizontal reed, and Kir made a mental note to remember the distinction, although she thought it would have been a lot more giggle-worthy had it been marked with a circular reed.

When she had finished stripping her clothes off in the disrobing hut, Kir returned to the bath where Queen Palinora was soaking.

"Kiriana! I was hoping you would join me," Palinora said merrily as Kir slipped into the rocky pool.

"The men's bath was just a little too steamy for my tastes." Kir placed her Guardian sword on the ledge behind her and leaned back against the wall of the relatively empty pool. She felt the unrealized stress in her muscles melting away. "I'd forgotten how wonderful this feels."

"It's been a while since you've enjoyed a public steam bath, hasn't it?" Palinora asked conversationally.

"Years. They're not very common in the backwoods parts of the world." Something tickled Kir's knee and she rubbed the skin, shooing away whatever had brushed against her.

The public bathhouses in Cornia where Kir was raised were mostly frequented by the middle and higher classes. They were exclusive members-only clubs, and favored meeting places for teenagers and adults alike. Such public baths were rarely found outside of large cities, and they usually existed in classier neighborhoods.

Kir was surprised and delighted to find that the Hilians appreciated such baths. Part of her wondered if the existence of the bathhouse in Hilihar was a deliberate biting-of-the-thumb at the oppression they had suffered. If it was, Kir couldn't help but raise a mental toast in applause. After years of watching their masters soak lazy muscles in the rejuvenating heat, the Libertines were finally able to enjoy the same luxury.

The use of magics in this bathhouse was exactly the same as in Cornia. The pool was heated by Inferno magic in a chamber below the stone floor. The weight must have been extreme, but the structure was built up on stilts and reinforced to accommodate. As far as Kir had seen, it was the only structure in Hilihar built entirely of such material. That fact, alone, spoke of the importance the people placed on their bathhouse. The expense and difficulty to transport so many stones across the Arshenholm Valley must have been tremendous. The pool looked large enough to comfortably support forty bodies. No small feat, considering they were perched atop a lake.

Although the room was similar in design to those in Cornia, the style spoke entirely of Hilian tastes. Cornian bathhouses tended to utilize marble, gems and lumanere for ornamentation, while the Hilians used natural elements like stone, driftwood, and flora. Walls of bamboo and reed comprised the perimeter of the room. Primitive, yet entirely reflective of the environment, and beautiful in its own definition of the word.

A modest stone waterfall on the far side of the pool trickled lazily, and Kir inhaled deeply at the relaxing sound. She closed her eyes and let her mind drift. Sometime later, Lili began to speak to an elderly woman who was seated nearby and they exchanged light conversation in the Dimishuan tongue.

Something tickled Kir's leg again and she sat upright, trying to determine what she had felt. The swirling heat made the water cloudy and opaque, limiting the distance she could penetrate with her eyes.

There it was again. A fleeting flicker just under the cloudiness. Kir moved swiftly to snare the object, but came up with a handful of nothing.

"Is there something in the water?"

"Oh, you are probably feeling the quen-tena. Skin fish. They're harmless," Lili said.

"Skin fish? Somehow that name doesn't sound so harmless," Kir replied, scanning the water again for the offending creature.

"They latch onto the bathers and consume the topmost layer— only the dead skin," Palinora explained. "It reportedly makes the skin smooth and supple. It is a mutually beneficial association between fish and beauty-seeker. The latching is painless, and most bathers don't even notice that the fish are there."

"I can understand the use of such things, but it makes it no less creepy," Kir commented. "Women sure do strange things to attain beauty, don't we?" She thought better of the comment, then added, "Well, not me. But women in general."

"Indeed," Palinora leaned forward conspiratorially. "Though, perhaps the methods we use to maintain beauty don't seem so extreme if we have someone to impress."

Kir smiled. The Queen was likely thinking of Guardian Arrelius. They had been lovers, living as a married couple during their exile. "It's pretty amazing that you've known him for so long and still look at him that way."

"Who? Oh, you refer to Inagor?" Palinora's eyes smiled back at Kir. "Yes, I suppose it is. So many people take their love for granted, and they forget why they fell in love in the first place. In our case, perhaps life in constant peril served to remind us every day of what we had to lose. We still feel just as passionately for each other, even after all these years. It's the kind of love that endures. I wish the same for you. Without the peril driving it, of course."

Kir's smile faded and her gaze fell to the water. A pang stabbed to her heart. "That is something I'll never know, I'm afraid."

"Of course you will, my dear. You are young. You have your entire life ahead of you."

"I'm not exactly 'marketable goods'."

"Love is not an auction, Kiriana."

Kir nodded but said nothing. In her mind, she knew the Queen was correct. She *was* young. But the life of a Guardian did not portend long-abiding happiness. In fact, it did not portend a long life at all. Kir was no longer seeking death, but the Soul Collectors hadn't turned their cold, yearning eyes from her. And even if she survived her Guardianship, there was no way she could attract a suitor. She was damaged and no longer a prize.

Palinora eyed Kir for a few moments. "Well, I am quite satisfied. The heat is delightful, but only in small doses. I shall retire to my room to freshen up before tea. I would like a slice of that scrumptious lychee pie sitting in the Kion's parlor, as well. The pastry chef here is quite masterful at his trade." She rose and started for the steps, then turned back. "You know, Kiriana, I remember the sweetest bakery pie I ever tasted. It came from a poor merchant's table, in a box that was dented and torn. And to think, I almost passed it up for the pristine, decorated box in the classy shop next to it."

As the Queen stepped out of the pool and glided gracefully toward the disrobing hut, Kir bit her lip and laughed silently. Palinora did love sneaky analogies.

When they were dressed, Palinora and Lili exited the bathhouse. Kir found herself, with the exception of the elderly woman seated a few feet away, alone in the steamy bath. She closed her eyes and leaned back against the smooth stone wall, listening to the soft and soothing trickle from the pool's waterfall. She fell into her own mind, clearing her thoughts and taking in the comfortable solitude.

After a few minutes, footfalls pattered softly on the floor, and she opened one eye to observe the latest occupant to the room.

The moment her mind registered the newcomer's identity, Kir's heart practically clawed its way into her throat. Walking around the perimeter of the pool was none other than Bertrand.

**-11-**

# Confluence

*Don't make an enemy of a misfit. He has*
*nothing to lose.* - Master Kozias

Bertrand's distant gaze did not stray from the stones at his feet and he made no acknowledgments to Kir. The boy walked purposefully toward the elderly woman. She issued a flat greeting when he plopped down behind her. His thighs formed a horseshoe around her back as he thrust his feet into the hot water at her shoulders.

Without a word, Bertrand's fingers closed around the old woman's neck and shoulders. A Healing light glowed from his palms. He worked expertly and swiftly, apparently addressing some ache or ailment the elder was suffering. The woman exhaled deeply in relief.

After a few minutes, Bertrand withdrew his fingers and the light faded.

The woman muttered something to the boy healer in Dimishuan, then rose from the water and made her way toward the disrobing hut. Bertrand remained motionless.

Kir sank low under the waterline until her face was partially submerged, hoping to avoid attracting his attention. Cowering and hiding was not her style, but then, Bertrand was not a typical adversary. She feared his penetrating eyes more than any blade or spear.

Kir looked to the doorway of the disrobing hut where her clothes awaited her, but she could not make it. Too many footsteps separated the edge of the pool from the safety that the hut would provide. She was stark naked and he was a twelve-year-old boy.

*If only there were a stray towel or robe nearby,* Kir thought. Her eyes darted desperately around the room in search of such an abandoned article. She was left disappointed. The steaming water was serving to shield her, but only bodily. It could not protect her thoughts. She was trapped at Bertrand's mercy.

There were two options: flee or stay.

If she left now, she'd be exposing her modest hull to his juvenile male peepers. On the other hand, if she stayed, Bertrand would likely begin another freaky conversation where Kir would fall victim to his penetrating gaze and icy brain-grip. She weighed the two options, trying to decide whether it was better to be naked of body or of mind. The longer she lingered, the greater the chance of him noticing her presence. *Not that he doesn't already realize I'm here. He can invade my head and hear my every thought.*

"I am not an invader," Bertrand said, still staring at the water.

*Well, there goes Option A.*

Kir sat upright and raised a contentious eyebrow at the kid. "Then, how did you know what I was thinking?"

"For the holes in your mind," he replied. "You're riddled."

Kir was about to comment that he was more of a riddle than she, but instead, she asked, "Holes?"

"I told you before. You are wounded," Bertrand stated, as though the answer was obvious. He continued to stare at his feet.

Kir remembered Bertrand making that statement in the Arshenholm Valley during their first conversation. She had decided that the observation must have been hypothetical, as she surely could detect no injuries unaware. Kir had wondered what he meant, but had long since dismissed it as more of his odd-talk.

Since Bertrand was there and the topic had come up, Kir decided to probe him for more information. It was unlikely she'd be able to make anything out of his riddles, but it was worth asking. "I am wounded. What does that mean?"

"Riddled," Bertrand replied. "Someone poked holes in your mind. I do not invade your thoughts. They spill out to me."

It was true, she was weak against Psychonic magic. Kir had always tried to safeguard her thoughts from prying Psychonic users, but they seemed to find ways into the crevices of her mind anyway. That she was so unskilled at guarding her brain gears had been a frustration for her in recent years, but she had not realized that there was more to it. The damage Tarnavarian had inflicted during her torture sessions must have gone deeper than she had realized.

The idea was jarring and sobering. She was a liability with such a weakness, and to learn that her mind was so readily open to assault? No wonder the child Jessia had been able to snare her so easily all those months before.

Kir swallowed hard and gathered her courage. "Can you fix me?"

Bertrand shook his head slowly, yet with a steady intent, like the rhythmic swinging of a clock pendulum. "Only you can."

"How? I am no healer, and I don't know the first thing about Psychonics. How could I ever fix myself?" Kir asked incredulously.

"Look to your patch."

"My patch?" It took everything Kir had not to shake Bertrand by the shoulders and beg him to speak straight, for once.

"Your crutch. Your talisman. You have used it before. Because it makes you strong," he replied simply, as though the answer was as clear as day.

"I still don't understand."

"You will," Bertrand assured her. Then, he said something that entirely threw her for a loop. "But I envy you."

Kir wanted to laugh and scream at the same time. "You envy me? You are the greatest healer in Septauria and you have an amazing power at your disposal. How ever could you envy *me*?"

"You do not know?"

Kir stared at Bertrand sternly. "Look inside my head and tell me that I have lived an enviable life. Say that with a straight face."

"The past is gone. Only now remains."

What did the present have to do with his proclaimed envy? Kir sighed, feeling the beginnings of a headache coming on. Talking to the kid was incredibly taxing, as it took so much effort to interpret his odd statements. "You speak in riddles."

As if in answer to her confusion, Kir suddenly felt a powerful surge of loneliness and heartache. She could see images swirling in her mind's eye: pictures of people whispering and pointing, children avoiding her with looks of disgust and fear and awe. She could feel their emotions, their reservations. Their reverence and their separateness.

Kir suddenly realized that Bertrand was sending her pieces of his own memory, but he was projecting it through the solidification of emotions that he had carried inside those terrible heartaches. The emotion-laden images he offered painted a clear picture of his life. And his own weakness. Bertrand was functionally different than other people, and the tragedy was that he knew it. He knew it, yet he was unable to grasp the social complexities that would allow him to function as a normal child.

Kir also realized that, despite the pampering and devotion he was granted, Bertrand had not a single person in the world who cared for him as he was. His abilities garnered him respect, while his oddities earned him avoidance and fear. Kir had been just one of many to issue him such a response.

"You're utterly alone. Your power makes you singular and while you're surrounded by people, you are the most ithinary creature in the world, aren't you?" Kir vocalized the realization.

"When one is singular, one shall know ithinary solitude everywhere. You know this. You were singular. You were ithinary. But no more."

"I understand," Kir whispered. She could not explain why a tear sprang to her eye. Perhaps it was an after-effect of the powerful sorrow embedded in the emotion-memories that Bertrand had projected to her.

"I envy you. Because you knew this life. And must know it no longer."

"No longer, because now I am part of something," Kir interpreted. "A brotherhood. With people who care for me, not for my abilities, but for who I am. And you've never known that."

"People only want me when they need me," Bertrand said, staring at his feet. "They flee when they can. They stay when they must."

"So, you have no true friends. Nobody sticks around for you, unless they're attending you out of duty. Why not?"

"Why did *you* want to flee when you saw me here?"

Kir hated when people answered a question with a question. "Well, honestly? I'm suppose I'm self-conscious. Because you can see inside me. I hate being vulnerable, and you make me feel that way," she admitted.

"And because I'm a *creepy little brat*. Most people find me so. And so they flee."

Kir felt a pang of guilt for having thought the phrase in Arshenholm, especially since Bertrand had "heard" it.

There were a few moments of silence. The babble at the base of the pool's waterfall was the only sound in the room.

Finally, Kir asked, "What did you mean by *they stay when they must*?"

"When there is circumstantial necessity," Bertrand answered. "Why did *you* stay in the pool?"

It dawned on Kir what he meant and the corner of her mouth turned up. "I see. My circumstantial necessity: I stayed because I'm naked."

The boy cocked his head. "A necessity I do not understand. I am a healer."

"I know that," Kir chuckled. "But I'm still naked."

"Why does that matter? Healers see all."

How did one explain modesty to a socially inept twelve-year-old? "It's just another self-consciousness on my part."

"Then, that is your circumstantial necessity," he responded.

"I get you, Bertrand. But, I'm no longer here out of necessity," Kir said, offering the kid a genuine smile.

"You are still naked. And you are still self-conscious," he replied matter-of-factly.

"Yeah, but like you said, you're a healer. I don't have anything you've never seen before. I'm staying now because I understand you. Because you've seen my weakness, and I've seen a bit of yours. Does that make us friends now?"

Bertrand stared at his feet with a profound look of pondering. The expression in his face was difficult to read, but he was likely trying to decipher her logic. She wondered if anyone had ever offered friendship to the boy in his entire life. "I do not know. Is sharing of weakness where friendship begins?"

"No. But sharing of understanding is. And I think I understand you now, kid," Kir told him.

"And I understand you more also. Not entirely. But more," Bertrand replied conclusively. He rose to his feet and started for the bathhouse door. "I will leave you with your self-consciousness."

When he was gone, Kir shook her head. She'd never had a conversation that was so confusing and enlightening at the same time.

As she stepped out of the hot pool and started for the disrobing hut, Kir realized that Bertrand's presence had not sucked the warmth from the room this time. Of course, she had been sitting in a steaming bath. But still, it was the first time she had talked to the kid that she wasn't freezing.

<h2>-12-<br>All Bets are Off</h2>

*Butt-naked and sweaty is a far better condition for wenching than for bathhouse politicking.* - Master Kozias

"Pay up, my fine fellows. Bully to His Majesty and myself!" Scilio exclaimed when the laughter had died down. "You predicted Kir's reaction masterfully, Vann. Even moreso than I. Applause. Between the two of us, we are unstoppable when it comes to character. A quality trait for the future King and his most brilliant adviser to possess."

Vann wiped a tear from his eye and bent over, clutching his aching abdominal muscles. He had not laughed so hard in ages and he felt rather guilty that it had been at Kir's expense. It was easier to laugh when it was happening all around you. Laughter was more contagious than the gingerpox. And Kir's expression when she fled the bathhouse *had* truly been priceless.

Inagor, Malacar and Ulivall divvied up their losings and distributed them to Vann and Scilio appropriately. Vann was granted the largest cut, as his predictions had been the most accurate.

Ulivall stepped away and scanned the empty pool with some annoyance. "I'm afraid the Master Prophet has not yet arrived. Forgive me, Majesty, but I must take my leave of you temporarily. The Circle awaits my input. Please make yourselves comfortable until Farning decides to show up."

When Ulivall was gone and the men had placed their clothes and weapons in the keeping baskets of the disrobing hut, they made their way toward the bath.

Vann stepped into the hot water and found a comfortable spot on the wall toward the mid-section of the pool. The Guardians followed suit, choosing places on either side of him. They waited for several minutes, taking in the soothing effects of the heat.

"This is really hot, but it feels great," Vann commented, more to himself than anyone in particular.

"Ah! This is your first steam bath?" Scilio asked.

"I've heard about them, but we were keeping a low profile when I was growing up. Joining the ranks of the upper classes would have drawn too much attention to us, so I was never allowed this luxury before. I think I could get used to it."

"Then, you'll be happy to learn of the massive steam bath reserved for the royal family in the palace, Vann," Inagor told him. "The pool itself is made of lumanere. The way it shimmers like glassy stone is quite beautiful."

"Truly?" Vann asked, delighted.

"If I told you half of the luxuries you will be granted at the palace, your eyeballs just might pop from your head," Inagor said.

"I don't know if I'll have time to enjoy such things. Doesn't a monarch have his hands full with the daily toils of running a country?"

"When you are King, you'll have a lot of administrators and bureaucrats at your disposal. And there's your court and the council of advisers. The Islandic Governors are responsible for their respective territories, so you won't have to worry about the 'nitty-gritty.' There will be plenty of responsibilities to keep you busy, that's true, but you will have more free time than you expect," Inagor assured him. "That assumption is based on the operations of your father, of course. I stood by your mother's side and observed for many years before we fled with you. The King spent more time on the hunt in Cornia than he did in the palace, in my opinion."

A cluster of air bubbles began to drift to the surface of the water nearby, lingering a moment before popping. Vann studied them curiously, then shrugged the attention away.

"My father will teach me, won't he?" he asked. "I'll be out-of-place there, having grown up amongst the people. I dare say learning of the palace from a book will be quite different than living the palace in person. I can't wait to meet him. All these years I've imagined what he's like. What our reunion would be. He lost so much when we slipped out of his life." He knew his eyes twinkled at the thought of his father. Soventine represented a romantic lost world that Vann only glimpsed from afar, but had longed to taste.

Inagor was silent for a moment. He and Malacar exchanged

glances, and Inagor heaved a weighty sigh.

Vann knew that sound. Inagor always issued that something-important sigh when he was about to reveal something, well, important. Vann could remember several of those instances throughout his life. He could understand Inagor and Palinora's over-protectiveness, but he still harbored a mild resentment and was growing tired of secrets. He was a man now, and would one day be King. He would have to make his desire known officially: he would tolerate no more secrets. Not by his parents. Not by his Guardians.

"Tell me," Vann said firmly. "What are you keeping from me?"

"It's been no secret, but we thought it best not to say anything. It is a rumor, after all," Inagor began. He glanced to Malacar and nodded, as though giving permission to divulge the revelation.

"Majesty, there has been word circulating for a while of the King's failing health," Malacar told him somberly.

"He's sick? Or, do you mean he's dying?" Vann felt a pang in his gut. Just when they were about to be reunited, he might be losing his father again?

"It is only a rumor, Vann, but it has been a persistent one for some time," Inagor said. "I pray you have time with him, I really do. But don't expect years. If the rumor is true, and I tend to believe that it is, we may be standing at your Ascension sooner than you think."

Vann inhaled deeply, trying to suck in air that the intense heat seemed to drain. "Then, we should not linger here too long. I need every day with my father. I've lost too much time with him already."

Inagor nodded tightly through a clenched jaw.

Another large cluster of bubbles rose to the surface, but this time, Vann was not the only one to notice.

Malacar waded toward the spot as Inagor and Scilio pulled Vann away. They placed their bodies in front of his protectively.

Reaching down through the opaque waters where the bubbles had surfaced, Malacar grasped something firmly and lifted the object from the water. He held a handful of moppy brown hair, which belonged to the head of an Alakuwai man. The man gasped for air, his hair still grasped firmly in Malacar's hand.

"How dare you approach His Majesty so—" Malacar began, but stopped as he studied the man's face. "Master Prophet Farning!"

## -13-
## A View From the Web

*The spider makes the perfect assassin. It sits as if no care in the world assails it and its prey is dead before it feels the sting.* – Master Kozias

The blood was not yet dry on the contract, and it smelled delicious. Soreina's long, graceful index finger blotted the sticky wetness. She drew it across her tongue, then closed her eyes and savored the salty metallic tang of the binding liquid. A smear remained on her digit, and she painted it on her lips, then pulled Six to her. She would have preferred One, but Six was handy and... ready. The sycophant traced the tip of his tongue along the smear, then engulfed her mouth with his own, kissing her greedily. Had she not been thirsty, she might have allowed his inching hand to continue its leisurely trail up her inner thigh. There was no pleasure to be had sans her favorite Beckett vintage, so she shooed him away to fetch a bottle.

Soreina loved these happy times.

These celebrations she allowed her subordinates following the acquisition of a new client were riotous, fiery and seductive. Soreina believed in rewarding behaviors with appropriate prizes, and the form entirely depended upon what type of behavior she was rewarding.

Naturally, her men feared and adored her. Their desires were her leash upon their necks. Soreina knew exactly what men desired. That knowledge, even moreso than her crafting with the Forbidden magics, was her greatest weapon. It had enabled her to become the most sought-after assassin in Septauria. No man could outmaneuver her abilities. She was nothing, if not exquisitely masterful at her craft.

Her generosity abounded tonight, as she had just made the deal of a lifetime. No other contract in her history, even those made with Soventine, himself, had been so lucrative, or so attractive. Attraction was, by far, the most important aspect of a prospective mission. Of the hundred or so offers each season, she had the luxury of selecting only the jobs that piqued her interest the most, and the longer she performed her work, the more difficult it was to generate that same passion anymore.

This particular venture would probably not be difficult, based on the intelligence Wardion had handed over in his tidy little folder. Soreina was not normally interested in "easy" but this was a special case. There were several ways she could play this, and the fun was in deciding just which angle to take.

The bitch was the most obvious path. Kiriana Ithinar nee Karmine would be a delightful means to the princeling's untimely demise. Her mind was pocked with holes, which would be easy to infiltrate. Of course, she was also something of a sister-in-pain, but Soreina had never really indulged her sentimental side. In fact, she doubted that it existed at all. The problem with going the bitch-route was that Karmine... Ithinar... whatever, was already broken. Where was the fun in shattering an already splintered mirror?

Option B was the big lout. Denian Malacar guarded not only the neck of the princeling, but a well of secrets, too, which would be easy to exploit. Galvatine would surely think it ironic that the former traitor-sentry would ultimately bring about the downfall of the very prince he'd betrayed the priesthood to protect. The drawback to this option, of course, was that Malacar had, according to the report, shown no interest in women, thanks to the psychotic bitch's blade that had uprooted his life. Soreina's job was so much more fun if she could enjoy her prey deeply and thoroughly before taking the fatal bite.

It would be Option C, she thought. The most captivating route to the prince's downfall would be the bard, Toma Scilio. Wardion's report made no mistake: the fop was a hands-down lecher. The most despicable and wonderful sort of rogue that Soreina could imagine. For there was no prey in the world more fun to toy with than a mark who chases the bite.

As an added bonus, Soreina had the Queen and her Guardian for the taking, once the job was complete, and Wardion had made no objections to the addendum. Soreina had never tasted royal blood before. She licked her lips at the delightful thought. And the two were lovers... Oh, the myriad wickedness that she could devise for the pair!

Wardion had insisted that his Keepers accompany Soreina, and it was a stipulation that was nonnegotiable. If it were any other job, she would have dejeweled the contract-bearer for insulting her with such a demand. Since this was a unique arrangement, she decided to allow the Keeper zealots along for the trip. Perhaps they would be of use, should she grow hungry for an appetizer.

Satisfied that the blood was finally dry, Soreina rolled the contract scroll and bound it with a scarlet ribbon. She placed it in a scroll box on the shelf, then turned gracefully and slipped through the room. Against the tattered darkness of the massive chamber, the flicker of Inferno lamps danced on the naked flesh of the men sprawled upon the floor, tables and fountain, exerting their manly passions on the four daughters of the last target.

The wenches had been a great catch, although three of them would probably not last the night. Soreina could see the defeat in their expressions. The fourth was a hardier breed and there was a beautiful, burning hatred in the woman's eyes. Hatred that Soreina knew all too well. This woman was a survivor, and she would hate until the very last.

The loss of the prizes would be disappointing, but such was a worthy sacrifice, if it kept the morale up, and her retinue satisfied. Their blood would keep for several months in the frost-cellar. Not that she expected to let it sit that long.

As her men continued in their drunken revelry, Soreina returned to her lush lounging seat to watch the spectacle. She was just about to recline, when she caught a glimpse of her glorious reflection in the mirrors that lined the far dark stone walls of the chamber. She paused briefly to bask in her own beauty, then slipped quietly into her seat, letting her ankle-length silver hair flow with wild abandon.

## -14-
## The Things that Bind

*Annoying children and river bottoms are a match
made for each other.* – Master Kozias

"Guardian Ithinar!" a young voice called.

Kir turned on the Kion deck to see a child, probably eleven or
so, scurrying toward her. A light band of golden skin around his neck,
where a collar once marked him as a slave, stood out in stark contrast
to his sun-glazed bronze body. He must have been a recent Libertine,
which was the Hili name for an escaped slave, freed of the collar.

"You found me," Kir responded, hooking a thumb at her chest.

"I have a delivery," the boy said. He thrust out a long paper-
wrapped object that was decorated simply with a breath of ithinar
blossoms.

Another gift from Slinky. Kir accepted the package, surprised at
its heavy weight. "Did you get a look at the man who sent it?"

"He was kinda shadowy and dark. He had a hood, so I couldn't
see his face. Maybe he was a *chadoda-suya.*"

Kir cocked her head. "What's that mean?"

"An ugly fu..." he paused, then bit his lip. Standing on tip-toes,
he stretched for Kir's ear, and whispered the forbidden word.

Kir's eyes spread like hoecakes on a griddle. "That's no
language for a kid. *Chadoda-suya*, was it? Do you know any more of
these great expressions?"

"Sure. I can swear fluently in four different languages," the boy
proclaimed proudly.

"Four? I'm impressed. I'm still trying to improve my vocabulary
in two. Maybe you can help me out," Kir suggested. "What's your
name?"

"Dailan the Nabber."

"Nabber? Not much of a name."

"Means I was a thief. My master taught me his trade and we
brought in quite a bit of graft. He weren't so bad. Spent a year with him
before he made a bad bet and lost me to another wenchin *kadda*. The
new master was right mean when he took to drinking. But he wasn't all
that bright. Took him an hour to teach me to pick a lock. Took me only
ten seconds to pick my own the night I escaped," Dalian said smugly.

Kir chuckled. She liked this kid. He was her kind of people.
"You're quite a dagnabber." She turned her attention to the package in
her hand. "Wager a guess?"

Dailan inhaled thoughtfully. "It's pretty heavy. Sword, maybe?"

"Let's find out." Kir ripped the paper away to reveal a branding
iron. She winced as the sizzle and smell of burning flesh assaulted her
memory. Had Dailan not been standing with her, she might have flung

the repulsive instrument immediately from her grasp. She maintained
rigid control of her emotions and, instead, channeled her loathing into
her tight grip. The metal was cool, and it could no longer hurt her.

"That brand matches the mark on your shoulder," Dailan said
warily.

"It surely does," Kir confirmed darkly, examining the head that
Tarnavarian had used to sear his royal crest into her. She inhaled and
pushed the lingering revulsion away. "But it just reminds me that my
master's dead and rotting. So this brand will never be used again."

Dailan nodded keenly.

Slinky had made his point with the symbol, and Kir could find
no reason to keep the vile object. Had Tarnavarian still lived, she might
have thought differently, as it would have amused her greatly to shove it
up a royal orifice or two. She would have to suffice with the wonderful
mental image. However, should the Guardians see the iron, it would
invite a slew of questions, so a practical means of disposal was in order.

Dailan's bare neck reminded Kir that he had recently been
released of his own master's mark. "When your collar was removed,
what did you do with it?" she asked.

"I let the lake eat it up."

"That's a good idea."

Kir strode to the Kion railing and leaned forward. She held the
branding iron out over the water and opened her fingers. The
despicable marker plopped and disappeared almost instantly as it sank
into the murky depths of Lake Hili.

"So long," Kir called to it, saluting in mockery. "May you rust
forever." She turned to Dailan. "Now then, Dagnabber. Four different
languages, you say..."

## -15-
## Inhibitors and Inhibitions

*Evil is in the eye of the rule-maker.* - Master Kozias

Farning blinked repeatedly as though trying to clear dust from
his eyes. He was small and wiry, at least three heads shorter than
Malacar. Red heat painted his face in splotchy islands that floated in a
sea of pale skin. Tiny, beady eyes were set back into his face, and they
darted around madly.

"What in the Five Layers of Hell did you do that for, you big
lummox?" he asked Malacar in a voice as wiry as his body. He slapped
at the Guardian's hand, which was still firmly gripping his mop of wet
hair.

When Malacar released him, Farning slipped back into the
water and his head bobbed for a moment like a cork in a washbowl. He
righted himself, planting his feet into the rocky pool bottom to stabilize

his balance.

"Captain Malacar, that was the rudest awakening I have ever—" Farning began, then stopped in mid-sentence. "Ah, Captain Malacar! No, *Guardian* Malacar, I see!" He snatched Malacar's vambraced arm and squinted an eye. He studied the vambrace closely, then distantly, as a Gem Master scrutinized a diamond. "Kion-Eska. Very nice. Very nice specimen. The Gods have been gracious. Welcome back, Guardian Malacar!"

Farning turned his attention to Inagor. "And Guardian Arrelius. Back from your jaunt. And with two new faces in tow."

Inagor bowed casually to the Master Prophet. He introduced Vann and Scilio with a formal edge to his casual presentation. Apparently, the Master Prophet had little use for show.

Farning glanced at Scilio first, eying him intently. "A Shunatar. Impressive."

"Shunatar?" Malacar probed.

Farning nodded absently. "It's the eyes."

"Oh," Malacar said, clearly befuddled. He made a questioning face at Scilio, whose expression was equally clueless.

"His purple eyes," Inagor whispered to Malacar, the tone indicating that it was more of a question than a statement.

Vann stepped toward the strange little man. "Greetings, Master Prophet. I have long awaited this day."

"Yes, yes. Chaos Bringer. Fine, fine specimen," Farning mumbled to himself.

*Chaos Bringer*? Vann shot a glance at Inagor, who shrugged uncertainly.

Farning squinted his eye and scanned Vann, crown to sternum, in obvious scrutiny. He made no bows or formal greetings, as was typical of a royal introduction. "Hmm... Young. Definitely a fawn in spots. Handsome, no doubt. Tall. More muscular than expected, based on previous reports. Brains?" he asked Vann.

"Excuse me?" Vann blinked.

"Well, maybe not as many brains as I'd hope. But at least he's intelligible," Farning muttered under his breath as he continued his analysis. "Mother's eyes. Father's constitution. Yes, I'd say you're definitely *him*."

Vann bit back a laugh. Was this man the genuine article, or was this another one of Scilio's pranks? A quick glance at the dumbfounded Bardian assured him that no trickery was afoot. It appeared that the rumors of Farning's eccentricity were not exaggerated.

It struck Vann that the man must have been holding his breath for quite some time. "Master Prophet, may I ask why you were under the water? I did not see you enter the pool, so I assume that you have been holding your breath for the duration of our bath," Vann commented.

"Of course I was, boy. Can't get good prophecy without a little deprivation now, can we?"

"Deprivation of what?" Inagor asked.

"Air, of course. Air to the brains. The best communes with the Gods come when you are good and drunk on deprivation," Farning replied.

Vann raised an eyebrow. "So, were you communing with the Gods? Did they have anything interesting to say?"

"Not a thing. I did get a magnificent euphoria from it, though I wasn't down long enough to really get into the prophecy-range. Thanks to Guardian Malacar's interruption," Farning grumbled. "Given another five minutes, I might have been rolling."

"Another five minutes?" Scilio asked dubiously. "Would you not have been drowned long before that?"

"Oh, no," Farning shook his head, sending droplets of water scattering from the ends of his moppy hair. "There is a method, you see. You must call upon your Healing magics. Stop your breathing. Slow your heart. Then, you can use your Healing magics to keep you alive whilst you enter the sacred world betwixt and between. That's where the Gods can meet you."

"Killing your brain allst the while?" Scilio said, his voice teetering on the edge of hilarity.

"But Master Prophet," Vann argued, "Why must you go to such extreme methods to commune with the Gods? Can you not have a Holy Chamber built here? Like those in the temples?"

The temple Holy Chambers were said to be the sacred rooms where the prophets communed with the Gods and transcribed the given prophecies. Such rooms were not of the world, nor were they the Heavens. They were somehow in-between. A limbo where prophecy was delivered.

"What kind of prophet do you take me for, boy?" Farning asked. He rolled his eyes and shook his head, as though Vann had just asked the most ridiculous question in the world. "One would have to be a God to accomplish such a thing. No, much better to enter the Holy State by deprivation. Or with cashnettar. The Hilians sometimes use such a method. But it's very expensive and hard to come by. Only grows in the wilds of Arcadia. Not many will venture there. Not with the Chaos in those wilds."

Vann had heard tales of the kaiyo in the Arcadian wilderness, of the Chaos that was bred there, but he had never lived on the island. He knew very little about the place, save what history reported, and what little Inagor would say.

The battle of Cerener Valley, which was fought in Arcadia, had secured the King's victory in the civil war, twenty years past. Arcadia had fallen quiet since that time, apparently licking its wounds after the defeat. While there were no more attempts at revolution, the island was still said to harbor terrible creatures of chaos.

"What does cashnettar do?" Vann asked.

"Brings you into a Holy state. Smoke just a puff and you can receive prophecy as easily as you can blink. The Hilians come here to their bathhouse to smoke and bake so the Gods will speak. The heat makes the delivery all the crisper. That's why they built the bathhouses. Well, that, and the heavenly luxury, of course. But mainly for the prophecy," Farning replied. He raised an eyebrow at Vann and studied him for several long heartbeats. "Would you like to tap your mantic gifts, boy? Would you like to speak to your Gods?"

Vann hesitated. He was suddenly beginning to question the entire process. Could one truly trust a deprivation or drug-induced state? How could Farning be sure that he was not transcribing some hallucinatory figment of his own warped mind? "I don't know, Master Prophet."

"Oh, fie-piddles. What are you afraid of?" Farning taunted.

"Well, for starters, I cannot cast magic. I have been marked, you see—"

"Oh yes. I had almost forgotten," Farning nodded sharply.

"It has been suggested that you might be able to remove the marks," Vann said.

For some reason, he was hesitating. Given what he had just heard, he was not sure he could really trust this Farning.

"Of course I can, boy! After all, I was the one who placed them."

Vann practically choked on his own saliva. "*You* placed them?"

"When you were just a pup. I needed a way to keep track of you, understand? But that old slug must have figured it out," Farning muttered something, and while Vann could not hear it, he was sure it was some manner of insult.

"Old slug? That would be Galvatine?" Vann reasoned.

"You're quicker than I thought," Farning said sarcastically, eying Vann again. "Yes, I mean Galvatine. He must have started sending those snake-handlers after you when he learned of the marks. But, that is no longer an issue now. As I can remove them."

"How do we accomplish that?" Vann asked.

"We? Oooh, no. It takes years of practice to achieve the title of Master Prophet, boy. You have a lot of work ahead of you before you can ever dream of attempting such a complex task. No, I will remove the marks for you. And the inhibitors, as well."

"Inhibitors?" Vann asked with a start.

"I placed the inhibitors to ensure that you were not tempted to cast at full strength," Farning explained. "Royals tend to display high levels of magics, you see, and powerful castings would have drawn attention to you. Therefore, you've been able to cast, but your abilities are somewhat muted."

"So, when you've removed the inhibitors, His Majesty will have full access to his magics?" Malacar asked for clarification.

"Isn't that what I just said?" Farning looked at Malacar as one glared at an annoying insect. "Yes, he'll have all of the Seven Typical Magics at his disposal. Healing, Offensive, Defensive, Natural, Creative, Elemental and, of course, the Prophetics." Farning checked off each category with his fingers as he spoke. "Controlling them, however, is another matter. The boy would do well to attend university. Some of the best teachers are in Havenlen, wasting their time instructing dimwitted students who will never have *half* the potential that this lad holds in his pinky. But then, once he reaches the palace, he will have an entire host of tutors at his royal disposal, and will have no need for public study."

Farning turned his attention back to Vann. "And that is the real trick, boy. Learning control of your magics is, in some ways, more vital than actually having the power itself. The greater the power, the greater the potential for good, but also for ill when wielded by inexperienced hands."

Vann understood. More harm than good had come to many who attempted use of their magics to a greater ability than they could control. A poor understanding of the magics one manipulated could lead to terrible mishaps, even deadly consequences. Like the man in Findelore who had pretended Master Healer's status without having real experience. He bore the talents but not the training, and seven people had died due to his ignorance before he was caught.

With a barely concealed look of horror on his face, Malacar whispered, just audibly, "Like Balinor."

The thought of Kir's unintentional massacre at Balinor sent a shiver down Vann's spine, despite the intense heat of the water surrounding him.

Most magic users who planned to fully master their crafts beyond their childhood Lessons ventured to Havenlen. The universities there were often the first stop on the path to adulthood for most young people of middle or higher classes, and the rare commoner whose magics were strong enough to secure him a sponsorship. Master status afforded the bearer a title of experience and garnered respect. The only way to achieve Master status was to study and train. Or to be extremely gifted in a given field, much like Scilio was a natural Creative.

"Now then, why don't you try to cast something?" Farning asked.

"Should you not remove the marks and inhibitors, first?"

Farning stared incredulously at Vann for several long moments. "Where have you been during this conversation? It's long since done."

"But, you cast nothing," Vann argued.

"I am no sideshow entertainer, boy. When one is a Master, one ought not needlessly showcase one's ability with meaningless mutterings," Farning replied. "Or were you not aware that it is the will and the thought that drives the ability?"

"So, I am free of the marks? That's it, then?"

Farning threw his hands into the air in exasperation, sending a spray of droplets outward in all directions. "Am I talking to myself here? Yes! Cast something, will you?"

Vann was torn between excitement and uncertainty. He felt as though he had been imprisoned in an invisible cell, and the jailer was only now opening the gate. On the other hand, he felt no different, physically, than he had just moments before. Could he be sure that Farning had, in fact, done as he claimed?

There was only one way to find out.

Stretching his hand, palm down, over the water, Vann muttered the incantation for a very weak Frost Wisp, careful to limit the strength of the casting. The last thing he wanted was to freeze their bodies in a chest-high pool of ice. Releasing the energy in a concentrated downward direction, he was amazed at how quickly the surface of the hot water began to crystallize into a layer of solid white. The heat of the water underneath fought a valiant battle with the icy crust and returned it to liquid rapidly.

Farning nodded, for the first time appearing impressed with Vann. "A royal, indeed. Your level of control is amazing for a novice lagging fourteen years behind his peers. Most fledgling Elemental casters could not manipulate a Wisp so clearly and so locally. They might have frozen half of the pool, or frozen nothing at all."

Vann smiled, impressed in his own right. "I always believed my Elementals to be weak."

Farning raised an eyebrow. "Hardly."

Vann's excitement was difficult to contain. It was as though he suddenly felt the magics alive within him, eager to burst forth. They had always been there, but for the first time, he truly felt as though he were one with his gifts. It was surely a perception brought on by revelation, as he still felt no measurable change in himself. But Vann was unbridled and released into the wind, and he yearned to fly.

"Now then, Chaos Bringer, is there some other service I can provide you before I return to my divine communion?"

"Chaos Bringer?"

The spark that had been driving Vann's excitement speared him in the heart at that vile name. Bile rose in his throat as the budding anger gripped him. He grit his teeth and stepped forward toward the prophet, determined to ask the question that had burned its branding marks into his soul. "Am I truly to be the Chaos Bringer? Or are you mocking me?"

"I never utter the word of the Gods frivolously," Farning said. "But it may not mean what you think it does."

"But you told my parents I am *not* the Chaos Bringer," Vann insisted.

"That depends entirely on what chaos means to you. I told them that you will not destroy the world—which is clearly what they feared. But never once did I say that you are not the Chaos Bringer. If they misunderstood me, perhaps their ears were closed. They heard what they wished." Farning threw a glance to Inagor, whose face blanched considerably.

"But Tarnavarian is dead. I can't kill him, so how can I invoke the prophecy?"

"Who said he was the only means to the prophetical end? You can't spill his blood, but there may be other means of ascendance. There are many paths through the forest, but they all come out on the other side."

"What good is prophecy if we cannot use it to change the future?" Vann asked, feeling his voice crack.

"Oh, prophecy is indeed used to change the future. But in this case, perhaps it doesn't need to be changed."

"How can you say that? How can you honestly say that the downfall of our world is acceptable?" Vann spat angrily. "I will die before I bring Chaos to Septauria."

"One of Galvatine's mindless acolytes could not have spoken it better," Farning scoffed.

"How do I even know for sure what the prophecy says? No one has ever been able to recite it to me verbatim. For all I know, it was fabricated," Vann argued.

Farning surprised every ear with a deep and barking laugh. "Fabricated? Boy, who do you think issued it?"

Vann stared blankly, taking a moment to register the implication. He choked out a single, accusatory word: "You?"

"Why do you think I ended up in exile? Going over the old slug's head and delivering that forbidden proclamation to King Soventine was the boot to my buttocks. My invitation out the temple door. Had I been a simple-minded fool like all those who remain Galvatine's obedient lap-dogs, I would have been happy to silently sweep the prophecy away with the blood of two dead princelings. But, as it stands, the Gods delivered the prophecy to *me*, rather than Galvatine or his pets, and I could not, in good conscience, let the matter lie."

"Why you? What makes you worthy of the *honor* of receiving so revealing and devastating a message?" Vann couldn't hide the loathing set into the creases of his question.

"The Gods obviously saw the greatness in me that others chose to ignore. It wasn't due to my upbringing—my parents preferred to find their Gods in the land around them. They were free and carefree, and the priests were a lifetime removed from their world. That's why it was a shock when I came into my Prophetics. Neither of them boasted the talent, that they were aware, and my abilities scared my mother. If they hadn't died soon after, I would have probably seen a very different life." Farning seemed swept up in his own story.

"I spent the rest of my childhood in the Citadel, under the tutelage of the priests, but my Prophetics were not deemed as worthy as

I knew them to be. My low ranking was an irritant in my younger years. Instead of receiving the divine communion to which I was entitled, I was made a collar smithy. Years spent forging expensive collars for the necks of slaves and criminals, and not a penny went to my pocket, of course. The collar smithing helps fund the priests, did you know? Their cassocks are crisp and their altars are shiny on the labors of collar smithies like me."

The oppressive heat and Farning's ramblings grated Vann's patience down to a thin wisp, and it took all Vann had not to tear through it. "The *prophecy*, Master Prophet. If you please..."

"Yes, yes. The prophecy. I'm getting to that..." Farning grumbled something about hot-headedness and slow wits, then continued. "I was in the bathhouse one day, minding my own business, when I slipped and hit my head. As I slid under the water, the call of the Soul Collectors beckoned me on, but I knew I had a greater purpose that had yet to be fulfilled. In desperation, I harnessed my Healing magics to keep me alive, though I was losing consciousness and about to drown. Somehow, I found myself in the embrace of the Gods, who assured me of my importance. They gifted me the Chaos Bringer prophecy, and I delivered it to the High Priests. They were aghast and forbade the issuance to the royals. I went over the priesthood and all its teachings to deliver the proclamation. Of course, it was hotly contested, but how can one argue with the divine word?" Farning's smug grin plastered itself across his face.

Vann found no hint of amusement in the tale. He inhaled a steady breath and wrapped his authoritative aura around his voice. He may be the Bringer of Chaos in time, but at this moment, he was the Crown Prince. "Master Prophet, I would know the words of this ill-fated prophecy that has overturned the lives of so many. I demand you recite it."

The snide comment that Farning was, no doubt, considering died on his tongue at the unmistakable power in Vann's command. He merely nodded and, without a moment's hesitation, began:

> *Marked by the Betrayer,*
> *Bound in the spilled blood of the King Ascended,*
> *Second to the Throne shall become the First,*
> *In the Chamber keep.*
> *Should that second remain,*
> *The world as now shall cease to be.*
> *Moonless, so to be blind are we,*
> *as the Bringer of Chaos is delivered upon you.*

Vann and the Guardians sat in silence, processing the words and trying to find meaning in them.

Suddenly and abruptly, Vann laughed. A mirthless, bitter laugh that erupted from the depths of his gut. "That's it?" Vann managed. "That miserable spatter of words?"

"What's wrong with it?" Farning asked defensively.

"The fate of all Septauria has, for fourteen years, balanced on a fulcrum as tenuous as a morning mist? That vague utterance means absolutely nothing!" Vann cried, beside himself with disbelief. "You deracinated my entire life, and that of my family, on your rambling, drunken poetry?"

Farning's face darkened. "Do not disparage the words of the Gods, *boy*. Prince you may be, but you are still a mere mortal. The will of the Gods is not lightly given, and you should not lightly cast it aside."

Vann plopped back onto his stony ledge seat and his brow fell under the weight of the churning thoughts. "Tell me, then, Master Prophet. What do *you* believe the words mean?"

The trickle of the waterfall and the pounding in Vann's heart were the only sounds for several seconds. The room was still and calm like a tomb.

Finally, Farning's features softened.

"And that is the correct question, Your Majesty," Farning inclined his head in respect. "Everyone is eager to interpret the prophecy as *they* see fit. The Hilians. Your parents. Even the High Priests. But it was *my* holy vision that birthed the words. Subject to *my* interpretation above all. I believe that you are the harbinger of change. And sometimes the broth of change needs a little chaos to stir the pot."

The rising anger that had been brewing within Vann began to subside. "Then, you don't see evil in this? You don't see evil in *me*?" Vann asked.

"Only those who oppose change see evil in it," Farning replied simply.

Vann remembered Kir making a comment, several weeks before, about the abolition of slavery leading to chaos. In light of Farning's belief, Vann wondered if, perhaps, his allegiance with the Hilians was the foundation for the supposed chaos that would ensue.

"What am I supposed to do? If I am to return to Empyrea, and survive the attempt, Galvatine assures me that I will enter the Chamber. That I will fulfill this wretched predetermined destiny. Is that what I should do? Walk right into that Chamber and embrace my fate? Have I no choice at all?" The words were heavy, embedded with the pain that Vann had choked back for so long.

He had spent most of his life hiding his fear of the future from those around him, from those few acquaintances he had been fortunate enough to know, from his parents, from even himself. Vann did not want to believe that he was destined to do anything but live out a normal life. He would have been sufficiently content to live such a life. Why could the Gods not be content with that, as well?

"It is your will that drives you. Do what you will," Farning replied. "Prophecy only gives us the potential. What we do or do not, that is up to us. But the world needs a Chaos Bringer every now and then."

It was obvious that they would learn nothing more from the man and Vann was entirely ready to remove himself from the oppressive heat of the room. He rose and bowed to Farning. "I will take my leave of you, Master Prophet. May your communion be fruitful."

"Yes, yes, Chaos Bringer. Now, if you'll excuse me…" Farning unceremoniously slid under the water until his chaotic mop disappeared below the steamy surface.

Vann blinked once at the empty space that Farning had occupied, then shook his head and started for the disrobing hut.

He might have been appalled at the exhortation to become the thing he so dreaded. But there was something that Farning had given him: the hope that there might be some light beyond the dark veil of the future, and that maybe he wasn't destined for evil after all.

## -16-
## I Swear

*Gentility of speech is what the nobles devised to separate themselves from the rest of us swearin' peons. But in my experience, actions are more blasphemous than words, and most nobles are, therefore, more profane than the whole rest of society.*
*Better to be profane in word than in deed.* - Master Kozias

The moment he opened the bathhouse door to the world beyond, Vann practically fell over. The rush of fresh air flooded his lungs and made the breathing so much easier. It was a curiosity how hot air could be so smothering and rejuvenating at the same time.

"Well, that was certainly interesting," Inagor commented as the men made their way back toward the Kion.

"Indeed. And now, we face the wrath of Ithinar. Courage, Guardians," Malacar said.

"Not a chance," Scilio tutted. "By Alokien's song, Kir will be as cool and collected as she can manage, so as to convince us she was unabashed."

"That's assuming she doesn't realize we lured her in there unawares," Malacar said.

"Oh, she knew," Scilio said confidently. "Realization lit her features just before she bolted."

"You seem pretty sure of yourself and I hope you're right. I don't fancy being at the receiving end of Guardian Ithinar's fury," Inagor said.

"No, Toma's correct," Vann put in. "He's good at reading people, and Kir will downplay any embarrassment. She tries to project a cool and unaffected persona."

Vann wondered what had become of Kir after she left the bathhouse. Or stumbled out, was more like it. He hoped that she had been relaxing with his mother. Palinora had spoken of her desire to spend more time with Kir, and it warmed Vann's heart they had hit it off. Perhaps that was too strong a statement, but Kir regarded Palinora fondly, and his mother seemed to have tagged Kir as her new 'project'. Kir had been surrounded by men for so long, she needed some female influence in her life. Perhaps she would start to behave less like a hardened warrior and more like a woman.

It was already happening. Vann had noticed the slight changes. The rough edges of her rustic vernacular were beginning to smooth just slightly and she had mellowed, especially since their rendezvous with the Hilians and his parents. And since the night she had divulged the story of her Psychonic torture at Tarnavarian's hands. It was as though she had released a bit of the burden in the telling.

With Malacar's aid, Kir had come to terms with her actions at Balinor, where she had killed sixty men. Even so, Vann could see the remnants of silent guilt she still harbored. He had tried to invite Kir to open her soul about that fateful night. If talking about the Chambers had lightened Kir's heart, perhaps sharing her memories of Balinor would help unburden her even more.

Even after all these months, Vann still did not know exactly what had occurred on that stormy field. Every time he broached the topic, Kir would shy away from the subject. She always promised to divulge the details when she was ready, but Vann had continued pressing her. He was confident that Kir would take another step in healing her soul when she was able to share Balinor with him.

He didn't expect her to dissolve into a flighty giggler, but he hoped that Kir could learn to accept the feminine side of herself again. That part that she was trying so desperately to deny. She regarded it as a weakness. In Vann's experience, femininity and strength were not mutually exclusive. The one did not prevent the other. And in fact, many of the strongest people he had ever known were women.

As the party approached the pier, Vann spied Kir sitting on the wide railing of the Kion's lowest deck and leaning against a support post. One foot was propped on the rail and the other dangled lazily over the edge. A Dimishuan child was straddled before her on the rail and they seemed to be engaged in a deep discussion. Every now and again, the boy would shake his head or move his hands in emphasis, as if correcting her.

*What could they be talking about?* Vann wondered.

Kir raised her head as the men approached. The corners of her mouth drew up into a partial grin and her eyes sparkled. "You're just in time," she called with a wicked edge. "I needed some subjects to practice on."

"Here we go," Inagor muttered. He shot Scilio an *I told you so* look.

"What are you doing?" Vann asked as he stepped off the gangplank.

Kir glanced sideways and nudged the boy. "*Kudu ganta ne.*"

The boy dissolved into cackles, throwing his hands over his mouth.

"Oh, just taking in my first lesson. This is Dailan, my tutor."

"And what, pray tell, is Tutor Dailan teaching you?" Scilio asked, although it was obvious that Kir had just spoken in the Dimishuan tongue.

"Dimishuan profanity," Kir replied cheerily, then added, "You *kadda tekano.*"

Vann withheld a laugh. "But, you are already quite adept at cursing. Why do you need to do it in another language?"

Kir shrugged. "Just trying to *be the people.*"

Vann sighed deeply. So much for his earlier notion of Kir's increasing gentility. He narrowed his eyes and played a jest in the scolding. "How vile of you, Guardian Ithinar. Corrupting this poor boy."

Kir rolled her eyes in exaggerated motion. She made an odd hand gesture and said, "*Gotea gadee neyah!*"

Dailan shook his head. "No, *neyah* means the front side. You want to say *neeyah*: the back side."

"Oh. I beg your pardon, Your Majesty. *Gotea gadee neeyah,*" she corrected.

"This Lesson sounds quite interesting. What does that phrase mean?" Inagor asked.

Dailan opened his mouth to speak, but Kir shushed the boy with a wave of her hand. "Let's just say that if we were in High Empyrea, I could have been drawn and quartered for telling His Majesty what he can kiss."

"Except that in High Empyrea, no respectable nobleman would know what the phrase meant in the first place," Malacar pointed out.

"Correct, *benai jekai.* Hence, the great benefit to knowing Dimishuan insults." Kir inclined her head to the men. "Thanks. That was the most fun I've had in ages."

"So glad we could serve as your sullying targets," Scilio said darkly as Kir swung her leg back over the rail and hopped to the deck.

She flipped a coin to Dailan, who caught it deftly and sped away down the ramp. "Same time tomorrow," she called as he hopped in a longboat. Waving acknowledgment, he paddled away toward the market row.

Kir turned back to the Guardians. "So, how much did you win, Ponytail?"

"I beg your pardon. I don't claim to know what you're talking about," Scilio proclaimed innocently. He thrust his thumbs into his pockets and his chin rose an inch.

"You can drop the act. I know you made money on me, so spill it. How much? I figure I'm entitled to half, since it was *my* action under consideration."

Scilio tugged at his collar. "If you are referring to your hasty retreat from the bathhouse, I assure you—"

"How much?" she interrupted.

"Twenty lorans."

"Great! Where's my half?" Kir strolled to Scilio and extended an open palm.

"I believe the street value is closer to thirty percent in such a case," Scilio stated flatly.

"Well, I say half," Kir said firmly, then threw in, "And I have a sword."

"Shall we agree on forty percent? I am practically broke. Besides, His Majesty has yet to report *his* winnings."

Kir threw a look of surprise to Vann. "Is that so?"

Vann swallowed and winced at Kir's hard glare of death. "As I am the Crown Prince, there are certain allowances I am afforded. I have no need of money, really, so you can have *all* my winnings, Kiri."

He opened up his money pouch and withdrew a string of coins, which Kir snatched greedily. She regarded the lorans and paused, then cocked her head in wonder. "Fifty? Wow, Stick. You must know me pretty well."

"After all that time you spent together in Southport, *alone...*" Inagor said, and Vann couldn't help but notice the emphasis he placed on the word, "...it's no wonder Vann knows you rather well, Guardian Ithinar."

Vann caught Kir's fleeting glance.

"We weren't there all *that* long," she grumbled. Turning her attention to the coins in her hand, Kir dropped them into her pouch. "Well, thank you fine *kaddas* for supplementing my dwindling funds. Feel free to wager on me more often. I'll be living high on the hog at your expense," Kir practically sang.

"I think I liked her better when she wasn't spewing Dimishuan profanity and grinning like the village idiot," Scilio muttered to Malacar under his breath.

"By the way, I was wondering," Kir added, as a second thought, "What would you guys have done, had I decided to join you back there in the bathhouse?"

Scilio raised his head smugly. "You would have been most welcome. I have nothing to be ashamed of."

Rounds of chuckles were shared, and Vann caught Kir's gaze again.

When she smiled at him, Vann thought his heart would melt. It was not a joking smile, nor was it a falsely plastered mask. It was a genuine display of happiness. Perhaps the first Kir had ever really exhibited since Vann had known her. Of course, he had just surrendered his money to her. She would certainly be happy to make a loran or two. But Kir's smile wasn't about money or her triumph over the situation. It was purely a mark of gaiety.

Vann basked in the warm and contented look on Kir's face and fell into the abyss of her ice-blue eyes that seemed as deep as the sky was large.

"Well, if you two are gonna stare at each other all day, that's alright by me. But I'm going to see about the evening meal. I'm starving," Malacar announced as he made for the stairs to the upper decks.

Vann shook away his trance.

"Who's staring?" Kir muttered a Dimishuan insult. She turned toward Scilio as the bard tried to follow Malacar up the stairs. "Full stop there, Ponytail," she said, grabbing his arm. "Square up."

"Very well," he sighed.

When Kir was satisfied with the money Scilio issued, she darted up the stairs after Malacar. It was obvious that she was trying to gloss over what might have become an embarrassing moment for the both of them, had anyone decided to press the issue. After all, Kir had been beaming at him, too, hadn't she? If that was, in fact, what had occurred. Perhaps Malacar had been too hasty with his observation.

Vann stood for a moment, fixed on the empty space Kir had occupied just moments before.

He had almost forgotten that Inagor was still behind him. "Well, shall we join them, Vann? We should update your mother and Guardian Ithinar on our meeting with Farning."

"That's right! I forgot to tell Kir that I can cast now."

"Well, let's get up there, then. There's debriefing to be done," Inagor said.

-17-
## Family Reunion

*There is a power in a name, stronger than the word that carries it.* - Master Kozias

The next morning, Kir found herself sitting in their longboat at the weekly Hilihar market. Like Vann, she had been anxious to explore the city in a more casual manner, and the market was the perfect opportunity.

Their longboat was anchored alongside that of the textile dealer who also happened to be a tailor, and one recommended highly by several attendants. Vann and Scilio had been hovering over the beautiful array of fine fabrics for almost a quarter-hour already, deciding which ones would enter into service as their Guardian tabards.

While they waited, Malacar's fingers expertly moved against a small sheet of paper, creasing and folding. He kept a weather eye on the market, never pausing to examine the progress. The paper was beginning to take on the shape of a dragon. He'd been known to make trinkets from scraps of parchment before, but now that he'd bought a stack of patterned paper squares at the last vendor, his tiny figures would be bursting with color.

"Before the festival this evening? That would certainly be expeditious," Vann commented to the tailor. He turned to Scilio. "I wasn't expecting the tabards to be completed so soon!"

"Lady Tressa is as adept at her trade as she is lovely," Scilio said smoothly, flashing the tailor a dashing smile. The woman blushed and turned her eyes away coyly, whether out of shyness or reverence, Kir couldn't tell.

Vann unwound a length of the richest sky-blue cloth Kir had ever seen. He and Scilio tested the quality and texture between their fingers.

"I will have it done," Tressa said to Vann. "This tabard design is simple and requires only a small amount of fabric. And I promise you only the best quality and workmanship, Your Majesty. I achieved Master Tailor status recently."

"Ah, a *Master* Tailor!" Scilio inclined his head and placed his hand on his chest in respect. "She crafts with the hands of the Gods, as she herself has been crafted by them. To hold your sculpted work of art against my flesh will be like holding your heart to mine."

Tressa bit her lip and her chin dipped between her shoulders. She looked utterly awash with delight at Scilio's honey-mouth. "Thank you, Your Grace."

Kir had to dig her nails into her palms to keep from snorting rudely at the innocent woman's awe of the fop. The Hilians were overly complimentary of Scilio, but *Your Grace* was pretty darn excessive. She glanced at Malacar, whose hand was covering his mouth and his chest was heaving in choked-back laughter.

"What do you think about this blue with that silver?" Vann asked Scilio, holding the fabrics together for consideration.

As the men continued examining the large selection of cloth, Kir cleared the humor from her throat and turned back to her observations of the busy market's patrons. Rows upon rows of vendor boats lined the waterways, with merchandise spread upon boards that extended outward from each vessel. Some boaters paddled swiftly down the lane, while others stopped at various vendors, with items for barter stocking the bottoms of their longboats.

"Lady Kiriana? Kiriana Karmine?"

Kir turned toward the sound of her name that tripped through the crowds of boats and people in the market. The voice tickled her familiarity, but a haphazard sifting through the past didn't place it.

"I heard someone call your name." Malacar slid across the boat to Kir's side, scanning the crowd with her. "Your *old* name. Trouble?"

Kir squinted her eyes in search. "I don't know..."

After a moment, she spied a Dimishuan man with long hair paddling toward them. His longboat was stocked full of exotic foods. The man waved a hand to garner her attention.

"Begads! It *is* you, Kiriana!" the stranger cried. As his longboat drew near to theirs, the man tethered them together deftly.

Kir gasped with recognition. "Corban?"

He nodded and laughed, pulling her into a strong, if awkward, embrace over the edge of his boat. "You finally made it, Kiriana. After all these years…"

"Corban?" Kir asked again weakly, shocked at the unexpected reunion. She had not anticipated knowing anyone in Hilihar and she was entirely unprepared for seeing her family's slave. Or—former slave, apparently.

"You are surprised to see me," Corban said as he released her.

Kir nodded and blinked, fumbling for words in flabbergastation. A million questions assaulted her mind at once. She wanted to ask how he had come to escape, how long he had been in Hilihar, how fared her other friends in Cornia… But all she could do was stare at him dumbly, reliving the memories of childhood that flashed in her mind theater.

"I almost didn't recognize you in Hilian attire," Corban said. He was positively beaming.

Kir laughed, suddenly overcome with belated elation. "I almost didn't recognize you with long hair, old friend."

"I always wanted to grow it out, but your father was ever so strict about such things," Corban chuckled. "Ah, the joys of freedom!"

"Aren't you going to introduce us, Kir?" Scilio asked.

Kir realized that Vann and Scilio had abandoned their fabric bolts and turned their attentions to the newcomer.

"Oh, of course," she replied. "I forgot myself. May I present Corban de Karmine. Suise Chef of Karmine castle."

"Formerly," he corrected. "I hope it does not offend you that I renounced the name."

"I'm not offended. I renounced it, my own self."

Corban looked to Vann and the Guardians. "So I've heard. And I also hear that you travel in good company."

"I reckon my manners have jumped ship today. Might I introduce His Majesty, Crown Prince Vannisarian."

Corban saluted and bowed low to Vann in formal tribute. Vann returned his greeting.

"And these are my Guardian kinsmen." Kir introduced Scilio and Malacar in turn.

"You are, in fact, a Guardian? I heard rumor of such this morning, but did not believe it to be true. I would have expected the world cast into oblivion before I would have dared think of you in such a position, milady," Corban commented, then hastily added, "No offense meant to His Majesty."

Vann shook his head politely and issued a knowing smile. "Not at all."

"A lot has happened in three years," Kir said guardedly.

Corban nodded and the merriment faded from his face. "Take in your sails. How did you hear rumor of me? I didn't think anyone would recognize me here."

"I have told your story to many in Hilihar. Your name is not unknown to our people."

"I see." Kir was not set and sure that being *known* was a good thing. It was her action, after all, that had led to Mirhana's death. Would the Dimishuans be aware of that? Would they blame her?

"You reside in Hilihar now?" Vann asked.

"I do. I earned the title of Master Chef and run my own establishment. I was honored to be chosen as executive chef for Your Majesty's welcoming festival this evening." Corban swept his hand above the food piled high in his longboat. "Behold, the core components for the feast. I have personally selected only the finest ingredients for you."

"I look forward to enjoying your culinary masterpieces, Master Chef," Vann said.

"I'm happy for you, Corban. You were always the best chef in Cornia," Kir offered. To bolster his ego, she threw in, "Even better than Master Chef Garner."

Corban raised a skeptical eyebrow. "Your flattery is appreciated, but overdone. There is not another chef alive who can match talents with that man's palate."

"I take issue with that. Your custards were much superior to his," Kir reminded him.

"That always was your favorite of my dishes." Corban turned to Vann and the Guardians. "Did you know little miss Kiriana would sneak into the kitchens and steal bowls of my custard pudding from the frostery? I would be short a bowl come dinnertime and Master Chef Garner would be so furious with me." He chuckled at the memory. "Who would have guessed back then that the mischievous little thief would grow up to be favored by His Majesty. And twice over!" Corban gestured to the Guardian vambrace around Kir's forearm.

Kir's smile faded. She wasn't entirely sure why, but the innocent comment stung. She had not exactly been *favored* by either of the Princes. In both cases, she was merely fulfilling a role that she had not chosen or entirely wanted. Corban could not have known that. Nor could he have realized what kind of invisible collar she had, herself, worn in those days, by nature of her noble birth.

She tossed the thought aside and changed the subject. "But, Corban, how did you escape? What about Melia and Jurnet? Are they here, too?"

Kir thrilled at the thought of seeing her old friends again.

Corban's two daughters were several years older, and they had always treated her like a younger sister.

"Did no one tell you?" Corban swallowed and his features condensed.

"Tell me what?"

"Jurnet was killed. In the slave revolt."

"A revolt? Jurnet...?" Kir's heart sank. Sweet Jurnet, with her keen intelligence and gentle heart. "I didn't know."

Corban nodded warily and tilted his head. "I thought you would have been informed of the revolt. You were, after all, at the center of it."

## -18-
## Messenger

*I hate it when people tell me it could always be worse. Of course it could. I could be dead. What I want to know is: Why can't it be better?* - Master Kozias

Copellian de Ellesainia rubbed his index finger between the crude hemp ropes that bound his wrists. The rope burns were beginning to scab and itched terribly. It would have been nice had the slavers decided to use magic-inhibiting binders, but they probably didn't feel it necessary, as Copellian's slave collar prohibited casting, anyway. He would gladly exchange the irritating fiber of the ropes for the binders' cool, smooth lumanere and metal.

More than his embarrassing capture at the hands of these ignorant buffoons, Copellian was annoyed at himself that his message would be delayed. King Soventine had trusted him with a vital task: deliverance of the summons to Prince Vannisarian. Copellian did not take the mission lightly.

It had taken him, and many of the King's entourage, by surprise when Soventine had requested Copellian as messenger. To task a slave with such an important mission, overseen by only two soldiers, seemed next to insanity, and there were several whispers that the King might finally have lost his wits from the sudden downturn in his health.

Copellian, though, understood why the King had selected him. As a former Libertine, Copellian was well familiar with the land in and around Hili. He was known and trusted there. He had been a soldier in the Hili army, and was a member of Grand Master Ulivall's clan before he had been captured by slave traders and sold to the palace. The King had taken Copellian's knowledge and past into consideration. It made perfect sense that he would be the one to go.

This was the chance of a lifetime for a slave, and Copellian wished so badly that he could stay in Hili when his errand was complete. But, despite the ripe opportunity, he had made a promise to his beloved, who waited in Cornia. And he was nothing, if not a man of honor. The only way to fulfill his promise and help her escape was to return to Soventine's service. He might wear a collar, but he had escaped his bonds before. He would find a way to do so again.

As for the two soldiers who accompanied him, their presence was mainly for protection to and from Hili. They would not be welcomed beyond the Hilian borders with him.

Had Copellian not been trained in the Hili army, he might not have caught the subtle clues that these men were not ordinary troops. There was no wasted motion in their movements, and their eyes seemed keener and more alert than most of the soldiers Copellian knew. He had not seen them in action yet, so perhaps he was reading too much into them. However, the King had only sent two, which lent credence to Copellian's suspicion that these men were more than they appeared.

Of course, he might have been entirely wrong. Because here he sat, after all, rubbing two-day-old scabs on his wrists and waiting for help that might never come. He'd give the soldiers until nightfall. He could wait no longer than that, and he was ready to move at the first opportunity.

A rustling in the brush nearby drew the attention of one slaver. As the man went to investigate the disturbance, a silent arrow from another direction thumped into the chest of the sentry nearest Copellian.

"So, perhaps I was right, after all," Copellian mumbled to himself. "Though, it took them long enough..."

When the scuffle was over and all ten slave traders lay dead, Captain Jurian approached with a knife.

"Caught with your pants down, huh? Literally," he smirked. "You'll never live this one down."

"Unless no one ever knows..." Copellian growled as Jurian sliced through the ropes. "I thought you two were supposed to be guarding my bare neeyah."

"We were. Just thought it was too amusing to interrupt. In honesty, they might have attempted to waylay us down the road, so this was a good opportunity to take them out while they were occupied with you," Lieutenant Trual said, approaching from behind and helping Copellian to his feet.

Copellian studied the two men, who seemed jovial and witty as any average soldier might be. Their eyes betrayed none of the mirth in their words. These men were highly trained killers, as was evident in the swift and one-sided battle that had just transpired.

It had all happened so fast, but there was one thing that Copellian did not miss. The cold and calculating expressions on their faces as they had commenced their butchery.

After Copellian had drank his fill from Trual's canteen, Jurian said, "I'm sorry we've delayed your errand, messenger. Shall we be off?" He offered an empty smile and turned south toward the waiting horses.

Copellian jogged after him, thankful for once to be in the company of killers.

## -19-
## Icon of Revolution

*Avoid becoming legendary.* - Master Kozias

"I don't know what you're talking about, Corban. I was involved in no revolt," Kir protested.

"Perhaps you are unaware of the events at Karmine castle after your capture, Kiriana. Your fight for our people inspired us to arms in the hopes of freedom."

Kir was aghast. "You *fought*? That's insane! How could anyone have defeated my father's guards?"

Virnard Karmine's Manor Elite had been chosen from among the best soldiers in Cornia. Attacking them would be unthinkable for anyone under warrior class status.

The chef's head hung. "We couldn't. Twenty of us rallied in your honor. All were slaughtered. All but me. Jurnet was killed accidentally by a mis-aimed arrow during the revolt. Melia, I believe, is still in your family's possession. I, alone, was able to escape."

Kir stared at Corban, dripping horror from every pore. Her previous joy was instantly replaced by a raw anger. How the slaves could have thrown their lives away so foolishly?

"What a waste," she spat. "You must have known you had no chance."

"Every one of us knew that, milady. And every one of us believed it was better to die standing against the institution than to live under its heel. You showed us that. You gave us the strength to fight for our freedom," Corban insisted.

"No!" Kir protested. "I was no abolitionist, Corban. I was no martyr for your cause and I wasn't trying to be a hero for you. Don't you dare place their deaths on my head!"

"Not their deaths, Lady Kiriana. Their hopes. Their dreams. They held you in their hearts until the very end. And personally, I would have gladly died there, as well. Yet, here I stand, living the life of a free man. Because of you."

Kir's comeback fumbled on threads of heartache. She was not the champion of abolition they had believed her to be. Her reasons for helping Mirhana were entirely selfish and she had never intended to become an icon of freedom. That the slaves had used Kir as a symbol sickened her, as she had unintentionally inspired them to their deaths. Sure, she wished them their freedom. But at the price of their lives?

"I wish you would not put me on your pedestal. I deserve no praise for what I did. I was a stupid, spoiled child who was fighting to keep something that belonged to me. So don't glorify my actions," Kir said sharply.

Much to Kir's surprise, Corban laughed deeply. "I seem to recall a ten-year-old little girl who would tiptoe down to the kitchens every night just to teach my starry-eyed daughters how to read. Against the order of her father. I'll never forget how I wept the night you were caught and beaten for that.

"And I recall a little twelve-year-old girl who used to write fantastical stories of imaginary worlds where the hero would shatter every collar. You did not tell these stories merely for fun, or to please Mirhana. Deep down, you believed in them."

Perhaps it was only a few years back, but it seemed to Kir another lifetime. She had been an idealistic dreamer back then, much as Vann was now. Her innocence had long since been murdered by reality. "That was a long time ago."

"Oh, not so long," Corban chuckled. He suddenly seemed to come to a realization and he scooped up his oar. "Speaking of time, I must hurry back to the kitchens. Forgive me, I have a deadline to meet. These dishes will not cook themselves."

Corban leaned across the boat and pulled Kir toward him again. She returned his embrace tentatively.

"It was truly an honor, Master Chef," Vann said. "I do hope we will have the pleasure of speaking again. I would enjoy hearing more stories of Guardian Ithinar's childhood."

Kir grimaced. There were several stories she hoped Corban had forgotten about. Somehow, though, she knew that the most embarrassing events were the clingiest barnacles of recollection.

"It would be an honor to share such treasured memories with Your Majesty," Corban said, bending at the waist respectfully. "Until we meet again."

Kir watched Corban paddle away, until he disappeared in the crowd of boaters. She should have been overjoyed to see him, but the news of the revolt had cast a shadow on their reunion. The slaves had died in her name. Kir had never dreamt that her own personal rebellion against the Crown would have galvanized such a revolution.

"Are you okay, Kiri?" Vann asked, placing a steady hand on her shoulder.

Kir bobbed her head wordlessly, wading through deep ponderings. The men were silent, allowing her to process the news Corban had delivered.

"I wonder why Tarnavarian never told me," Kir spoke the thought aloud. "It seems like the deaths of twenty friends would have been ideal ammunition to use against me."

"Probably because you were the spark that lit the uprising. Although it was easily snuffed, that revolt was a victory for you, Kiri. People followed and revered you. Tarnavarian would not have wanted to give you any such pride to cling to," Vann reasoned gently.

"Somehow, I don't feel proud of anything," Kir sighed. "It just feels empty. They were wenchin fools, and I can't stomach that they threw their lives away for nothing."

"Nothing? Can you honestly look at the contentment and joy in that free man's eyes and say *that* is nothing?" Malacar suggested.

Kir couldn't argue. "I guess not."

"I wish I could bottle and soak myself in your charisma," Vann commented. "If the Hilians believed in me as much as your family's slaves believed in you..."

"They'd all be dead on a battlefield right now." Kir shook her head wearily and rubbed her balled fist against the palm of her opposite hand. She belatedly registered the first part of Vann's statement and laughed. "Charisma? That's the first time I've ever been accused of being charismatic. Now, having a flash fire temper? I've heard that a time or two."

The men chuckled and each gave her a supportive nudge. Kir allowed them a grateful smile and nod to reassure them.

When they seemed certain that she was okay, Scilio and Vann turned back to the fabric bolts. Kir watched as they made their selections, but she could not focus. She kept thinking of the revolt and imagining a bloody arrow protruding from Jurnet's chest. Part of her wondered if she was destined to bring death to everyone she knew.

-20-
## Chaos on the Water-Mart

*I never pray. Who wants to be noticed by the Gods?*
*The ant that stands out is summarily squashed.* - Master Kozias

Alokien pulled his body upward and untangled himself from the twisted sheets that half-covered the straw mattress. The Hilian woman who had pleasured him was still asleep beside him, snoring lightly, despite the mid-afternoon sun baking the lake waters just outside the door. He shouldn't have been surprised. She had been quite an exuberant little hellion. All night. And all morning. It was no wonder that he had exhausted her.

Alokien rose and found his balance slightly off-kilter. He was not accustomed to this body and it had been so long since he had taken a human host. It took time to acclimate to a borrowed form. Not that he hadn't enjoyed several hours already in this particular man, but walking and standing upright were two activities that had not been foremost in his thoughts. One did not need to walk or stand when engaged in other bedly preoccupations.

If only he had more time, and more magic. But the magic was too difficult to harness, and nearly impossible to maintain. Otherwise, he would not be in such a hurry. He knew that the magic could not sustain him in this mortal capsule until the festival, as that was still several hours away. For what little time was left, Alokien was not about to waste it in slumber.

He sat lightly upon the bed and pulled on the barbaric half-breeches that the Hilian males wore. He would have preferred to saunter around in the buff, to create as much of a stir as he could manage. However, it would not do to draw too much attention to himself just now. There was a time. Oh, there was a time! But he had not the energy to spare, as his mind of late was too preoccupied with other matters. With Soventine and the princeling. With Galvatine and Farning. With Arcadia and all his other pawns. There would come a day that he could make another stir. Entice another frenzy. Cast another chaotic die and watch the wonderful beauty of change. And thus, creation.

He just had to bide his time. What was the passage of a few months to one who had known eons, after all?

Bending at the waist, Alokien leaned over the sleeping woman and placed a purple lotus blossom on the pillow. He couldn't help taking in her beauty and her scent, musky and fragrant. The curve of her breast and hip. The smooth golden skin. She was a fine specimen. A pleasure, indeed.

"Your prayer is my Heavenly command, lovely lady. May he be strong," Alokien whispered in her ear. Even as she slept, the woman's supple lips turned up into a satisfied half-grin pressed against her soft down pillow.

Alokien scooped up a small muslin sack filled with items that he had purloined from the woman's pantry and slipped from the dark room. He squinted in the brightness of the sun as he stepped onto the planks outside the rustic dwelling. When his eyes had adjusted, he took up the oar of a nearby longboat and began to row toward the market swiftly. He had to make haste if he was to experience market day. The magic was ebbing away with every stroke of his paddle and he had precious little time.

As his longboat glided by one food vendor's craft, Alokien reached for a pouch of extraordinarily hot spices, normally used for smoking meat, and casually dumped its contents into the depths of several soup kettles.

At the next station, a seafood vendor turned to tally up his stock at the rear of his boat. Alokien swiftly moved in and used the man's distraction to his advantage, lathering the display of fish with a foul-smelling potion meant to increase the speed of hair growth to all parts of the body.

The third victim's wares were ignited with a spark, thanks to some dry tinder and a weak Inferno wisp.

And on he continued...

It was not as though he were doing the people an overall injustice, really. He was merely providing for them. Providing the foundation for the Creatives. Nothing could be born from nothing. It was his duty to create. To give his people that spark of inspiration. And so, Alokien continued as swiftly and efficiently as he could manage.

Several more vendors would come to learn of his mischievous entertainment in the minutes and hours to follow, but somehow the joy that he once took from his pranks, and the hopeful prospects of creative tales derived from them, was absent on this occasion. He simply could not focus. His thoughts kept drifting back to the elusive princeling.

No sooner had he finished uttering a Banishing spell to the seams of the garments on the nearest haberdasher's table, Alokien felt the oddest manner of tingling at the base of his neck. He rubbed at the spot vigorously, then realized that the sensation was not a physical manifestation, but a sensory perception. Someone was nearby.

Someone important.

Alokien craned his neck and spied him in the space of a breathless gasp.

The princeling.

And he was sitting in a longboat no more than fifty paces away.

Alokien felt his Dimishuan host's heart flutter. What a sensation, to be human! He studied the young man with yearning. How handsome and striking. How deliciously tempting. How desperately Alokien wanted him!

The magic began to unravel then, and Alokien grasped desperately at the threads. They were as fleeting as a kiss of breath on the wind, and he could not maintain his grasp.

As his consciousness was pulled away from the physical plane and the host to whom he had been anchored, Alokien caught one last glimpse of the princeling.

How powerful the young prince must have been! For even as Alokien's essence was emancipated from his host and faded from the world, the princeling could see him, was staring at him, as though his dissipating aura were an apparition. Their eyes made contact just before he vanished completely.

Alokien felt himself smile in anticipation of what was to come.

## -21-
## A Woman's Opinion

*There's a funny thing about a God's sense of humor. He's usually the only one laughing.* - Master Kozias

"I thoroughly enjoyed our afternoon together, Kiriana," Palinora said from her seat in the Kion parlor. "We must do this more often." Her voice was melodious and cheerful, much more like that of a teenager's, rather than of a thirty-nine-year-old Queen.

It had been a roaring good time for Kir, too. A welcome

distraction from the disturbing news that Corban had delivered. Their afternoon excursion in the market had proven to be relaxing and entertaining, and Kir was surprised that she could find enjoyment in such a mundane task as shopping. The Hiliiharian market was very similar in concept to the average market in the rest of the world, but the exotic edge of wild culture gave the flavor of her surroundings a hint of spice that Kir loved. It was foreign and thrilling.

"I'm glad you decided to come out," Kir said. "It gave me a chance to find that gift without the guys hanging all over my every movement. It's better when a gift is a surprise."

Kir and the men had been shocked when they'd heard Palinora's voice calling to them from the longboat across the waterway in the market. The Queen had reported earlier that she planned to relax in her room on the Kion until the festival, but apparently she had changed her mind. When their longboats drew together, Palinora had asked for Kir's attendance to "offer a female opinion," and Vann had happily excused her.

What "female opinion" Palinora had wanted, Kir still had not determined. The Queen seemed less interested in shopping for herself as she did in fawning over Kir.

At first, Palinora's attention was irksome, but as the afternoon had worn on, Kir felt herself loosening the reins on her aloof attitude. Palinora was far too exuberant to allow Kir's charade to go on for long, and it only took a few minutes for her to start kneading away at the hard stoicism Kir was projecting. By the end of the excursion, Kir felt less like a Guardian and more like a giddy schoolgirl.

Of course, it didn't help matters that the market had been plagued by an odd string of misfortune. Kir and Palinora had practically been reduced to giggles—well, perhaps not *giggles*, exactly—as they passed a vendor's booth overrun with water bugs. The poor man who owned the spread was frantically trying to shoo the bugs away, even going so far as to barrage them with minuscule Wind Wisps. The bugs were worked up into a frenzy over whatever merchandise was spread upon the vendor's table and they kept coming, swarming over the wares until Kir could not make out what the vendor was actually selling.

As they had passed another vendor, they could hear him speaking apologetically to a customer. From the context of the situation, it sounded as though there was something wrong with whatever he had recently sold to the customer. The patron pointed angrily to several large kettles that were suspended off the side of the vendor's boat, and he flapped his arms like an angry waterfowl. He then proceeded to spew a string of phrases that Kir recognized instantly from her lesson with Dailan.

*I knew those lessons would come in handy*, Kir thought triumphantly.

The occurrences continued as the afternoon had worn on. When Kir and Palinora exchanged musings on what chaos had been unleashed around them, Inagor, seated behind them at the oar, simply answered with the standard joking reply, "Must be that Alokien."

Kir had always thought the phrase unfair. After all, why blame the poor God for every little thing that went asunder in the world? But long had the phrase been used to explain why things went wrong, and it had become the standard answer for unexplained problems. Whenever a magical device ceased functioning or when something broke unexpectedly, the quick and easy blame was always jokingly cast to Alokien.

Despite the chaos, or maybe because of it, Kir had enjoyed the afternoon and she now found herself sipping tea in the Kion's parlor, awaiting Vann's return. She shifted on the bench in anticipation as she suddenly heard a chorus of footsteps approaching. The door to the forward deck swung open.

"Ah, you beat us back," Vann commented.

Kir and Inagor rose respectfully as Vann strode purposefully to the sitting area, tailed by Malacar and Scilio. All three carried canvas sacks that looked to be loaded with booty. Vann leaned forward and offered Palinora a peck on the cheek. "Did you have any luck in the market, mother?"

"I did, indeed," the Queen replied, throwing a wink Kir's way. "It always helps to have another woman's opinion on matters."

It struck Kir odd that Palinora hadn't purchased a single item at the market. She wondered if the Queen had simply wanted her around for girly social reasons, rather than functional ones. Her royal Sneakiness was likely trying to break down Kir's warrior-mentality with a little female-bonding.

"I'm glad she was able to assist," Vann said.

"Excuse me, Majesty?" Lili poked her head through the parlor door. "The tabards have arrived. Shall I deliver them to your chamber?"

Vann nodded. "Please do. We'll be there shortly to dress for dinner."

As Lili nodded compliance, Palinora called to her. "When you are finished, my dear, please attend me. The hour grows late, and this mound of hopelessness demands attention," Palinora sighed, patting her hair. "The humid air simply wreaks havoc."

Lili nodded and slipped away.

"I will take my leave now," Palinora said. She grasped Inagor's offered hands as she rose. "Kiriana, thank you for a marvelous afternoon. When you are dressed I will do something with your hair, as well." She twirled her finger around a stray strand of Kir's bangs. "Ringlet curls, perhaps?"

Kir shrugged noncommittally, clenching her jaw. It was one thing for the Queen to treat her like a woman when removed from the presence of the men. But Kir was a Guardian, and Guardians did not play dress-up with Queens.

"We'll play with it and see what works," Palinora said, seeming to recognize Kir's discomfort. She patted Kir's arm and turned toward the inner hallway leading to the bedchambers.

Inagor hung back for a moment and whispered in Kir's ear, "That's the most relaxed she's been in months."

As Inagor strode after the Queen, Kir returned to her seat. It stood to reason that Palinora had been under considerable stress since her capture and Vann's disappearance, but the woman was a noble, born and bred. Palinora wore her mask of unaffected calm as expertly as if she were in the court. Kir had previously believed that Palinora had been trying to girlify her with some manner of bonding, but could be the opposite was true. Maybe she wanted Kir's attendance for her *own* benefit? To ease away the edges of tension that had been riding her shoulders and heart for months.

Either way, it didn't matter. Kir had actually enjoyed herself, and was glad for the afternoon.

"Sounds like you had a good time," Vann commented, sitting next to Kir on the bench.

"Yeah, the market was alive with chaos this afternoon. It was pretty hilarious."

"In your location, as well?" Scilio asked. "We did notice quite a bit of trouble. As though someone was playing pranks on half of the vendors in our region. Quite inspiring. I may write a poem on it. *An Ode to Chaos on the Water-Mart*. I even have an ending for it. But I have to think of something that rhymes with *It all sank to the bottom*."

"You missed the excitement, Kir. These two are seeing ghosts now," Malacar reported, making no effort to hide his amused skepticism.

"It's true!" Vann insisted. "It hovered over a man, and had purple eyes that put Scilio's to shame!"

Scilio wrinkled his nose. "I beg to differ. *My* eyes are nowhere near that frightening."

Kir sniffed at the notion of ghosts. "So what did you guys find? Your bags are loaded."

"Malacar found a long daggery knife he fancied—" Scilio began.

"Arcardian toothpick," Malacar clarified for Kir's benefit.

"—but I believe I was the most blessed by my luck." Scilio pulled a garment from his sack and flapped it smartly to remove any folds that may have creased the fine fabric. "The Hilians, it seems, have a keen eye for noble styling."

Kir studied the tunic suspended from the dandy's hands. It screamed of Scilio's tastes, boldly refined and elegant. Foppish as a peacock. "It's very... popinjayish, Ponytail. Suits you to singing."

She was surprised the Hilians would bother making such fine garments, considering the fact that she had not seen a single Dimishuan wearing anything of the sort. Such articles were only worn by noble-born Alakuwai dandies.

"They sell and trade some of their wares with independent agents, especially those from the Underground," Vann answered her musing. "These types of expensive items bring in top loran in the black-market trade routes, so they make them for just such barter."

Kir raised an eyebrow and glanced at Vann from her periphery. Had he heard her thoughts? Gods, but she would have to endeavor to guard them that much more! Now that Vann had access to his magics, he would likely be able to utilize his Psychonics without even trying. No doubt he was talented in the field, as those types of skills tended to run in families. Kir was well aware of the magnitude of said talents in his bloodline.

She really must find this talisman Bertrand had talked about.

When Kir didn't respond, Vann probed, "What about you? Did you find anything interesting in the market?"

"Well, reckon I did. Something for you, truth be told," Kir said. She reached into her muslin sack and produced an object wrapped in brown paper.

"What is it?" Vann asked.

"Nothing much, really. Just a little something I stumbled upon," Kir replied nonchalantly.

"It's still a few weeks until my birthday, Kiri. You didn't have to get me a gift," Vann told her. It was a poor attempt at scolding, for he sounded absolutely thrilled.

"Just consider it a token of congratulations. On being able to use your magic now." Kir hoped she wasn't bleeding enthusiasm. She didn't want the gesture to be misinterpreted.

Vann thanked her sincerely and unfolded the corners of the paper, revealing a handsome leather-bound journal. His initials had been embossed into the smooth cover.

Kir had known it was for Vann the moment she had laid eyes on the journal. Most of the lorans she had received from Vann and Scilio had been used up on its purchase as she had nothing worthy to trade. Lorans, it seemed, were worth very little in Hilihar, the citizens having few outlets in which to spend or exchange them. Leather was also quite expensive, due to the lack of farm beasts in Hili. What little leather the Hilians were able to procure was usually employed in their armor, so the leather book was quite a luxury.

Vann inhaled an acute little breath and smiled as he rubbed his thumb over the scripted characters on the cover. "You did this for me?"

Kir masked her delight with a casual shrug and leaned back on the bench. "Well, I figured the Bardian was so busy scribbling in his own all the time that you needed one for yourself."

"I love it. Thank you." Vann squeezed her hand lightly in gratitude, then turned to his own sack. "I have something for you, as well. I wish this gift could compare to yours, but it is practical, if nothing else."

Kir accepted the paper-wrapped package from Vann's hand and tore into it. Inside, folded neatly, were three tunics and breeches. The shirts were of a light and airy fabric, sporting a design similar to the old lace-up variety she had always preferred in the past. These tunics were a tad more delicate in their style, with ruffles at the cuffs and collar. They also looked to be more form-fitting rather than loose and flowing. It was a definitely feminine take on what would otherwise have been a very masculine style.

"What do you think?" Vann asked as Kir turned the garments over in her hands, then held them up against her front.

"I think your taste in women's clothing is scary. And I think I rather like it," Kir said in approval.

"The shirts are long enough to wear your sword belt over them at the waist. They should be pretty comfortable," Vann commented.

Kir placed the articles in her sack, trying to hide the overzealous joy that tickled her heart. "They're perfect. I couldn't have picked out anything better."

Scilio chortled under his breath. "We know. That's why *we* did the shopping for you."

"With the tabards, I guess we'll all finally look like half-decent Guardians for once, won't we?" Kir said.

"Just in time for the celebration tonight," Vann agreed.

"Oh, that reminds me!" Scilio exclaimed, snapping his fingers. "I have something to pass along to you as well, Kir."

He rummaged through his own muslin sack and closed his hand around some obscure object, then smirked. "They were handing these out to all the little girls in the market today. Some trinket souvenir for the festival."

Scilio withdrew a primitive doll made of woven reeds from the sack and dangled it derisively before Kir. "I snatched one up, since I heard rumor once that you just adore playing with dolls."

Kir groaned inwardly. It had been an innocent encounter a few months ago, when she had taken a moment to exchange pleasantries with a young Dimishuan girl in Mercaria. Malacar and Vann had witnessed Kir 'playing' with a doll and she had expected them to run to Scilio with their hilarious news. When nothing had been mentioned, Kir had honestly thought that the subject had been forgotten, or never broached in the first place. She knew for sure now that they were busybody quidnuncs, after all. Blabbing away their gossip to add to the bard's arsenal of taunts.

To demonstrate her displeasure at Scilio's remark, Kir scowled and whipped out her shortsword, arcing the blade accurately through the air to cleave the doll into two pieces.

Scilio regarded the head and torso of the bisected reed doll, still outstretched in his hand as it unraveled. His features contorted and he shivered. "Remind me never to gift her a puppy."

Kir narrowed her eyes. "Who did you say likes to play with dolls?"

"I suppose I overheard a false rumor, Guardian Ithinar." Scilio patted the air in jest. "You like to play with *swords*. I stand corrected."

Kir raised her chin in mock triumph and sheathed her blade.

"My heart leaps that your aim is true. I value my hands as greatly as my eyes, for without them I would be hindered in my most preferable of occupations," Scilio noted, wiggling his fingers suggestively. "Majesty, may I make a suggestion? Upon your Ascension, you might consider enacting a law that prohibits *crazy* women from having access to pointy weapons."

Malacar's head shot up and his brow fell into a hard triangle of anger. "What was that crack?"

Scilio, apparently missing the edge of fury in the tone, threw Kir a sarcastic grin. "That lunatic females with swords are dangerous to the population. It is on our own heads if we allow them to gallivant around, endangering our children." He dangled the unraveled reeds out to make his point. "No child is safe in their care."

Kir had noticed Malacar's inexplicable mood change, but she was unprepared for his instant eruption. He launched toward Scilio and balled fist connected with slender jaw.

## -22-
## The Paths of Atonement

*I hate putting a sword in a woman's hand. Her tongue is sharp enough, and anything else is redundancy.* - Master Kozias

Scilio stumbled backward over a chair and landed on his hip.

"Malacar!" Kir yelled, leaping forward. She seized his arm at the elbow, needing both hands to hold back the fury in his strength. "Staunch your flamin' fumarole!"

"Never joke of such things in my presence," Malacar boomed. He shook Kir free and stalked toward the door to the outer deck, slamming it behind him.

Vann was already kneeling at Scilio's side, helping him apeak.

"What in the wenchin furies was that all about?" Kir asked. She and Vann each took an arm and hauled the befuddled Bardian to his feet.

"What did I say?" he asked groggily, probing his jaw gingerly with a wince.

"I've never seen him like that," Vann said. "That statement sure set him off."

"If he was defending your honor, Kir, he could have simply insisted I guard my tongue..." Scilio muttered.

"I don't think it was *my* honor he was defending, Ponytail.

Malacar guards his demons carefully. I think they just came roaring out for a moment."

"Maybe I should talk to him," Vann said, frowning deeply with concern. He uprighted the overturned chair and ushered Scilio to it.

"Let me. This is a good chance to practice your Healing," Kir said, grimacing in imagined pain at the knot on Scilio's jaw, which was just beginning to swell. "The Shunatar won't be attracting any lady friends tonight if his kisser's as big as his head."

"Many thanks for looking after my love life." Scilio tried to project a smile, then thought better of the effort.

"I'm only looking after myself. It's so much more peaceful when you're out of my hair." Kir slipped out the door and walked the length of the deck, searching for Malacar. She finally found him, leaning on the railing off the ship's port bow, his hands clasped in front of him. He bore a distant look that held the agony of ages.

Kir approached the railing and cast her own gaze onto the Hiliharian waterscape. She kept several feet of distance, so as not to trample on his tender personal space.

"Did you come to pry my soul open?" Malacar asked. His voice was laced with bitterness, but moreso with guilt.

"No. Your demons are your own," Kir stated simply. "Just wanted to make sure you were alright."

"I'm fine," he barked.

"Sure. If you need to talk—"

"I don't think so," Malacar interrupted.

"Alrighty then. Just let me know if you ever do. I figure I owe you one for helping me get over Balinor, and I hate being beholden to anybody. Don't let my debt go unpaid too long. I'll leave you to your brooding."

"Is he okay?" Malacar asked as Kir turned to walk away.

"Toma? He's fine. Just boggled. He never means anything by his joking. You know that."

"I am ashamed to have dented my honor on his innocent jaw."

"*Your* honor? You couldn't chip that with a diamond-plated chisel."

"His comment propelled me back to a bad time. I apologize. It will not happen again," Malacar said resolutely.

"That's good. But I'm not the one you should apologize to."

Malacar nodded solidly. After a moment, he spoke again. "Do you believe in the Five Layers of Hell, Kir?"

Kir leaned back, propping her elbows against the railing. She watched the purple deck banners as they wavered in the same wind that tousled her hair lightly. Malacar's past was not for her to pry into and it was unlikely that he would share the story of his torment, anyway. Still, Kir couldn't help wondering what had darkened his soul.

"I ask myself that question almost every day," she said solemnly.

"Have you come to any conclusions?"

"I think we're already stuck in the first level, Denian. I wonder every day where I'm going when I die. I'm not altogether convinced that it could be any worse than where I've already been."

"I don't know if there can be anything worse than what we already face in this world. It's hard for my limited imagination to wrap itself around the concept of a place worse-than-here."

"I don't know much about the workings of the world, but part of me hopes that there *is* a place for punishment in the afterlife," Kir said candidly. "It doesn't seem right that there wouldn't be. Because there are so many evil men in this world. Men who do terrible things and die old and comfortable, and never get the justice that they deserve. It doesn't seem right that they don't suffer the agony that their victims do. I pray there's a level or two of damnation, just for them."

Malacar seemed to ponder the idea for a moment. He cast his gaze upward to the clouds that hung on a hazy blue sky. "I can agree with that sentiment. But I wonder where the threshold lies. At what point do the Gods allow for evil deeds to be dismissed in justification?"

"I've wondered that, too," Kir said. "In my case, would killing Tarnavarian have been judged evil, since it would have been removing his own brand of evil from the world? I don't know. It's still killing. But before that, before I ever committed to his murder, there were the people I killed at Balinor. It was not intentional. So, is it evil, despite the accident? It's still killing. Am I condemned for the sake of their lives?"

"Maybe the Gods allow different levels of acceptance for different kinds of murder. The Crown grants such a distinction, after all," Malacar suggested.

"What do you mean?"

"When I was a Private, I was stationed in northern Havenlen," Malacar began. "Taxation protests led to several small revolts and the King ordered them silenced. Our battalion decimated the revolution. We executed the leaders and outspoken protesters. Those murders were justified by the Crown, as such insurrection would have lead to instability in the country. Two weeks later, a corporal who had personally taken part in the executions went home on furlough and murdered the man he found in bed with his wife. He was hanged for that. At the gallows, he pointed out the irony in allowing him to kill a stranger for his country, but not the thief of his own love."

"The same could be said for soldiers on the field of battle. The Crown allows murder in that circumstance," Kir reasoned.

"That's exactly my point," Malacar confirmed. "Maybe such is the way of the Gods, as well. Perhaps some acts are excused because of the circumstance or the intention. Just as soldiers need not suffer to atone for the lives they take in battle."

"Does suffering really lead to atonement?" Kir asked. "The

priests teach that it does, but who's to say? I sometimes wonder if it's true and if I've suffered enough. I seek redemption, but to whom, I don't know. Not to the Gods. When it comes right down to it, it was not the Gods I wronged. It was the men I killed. I can't give back the lives I've taken or all the blood I've spilled. Even if I spend a hundred years wandering like Ithinar, it can never reverse the evils I did to those men—they're already gone. And so, I'm just trying to do the best I can to be better, and hope that it's enough in the last analysis. That's the only way I can figure to change things. Vann's given me that chance."

"You don't look to the Gods for salvation?"

"The Gods don't save us, Denian," Kir said softly. "It's never been in their job description. We have to look out for ourselves. I kinda see Vann's Guardianship as my means of absolution. It's ironic that my path to redemption is paved with the blood of the men I kill in the name of Vann's safety. So, in seeking atonement for murder, I murder for atonement.

"But even after trying to make up for my wrongs, maybe my soul is already too tarnished to qualify for salvation. I am a Guardian to protect Vann, but the one who needs to be saved, who *wants* to be saved, is me."

"Maybe you already have been saved," Malacar suggested. "Your honor has been restored through the Guardian title, so perhaps your savior has been in that fact."

"My honor?" Kir tossed that around in her head. "I don't know if Ithinar's honor comes so cheap. Honor was something I'd read about in books. Something you warrior class boys wore on your sleeves like badges. I never realized how much I had until it was gone. Or how much I'd miss it until I wanted it back. Somehow, I don't feel like I've regained it by just making a promise and swishing around a sword. It's a lot harder to rope and tie, and my hands are too slippery. I think I'll spend the rest of my life trying to grasp for a hold-on."

"Intentions should count for something," Malacar said.

"I sure hope the Gods think the way you do," Kir chuckled. "Cause if the weight of want-to is the measure of goodness, they'll think me Holy. I could be the Goddess of Good Intention."

It warmed Kir's heart when Malacar laughed. Ten minutes prior, she would have never guessed he could crack a smile through the wall of anger he'd erected.

"All in all, it's a waste of time to worry about the hereafter, Denian. What's done is done. There's no crime we've committed in this life that can be as bad as the things Tarnavarian did. Or men like him," Kir said, trying to project an optimistic confidence she wasn't entirely sure she felt.

"You're probably right about that," Malacar admitted wearily.

"But here, I've been going on about *my* demons and insecurities, when I really came out here to see about yours. I haven't paid off that debt, you know."

"You owe me nothing, Kir. Part of a Guardian's job is getting his brothers through difficult times, on the battlefield *and* off," Malacar said, waving a hand in dismissal of her notion.

"You had some pretty thought-provoking questions. Were they more concerned with your own soul, or someone else's?" Kir asked tentatively. She wasn't sure just how far she could push the limit.

It took several moments for Malacar to finally respond. "Perhaps both," he said, running his hand through his hair.

Another few moments of silence passed. Kir knew that even though Scilio's comment had been a joke about her, Malacar's outburst was not. There was something tragic and sorrowful in his past that clung to him. What else could drive a man to ask such profound questions? But then, Kir was rather surprised at herself. She had voiced such personal reflections on what had once been, and still was, a dark and foreboding subject.

"Damnation," she said suddenly. "How in the wenchin furies did you manage to get me all philosophical-like? You got me spilling my ponderings without even having to torture me."

"You are more philosophical than you credit yourself."

Kir leaned toward Malacar and lowered her voice conspiratorially. "Just don't tell the guys, okay? I have a reputation to maintain, and it doesn't include looking all mawkish and introspective. That's our little secret, got it?"

Shaking his head, Malacar slapped Kir on the back in camaraderie, the strength in the blow sending her forward a step. "Someday you will get over those ridiculous notions of masculinity, Kir. You have nothing to prove to us."

"Maybe not, but I'm still a Guardian, and that means emitting a resounding image of strength and confidence. Kinda hard to project such a representation if I become the sentimental-heart-on-my-sleeve type."

"You needn't worry about that. You exude Guardian-ness." Malacar pulled Kir into a grateful embrace. "I'd better get back. I should offer my apology to Toma. Thank you for this engaging conversation. You may not believe it, but it helped."

Kir wrapped her arms around his waist. "I'm glad. You know, I wish I could have met her. Sounds like we had a few things in common."

Malacar released her and looked askance. "Who?"

"Whoever the crazy sword-toting woman was that you loved enough to fight for like that."

He started walking toward the parlor. At first, Kir thought that he might not answer. Did she hit that tender nerve?

Just before he disappeared around the corner, Malacar stopped. "No. She was nothing like you." His voice was pained, but held no anger.

Kir silently cheered the fact that she had surmised correctly. She would have looked dumb as dirt if she'd missed the mark on that observation. Only love could drive someone to such blind fury to protect a memory.

Kir wondered if Malacar had fallen in love with someone in his squad. The warrior class did produce female combatants. They had to be tough, perhaps even tougher than the men, but they were afforded the same respect as their male counterparts.

It was not Kir's place to go prying into Malacar's past, but at least she had another clue. Malacar had loved and lost. Another tragedy.

She crossed to a bench on the bulkhead and sat, opting to allow Malacar time to issue his apology without her standing there. It would seem more heartfelt if it appeared to come with no coaxing or influence from her.

Kir scanned the Hiliharian waterscape and observed the busy people who went about their lives, unaware of her vigil. Several longboats glided swiftly by. People came and went, living out their lives as best they could. The farther ones, bent over their crops or wringing out freshly washed clothing, looked like ants at the distance: tiny and unimportant. Was this what watching the world was like for the Gods? Did people appear ants to the Gods, too?

Kir grimaced at the thought and cast it away. It was much too depressing, and she was in much too good a mood to allow it. Despite her conversation with Malacar—sharing thoughts that normally would have found her brooding and dark—her heart was light and airy. Like the soft and perforated insides of a steaming loaf of crusty bread. She chuckled at the comparison and wondered why her Creatives were so accessible and ridiculously poetic today. Maybe she had been bitten by a muse-fly.

Kir inhaled deeply, lacing her fingers behind her head, and leaned back against the wall. She basked in the peace of the moment.

Then, she was sucked backwards.

## -23-
## An Obsidian Visitor

*Betrayal is the shield removed at the death stroke.* - Master Kozias

Kir's mind seemed to collapse in on itself. It was not a bodily sensation, but more of a Psychonic one. She felt like she had imploded inward and suddenly stood in a grayish-blue nothing, hazy and misty and cold. The Kion was there, but it wasn't. The deck she stood upon was still supporting her, but in some other level of being.

Was this a Prophetic vision?

"You must not trust the King," a deep voice said from behind.

Kir spun and her shortsword was in her hand before she had really registered drawing it.

A figure appeared from the shadows. He was a tall, beastly man, bulging with muscle that was evident even beyond the fuzzy haze that obscured his details. He reminded Kir of Inagor, but there was something different about his aura. He felt darker. Harder. Colder.

Kir studied him, trying to finger his identity. Most of his features were muddied in gray-blue shadow, but she could make out his green eyes. They seemed to glow, like firelight reflected in a wolf's eyes.

His clothing was blurry, but she could see, with stark clarity, the gleam of a vambrace on his forearm.

It was black. As black as a moonless night.

It was their phantom Guardian compass! Months ago, this same man had pulled Vann into a similar vision. He had directed them to Hili, but his identity and intentions were still a mystery.

"I don't trust the Crown," Kir replied, simply.

"You are walking the prince to his fate. You must *not* trust the King," the man repeated.

"Who speaks, that I might trust *you*?" Kir asked.

"Is the vambrace not proof enough?" He held his fist-clenched arm upright for her consideration.

"Not when it looks black as death," Kir replied evenly. "I don't issue trust easily where my Prince is concerned."

"My distance is great, and so the magic is dwindling. But if it is proof of my identity you require, accept this."

The man blinked softly, purposefully, and stepped toward her, as though entering a field of light that had not existed a moment before. His tunic came into focus—he had willed her to see it, she realized.

No, it wasn't a tunic. It was a Guardian tabard. Of crimson and gold. The embroidered dragon-wrapped royal sword and shield on the front panel matched the brand on her shoulder.

Kir choked back a gasp. "You were Tarnavarian's Guardian?"

The man nodded wordlessly.

Kir realized, then, that she was not in the clutches of a vision, but in the embrace of the Guardian magic. This was an aspect of the Bonding.

"Are you the one? Did *you* kill Tarnavarian?" Kir asked, her heart fluttering with excitement, mixed with a pang of jealousy and—was it a twinge of fear?

The Guardian nodded again, still holding his vambraced arm aloft. "And this is my mark of betrayal."

"It is said we cannot harm our Guarded. How is it possible that you *killed* yours?"

The man's voice hardened to an icy level. "I have no time for this. The distance is too great for me to maintain the Bonding for long. You must know. The King has ill designs on your Guarded—designs that will affect all Septauria. I can trust this to no one else. You alone suspect the depths of the Crown's treachery. Keep the prince from Empyrea upon the moonless night to come. At all costs. Or he will suffer the same fate as Tarnavarian. At my own hands, if need be."

Kir felt a flurry of emotions, starting with exhilaration, for this man had just confirmed her suspicions about the King. The excitement was short lived as the emotion gave way to alarm, and finally congealed into intense fury. "We may share a common goal where the Crown is concerned, but you will not threaten my Guarded. You may have killed *yours*, but I'll be damned to the Five Hells before I'll let you lay a hand on mine."

"You cannot take me," the Guardian replied coolly.

Kir flicked her wrist sharply, bringing her shortsword up into a battle stance. "My shiny twenty-four inches says otherwise," she snarled.

The Guardian Betrayer pulled a large black broadsword, a tainted Guardian sword, Kir realized, with practiced ease from the scabbard strapped to his back.

"Come, then," he said, in a frighteningly casual manner.

Kir appraised the man as best she could in the surreal haze. She wondered how much of his image he was allowing her to see. Was she making a mistake by challenging him in this, his own controlled environment?

The thought died instantly as he lunged.

Kir's counterattack formed swiftly in her mind, but the man was too fast. A blur of movement against a field of shadow. In the space of a sharp gasp, he was behind her, his vambraced arm wrapped tightly around Kir's shoulder and his left hand gripped her throat in a death-like vice. His sword arm circled from the other side, high above her head, and the razor tip of his blade rested precariously at the cleavage of her breasts. One brief flick of his wrist would drive the sword through her heart. He held her solidly for a few tense, forced breaths.

Kir could not move. Could not act. She was entirely at his mercy.

"You are good. But you are not ready for me," the Guardian whispered in her ear.

When she felt his grip slacken, Kir whirled out from under his hold and rolled away, crouching in a defensive stance. She struggled wrenchingly with indecision. She wanted to charge him and engage, but he had made his point. It would do no good to die inside her own mind. There was no hope of victory, when the circumstance and environment played entirely to his advantage.

Besides, the Guardian was an ally of sorts—as jealous as Kir was of his action, he had still removed Tarnavarian from the world. This man had done her a favor—by dispatching Tarnavarian, he had probably saved her life. If the Guardian had wanted to kill her, there had been nothing between his blade and her heart but a breath of fabric and a few inches of flesh and bone.

Kir let her stance waver. She thrust the tip of her blade downward into the floor, submitting. It was not easy to yield, but what choice did she have?

"I am spent," the Guardian said, suddenly weary. "You have been warned."

"I would have the name of the man who so easily bested me," Kir managed through her clenched jaw.

"I am Guardian—" he paused, reconsidering. "I am Ashkorai."

The Bonding faded away, leaving Kir alone on the Kion bench, her sword still sheathed beside her. The colors of the world, vibrant and crisp, had returned with the sticky heat. She steadied trembling fingers with a calming breath.

Although Kir's nerves settled quickly, the enormity of the warning did not abate. She was in a humdinger of a spot. Soventine was still on a golden pedestal that Vann had sculpted in his mind. Kir knew what parental betrayal felt like, and it was a hurt that no shield was strong enough to deflect. It would be impossible to guard him from that. He wanted so desperately to return to Soventine's side. To take his place as royal heir, and to make his mark on the world.

Kir had to find a way to hinder him. To keep Vann from High Empyrea, his father, and soul-shattering betrayal. From his fate. Failing that, she had to find a way to protect him, from not only the Keepers, the priests and the King, but from Guardian Ashkorai, as well. Likely, against Vann's own will.

Kir chuckled mirthlessly to the Gods. "That's not much to ask."

# Invitation to the Dance

\* \* \*

## -24-
## Banquet of Strange

*I would rather share my fire with a cook and his*
*onions than a king and his gold.* - Master Kozias

"Your Majesties and honored guests, on behalf of the Hilian people, I invite you to partake in the flavor our culture," Trenen said. The Elder stretched his arm toward the presentation table. The display showcased a portrait of the evening's fare, a visual menu of the feast to come.

Kir had never seen a more exotic spread of weirdness in her entire life. If Corban and his kitchen staff had cooked anything remotely Alakuwai in origin, she didn't recognize it. The dishes were gussied up with more flare than a street corner slattern. Kir took a fit of cackles at a vase of gruesomeness that she affectionately termed the "eyeball bouquet." Grilled and seasoned eyeballs of various sizes were impaled through skewers like an arrangement of flowers.

Another dish that kicked Kir to knee-slapping was the "frog-kisser". The plate sported a giant frog, at least thrice the size of her hand, its arms spread like it was wanting for a hugging. The animal's torso had been hollowed out and served as the make-shift bowl for the meal, a mushy stew of frog meat, vegetables and rice.

The Hilians were extremely creative when it came to the presentation of their dishes, and there was an essence of humor fashioned naturally into them. While Kir was delighted by the exotic display, Scilio was bone-blanched to horror.

"Sing a merry eulogy in my name if I do not make it out alive," he whispered in Vann's ear.

Kir dug her nails into her palm to staunch a snicker fit at the pampered priss' plight.

"Nonsense. You should try the moss paste. It's a treat," Malacar said.

The twitching of Scilio's nose at the suggestion might have led Kir to believe that they were not on speaking terms, but she knew Malacar's humble apology had been readily accepted.

The Bardian mumbled something unintelligible and turned his gaze away from the display. It came to rest on two young female attendants who stood by at the doors, waiting to serve the meal. They were well endowed and the smile instantly returned to Scilio's face.

The party took their seats as directed by their ushers. Kir had been pleasantly surprised to learn that the Guardians were considered guests. She had fully expected to stand guard behind Vann for the entire twelve course meal, as was typical of a Guardian's duty, but the Hilians insisted that the entire entourage be accommodated with every comfort afforded the royals.

Kir sat at an honored place alongside her brother Guardians. They were dressed in their new tabards, and Kir found that she actually liked wearing the article. It solidified her sense of belonging with a pride in Guardianship she'd never really experienced before. The sky-blue tabards were masterfully crafted, trimmed in silver, and they sported an embroidered silver dragon in the center panel. The sleeves were cropped short but loose, and the bottom hem cut at mid-thigh. Scilio and Vann had done a dandy job in the design.

Inagor had donned his own tabard for the occasion, as well, and had commented that it would be appropriate to wear them while on duty from here on out. His tabard was kinda-sorta similar, but longer in the sleeve and shorter in the panel than Vann's design, and Palinora's royal crest was more delicate than Vann's bold silver dragon. The tabard, of winter butter trimmed in goldenrod, reminded Kir of a springtime sunsplash, and the royal colors fit Palinora to a tea, from her hair right down to her warm smile. It looked mighty fine on Inagor, too.

Although her rump was comfy at the moment, Kir knew she couldn't let her guard down. Sitting at the royal table did not negate her duties. She stole a glance at her surroundings, unwilling to relax her attention to Vann's defense, even here. One could never assume that attack would not come, even in promised safety.

She did not want to be lulled into a false sense of security, especially since Slinky was slinking about. He had easily infiltrated the supposed safeguards that the Hilians had established, and who could say that he was the only one to have accomplished such a thing? No place was entirely impenetrable. There was always a weakness to every door. A flaw in every lock. There was no true fortress.

The Pavilion of Freedom was only partially enclosed. The eastern-most half connected to a large building. Several servants scurried in and out of doorways to the kitchens housed in the structure. The building's roof concaved over the pavilion halfway, forming an archy V-shaped ceiling over the diners. The western-most half of the pavilion was open to the sky above, which was already dissolving into evening pastels of sunset. Two platform stages, slightly higher than the floor, were offset on the open outer edges of the pavilion, just against the waterfront. Drums of various sizes and shapes were arrayed across the stages, and the percussionists stood by quietly in wait.

In addition to the head table of the royal party, which was situated nearest the kitchens, there were two long guest tables that ran the length of the pavilion. Kir recognized a few of the counselors amongst the scores of unfamiliar faces seated there.

Elder Trenen joined Vann, Palinora and the Guardians at the head table, along with Bertrand and Ulivall. A small Alakuwai man with snake-like beady eyes was the last to arrive. Every Hilian rose upon his entry, just as they had when Vann had entered. When he was announced as the Master Prophet Farning, Kir understood why he had received such a royal welcome. Farning was revered as something of a savior to the Hilians for popping their collars.

Farning took his seat at the opposite head of the table from Vann's party and immediately commenced to harassing the attendants for wine. He was delivered a goblet of the finest Hilian vintage. As the sommelier turned to fill Scilio's goblet, Farning snatched the bottle from the unsuspecting man's hand. The prophet shooed him away and plopped the bottle on the table before him, apparently intent to set his own pace.

Kir smirked and turned her attention to the rest of the pavilion. She overheard the two buxom attendants, hushed chattering over their giggles, and one mentioned the Fer Waidan as she pointed to Scilio.

One of the many entrances to the Fer Waidan was located behind the kitchen. It was an elaborate maze of interconnected walkways. The planks of wood snaked through the water for leagues, like a spiderweb in seemingly random pattern. The primitive paths had originally been intended as walking trails, but so many romances had been sparked there, it had earned the name Fer Waidan, or *Path of Lovers*. There was a seemingly infinite number of routes one might take. Strategically placed bench decks and inferno lamps pocked long strips of buoyant gardens. Fireflies hung in the air like candles, blinking slowly in chaotic harmony. The planks were only wide enough for two bodies to walk side-by-side, pressed closely together. Inviting hand-holding and whatever else came with it.

The scope of the place lent itself to privacy for those couples wanting to be discreet in their rendezvous. Kir decided they should keep Scilio away from the Fer Waidan, lest he wear out the paths.

After a few minutes of humming conversation, Trenen rose. "Yesterday, our honored Circle made hue on a matter of some importance to the future of our people, and the destiny of Septauria."

Vann's hands tightened around the serviette in his lap. This was the announcement he had been waiting for.

"His Majesty has presented the Circle with a treaty of allegiance. I am pleased to announce that the Hilian people have decided to extend our friendship. While we cannot offer allegiance in a financial, political or military manner at this time, we will provide an entourage to accompany Your Majesty to High Empyrea. When you are established in the court, the Circle will reconvene and sit again on this matter." Trenen bowed to Vann, then returned to his seat.

Vann's face did not stray from polite interest, but Kir knew he was disappointed. The Circle seemed to be taking the safe route, avoiding commitment, but still keeping friendly ties open. It was probably a smart move on their part. After all, Vann hadn't even set foot in High Empyrea. They could not know what the future would bring for him, and what his destiny as the Chaos Bringer would mean.

Vann rose graciously and offered a smile. "I am sincerely honored to consider myself friend to the Hilian people. Your hospitality has exceeded any expectation, and I wish to offer my humble thanks to the people of Hilihar for sheltering my mother in these perilous months. I do not require your financial or military backing to do what is right. Therefore, I make this promise. Upon my arrival in High Empyrea, I will issue a formal proposal, requesting official recognition of Hili as an independent territory. Although I am soon to depart from your company, a piece of me will ever remain in Hili, and I look forward to many years of peaceful negotiation with you."

When the gentle applause had ceased, Trenen rose once again. He presented Vann with a pendant that looked like those worn by the counselors. "Your Majesty, this Hue Pendant is a token of our friendship. It is a symbol of leadership, but also something more. May it always sing to you the voice of the people."

Vann accepted the pendant humbly and issued his salute of thanks. He slipped the pendant's woven chain over his head. "I have a gift to present, as well. Please accept this presentation as an offering of exchange, from our culture to yours."

Kir cocked her head. Thanks to the mage attack in the Arshenholm Valley and the whirlwind of events afterward, Vann and Scilio never had a chance to complete the skit they were planning. Kir hadn't realized they had cooked up something after all.

Scilio rose and accompanied Vann to a forward stage. Lili moved in, almost from nowhere, and handed Scilio a lumachord, the stringed instrument most bards preferred.

"This is a traditional Alakuwai song, dating back ages. May you find harmony with this message of peace," Vann announced.

He and Scilio had shared countless conversations about music, but Kir had not once heard Vann warble a tune. She hoped he didn't embarrass himself. Whose voice could compare to Scilio's?

The Bardian strummed the lumachord and began the ancient song as the instrument bled ribbons of light to accompany the mood. He sang an opening verse, masterfully weaving in his magic. When Vann took up the next verse, Kir liked to have choked on her wine. His mellow tone stole her breath right away.

At the chorus, Vann and Scilio began to blend their distinct styles in harmonious concordance. Where Scilio's tenor flowed with wild direction and an unconventional edge that bordered on genius, Vann's high baritone was classic and rich, much more mature than Kir would have expected from his stick frame. The contrast between the two voices was astonishing. They seemed to blend the old and new into the same song, like it had been around forever and like she was hearing it for the first time. Kir was so taken at the tone and depth of Vann's voice that she never wanted the song to end.

When the performance was over, the applause was unconstrained. Kir joined in enthusiastically as the pair bowed and returned to their seats. She wanted to praise Vann's amazing performance, but the eruption of chatter and laudation around them drowned out any attempt. Several guests jumped from their seats to approach the royal table and offer salutations. It was entirely unusual. Kir had never seen the like at a formal dinner. But then, the Hilians did have their own way, which seemed less formal and uppity than the Alakuwai nobility would have suffered. Yet another reason Kir liked Hili.

Since the table was overrun with gushers, Kir decided to save her own compliments for later, when she could issue them in private. After a few minutes of animated conversation between Vann, Scilio and their newfound fans, Elder Trenen rose and waved a hand for attention to usher everyone back to their seats.

"May I present Master Chef Corban," he announced.

"Honored Counselors and distinguished guests," Corban said, "We have spared no effort to bring you the pinnacle of our people's cuisine. With this, let us begin the feast!"

With a sudden boom, the drums began hammering an exotic rhythm into the evening air. The sounds reverberated off the angled pavilion ceiling and tickled the eardrums to itchy.

Just beyond the stages, two barges swept in and sidled up to the pavilion. Each flat-decked stage boat supported forty elaborately-costumed dancers that were moving in united motion to the drums. The performance reminded Kir of the Dimishuan dances she'd participated in as a child. Her feet remembered the old steps, long thought forgotten, and she had to stop her legs from moving with the cadence.

Corban knelt at Vann's side. "Majesty, I am pleased to make your acquaintance once more. Thank you for the beautiful song. I've not heard that one in years. You should have asked Kiriana to accompany the performance with dance."

Vann's jaw dropped like a hungry baby bird. "Dance?"

Kir shot a warning at Corban and shook her head.

Scilio repeated Vann's question with smug mirth written across his face. "Why, Guardian Ithinar! When were you planning to divulge this delightful ability?"

"At our sword practice tomorrow, I'm thinking," Kir huffed.

"Guardian Ithinar is a dancer?" Vann asked Corban, obviously probing for more information than Kir was willing to spill.

"Quite accomplished. How many medals did you win in tournament, milady?"

Kir's head fell into her hand. She hadn't intended for the men to learn of that tidbit of her life. After all, Guardians did not dance.

"Dunno. Didn't keep count," she muttered.

"I knew it!" Scilio poked her in the ribs with an index finger. "I knew you were holding out on us. As I've said, we Creatives can sense it about another."

"You're about to sense how creative my *sword* can be."

"I must return to the kitchens, but if I can be of service, please summon me," Corban said, tossing Kir a knowing smile. He bowed and slipped away.

The meal began as any formal banquet, though Kir had never attended one that included drums and dancers. The evening was conducted in the standard manner, with each course served promptly and each empty plate whisked away before the next was delivered.

During the first course of a strange soupy concoction, Scilio hardly touched his bowl. The form of Kir's bathhouse revenge began to take shape in her mind.

She leaned sidelong toward the ashen Bardian, cupped a hand to her mouth and whispered, "You're going to offend them."

"How so?" Scilio asked sullenly.

"Didn't anyone tell you?"

"Apparently not. What, pray-tell, have they neglected to divulge?"

"The Hilians are altogether funny about wasting," Kir said soberly. It wouldn't hurt to spin the truth a sliver. "You have to eat *everything* on your plate or they'll take it as almighty rude. It's the gravest insult, leaving untouched food. After all, some Godly creature had to die to provide your fare. So, eat it. Don't you dare embarrass Vann!"

Scilio's face turned a lovely shade of swampy. He studied the morsels bobbing in his bowl and inhaled nervously. Kir only hoped that her revenge didn't backfire and cause him to vomit all over the table.

But then, that in itself, would be downright hilarious.

"You can do it, Ponytail," Kir urged, inserting the hollow eating utensils called tanadas into her bowl. "Just pretend it's something you like. Don't think of it as eyeballs and testicles..."

Scilio squeaked and dropped his tanadas. "Eyeballs and *what*?"

"Oh, I'm just funning," Kir snorted. As Scilio began to sip the broth, she added, "The testicles come later. They wouldn't taste right in this kappa-blood broth."

Kir swore she saw a vein pop in his head. He struggled, but managed to empty the bowl.

When the next course of bite-sized appetizers was delivered, Kir found the roasted meal-worms, served in a curved shell, to be her favorite on the plate. She swiped a few of Scilio's and refused when he offered over the rest. His face puckered to pruney with each "crunch" of his jaw on the tiny larvae.

The eyeball bouquets were brought around and the diners were encouraged to pluck their own from the arrangement. Scilio hesitated, so Kir cleared her throat to remind him of his duty. He chose the smallest one. Kir picked several to hide in the folds of her serviette.

With effort, Scilio swallowed the orb whole and washed it down with the remainder of his wine. Kir motioned for the sommelier to refill his goblet.

Throughout the course of the meal, Kir made sure to drop an

eyeball onto Scilio's plate whenever he would close his eyes or divert his gaze in disgust. Every time his tanadas found a new addition, he would glance around suspiciously. He would finally submit and choke down the item, followed by a long chug from his goblet.

Kir issued occasional words of encouragement, and she knew he suspected her treachery. When probed, she feigned innocence.

"I have no idea where that eyeball came from. Maybe it was hiding behind that Kappa-claw garnish. It's kinda funny how they stare at you..." Kir poked her tanadas at the meaty part of the orb on Scilio's plate.

He slapped her hand away and shuddered. "Demented scapegrace. How I long for some juicy caviar toast, followed by a nice squab, on the blushing side of rare..."

Kir wasn't quite sure how fish eggs and a bloody pigeon carcass could be more appealing than anything else on his plate, but she kept her contrary notions to herself. Nobility liked to believe its weirdness was somehow grander than everyone elses' weirdness.

When her stash was depleted, Kir began slipping the most unappetizing bits of her own meal onto Scilio's plate. She couldn't wait for final course. There were some choice entrails, juicy and plump, that she had snatched from the central table decoration. They would look colorfully morbid folded into his dessert.

As talk hummed and the meal was on the wrap-up, the dancers began another performance that held the tables' rapt attention. The dessert course was on the way, and Kir readied the grisly garnish. Just before it was presented, a hand tugged on her sleeve. She turned to see Dailan standing behind her.

"Got a delivery for you, Guardian Ithinar," Dailan said. The boy handed over an oblong box, bound in ithinar.

Kir's heart fluttered in excitement as she slipped the container into her lap to keep it hidden from view. She removed the flower and placed it on the table, then opened the lid to reveal a dance card and a single Cornian cigar.

The dance card was empty, save one name in elegant script. Sandavall Xavien.

"I think it's time to dance," Kir chimed.

## -25-
## Dance of Blades

*It is better to assume your enemy knows your every move.*
*For he just might.* - Master Kozias

Kir's heart did a little frolic against her ribcage. Slinky was ready to face her! Blood pounded in her ears as battle-lust overwhelmed her senses.

She abandoned her serviette, still bulging with entrails, in her seat and used the royal party's distraction to slip away unnoticed. Dailan stopped beside the kitchen building.

"Where is he?"

"On the Fer Waidan," Dailan motioned directions, then handed over a gunny sack. "He wanted you to bring these."

The sheathed shortsword and silver hair comb within plowed a furrow in Kir's brow. They were her own. She had left them in Vann's bedchamber aboard the Kion. Which meant Slinky had infiltrated the room to collect them.

*All he had to do was ask,* Kir thought bitterly as she shoved the sword in her belt and tucked the comb into her pouch. Slinky was grinding home a point—assuring Kir that he had control over the situation. The thought was irksome, but Kir pushed it aside. She couldn't allow herself to be rattled before the battle had even begun.

"Keep this safe for me, Dagnabber." She pressed her Guardian sword into Dailan's hand and waved dismissal. He scurried away through a kitchen door.

After a centering breath, Kir set upon the path around back of the kitchen. Her silhouetted opponent stood a few hundred feet away, in the shadows between Inferno lamps just beyond the Fer Waidan entrance. His head was bowed and his fingers laced.

Kir could almost taste the raw excitement on her tongue as she lilted along the planks. Without entirely realizing it, her footsteps had fallen into rhythm with the beating of the exotic drums that resonated through the air.

"I was wondering when you'd finally ask me to dance. It's not polite to keep a lady waiting," Kir called. She hoped her voice wasn't over-laced with enthusiasm, but it was nigh impossible to contain the battle lust that welled up like a flashing flood.

"It seemed an appropriate time," the man called back. His voice was airier than Kir had imagined it would be. "It is a party, after all."

Slinky stepped into the lamp light. He was fully cloaked in the familiar black robes that Kir so despised and his hood was drawn around a white oval mask.

Her feet stuttered in alarm. "You're a mage?"

The Keeper lowered his hood and tugged away the mask, revealing a face that was almost too comely. He had slender features, gentle angles, and a smooth, pale complexion. Kir noticed immediately that he was not wearing his usual hat, and his long tawny-brown hair mimicked her own favored style, pulled back into a ponytail at the nape of his neck.

"I prefer to think of myself as a Keeper of Magic. Or a student of magic, rather," the mage replied cordially. "But tonight, I cast aside my robes. I belong only to you." He ripped the cloak away from his body and dropped it to the planks at his feet with deliberate flair.

If Kir was aghast at the robes, she was even more blazerstruck at what lay beneath them. The man was outfitted in the crimson and gold tabard of Tarnavarian's Guardians.

"You're his Guardian, too? Wenchin furies, but who ain't?" Kir cried, throwing up her hands in disbelief.

"Do you like it?" the mage asked coyly. He pinched the tabard at the shoulders, between his fingers and thumbs, as if showing off his prize. "I haven't worn it in three years. The moment I saw you, I knew I simply *must* pull it out again. Funny, isn't it, how fashions tend to run in cycles?"

Kir blinked. "Whatever you say."

In light of the revelation, she needed to warn the Guardians. Slinky was a mage—he would undoubtedly be after Vann. He had unhindered access to Vann's bedchamber, and not a soul in the royal party had any inkling of danger. Kir cursed for not having erred on the side of caution. She could chide herself later, after she had sent him to tea with the Soul Collectors.

Slinky seemed to be reading Kir's thoughts. "Oh, fear not. I have no intentions of pursuing the prince. Yet. The Soul Collectors will be escorting *you* to tea before I endeavor an attempt on Vannisarian."

"So much for your dogma. I thought mages had to abide by their covenant."

"Perhaps I am not quite as devout as my brothers. I see my association with the Keepers in a more self-serving respect. What I take from their teachings, I use for my own personal gain. Selfish, I don't deny. But then, aren't we all ithinary creatures, in the end?" Slinky beamed.

Kir glared at the mage for a silent, stalking moment. When she couldn't glower his smile away, she saluted him tersely and nodded. "Well, let's get at it, then. Unless you're of a mind to talk me to death."

The man bowed deeply, almost mockingly. "I, Sandavall Xavien, am at your service, milady. I have long awaited this moment."

Xavien turned his body to minimize his profile and took his stance.

Kir squared her shoulders and flicked the catch of her shortsword to disengage it. "By Nomah's honor," she saluted.

"I favor Alokien, myself," Xavien returned.

There was a long, dramatic pause of deafening silence, contrasting the intense heartbeat of drums that rattled the air.

Kir and Xavien stood motionless, sizing each other. At that moment, Kir noticed that Xavien's eyes were a match for Scilio's. They were as purple as the deck banners on the Kion! Kir made a mental note to ask Scilio if Slinky was his long-lost brother. There was a vague similarity between the two. Not just in their hair and eye color, but in their carriage and auras.

Finally, Xavien attacked. His twin swords were in his hands with a casual, expert speed. He leapt from his plank to Kir's, closing the distance in an instant.

In the space of a heartbeat, Kir had already sized the lengths of Xavien's blades, confident in her initial defense and counterattack. His shortswords looked to be two inches shorter than her own, and he seemed to favor his right side. Kir figured him for a right-hander and her strategy would play to that knowledge. As Xavien landed gracefully before her on the plank, Kir met his glancing blow off her sword with a parry, then moved to his left to strike at his weaker side.

"I have no weak side," Xavien chortled, countering her move with his left blade as he simultaneously slashed with his right. Kir sidestepped to dodge the edge of the blade, which should have been easy enough. But when her deltoid stung with a sudden flash, Kir knew she had misjudged the blade's length. It shouldn't have been possible. Her arm should have been a good inch outside his range.

Kir jumped back into a handspring to put distance between them and to buy a few seconds to reevaluate her tactics. A line of blood stained the sleeve of her tunic, and she cursed. "This was a brand new shirt."

"I do so apologize for ruining a gift from your beloved princeling. He has superior taste," Xavien smirked.

Kir thought furiously. What was the trick? Xavien had been able to score a point in the first assault, but it should not have happened. Kir knew exactly where the tip of his blade was. There must have been some alteration of his weapon. Perhaps it could change its length by some magical means? Or...

## -26-
## Clarity of Mirrors

*The best way to survive a fight is to not be where the pointy end is.* - Master Kozias

Kir eyes walked the length of Xavien's blades with careful scrutiny. A smear of blood seemed to hang in mid-air beyond the apparent tip of one. It trailed the outline of an unseen edge, and Kir instantly realized the deception. There was no magic involved. Only a simple illusion. The true ends of the blades seemed to be made of some translucent material like glass, which extended two inches beyond the false tip. It was a clever trick, but it would only work once.

"Ah, I see you have discovered my little secret," Xavien crooned.

"Yeah. But you're gonna need more than flim-flammery to beat me," Kir returned.

Xavien laughed too heartily to be reckoned dangerous. "Oh, I assure you. I've only just begun."

Fully confident now in what she believed to be Xavien's only advantage, Kir flipped toward him. She brought her sword into a series of continuously flowing arcs, only to see each one countered expertly and easily. The two opponents fell into a rhythm in time with the pulsing drums, and Kir found herself wrapped up in the battle. That Xavien could counter her every attack was exhilarating, proving that he was a most worthy adversary.

It occurred to Kir that she had been waiting for just such an opponent. Without Tarnavarian to focus her obsessions, she needed this adversary to make her feel alive. She loosened the reins on the gravity of the situation and began to enjoy the steady ecstasy of combat.

The dance continued for some time. Kir met Xavien's twin swords with her own blade, and her vambrace served as a shield. On occasion, she attempted to strike Xavien with the armguard, but he always seemed to move a half-second too soon.

Their styles were remarkably similar, which was a curiosity. Why would a former Guardian attempt to master an entirely new style of fighting that relied on speed and agility over strength and power? A broadsword, like the Guardian sword, required the latter. Xavien either had an interest in unique battle styles, or he had specifically mirrored Kir's own.

Xavien managed to draw blood several times, though none of the wounds proved to be severe. Kir's agility was the only thing keeping Xavien's blades from scoring a major hit, and she narrowly escaped such a strike more than once.

They leapt back and forth, jumping across short stretches of water between the planks of the Fer Waidan, trading blows like the ebbing and flowing of a tide. Kir had rarely been able to use her gymnastic abilities, and she found herself thrilling at every flip, every tumble, every handspring. Xavien was almost as acrobatic.

After one clashing of blades, the two opponents ripped apart and Kir crouched as her feet skid backward across the plank. She wiped sweat from her forehead with a quick flick of her wrist. Xavien crouched as well, taking the brief moment of pause to throw a barb. "Perhaps you need a moment to compose yourself, Princess. You look a bit peaked from the humidity. Might I offer a cool refreshment?"

"Actually, I was thinking about turning the heat up a notch," Kir replied evenly.

Inferno magic wrapped itself around her shortsword as she readied her specialized attack, the Fire Star. When she launched it, Xavien crossed his blades at his chest. Kir's Fire Star was drowned in twin torrents of water that erupted from the lake around her. Her flaming blade never came close to the target, as she was forced to throw a Shield up to prevent the deluge from soaking her. The last thing she needed was to be weighed down in battle.

Xavien answered Kir's failed signature move with his own. "Frozen Throne," he summoned.

The lake water surrounding the planks at Kir's feet seemed to rise up like a fountain. She tried to jump back, but tendrils of water grasped at her ankles and began to solidify into ice, fixing her legs in place. Suddenly, six spears of ice bellowed forth from the frozen immobilizer. Kir's instant Inferno met them before they impaled her, though one did survive the heat and skimmed along her outer thigh as she twisted, leaving a jagged gash. Kir quickly dissolved the ice that rooted her to the plank, ignoring the blisters on her legs from her own Inferno Wisp. She sprang backwards and crouched, thinking furiously.

Xavien had predicted her attacks. He had vanquished her Fire Star. Kir was running out of options. She needed to establish an advantage. Xavien was meeting her move for move and he was toying with her. Their mastery levels were not all that different, so she should have been able to score more hits, but Xavien was anticipating every motion and attack she made.

*He must be a Psychonic*, Kir reasoned. How else could he be reading her every thought? If she could find her talisman and close the holes in her mind, Xavien would have no advantage. Kir could fight him on equal ground.

Xavien seemed to be enjoying the battle, and perhaps he was prolonging it for just such a reason. The minor wounds he had dealt were not severe, but enough of them would begin to sap her energy. And eventually, he would grow bored and end the battle. Which meant that Kir simply *had* to find her talisman before that happened. Her mind began to race, retracing her conversation with Bertrand for any clue.

*Find my patch... find my crutch... a patch is something you cover a hole with. A crutch is something you lean on when you're too weak to stand on your own. But what does that mean? Betrand says I've used it before. There's nothing I have in my dunnage that serves to do both...*

Xavien's sudden lunge diverted Kir's attention from the evasive answer and she whirled around. Without really thinking about it, she flicked her sword and sliced through the leather lacings that bound his ponytail. It was an instinctive move she had developed, meant to burden the opponent with his own unruly hair falling into his face. She never really registered doing it, so Xavien did not anticipated the tactic.

As his long hair fell around his shoulders, Xavien tumbled out of Kir's reach, then erected himself and bowed gracefully. "Well done, Princess. You have a highly developed battle instinct. However, this is one advantage I am delighted to withdraw from you."

Xavien slipped his fingers inside a pouch that was hidden beneath his tabard. He produced a single silver hair comb, twin to the one in Kir's pouch, and held it up for her appraisal.

"I was hoping I would get to show this off. When you're dead, I will reclaim the other. They should have been mine from the start." He quickly bound his hair with the comb. "I was sanguine that you would wear yours, as well."

Kir stood for a befuddled moment, then she traded him a grin. By wearing the comb, Xavien was inviting a contract of sorts, marking Kir as his equal and his opposite. She began to understand him, as much as the sun could understand the moons. Her hand reached up to the elaborate styling that Palinora had gussied hours before. She loosened the pins, allowing her own hair to fall free. Xavien watched with gleeful intensity as Kir rebound her hair with the matching comb.

"I was wondering where the other one was," Kir's voice dropped a sarcastic notch. "So, you think these should have been given to you. That's why you have a bone to pick with me, is it? Did I steal your man?"

Xavien's smile faded. "The fair princess had little respect for what she held in her very hands. Whereas you loved what Tarnavarian represented to you and your future, I loved *him*. You had his hand, but I had his heart."

"What you loved was a butcher," Kir spat.

"What I loved was a genius that not you, nor even his father, ever recognized," Xavien replied coldly.

"If you wanted him that badly, you coulda had him."

"Oh, I did. Many times. But I could never wear your combs. I could never give him an heir. I could never have what you threw away," Xavien said.

"You were his Guardian. Wasn't that enough?"

"You are Vannisarian's Guardian. Is *that* enough?" Xavien tossed back.

Kir swallowed as her heart squirmed in her chest. *He doesn't know what he's talking about.*

"Of course I do," Xavien said, answering her thought. "I can see your blind heart with the clarity of mirrors. How do you think it was so easy for me to infiltrate your dreams? Which, by the way, I thoroughly enjoyed, I must tell you. You were quite the willing prey. Your mind opened to me like a whore to the thrust, and I relished the raping of it."

Kir clenched her fist in quiet fury around her sword.

"You wanted it," Xavien continued. "You were so anxious to punish yourself that I barely had to make the suggestions. Your tainted mind created the grisly imagery all on its own. I particularly loved the dream of the dead princeling as a smorgasbord for carrion crows. Poetic horror put to beautiful illustration. I was touched. Oh, how I miss frolicking in the playground of your dreams!"

Kir took a deep breath to quell the fire in her gut. "I was gonna kill you quick. Now I'm gonna bleed you. And I'm gonna enjoy it," she hissed between clenched teeth.

"I'm not the one dripping on my boots." Xavien flicked Kir's blood from his swords for effect. "The day I discovered you were still alive, I joined the Keepers to learn every technique possible to prepare for this day. I have come to you, Princess. I have come to you as your death."

"Seems like you're more interested in jawin' than killin'. You had advantage over me—coulda pulled your sword across my throat whilst I slept. And yet, here you stand, trying to talk me into my grave."

"You have misjudged me, dearest," Xavien tutted. "When I kill you, you will be facing me. You will have your sword in your hand. I will not allow you to die without knowing who killed you. And why."

Kir inhaled sharply. She had thought the same thing about Tarnavarian. Her only desire had been to watch the prince's eyes as they registered the recognition and the realization in the moment of his death. Xavien was obsessed with Kir in the *same* way she had been with Tarnavarian!

It struck Kir that Xavien's grudge went deeper than mere jealousy over a lover. There was more to his hatred than being the collapsed point of a love triangle. This grudge was extremely personal.

When Xavien attacked again, Kir barely deflected his blade and she returned with a strike of her own. They traded even blows as they bounced around the nearby planks, but Kir was suddenly ground into the harsh reality. She found her concentration unfocused. Xavien had infiltrated Kir's mind, her dreams, even her heart. He could read her as though she were an open scroll, and that advantage was the greatest any one opponent might have over another. She had no hope of winning this battle. Not as she was.

Kir detected a hint of victory in Xavien's face. He was reading her insecurities. Yet another advantage for him.

She would not give up, but Kir resigned herself to the inevitable —she would likely die here. She took consolation in the fact that she would die at the hands of a worthy opponent. At least that was something.

Vann's voice suddenly assailed her mind: *You would serve me better by choosing to live for me, instead.*

Kir blinked. She pictured Vann and somehow, it felt as though he were scolding her for accepting death so readily. Kir swallowed against instant guilt at the thought of leaving Vann. Perhaps the Guardian magic was prohibiting her from welcoming her own demise. Inagor had alluded to such a thing before.

Vann's dazzling image was warm and comforting so Kir decided to cling to its comfort, much as she did every night to dispel Xavien's grisly nightmares. Its shield seemed to block out the night somehow, and she had come to rely on the Princey Charm in her most ithinary moments. It walled off the torment and bolstered her strength. In a way, Vann had served as Kir's Guardian.

She rolled her eyes at her own idiocy as the comprehension struck. Her Princey Charm. Her patch and her crutch. It wasn't an object or trinket. *Vann* was her talisman! She laughed heartily and slapped her head, feeling a wave of confidence wash over her spirit. "I can't believe I didn't think of it before. That's why you haven't been in my dreams lately. I've been using my talisman to plug the holes all along."

Xavien's cocky grin flipped upside down. "Oh dear. As much as I was enjoying our engagement, Princess, I had expected to defeat you before you grasped that tidbit of enlightenment."

Kir narrowed her eyes and took a high stance. "Mind your step, Keeper Xavien. The tide's turning. And I'm about to drown you in it."

**-27-**
# The Turning Tide

*Hate is not the absence of love. No one can truly
hate who has not deeply loved.* - Master Kozias

"This Crown of Seven Fruits is the most delicate concoction I've ever tasted," Vann commented to his mother as he politely licked the cream from the discs of his tanadas. He marveled at the sparkling spun-sugar structure of the crown sculpture, which formed a hollow dish for the layered dessert.

"Indeed. Master Chef Corban is most adept at his dessert dishes," Palinora agreed. "Even after all these years, I can still remember the creative masterpieces he served at the Karmine estate. They were far and away the best in Septauria. Soventine tried to purchase Corban from the Karmines years ago, but Virnard would not hear of it."

Vann had almost forgotten that his parents had been close to Kir's family. He wondered what might have happened had he grown up in the palace. Might he and Kir have been childhood friends in that other life? It was ironic, how the Gods toyed with men. What unknown force had brought them together in the Hatchel Wood that morning? His fate had been intertwined with Kir's, before either of them were even aware of the others' existence.

Vann pulled himself from his musings. Kir dominated his thoughts these days. He glanced to her empty seat and frowned. "I hope Guardian Ithinar hurries back before she misses this final course. She's been looking forward to it all day."

While Kir had not spoken of it, Vann had sensed her excitement. She had been harboring quiet anticipation of the feast for hours, and she was particularly enthusiastic about the dessert. It brought back memories of a happier time for her.

How odd that he was suddenly so receptive to Kir's mind. Ever since Farning had unburdened him from the Inhibitors, Vann was distinctly aware of a connection with Kir. He could sometimes hear her thoughts verbatim and he seemed to have a heightened awareness of Kir's moods and notions. They came not so much in words, but translated in patterns of nearly tangible feeling and ideas. He was unable to sense the same level of openness in anyone else, so it was a puzzle. Kir was such a guarded soul, Vann had entirely expected her mind and emotions to be an impenetrable wall.

Malacar regarded Kir's empty seat with concern. "Guardian Ithinar has been gone for some time, Majesty. Perhaps I should check on her."

"If she is powdering her nose, I doubt she would appreciate your intrusion. If she does not return soon, I will see about her," Palinora said.

The next performance began on the stage-barges, a strong and pulsing rhythm that was alive with energy. Vann found himself enthralled as the dance enchanted his every sense. Sometime into the performance, he blinked to awareness. Something was nagging at the back of his mind—a glimmer of hopelessness. It wasn't emanating from his own thoughts; it seemed to be coming from Kir. Vann stretched out to her with his Psychonics and was inundated with a sense of loss, wrapped in bittersweet acceptance of fate. Kir was anticipating...was it death?

When Vann glanced to Kir's seat and found it still empty, his heart tumbled in his chest. He didn't know what she was facing, but she was clearly in peril. He couldn't let her surrender to despair. Thrusting his determination into the magic, Vann issued a defiant reminder of her duty to live. He only hoped she would be receptive to the message.

"Guardians, with me," Vann ordered hastily, springing to his feet and trying to keep his nerves from the edge of panic. "Guardian Ithinar is in mortal danger."

The men barreled from the table in a flurry. Vann raced toward the kitchens with the others on his heels. Ulivall motioned for two nearby sentries to join them. After a quick search turned up no sign, he led the party out a back door toward the Fer Waidan.

Corban and Counselor Ferinar were standing beside Dailan, who was perched on the railing of the kitchen's back deck. The boy clutched Kir's Guardian sword tightly, and his attention was fixed on the Fer Waidan. The men only briefly glanced up in acknowledgment of the royal party, before turning their riveted gazes back to whatever held their interest.

Vann followed the trail of their eyes. Kir was standing on the planks of the Lover's Path, her shortsword poised in graceful stance above her head. A stranger, clad in a red and gold tabard, stood on a plank several yards away, facing Kir in a battle stance of his own.

With lightning speed, Kir launched. Vann sensed a connection between the two opponents, as though they were bound by some invisible nexus. They spun and flipped from plank to plank, clashing and repelling like two spinning tops. Both seemed to be equally matched, and both exhibited moves that seemed at times to defy gravity. Kir used her vambrace to offset the opponent's second blade, as he was armed with double weapons to her one. Even so, she kept pace and managed to score several points.

After a few moments, Kir noticed her audience. She hesitated when she spied Vann. "He's a Keeper!" she called. "Guardians, protect the Prince!"

"Understood!" Malacar answered.

Inagor stepped to Vann's side and gripped his arm, ready to whisk him away in an instant.

"We have a mage breach. Enact procedures," Ulivall instructed a sentry, who banged fist to chest and retreated.

The mage's unexpected Blazer Wisp crackled along the planks, forcing Kir to handspring backwards a safe distance. The plank upon which she landed wobbled and dipped under the water, throwing her landing into an arm-twirling fight for balance. She quickly regained stability, but the Keeper took the distraction and leapt forward. Malacar rushed in to her aid.

"No!" Kir called, seeming to sense his approach. "*I* am his opponent." She sprang toward the oncoming man, meeting his blades with sparks.

Malacar skid to a halt, respecting her warrior's claim. His hand remained on his weapon's hilt. Vann and the others moved in behind him to get a closer view of the battle.

The tension in Malacar's stance indicated that he was wrestling with indecision. Finally, he drew his new Arcadian toothpick from its hiding place beneath his tabard. He stepped toward the dueling pair.

"Ithinar!" Malacar shouted, tossing Kir the dagger. She whirled and snatched the blade from the air without missing a beat. Her body continued in the spin, fluidly bringing the new weapon around to catch the mage's.

Sudden explosions of color erupted in the skies overhead, and Vann looked up to the display. He had seen fireflowers before, but somehow, the grandeur of these seemed enhanced by the magnitude of the battle. It was breathtaking and overwhelming all at once.

Kir and the Keeper fought and twirled in rhythm with the hammering drumbeats, their blades sparking fireworks of their own kind under the canvas of color suspended above them. The entire picture seemed mythical to Vann, as though he were removed from the scene. The pulsing drums, the cracking reports of the fireflowers, the haunting glow of the low-hanging moons, the aura and the essence of the Fer Waidan: all created a surreal backdrop behind the magnificent dance of blades. Vann lost track of time, so engrossed was he in the scene.

When their swords locked, Kir spoke to the mage. "Folks don't get to hating for no good circumstance, Xavien. My engagement to Tarnavarian was about as brief as blinking. I just gotta know. What drives a man to so deep a hate? Did I spill wine on your dress or step on

118 · *H. Jane Harrington*

your flowerbed, or something?"

Xavien's jaw clenched as he disengaged and pushed away. "You killed my love."

Kir cocked her head. "Much as I'd love to take credit, Ashkorai stole that honor from me. Go toss some of your hatred on him. And make sure you smack him around some in my stead."

"Oh, I have a date with Ashkorai, once we finish our dance. But you hold a special place of contempt in my heart, Princess. Your shovel leveled more than the Crown Prince. It was the deathblow to my Guardianship. And to his affection. Tarnavarian cast me aside as useless when I failed to prevent your shovel bashing his temple."

"I don't recall you even being there. How could you have prevented it?"

"You still don't remember me, do you?" Xavien almost looked disheartened.

"Other vivid details stand out more about that night. Sorry, but you ain't one of 'em."

"But for a cigar and a smile..."

Kir inhaled sharply. She hadn't been able to figure why Xavien used a Cornian cigar for a calling card, but a lost tidbit of recollection grew sharper in the dim recesses of her memory.

"You were the Guardian standing outside the stable doors," she realized. "I gave you a cigar—"

"You bought me off."

"I didn't plan it that way. I just wanted to spend a private moment with Tarnavarian, without eyes and ears bathing us in scrutiny. I only suggested you enjoy the cigar in the gardens so we could be alone for once. If not for that cigar, the whole outcome of both our lives might have been different, I reckon."

"But for a cigar and a smile," Xavien repeated. "For my negligence of duty, Tarnavarian turned me out into the streets and stripped me of the only bonds I cared about. It was all for your little revolution. You brought about the downfall of my world."

They clashed again, but this time, Kir must have seen an opening. Her sword arced downward, slicing a deep gash into Xavien's trapezius. He stumbled back, grimacing and clutching the gaping wound above his shoulder.

"You brought that downfall on yourself, Xavien. You were his Guardian. If you hadn't let a little girl buy you off with a cigar and a smile, you would'a been there to protect him from that shovel. So don't blame me for your mistakes. I got enough of them on my conscience. I ain't taking responsibility for yours, too."

Xavien stood silently for a moment, watching his blood drip on the plank at his feet. "Perhaps when you realize your love, you will understand what it is to lose it," he panted.

Xavien attacked again suddenly, and Kir hurled aside to dodge the fury of his Inferno. She rolled into a somersault and, in the midst of the move, closed her fingertips around the fabric of the cast-off mage robe that had been lying on the plank.

When Xavien lunged, Kir sidestepped narrowly and threw the robe around his head to obscure his vision. She plunged her sword deep into the fabric, but the cloak seemed to implode on itself, sucking the Keeper into a void. Engulfed in the cloak, he had dematerialize into nothingness, right under Kir's hands. She fell forward, having lost her stability against the body that was instantly gone.

"What the—?" Kir began.

As quickly as he had disappeared, Xavien rematerialized behind Kir, with the cloak draped around his shoulders. He brought his sword up to issue a killing blow to her back.

If ever Vann could have tasted his own heart, it was now, for it was surely lodged in his throat. He tried to push forward, beyond the wall of muscle that was his Guardians, but utter terror froze him in his tracks as time seemed to crawl steadily to a halt. Xavien's blade was careening toward Kir's spine and in the next breath, she was about to take her last. Vann stood, rigid, immobile, unable to watch and yet, unable to take his eyes away.

His chest contracted painfully in the realization that he was about to lose it all. Vann's heart was bound with Kir's, to a degree he was only just beginning to grasp. And now, as he bore the excruciating stretch of infinity, he knew that he could not live without his heart, any more than he could live without air. If Kir died here, he would surely follow, for no body could live as an empty shell. Kir filled him. She completed him. A red thread of fate had wrapped itself around his pinky and it had knotted right around Kir's at the other end. He could not disentangle his soul from hers. She gave him the roots of the earth and the wings of the sky.

He loved her.

Vann's mind had churned him to this point in the space of a heartbeat, and it coursed through him, ripping him from the clutches of panic.

"Behind you!" he screamed.

There was no hesitation in Kir's motion. She spun, just as the blade made contact. She managed to dodge the majority of the strike, but the blade skid along her ribs, slicing a deep gash through the tabard. Kir staggered backward and winced. Then, she grinned and acknowledged Xavien with a salute.

"So that's the trick. You cloakers got everyone thinking you're almighty powerful with your shadow-hopping. Turns out the magic's all in the robes, ain't it?" Kir bobbed her head. "They're nuthin more than magical devices, harboring some kind of arcane spells in their folds that allow you to jump space. Impressive, I'll give you that. But without that cloak, you're just a regular caster like the rest of us. Takes some of the mystery outta you guys."

Xavien's strength seemed to falter and he dropped to a knee, thrusting the point of one sword into the plank to steady himself. The battle was drawing to an end. The injured Keeper would soon pass out from the copious amounts of blood that were spilling down his shoulder.

Ulivall motioned to the twelve warriors who had slipped up behind the royal party. He signaled the cohort with silent hand gestures, directing them to move in and capture the mage at the moment he fell.

"Our audience appears anxious to make my acquaintance," Xavien commented heavily. "Let us continue this dance further, my dear. When we are both refreshed and ready to begin the steps anew."

"Sooner than later, I hope," Kir panted.

"Do take care not to die prematurely, Princess. You are first on my dance card, and I will suffer no other to kill you in my stead."

"Oh, don't worry. I don't plan on kickin' it 'til I have your tabard hanging on my trophy wall."

As Xavien disappeared into the darkness of his cloak's vortex, Kir seemed to have a sudden notion. She dropped to a knee and flung the long dagger at him.

## -28-
## Playing in the Mud

*There is surely no hurt that cannot be cured*
*with a fine wenching. - Master Kozias*

Malacar's dagger disappeared into the void after Xavien, and Kir cursed. "Wenchin furies. Well, I hope it gave him a belly-ache, anyway."

Vann could contain himself no longer. "Kiri!" he cried, ignoring protocol and formality. He pushed between thick shoulders and raced along the planks toward her.

Kir rose and turned to Vann, oblivious to his gut-wrenching worry. She grinned widely, like a child stepping into a confectioner's shop. "That guy's pretty wenchin strong!"

The stars in Kir's eyes twinkled; Vann might have thought she had just been frolicking through a field of flowers, rather than fighting for her life.

"You don't have to seem so happy about it," Scilio called.

Kir met the men half-way. She was winded, but giddy and fidgety, as though she were withholding some reserve of energy she had not already spent.

"You're hurt," Vann said, his voice catching in his throat as he realized the multiple crimson trails across her arms. He was certain Xavien had sliced Kir deeply across the ribs, but the tabard betrayed no such evidence.

"I'm fine," Kir returned casually through rapid breaths. "That was the most exhilarating battle I've ever had!" She chuckled silently. "I must be moving up in the ranks, to have acquired an archenemy."

Inagor stepped to Kir's narrow plank, which was already overly crowded with bodies. He lifted the bottom hem of her tabard to reveal a dark splotch spreading across the side of her tunic. So she had been wounded, after all.

"I believe you've sprung a leak. Perhaps we should have Bertrand join us in the kitchen's lounge," Inagor said with mild concern.

Ulivall produced the mute-flute that Vann had seen him blow once before, when Malacar had been injured. The Grand Master puffed on it a few times before replacing it on his belt. He turned to his warriors and dismissed them to guard posts around the pavilion's perimeter.

The party began walking back toward the kitchen building. Vann tucked himself firmly at Kir's side to offer aid, should she require it. Despite her dismissal of the injuries, she was still bleeding and liable to collapse from shear exhaustion.

A sizable audience had congregated on the deck. They were mostly guests and kitchen staff, and every one of them seemed enthralled at the battle they had witnessed. Vann spied his mother standing among the crowd. Palinora's brow was knit with concern. Vann nodded in assurance and her clenched features eased just slightly.

As they walked along the narrow planks, Kir inspected her tabard and cocked her head in wonder. "Now that's something. There's no blood on it. And, where's the slash...?"

"Those tabards are repellent and self-healing. Master Tailor Tressa worked Natural magics into the cloth. They call the technique Lotus Leaf," Ulivall reported.

"Repellent?" Kir made a noise of impression. She paused and stuck her fingers into the blood soaking her side, then flicked them at the tabard. When the droplets congealed into tiny balls and rolled off the fabric, Kir gasped in astonishment.

"Wenchin furies..." she breathed. She tried it a second time, clearly amused as the blood, once again, tumbled away.

"If you're quite done..." Malacar chuckled, nudging her along.

"Don't step on my bliss, Malacar." Kir smiled dreamily. "I've had a wonderful night."

Vann shook his head. "Kiri, you are the only person I've ever known who would prefer dueling to dessert."

Kir frowned for the first time. "Oh yeah. Dessert. I missed it, didn't I?"

Ulivall laughed. "I'm sure the Master Chef can remedy that, once we see to your wounds."

Kir's balance wavered. She almost stepped off the plank, but Vann caught her quickly.

"Reckon it's finally catching up to me," Kir said sheepishly. She allowed Vann to aid her as they walked, but the satisfied glory never left her pale face.

When they reached the kitchen deck, the crowd parted for the royal party. Vann could make out whispers and hushed comments of awe from the observers.

Malacar slipped up to Kir's other side and wrapped an arm around her waist for support. The big man had become quite protective of Kir, Vann noted with a smile. And to think that they had once been at each others' throats, as well! Vann relinquished Kir to Malacar's care, and she was led into the kitchen building. He hung back to collect her Guardian sword from Dailan and issued a quick word of thanks to the boy for keeping the weapon.

Opening the back kitchen door for Vann and Palinora, Ulivall nodded and said, almost to himself, "Kiri. How appropriate."

"What do you mean?" Vann asked.

"There is a tree called kiri. The more you cut it down, the stronger it grows back."

Vann smiled. Appropriate, indeed.

\* \* \*

Kir stumbled drunkenly into the kitchen lounge, but thanks to Malacar's steady grip, she didn't fall. He lowered her into a waiting high-backed chair and removed her belt, then eased the tabard over her head as the royal party filtered into the room.

"I think I lost your new Arcadian toothpick," Kir said apologetically as Malacar gingerly inspected the deep gash across her side. He pressed a kitchen towel against the wound to staunch the bleeding.

"It was worth the loss. Though, it was dishonorable to attack a retreating foe in such an underhanded manner," Malacar scolded.

"I know. But when you play in the mud, you play dirty. Something you honor-bound warrior class boys never learn. I honestly didn't plan for it to kill him. I wouldn't be able to face him again if he died tonight. I mainly wanted to confirm a suspicion."

"What suspicion?" Scilio asked, settling himself in a seat nearby.

"The mage cloaks open a portal of some kind that allows things to pass through. It's not the Keeper that shadow-hops. It's the magic-infused robes he's in contact with. I felt the magic in the fabric activate under my hand when Xavien summoned it. In fact, I thought the cloak's vortex was going to swallow my sword when I stuck it where Xavien's head used to be. To be sure, I chucked the dagger to see what would happen. It disappeared into the rift when it contacted the cloak. "

Vann knelt at Kir's side and placed her Guardian sword on the floor. His face was scrunched with worry. "Who is Xavien, Kiri? Tarnavarian's former Guardian, obviously. But if he's a mage, why did he come after you, in my place?"

"Because we're flip sides of the same coin," Kir sighed, feeling her energy seeping away. "I guess I have some explaining to do."

Bertrand's entrance into the room interrupted the conversation. He lingered in the doorway. His nervous eyes darted around, then chased dust along the floor. The number of people in the small lounge seemed to overwhelm him.

Kir waved him over. "It's okay. They won't bite."

Bertrand raised his eyes slowly, like his face was stuck in a barrel of molasses. His hesitation lasted a moment before he shuffled to Kir's side. "You're not dead," he stated flatly.

Kir might have scoffed at the ridiculously obvious statement, but she was able to garner the underlying meaning behind the words that were more of a function of relief than of observation. "No. Were you worried?"

"You found your talisman," Bertrand said, ignoring her question.

Kir resisted glancing at Vann, for fear of announcing its form too evidently. "You were right. It was with me all along."

Bertrand left the statement lie and began inspecting the crimson marks of Xavien's affections. As he probed her ribs, Kir's head went for a swim, as though she had just consumed a night's worth of ale.

"Your pardon, Master Healer," Vann touched Bertrand's shoulder lightly. "Might I assist in some way?"

"My Healing talents are above all," Bertrand replied shortly.

Vann winced.

After their talk in the bathhouse, Kir felt familiar enough with Bertrand's odd speech patterns, and she realized that the child wasn't actually bragging, as she might have thought. He was stating that he simply didn't need help.

"That's true, Bertrand. They are," Kir affirmed. "But His Majesty has just come into his Healing magics, and he'd like to learn. I bet you'd make a great tutor. Will you teach him?"

Bertrand teetered on his hesitation.

"Maybe His Majesty will need his Healing to save my life someday. Who better to teach him than the best?"

That seemed to tip his favor. "I will. Because my Healing talents are above all."

The boy took Vann's hand and placed it over the deep canyon in Kir's side. "Inside out. That's the way to heal. Always inside out."

As they worked, Kir focused her breathing to a controlled point and disconnected herself from the fire that came along with healing.

She never thought her year in the Chambers would have any benefit, but for once, she was thankful to Tarnavarian. His torture had left her with a very high tolerance for pain.

Bertrand and Vann seemed to be communicating on another level through the magic that glowed from their palms. When the deepest wound was sufficiently knit, they moved on to the others. With each subsequent injury healed, Kir felt Vann's essence more and more, until she realized that Bertrand was no longer involved in the process. Vann was entirely self-sufficient, and Bertrand had allowed him to finish the task.

The healing took the better part of an hour, and during the last half, Kir began to drift. She wasn't really asleep, but her consciousness balanced on the cusp of cognition. Light conversation hummed in the background, lulling her into a peaceful contentment. She was vaguely aware of Lili entering the room with a supply of bandages, and Kir thought she heard Corban's hushed voice, as well, but she didn't open her eyes to confirm.

After some time, Vann whispered in her ear. "Kiri? We're done."

Blinking the fatigue away, Kir sat upright. She stretched and flexed her arms in assessment. "Not bad, Stick."

"Don't stress them too much," Vann cautioned. "A few of the wounds were rather deep. They'll reopen if you're not careful. The mending should be stronger by tomorrow night."

"Tomorrow? I can't complain about that. Xavien's gonna be laid up a lot longer than a day," Kir smiled in satisfaction and eased herself back in the chair.

"That's for His Majesty's crafting. In mine, you'd be fully healed already," Bertrand commented frankly. He was crouched on his haunches, rocking on his feet as he fingered his shell pendant, and his eyes were studying the floor.

Vann proceeded to wrap a final bandage around Kir's arm. He smiled, in spite of the barb. "You never told me you dance," he commented as he tied the ends of the cloth snugly.

"You never told me you sing," she shot back.

"Don't we all harbor an infinite abyss of secrets?" Scilio commented dryly. He handed Kir a serviette, which was peeking entrails from the folds. "Perhaps you want this back. I'm sure these delectable delicacies would taste divine in your dessert."

Kir tried to feign shock at the implied accusation, but dove into barrels of laughter instead. "You shoulda seen your face, Ponytail. It was worth a keg. So now we're square for the bathhouse."

"Well played," Scilio said, inclining his head. "At least I shall go to bed on a full stomach." One of the buxom attendants slipped into the lounge with a tray of beverages for the royal party. Scilio did not miss her low-cut neckline, or the suggestive glance she threw his way. "Or, on *someone's* stomach, anyway."

When the attendant had gone, Inagor rose from his seat beside Palinora. "Speaking of secrets," he began seriously, "you have kept an important one, Guardian Ithinar. Now that you are once again whole, we have some things to discuss. Please enlighten us about this Guardian-turned-Keeper."

### -29-
# Admission and Admonition

*Always accept constructive criticism from a superior with grace.*
*I killed mine once, and I'm still paying for it.* - Master Kozias

Vann frowned. "As curious as I am, Kiri needs to rest, Inagor. She lost a lot of blood and that can't be instantly replaced by magic. Bertrand showed me how to expedite the process, but she's totally exhausted. Let us postpone this conversation until tomorrow."

"No, I'm fine, Vann. Guardian Arrelius is correct. I do owe you all an explanation, so we might as well get it over with."

Vann nodded hesitant approval. "As long as you're up to it."

Kir laid out Xavien's story, including every detail she could recall in regards to his pursuit and the battle. She told of Xavien's Psychonic abilities, and how he had accessed her dreams through the "holes" in her mind. She recounted how she had discovered a Psychonic stopper of sorts, based on the help Bertrand had given, but she intentionally neglected to mention the actual form of her talisman. It was not a necessary bit of information, anyway.

She also offered up her own observation that Xavien was singular, even for a mage. The fact that he could shadow-hop repeatedly, which was especially evident in the last moments of their battle, meant that he had abilities that were either inaccessible or unknown to the other Keepers. Mages were only known to shadow-hop twice, at most, in a given period of time. Xavien must have tapped into a massive mana reserve, to be able to utilize such powerful magic so frequently.

A nagging feeling told Kir that she was forgetting something in her narration, but her drowsy mind couldn't grasp just what detail of the battle she had misplaced. She shrugged it away and decided to ponder it when her head was a bit less fuzzy.

When she had finished her report, Vann looked concerned. "Kiri, he'll keep coming for you. He won't rest until one of you is dead, will he?"

Kir tried unsuccessfully to hide her utter delight at the thought. "No, he won't. He's totally obsessed. Now that he's lost his Psychonic advantage over my mind, he'll probably find another creative element to use against me. I can't wait to see what he'll have up his sleeve next time."

Inagor placed stern hands on his hips and blew out a sharp breath. "Guardians, I understand that the circumstances of your Guardianship have allowed neither time, nor opportunity, for orientation. You are warriors of the highest caliber, but I have obviously been wrong in my assumption that your training can wait. Grave mistakes have been made and we must address those issues without delay."

Kir grimaced, ready for the criticism.

"First of all, Guardian Ithinar. You have been aware for some time of Keeper Xavien's stealth and presence, yet you chose not to alert your brother Guardians, let alone the regional security which, in this case, would be Ulivall. What have you to say for yourself?"

Kir nodded solemnly, accepting the reprimand. "Had I known Xavien was a cloaker, I would have done just that, Guardian Arrelius. But you are absolutely right. I should never have assumed Xavien was not a threat to His Majesty. He was specifically targeting me, and I didn't want to pull you all into my problems. The demons from my past are my own. I don't want them to burden anyone else. That's all I can say in my defense."

"Guardian Ithinar, your troubles are no longer yours alone," Inagor replied, the caustic edges of his tone dissolving. "From the moment you gave yourself to the brotherhood, you lost the privilege of suffering in ithinary silence. We all shoulder the burdens of our brothers. How else can a wheel turn, without the stronger spokes alleviating the stress on the weaker ones? Never feel as though you must take on a foe, or your troubles, alone. We share in our tribulations, as well as our triumphs."

There it was again. That warm and fraternal sensation. Kir's vambrace tingled just slightly, and she bowed her head in acceptance. "I understand."

"Now then, Guardian Scilio," Inagor said. "Do you recall the events in the Arshenholm Valley on the night of our rendezvous?"

"I knew I was next," Scilio sighed. "I do, Guardian Arrelius."

"A Guardian never leaves his Guarded during a time of crisis. Not even to save the life of another. When you abandoned His Majesty to assist Guardians Ithinar and Malacar, he was left vulnerable, with no protector. This is our single most sacred rule: a Guardian's first duty is to his Guarded. At the expense of all else."

Scilio bowed his head in submission. "Lesson humbly accepted."

"Now that those issues have been addressed, I am satisfied," Inagor said. He leaned back against the wall and crossed his arms.

"Returning to the subject of secrets," Vann said, "I've been thinking a lot today. There was information withheld from me over the years and I understand the desire to protect me from the world in its ugliest forms. However, I am making it officially known. Henceforth, I will tolerate no more secrets. From anyone." He threw a meaningful look to Palinora and Inagor. "If there are important revelations that have not yet been divulged, now is the time."

There were a few moments of uneasy silence. Kir knew she held one giant whapper of a secret, and she had been wrestling over it for hours. She honestly wanted to tell Vann of Ashkorai's warning, but another part of her was wary. Initially, she had decided to keep the information to herself for the time being. She had even determined to delay Vann's arrival in Empyrea, just for safe measure.

The command in Vann's voice was unmistakable, so Kir cast her plans away. It was best if he knew about Ashkorai's assertions and threats. Vann had been sheltered enough. It was time for him to make his own decisions. If nothing else, it would lend one more log to the fire in favor of caution where the King was concerned.

When no one spoke, Kir raised a timid finger.

"Kiri?" Vann asked, dripping surprise from her name.

"Well, I kinda have something else to divulge. Timing just never seemed right, with everything else going on." All eyes were parked and probing on her. "I was paid a little visit today. By our friend with the black vambrace."

"In person, or through a vision?"

Kir tried to fit her meeting with Ashkorai into a neat little package, and she concluded, "The vision seemed to be a function of Guardian magic. I think he has some Prophetics. Maybe that's how he can project these visions through the Bonding."

Inagor paced the floor in deep thought. "So Ashkorai killed Tarnavarian. To be perfectly honest, I'm surprised. There's never been a more honor-bound warrior. What hellfire has been stoked in Empyrea to blacken a Guardian like him? I simply cannot fathom."

"You know him?" Vann asked.

Inagor nodded darkly. "I knew him, yes. Many years ago."

When the Guardian did not speak further, Palinora said, in a measured voice, "Ashkorai was at Cerener Valley, Vann. He was one of the Sanguinary Tides."

Vann nodded in understanding and stared at Inagor with an intensity Kir had rarely seen him exhibit before. "I see," he said coldly.

Kir had never heard of the Sanguinary Tides, but she did not ask for details, fearing her lack of knowledge would make her appear a fool. She could read up on the history when they reached the capitol.

"Whatever his story, Ashkorai spewed a pretty pointed threat. I don't think he means to harm Vann without cause, but there is definitely something going on in High Empyrea that's worth killing royalty for. It's all wrapped around the Chaos Bringer," Kir said carefully. "Whether or not we believe his claims of the King's treason, we must be on our guard against Ashkorai regardless."

"Considering he still has the vambrace and access to the Guardian magic, we can't be too careful," Inagor agreed. "I need to think on this matter. Thank you for presenting it, Guardian Ithinar."

"What do you want to do, Vann?" Kir asked. "If we continue to High Empyrea, you'll be adding one more enemy to the list. And, if Ashkorai's correct, the King is at the top of it."

"Nothing can scare me away from Empyrea," Vann said firmly. "Ashkorai may have led me to Hili, but his intentions may well have been to secure my trust in him. I refuse to believe the assertions of a traitor to the Crown. My father has no motive to bring me harm. I fear him no more than I fear Ashkorai's threats. Stumbling through brier patches for fear of the field bees never accomplishes anything but prickles. I'll walk the fields," Vann said resolutely. "And if the bees sting, I'll squash them."

Talk turned to lighter subjects, mostly revolving around the festival. Ulivall explained that the celebration would continue throughout the city, and would last late into the night.

Kir leaned back into the plush cushion of her chair, listening to the chatter. She didn't remember closing her eyes, but she realized she was drifting off when Vann pulled a blanket to her chin. She did not recall being carried back to the Kion in Malacar's cradling arms. She did not stir as Lili and Palinora dressed her for bed.

All Kir knew was Vann's talisman, and a warm, black nothing.

# Welcome to the Family

* * *

## -30-
## Transparency

*Not all battles are of the blade. The most profound campaigns are those a warrior faces weaponless and exposed, with only will and heart for arms. Our victories here are the mark of character, and the demonstration of true courage.* - Master Kozias

Kir lay on her stomach at the edge of the deck, arms crossed under her chin. The rain was pattering on the waters of the lake, to her fixation. The way the tiny drops plopped in chaotic rhythm, individual and yet part of the whole. Kir studied it intensely, trying to find pattern in the chaos.

"It's raining," Scilio commented from the bench where he sat guard.

"I know," Kir replied.

"You have an extreme distaste for the rain," he added.

"Yup."

"In fact, you rather hate it," he amended.

"That too."

Kir didn't have to see Scilio's face to know he was flummoxed. She did hate the rain and normally wouldn't dare consider laying in it.

The men had been overly concerned about Kir from the moment she blinked awake in her cot on the Kion. They did their dangdest at keeping her in bed, insisting that she needed time to regain her strength after the previous night's battle with Xavien. It was a ridiculous notion. Bertrand had taught Vann well in their brief session, and Kir already felt completely healed.

Malacar had brought lunch on a tray. Vann had propped her up with an assortment of plush, downy pillows and handed her a book, *Unification of the Taurian Isles: The Story of Loran, the Corsair King*. Scilio had even offered to massage her feet. The men had doted on her annoyingly, working every angle, presenting every possible bit of logic for why Kir should remain bed-bound. They also mentioned that her clothes had been whisked away for (what Kir knew was unnecessary) cleaning, leaving only the silken nightdress she wore. They seemed spit-sure that she would not leave her comfortable cot while clad in only the thin wisp of a gown.

Their ridiculously overattentive behaviors had tipped her off. There was some other reason they wanted to her to stay in bed, beyond unfounded concern for her injuries.

Kir had ignored their urgencies and pushed through their bodily barricade at the door, walking barefoot and nightgowned toward the deck.

The minute she stepped outside, she understood their apprehension.

It was raining. And all three men winced in anticipation of her reaction.

Kir had surprised them when she stepped right out into it, allowing the rain to patter on her head and run down her unbound hair. She blinked droplets from her eyelashes and stood silent and still for a few minutes, listening. Then, she trod over to the edge of the deck and planted herself on her stomach, where she had been laying ever since.

She still hated the rain, but it, too, was an adversary. She would face up.

Scilio had been quiet for the entirety of Kir's battle with the shower, but he was obviously getting bored of watching her lay there.

"Perhaps you are aware that I am getting soaked, as well?" Scilio pointed out.

"Nobody said you have to babysit me."

Scilio cleared his throat. "Well, actually, Malacar insisted I keep you company. And he included words like 'Mercarian jewels' and 'crushed'. In the same sentence, no less. For being an inarticulate lout, he certainly can script some vivid imagery at times."

Kir chortled. "Well, we can't have that. You're better suited to tenor than soprano." She sat up and stretched, then sauntered to Scilio's side. "Let's go dry off. I've bested my bully for today."

When Scilio looked up, his eyes bulged and he grit his teeth like he was cutting them on sandpaper. He cleared his throat and darted for the closest passage. Kir hustled after him.

Rounding the corner of the bulkhead, she found Vann and Malacar at the other end. She reckoned Vann had concluded his latest engagement and was coming to check on her.

As she approached, the men skittered to a halt, all bug-eyed and contorted—a perfect match for Scilio's face only moments before. They examined the ceiling, then the deck, babbling incoherent nonsense. Their hands flapped in odd gestures Kir couldn't translate. Then, they scrambled away quickly through a doorway toward the parlor, practically falling over themselves.

An unspoken question to Scilio was met with an unspoken answer. His gaze shifted from Kir's face to her gown and back again. After a split-second of awkward vacillation, he darted toward Vann's bedchamber, spouting gibberish of his own.

"Rain sure does make folk crazy," Kir muttered as a flash of lightning cracked the sky.

Kir's baffled mind tried to wrap itself around the meaning of the odd behaviors. Then, with the bark of thunder, it struck her. She glanced down at her nightgown and squealed in mortification at its water-induced transparency.

Springing after Scilio, Kir thrust herself into the bedchamber. She dove for the safety of her cot and pulled the blanket well over her head. Then, taking a calming breath, she peeked over the edge.

Scilio was busying himself with his market-day finds, pretending not to take notice of her entrance.

Kir scolded her cheeks for flushing. This situation was yet another form of adversary; it would not best her. She inhaled deeply and donned her leathery warrior's persona.

"Kinda chilly over here," Kir remarked.

"I noticed," Scilio smirked. Then, his eyes spread like hoecakes on the fry and he amended, "I mean, your clothes! Actually, I saw an attendant return them recently."

It was a pathetic attempt at lying, especially for a thespian, but Kir did not point that out.

Scilio reached under his cot and fished out a sack. He handed it to her apologetically.

Kir decided not to call the deception. Instead, she would master the situation.

"I'm offended, Ponytail," she joked. "I thought you liked looking at women. So, why did you run away, when you had a chance to gaze upon your favorite view in the world? Am I that hideous?"

Scilio cleared his throat seriously. "Oh, the beauty of the woman is not in question here. Quite honestly, I tried. But an image of your sword kept assaulting my mind's eye."

**-31-**
**A Matter of Petition**

*We cannot choose our blood, but we can choose how to spend it.* - Master Kozias

When they were dressed and ready, Kir followed Scilio toward the parlor. As if struck by the divine inspiration of Alokien, Scilio strangled a cackle that bounced around his windpipe before he cleared it away. Kir would have ignored it, until it happened again.

"Keep those hyenas in your throat long enough, they just might chew their way out. What's struck you so all-fired funny?"

"I was just reflecting on your spectacular battle last night," Scilio replied.

"And that's giggle-worthy because...?"

"Because the enormous amount of gender confusion between the respective opponents paints a picture of ironic hilarity upon the canvas of my mind."

"Gender confusion? That's the grass calling the dragon green, ain't it? Not even Xavien's as girlified as you," Kir countered.

Offense tainted his expression. "I may love the bedchamber, but never have I entertained a man in it. Does it not bother you that your archenemy is something of an androphile?"

Kir shrugged. "Nope. What Xavien does in his bedchamber's

none of my anyhow, any more than what I do in mine's his."

Scilio's grin spread like melting butter, but Kir ignored the perversion that was likely painting across his letchy mind's proverbial canvas and continued. "Or *yours*. Besides, I don't reckon we can choose who we fall in love with. Why folk label and judge and concern themselves with other peoples' private business is beyond me, when it don't hurt or hinder their own selves in any single way. Xavien's chosen a warrior's path and he's worthy of that choice in my eyes."

"Point taken," Scilio admitted. "It's such a shame to think of what he's missing..."

"He's probably thinking the same thing about you. To each his own and then some. I don't care a lick about Xavien's preferences. I'm just happy to have a worthy opponent to fuss on."

"I'll sing a song of obsession for us," Scilio said merrily.

"Come again?"

"Obsession drives our passions, you and I. We both find our purpose in that which fuels our souls. We are kindred in such."

Scilio had nailed her flush in a whack. Mirhana had long filled that role in Kir's life, then vengeance in her place. Obsession had kept Kir rooted in sanity throughout her life.

"You're square on. I never thought the two of us would find common ground to walk on. Your obsession is wrapped in flauntin', falutin' and philandering. Mine is unsheathed at the end of Xavien's blades."

"Though as Guardians, we now have one obsession that overrides them all. Let us both be wary that we do not sacrifice the one that matters for the thrill of the other," Scilio said in a measured tone.

"Agreed, but you can put away your big-brotherhood. I took my scolding well enough from Inagor, and I won't repeat the mistake. Vann comes first and always will for me," she assured him.

Kir pushed the parlor door open and made her way to a chair beside Palinora.

"And so, we have very few leads, Your Majesties," Ulivall continued as Scilio slid into the seat to Kir's left. "There has been no determination on how the Keeper was able to breach our protections, and a thorough inspection of the magic has offered no clues. The shadow-hopping should not be possible within our borders, but we will continue to investigate. All I can offer is my sincere apology regarding this matter, and my assurances that security is on high alert. If Keeper Xavien makes another appearance, we will be ready for him."

Kir knew Xavien wouldn't try again. Not for a while. He would bide his time and wait for the perfect moment, then he would contact Kir for a rendezvous. She understood his mind on another level. There would be no covert attempts at assassination on his part. Xavien thrilled for the battle as much as Kir did.

"Thank you, Grand Master," Vann replied. "I appreciate your

diligence in this matter."

"Good afternoon, Guardian Ithinar," Ulivall greeted. "You are feeling better, I trust?"

"Fit and feisty," Kir assured him.

"I am glad to hear that," Ulivall said. He produced a package wrapped in brown paper from the nearby table. "I have something for you. I probably should have waited, but with all the other offerings coming in, I feared mine would be lost in the multitudes."

"What's this for?" Kir asked, utterly perplexed at the gift.

Ulivall's usual stoic mask was gone, replaced with a warm sincerity. "It is a custom for our people. We offer a gift of petition to a newly welcomed member. The offerings are already piling up on the lower deck, as so many are eager to adopt you into their clan."

Kir had to pick her chin up off the floor. She was well familiar with the clan-bonding customs of the Dimishuans. As most slaves were removed from their biological families upon sale, they had developed their own honorary system of clanship, where the new slave in a household was adopted by one of the established families. Some smaller estates only had one or two clans, while larger ones, such as the Karmines', had as many as twenty.

Customary adoptions began with the offering of gifts by the respective clans, as most newcomers had little in the way of possessions. The adoptee was then allowed to choose which family he or she would accept, which was announced at a welcoming celebration. The system allowed the slaves to establish strong family bonds in place of blood ties.

"I'm being petitioned for clan-bonding?" Kir asked. "But, I'm not Dimishuan."

"Not in blood, but the Circle held session this morning and in the course of proceedings, you were nominated for Hili citizenship. There was unanimous approval, which is very rare. As of today, you are an official resident of Hili. I probably should have allowed Elder Trenen to tell you, but it's not a secret. In Hilihar, gossip travels faster than flood tide."

Kir swallowed hard against the lump that jumped into her throat. "This is quite an honor."

"Only Master Prophet Farning has received the same." It sounded like a trickle of pride leaked its way into Ulivall's statement.

"But, why me? All I've done's fight a cloaker. That's hardly worthy of accolades."

"Master Chef Corban has been romancing your story for some time. Sacrificing ties to your own family for the sake of one of ours has endeared you to many. Your battle last night earned you an instant fanbase. Almost every counselor witnessed it, and they were enthralled. You have been all the talk in Hilihar, and have even been endowed with a name of affection—Saiya Kunnai. It means Little Whirlwind."

Kir grimaced. The last thing she wanted was celebrity. She'd rather blend into a crowd than stand out in it. Master Kozias always said, *Notoriety is a fast route to a short life*, and Kir had tried her best to avoid it. For some reason, notoriety and trouble seemed to stick to her like dog dirt on a boot. She tended to accidentally step into both, and neither were easy to scrape away.

Vann and the Guardians seemed touched. And a tad bit amused.

"Come to think of it, she did look like a whirlwind," Inagor noted to Scilio, who bobbed his head in glee at the poetic comparison.

"I don't know what to say, Ulivall," Kir managed. The lump wouldn't swallow down. It had been a long time since anyone had borne a look of pride at the prospect of tying kinship knots with her.

"There is no need for words. As for my petition, I'm afraid my own clan is small. I've never had much time to devote to relationships, so a handful of my warriors have been my only family. There are eleven of us, all men, and I serve as the clan patron. I know that cannot compare to what Corban's clan can offer, with a large and well-established family unit. But I offer my clan for your consideration, anyway," Ulivall said humbly.

Kir opened the folds of the package to reveal a breathtaking Hilian outfit: a halter top and flowing pants that could easily be mistaken for a long skirt. It was similar to the crimson set she had borrowed from Lili, but these garments were much more elaborate in their detail and they shimmered in shades of iridescent indigo and midnight blue.

"You may venture to Empyrea and beyond, but you will always have a home here with our people, Saiya Kunnai. May this token remind you of your new heritage." Ulivall said over a graceful bow and salute.

"It's beautiful." Kir held back any speechifying for fear of her voice crackifying.

Ulivall smiled genuinely, then the mask of leadership returned to his face and he addressed Vann and Palinora. "I must return to the investigation, but please summon me if necessary, Your Majesties." He excused himself and exited the parlor.

"And so the cast-off of one foolish family becomes the sought-after treasure of a wiser one," Palinora commented pensively. She smoothed a hand over Kir's hair in a motherly gesture. The mushy affection that had inundated the room should have bothered Kir, but for some reason, it felt very natural, and surprisingly comfortable.

Lili poked her head through the doorway. "Excuse me, Guardian Ithinar? I have a delivery for you."

"Why is *Kir* lavished with all the gifts?" Scilio grumbled jokingly, nudging her in good humor. "No respect for the Shunatar."

Lili carried a large covered dish to the serving table and proceeded to scoop spoonfuls of its contents into a smaller bowl. She presented it to Kir, along with a note.

"Master Chef Corban sends his warmest regards," Lili said. "He made this especially for you, since you missed dessert last night."

Kir's heart tickled a chuckle that escaped her lips before she could cork it. Corban had whipped up a batch of her favorite custard. She inhaled the familiar scent, startled at the forgotten memories it stirred up.

Scilio snatched the note from Kir's lap as though it were a love letter. He read, "Affections to our Saiya Kunnai. If His Majesty would excuse you, please join me for a day of shared memories and reflection two days hence. Dailan will escort you to our rendezvous point. Awaiting your reply. Faithfully yours, Corban."

"That's a good idea," Vann said. "I only need one Guardian on duty during social appointments. You should take the day and enjoy it, Kiri."

Kir nodded absently and grabbed the note back from Scilio's fingers. She added a punch to his arm for invading her private messages and airing them for the public.

Her attention turned to the bowl of custardy pudding, layered with delicate slices of fruit. She licked a ribbon from the tanadas, savoring the delectable creaminess. It was even better than her memory had sugar coated it to be. After sucking down the bowl, she accepted seconds.

The men watched her pleadingly. Their tongues were practically lolling from their mouths in envy. Finally, when she could take no more of their doe eyes, Kir waved her hand. "I can't eat all that. Anybody wanna share?"

She hardly needed to ask.

As Lili served the remaining dessert, Kir studied the note. It would be nice to talk with Corban, but she wondered if there was something else at play in his request. It was suspicious that he had chosen a meeting place away from the Kion, and that he hadn't mentioned the specifics. He was likely planning to coax her into accepting his own clan's petition.

Scilio cried out in ecstasy. "Food! Real food! Fit for the consumption of man!"

"And no eyeballs, entrails or testicles in sight," Kir mumbled under her breath with a grin.

# -32-
# The Face of Despair

*Memories roused up, like the dead, are best left to rot.* - Master Kozias

The next morning, Kir learned that Vann had chucked the day's appointments. He wanted to practice his newly unlocked magic. There would be no opportunity unless he took it, and he needed guidance from the Guardians.

Ulivall offered the use of an unoccupied army training field, which had more right to be called a muddy obstacle course. The trees, vines and boggy earth proved much more true to war than any flat, dry, landscaped training ground the royal army might have preferred. What better place to practice for the unpredictability of battle than in a place that threw unpredictability in your face?

While Palinora and Lili watched from over mint teas and under a twisty-vined canopy on the unmucked edge of the field, Inagor roped the morning with combat training. He was a good instructor and Vann was an even better pupil. It took no time for Vann to grab knack of the Elementals. The Guardians joined in, practicing dual castings in partners, using one Elemental to bolster another. The lesson bled into Defensives, which were not as flashy but much more important for Vann to hone.

After a light lunch, the afternoon found Inagor guiding them through different aspects of the Guardian Bonding. Kir hadn't realized that there were so many layers to the magic. While her heart sang when twirling with her blade or frying hay-stuffed targets with Infernos, it positively soared in the embrace of the Bonding. There was no warmer, cozier place than wrapped in the sturdy cloak of brotherhood.

"Now that everyone is comfortable accessing the Guardian Bonding, we can move to the next step. Let's look at the Bonding from Vann's vantage," Inagor instructed. "Your Psychonics can connect you to your Guardian's mind, Vann. I want you to focus on accessing memories."

"Won't this be difficult? From what I hear, it's not easy to utilize Psychonics. Most people instinctively guard their minds."

"Of course, but they can willingly drop their defenses, or they can be forced into doing so through torture. But I don't think you'll have to torture us for access today," Inagor said wryly. He waved Palinora over.

The Queen, clad in travel wear, navigated around magic-blasted holes and slippery mud patches until she reached the group. Kir wondered how Palinora managed to look the picture of perfection in all the sticky, humid, slip-slobbery grime.

"Do I get to play, too?" Palinora cooed. "You've been having all that fun without me."

"It would be a marvelous moment in my memoirs to bear witness to the Queen of Septauria throwing Wind Wisps at empty bottles on a pole," Scilio said suavely. "But it would be even grander to share some of my most treasured memories through your Psychonic gift. Would you care to take a tumble through my world?"

"Entertaining as that would be..." Inagor began, scratching his head.

"...we all know what your world is already. I think we can pretty much guess what those treasured memories are about," Malacar finished. "I don't want to have to arrest you for perversion of the royal family."

"Pity," Scilio sighed. "I had such an abundant variety to share, too."

"A lesson in Psychonics through the Guardian Bonding," Palinora said thoughtfully. "That would be most useful. Magics of the mind are not very easy to utilize. People are guarded. And it takes a tremendous amount of energy to harness this magic in the first place. In the Bonding, however, it's different. You are already connected to your Guardians, and they are not putting up a mental block to you, so it requires less energy and focus."

"Can you show me?" Vann asked.

"Inagor and I have connected on a number of occasions. I will access one of his recent memories. If you all will relax your minds, I will pull you in. Be aware—as you are linked to the memory's emotion, you will see and feel everything that Inagor did in the moment. If he was happy, you will feel it, too. Sad, the same, and so on."

*The mossy greens and browns of the forest backdrop faded into a grayish-blue haze as Kir felt the magic wash over her. The Guardians were beside her, not in a physical manner, but more in a sensory one. The scene unfolded to a familiar table. A sommelier filled Inagor's goblet with a dark Hilian vintage. Vann and Scilio were on the stage.*

*"This is a traditional Alakuwai song, dating back ages. May you find harmony with this message of peace," Vann announced.*

*Scilio strummed the lumachord and began the ancient song as the instrument bled ribbons of light to accompany the mood. He sang an opening verse, masterfully weaving in his magic. When Vann took up the next verse, Inagor was overloaded with paternal pride.*

*At the chorus, Vann and Scilio began to blend their distinct styles in harmonious concordance. Palinora's delicate fingers slipped over Inagor's callused hand and she leaned her head against his shoulder. His chest heaved in a helping of deep contentment and absolute love. There were no palaces or royal courts to constrain so simple, beautiful an act as her hand on his, and their hearts entwined.*

The Bonding evaporated around them, thrusting them back into a world of lush green.

"After that precious moment, I'm almost ashamed of the memories I was planning to offer..." Scilio muttered into his hand.

"The important thing to remember is that memories are not rigid captures of a moment in fact," Palinora said. "Time erodes them. Perception twinges them to fit a belief or need. The same event will be very different when viewed through the recollections of different people. Sometimes memories are intentionally altered, but you can often recognize the patches."

"Now then, Vann. It's your turn. You will partner with Guardian Ithinar for this task," Inagor instructed.

Kir inhaled deeply, nerves a'jangle at the prospect of Vann dancing around in her head. She steeled herself and nodded. "Ready as ready gets."

Her mind slackened and she dropped her talisman, letting the vambrace guide her back into the Bonding. Its strength and essence encompassed her as the world dissolved into a grayish-blue haze. A vortex of memory began to swirl about them, and Vann seemed lost as to direction and control of his newfound ability. He stumbled aimlessly through Kir's mind, as though his hand were fishing to snag a random minnow from a pool of thousands.

Without warning, an image coalesced into stark, horrific reality. It was a face Kir would never forget, and a moment she wished she could.

*Kiriana cowered in the corner, trying to hide her naked and battered body. She clutched the newly forged lumanere collar around her neck. Tarnavarian, in all his prim and immaculate perfection, towered over her. In one hand, he held a shovel. From the other, he dangled an object wrapped in a blood-stained sheet. He let the folds tumble away. The fabric unfurled like a terrible ithinar bloom, opening to reveal its dread center. Long black hair encompassed the round thing that fell from the blossoming wrappings. The object bounced off the painful brand mark that festered on Kiriana's shoulder, and it rolled to a stop at Tarnavarian's foot. It was a severed head.*

*Mirhana's dead, empty eyes stared at her...*

*Tarnavarian laughed cruelly. "You're adept at using a spade. Now you can bury your little pet in your cell and she'll always be with you." He slammed the shovel against Kiriana's temple, then dropped it as she hit the wall.*

*She slid to lay upon the cold dirt floor, unable to move. The blow had stunned her, maybe even injured her brain. She could not turn her head, could not close her eyes, could not even muster the breath to scream.*

*Mirhana's empty eyes stared. And Kiriana could do nothing but stare back...*

Kir screamed and recoiled, ripping herself from the clutches of the Bonding. She didn't remember throwing herself against the nearby cypress, or sliding to the dirt. She must have covered her head because when she regained control, she was huddled against the scratchy bark.

Vann's hands gently pulled her to his chest. "It's okay, Kiri," he soothed, fighting back a waterfall in his own eyes. "It's over now. I'm so sorry..."

Kir blinked to awareness and glanced around the verdant foresty field, ensuring that the gray-blue haze was gone. Vann's hands trembled, but his cradling arms remained fixed around her.

"I'm okay," Kir shuddered a breath. "I'm fine now."

"By the Gods. This is all my fault," Palinora stated through her hands that had clasped her whitewashed face.

Inagor pulled her to his breastplate and whispered something soothing that Kir couldn't catch.

Vann wiped his hand over his eyes and composed himself. "No. It was my doing. I jumped into a whirlpool and was sucked away."

"We should have warned you. Be very specific about what you are trying to access. For my part, Kir, I humbly apologize for not anticipating this." Remorse laced Inagor's words.

Kir waved her hand in dismissal of the notion. She wiped streaks from her face and patted Vann firmly on the shoulder. "Don't fret on it. It's long past and done. I'm kinda surprised it still has a hold on me, after all this time."

Vann did not release her, even when she tried to stand. "It's not long past and done for me," he whispered.

Kir glanced past Vann's shoulder, taking in the remnants of horror that were still etched on every face. Malacar was rubbing his forehead in a daze. Scilio sat in the mud, head in his hands, next to the partially digested remains of his lunch.

They had not just *seen* the vision, but they had lived every ounce of monstrosity with her. The Bonding allowed the emotional connection to manifest like a physical pathway, becoming as real as if they had been there themselves. For Kir, she'd had three years to cope and overcome it. The others had only just been subjected. They were unaccustomed to being thrust into such raw, unadulterated terror.

If they dwelt on the shock, they would be unable to get past it. Kir would have to be the strong one.

"Let's get back at it," she said, detaching herself from Vann and forcing her unsteady legs to rigidity.

"Perhaps... we should resume this exercise later," Palinora recommended. She steadied her stuttering breathing and shook off the effects, pulling away from Inagor to prove her grit.

If they stopped now, Kir would not be able to face her own fears, and she was not about to be bested by the past. "No," she insisted. "I need to go back in. We *all* need to."

Kir stared at Inagor intently, unyielding. He finally submitted. "Very well. If you think yourself able..."

"I do, and we must. If we tiptoe around it, we'll always be afraid of it," Kir replied firmly. "Fearing our own weapons only advantages our enemies."

Malacar pulled Scilio to his feet and slapped an encouraging hand on his back.

"This time, we'll find a happy one." Kir forced a smile and urged Vann up. "I'll even let you pick the one of me in a wet silk nightgown, if that helps."

The remaining session was fruitful. Vann was able to successfully access two of Kir's memories. She had given him specific instructions on which events to target, and he found no difficulty in pinpointing those exact moments. The carefully chosen memories were limited to her time with the Guardians, so there would be no more surprises or embarrassments.

After Vann had pulled scenes from Malacar and Scilio, Inagor called the day to a close.

When the Guardians started toward the longboats, Vann held Kir back. "Kiri, now that I can call upon memories, maybe we can practice again sometime?"

"Sure. Let's access a few of yours next time."

"Of course. You know, if there's ever a memory you'd like to show me, please don't hesitate. Sometimes it helps to share your torment," Vann said, taking Kir's hand. "I feel closer to you, somehow. Knowing more about you. About your past."

Kir swallowed in discomfort, whether from the change in the atmosphere or the prospect of divulging her most terrible memories, she wasn't sure.

"I can handle it," Vann continued. "Anything you want to share. I'll be here for you. I just wanted you to know that."

Kir was surprised, after the first memory they'd accessed, that Vann would be willing to experience such terror again. But she also realized that this was his way of offering to shoulder some of her own pain.

*That must be why he's been pushing me to share Balinor,* she thought. *It's not to satisfy some morbid curiosity, but a genuine attempt to support me.*

"I appreciate that, Vann," Kir said, squeezing his hand. "Maybe someday we'll take a swim through the memory maelstrom together. Maybe someday I'll even show you Balinor."

## -33-
## A Sub-Rosa Tea

*Never shake hands with a smiling man of influence. He'll yoke you in a collar much stronger than lumanere.* - Master Kozias

Kir threw a glance back to Chaiman, at the oar of her longboat. "How far out are we meeting Corban? This Godsforsaken swamp is on the unhealthy side of remote."

She did not expect an answer, so she was not disappointed when Chaiman shrugged apologetically and remained silent. The language barrier would extend the mystery of Kir's journey a little longer.

Kir glanced around and grimaced distastefully. On either side of the boat, the vegetation had become much more primitive and uncultured, with even the sun seeking a retreat. Unlike the well-tended paths the royal party had traveled to Lake Hili, this place was all murk, glum and brume. It was much more on par with what Kir had expected from a swamp. She slapped at another mosquito and growled.

A nagging hint of wariness was teasing her to the edge of concern. This was not a typical rendezvous. If Corban had planned to meet over tea, they might have done so anywhere in Hilihar. Instead, Chaiman had continued to paddle onward and farward, right to the wetland borders of the lake. Dailan had scurried away on other errands after delivering her to Chaiman's longboat, so she had no translator and no way of knowing where she was going. She drew a rough map in her head as they traveled, just in case.

After some time, the swampy waters gave way to muddy patches of land, and Chaiman steered the boat into such a bog. He handed Kir a pair of high boots and commenced tugging on his own.

They sloshed for twenty minutes. Every now and then, Kir was forced to skirt a snake, but no trace of human activity seemed to exist in this isolated mudhole. The ground firmed as they walked, and eventually it became hard and sturdy. The environment was no prettier than the swamps, but at least they weren't sinking in gunk anymore.

Before long, Chaiman stopped short. He held an arm to Kir in warning, then called out to the tree line and waited. A man stepped from a well-hidden picket and barked sharp words to Chaiman.

"Saiya Kunnai," Chaiman answered, motioning to Kir.

The sentry instantly bent at the waist like the broken stem on a dandelion. It was a deep and respectful bow, of the kind she might have expected on her father's estate in Cornia. Chaiman nodded approval and Kir followed him past the picket. As they crossed, a fuchia flicker on an invisible wall of air allowed them access through the magic-laced Lock Barrier that was meant to keep unwelcome guests out.

Voices echoed through the trees, and in minutes they came upon a clearing. The perimeter was hugged by tents. The open center of the encampment was busy with activity. Groups of men, arranged in individual circles, were engaged in sparring matches. A handful were practicing forms with their blades, and a row beyond looked to be flinging arrows at hay targets.

"Ah! Kiriana!" Corban called. He trod toward her with a warm smile.

"Is there a reason you dragged me out to the dung pit of Aquiline?" Kir asked, making no apology for the annoyance that permeated her voice. She fought her hackles from jumping to the rise.

"Deception was not my intent, but I will explain in due time," Corban returned humbly.

Another familiar man approached behind Corban. "Guardian Ithinar. Or, Saiya Kunnai, as many are calling you. Welcome to our headquarters. I am Counselor Ferinar."

"I remember you, Counselor. You were the mouthy one."

"I have always been outspoken, sometimes to my fault. It is in my nature. I hope you were not offended," Ferinar said.

Kir shrugged. "A man has a right to speak his mind. But getting on to matters concerning me, I'm not savvying this parlay. Why am I here?"

Ferinar and Corban seemed to have a full conversation through their eyes.

"This way. We have much to discuss," Ferinar replied simply.

Kir followed them to the largest tent in the encampment. Her mud-caked boots were left outside, in favor of woven indoor slippers. The inner chamber was bare, save for a cot, some basic cooking utensils and a woven case. Three floor mats awaited the trio around a fire pit and tea set.

They settled onto the mats. Ferinar poured tea and offered Kir a cup.

"This is your favorite variety, if I recall," Corban mused.

When Kir sniffed the liquid, a suspicious eyebrow popped up. "Gradhia Dark. You have a good memory, Corban. But this is pretty expensive tea, and hard to find. It's only processed in southern Arcadia."

"Indeed," Corban replied with a knowing smile.

Kir grit her teeth. There was some manner of politicking going on here. Why else would they be lavishing Kir with a leaf that cost enough to feed a family for a week? They were trying to win her over with sentimentality. Kir sipped at the tea and watched over the rim of her cup as her hosts poured their own.

"I see the Grand Master has already offered his token of welcome," Corban noted, gesturing to Kir's outfit. There was some spark of underlying meaning in his tone that Kir could not translate. "Our styles become you."

She nodded darkly. "I thought it appropriate to outfit in Hilian flair, since I was under the assumption we'd be chatting over tea in your home. Had I known I'd be muck-walking and pest-slapping, I might have dressed to the occasion."

The men chuckled, apparently unwilling to rise to the bait.

Kir considered diplomacy, but she had little use for circumspection. The straight blade hits quickest.

"So, you're building a secret little army. Pretty good location for it. Being situated in the middle of Hell keeps it hidden from prying eyes, no doubt," Kir commented, then added carefully, "Such as Ulivall's."

"Before we explain ourselves, might I ask for your discretion?" Ferinar requested. He offered a single rose and waited for her response.

Kir paused for a heartbeat, then clasped her hands into her lap firmly to refuse the time-honored symbol of secrecy. "That's a promise I can't honestly make, Counselor. I consider myself a trustworthy individual, but understand that I am bound by the Guardian Oath. If anything discussed here were to threaten His Majesty's safety, I would be forced to divulge the pertinent information."

"I assure you, we are involved in nothing that would bring harm to His Majesty. On the contrary, Hili's Circle has pledged our friendship to the Prince," Ferinar soothed. "The enterprises here will only be to His Majesty's benefit, and to that of the kingdom as a whole."

"Then, on my honor as a Guardian and the secrecy of the rose, you have my word," Kir said, plucking the flower from Ferinar's hand. Her finger pricked on a thorn and she rubbed the blood across the stem, as was customary for a blood oath.

"As a Guardian..." Corban repeated cautiously. "About that, Lady Kiriana. I'm surprised, knowing your history with the Crown, that you would allow yourself to be enslaved to it."

"It's not as though I chose this path. It was chosen for me," Kir replied, handing the rose back. "A convenient deception. Not much different from how I was duped into coming here..."

Ferinar and his keen political brain must have seen the exploitable opening in her statement. "Then, might I ask, why do you remain loyal to a man who manipulated you into servitude?"

Kir cursed herself for being caught in the trap of her own jaws.

"Have you never sidestepped principle for the sake of survival? His Majesty was only trying to protect himself, and me, from the many dangers that were clawing at our throats. His deception was a matter of pure survival, and I do not fault him for his ploy. I doubt I would have done different, were I in his shoes," Kir defended.

"Don't think I judge, milady," Corban said gently, "but I saw what the Crown did to Mirhana, and to you. They ripped every innocent twinkle from those sweet childrens' eyes. I've mourned that loss every day since. I still don't see how you remain loyal, after all the evil the Crown has visited upon you."

"I'm not loyal to the Crown," Kir stated firmly. "I'm for Vann."

Ferinar sipped his tea thoughtfully. "Are they not one and the same?"

"No more than Ferinar and the Circle are one and the same. And I don't see the rest of the Councilors sitting around this sub-rosa tea with us."

"You speak of the Circle as though it compares to the Crown. The Circle represents the will of the people, but the Crown represents the will of one. When Vannisarian is King, he will not need to hear the voices of the people, as his will rules all," Ferinar returned coldly.

"You're stitching together a garb without tailoring it to the wearer. Vannisarian came up as one of the people, and he'll rule from them and for them. I've never met a man better suited for the job, and I'll die defending that belief."

"One taste of life in a lumanere palace will forever taint the flavor of the humblest man," Ferinar countered.

"Look, Counselor, I didn't come here to debate political theory. You're biting at the hand trying to remove your collar and I won't stand for any more verbal fencing with you. If you have a purpose in bringing me here, make it plain. Or fetch my escort and send me back," Kir stated sharply.

Corban held up a calming hand. "Please, milady. We meant no disrespect. The prince is very fortunate to have such a passionate defender. Even if I don't know him, I do know you. I know your heart. If you tell us that Vannisarian will honestly help our people, then we will trust your word."

Ferinar said nothing, staring at Kir silently over his tea.

"I tell you that. I believe in him, Corban. He's my Mirhana now. This vambrace may be another kind of collar, but I wear it willingly," Kir said.

There were a few moments of profound silence. Finally, Ferinar spoke. "As you stated, we did not call you here to debate politics. Allow me to apologize for my rude behavior. As I've said before, I can be overly forthright when my passion sweeps me away. In actuality, we have a very serious matter to address, which is why we invited you here. You have been a friend to our people in the past, and I'm humbly asking for your aid, once more."

Kir wanted to squirm. Their perception of her as some kind of liberator was not necessarily a role she desired. Her little rebellion had been a personal one, and it had cost the lives of too many. It was nothing to be proud of. "What help do you believe me to be?"

## -34-
## Kappa Call

*Love: Mortal enemy of the warrior's heart. It binds to your weakness while keeping you blind to its danger. Not blade, nor arrow can pierce its immalleable hide. Avoidance is the best strategy. For once caught in its unyielding clutches, you are certainly doomed.* - Master Kozias

Vann scooped up a cucumber slice from his wooden bucket. After a minute of careful calculation and an impressive wind-up, he flung it into the cattails, putting as much power behind it as his arm could muster. He turned on the bench seat of the flatboat and smiled, impressed with his own toss.

"Top that, Your Highness."

Palinora daintily plucked a slice, then held it at lip-level. She blew lightly, casting a Wind Wisp, which propelled her tidbit a good ten meters beyond Vann's mark.

"I believe I won that round," Palinora said.

"Of course, since you backed yours with an illegal casting. That was rather unsporting, to use magic," Vann frowned.

Palinora pursed her lips and lowered her eyes demurely. "I do not recall there being a restriction on the use of magics in this game."

"I thought it was implied," Vann pouted in jest.

"One cannot cheat against a nonextant rule, dear one."

"You've been hanging around Kiri too long, mother. Not that I'm complaining. Too bad she's missing the fun."

Scilio chuckled. "I, for one, am delighted to be free of our unrefined sister. Were she to grace us with her presence, I can visualize her barbaric behavior. There she be, leaning devilishly over boat's edge, cucumber extended, and calling allst the while, 'Here, kappa, kappa, kappa,' with her sword at the ready to whack a hapless beastie should one draw nigh. And worse, she then would turn to me with the grisly entrails and proclaim, 'Chow down, Ponytail!'"

The entire party laughed uproariously at Scilio's impression.

Palinora called him to her side and praised his theatrical genius, which led them into a lively conversation about his past thespian endeavors. Malacar and Ulivall were engaged in their own discussion, so Vann moved to the open seat beside Inagor and sank his hand into the cucumber bucket.

The flatboat touring vessel continued its leisurely cruise along the wetland's edge. In response to Vann's request to partake in some of the activities common to an average Hilian resident, Ulivall had suggested they participate in the weekly Kappa-Call. Kappas were common in the wetlands and had been known to cause trouble, even kidnapping an occasional child, so the Hilians always took time to assuage kappa hungers with the beasts' favored food. The cucumber tosses seemed to appease the kaiyo, thereby eliminating their desire for other sustenance.

As they continued tossing their slices, Inagor remarked, "You know, I could never imagine your father doing this."

"You think it a weakness? For a royal to engage in such menial activity?" Vann asked carefully.

"On the contrary. Marks your strength. Too often the Crown overlooks the very people it's intended to protect."

Vann stared at the cucumber in his hand. "You knew my father. Do you think I'll disappoint him as an heir?"

"I think you'll learn a lot from Soventine, but he may try to remake you in his image. Don't ever forget who you are, Vann. That said, I don't think he'll be disappointed. You have so many strengths to offer the Crown. Soventine will not overlook that. And it will be good for you to return anyway. You'll have a real father, again." Inagor's eyes betrayed a glimmer of loss.

Vann shook his head. "No. I'm returning to the King. But as far as I'm concerned, I've always had my real father with me."

Inagor's jaw clenched. He seemed sincerely touched. They had shared so few conversations of this sort, and Vann regretted that.

"When we reach Empyrea, will things be different between you and mother?"

Inagor grasped Vann's shoulder warmly. "Now, don't you worry about your mother and I. Things didn't change all that much after we left. I don't see why they would change when we return."

Vann's toe nudged his canvas sack, which contained several of his personal effects. The edge of his leather journal poked out through the opening and he stared at it, wishing Kir was there to share the day. Even amongst his family and Guardians, it still felt as though something was missing, and Vann knew exactly what that *something* was. He could hardly think without his mind straying right back to her.

"How did you know..." Vann bit his lip, trying to summon the courage to ask such a personal and potentially revealing question. "How did you know you were in love with mother?"

There was no hesitation in Inagor's answer. "When our hearts collided, and we could never again separate out the pieces."

"I didn't think you were a Creative," Vann choked out in delight. "Only a poet could have scripted such a profound thought."

Inagor smiled. "Your mother must be the muse to my creativity. My every waking thought is of her. She dominates my worries, my hopes. My dreams and desires. I had this perfect idea of what my warrior's life would be, then she came along and spoiled it all. And I was entirely okay with that. That's how I knew I loved her."

"But, is it possible that the Guardian magic can heighten such a feeling?"

"It can't influence emotions. Those are your own. The magic only binds your feet when you want to run away," Inagor answered.

"Why would you ever want to do *that*?" Vann commented under his breath. His cheeks suddenly flushed and he ran his hand through his hair.

"Why, indeed," Inagor smiled knowingly.

"How did you handle it? When you realized how you felt?"

Inagor inhaled thoughtfully and rubbed his chin. "I marched to her side as though I was going to battle. The field of honor was her heart. It took courage, but most of all, it took honesty. I only wish I had found that fortitude sooner."

Vann nodded. He knew exactly what he would do. The Fer Waidan was the ideal setting. When Kir returned, Vann would gather his courage. He would be assertive. He would be stouthearted. And most of all, he would be honest.

## -35-
## Cabal

*Use what you got. To the man dying of thirst,*
*even piss tastes sweet.* - Master Kozias

"Slave revolts have become more frequent in recent years, thanks to the diligent work of the Underground," Corban told Kir. "But despite their increasing occurrences, the success rates of the revolts have not improved. We are losing too many of our own. We can encourage revolution, and though we have the will to fight, we don't have the tools to wage this war."

Ferinar took over. "Our people are taken with you, Saiya Kunnai. Ulivall's message eagles brought reports of your prowess before you arrived in Hilihar. Such stories are often embellished. But when we saw you on the Fer Waidan, we knew the words were no exaggeration. You share in the passion of our people, and you can give us what we lack. We ask for your aid. What advice or training can you offer us to strengthen our hope?"

Kir swirled the liquid in her cup. She drank it down quickly, then stated flatly, "Any aid I give you only encourages more death. Revolts will not ultimately lead to abolition. I tell you that your only hope lies in Vannisarian's support. It might not happen the day after he ascends the throne, but I have no doubt he will find a way to free your people."

"I understand you do not encourage revolt. But even if you do not help us, we *will* fight for our freedom," Ferinar said.

"And you may die."

"Better dead than slave forever."

"As long as there are slaves, there will always be revolts. At least if you help us, we stand a chance of surviving to the end. If I'd had some manner of formal training years ago, perhaps Jurnet would be sharing this tea with us today," Corban said, placing a hand on Kir's arm.

That notion strummed a chord on Kir's heartstrings. "Why me? Why not Ulivall?"

"Our esteemed general is caught up in Farning's suggestion that the Chaos Bringer means our freedom," Ferinar scoffed. "The practical among us harbor doubts. Besides, Ulivall is too trusting in the Prophet and too passive for his own good. If he had his way, Hili would remain a place forgotten by the Alakuwai, but for their bedtime tales. We would never achieve independence in the eyes of the world. Warrior though he may be, Ulivall has no thirst for war. He wants peace so badly he would believe anyone who offers him a cup of it."

"And if Vannisarian succeeds in uncollaring your people? Would all this be in vain?" Kir asked.

"That is the most ideal outcome we can hope for. As the

Alakuwai say, 'Hope for the best, but plan for the worst'," Ferinar replied.

Kir allowed Corban to refill her cup, and she stewed and seasoned for several moments. There was more going on here than they were admitting. Inspiring captive slaves to coup was all well and good, but such work was the dealing of the Underground. Armies were intended for war, not covert operations.

"You can't tell me that this little militia you've collected is meant to inspire slaves to revolution. What do you have planned? An all out war? Do you honestly think a handful of bitter men can defeat Soventine's army? No matter how well trained you may become, you are no match for his shear numbers."

"If our plans come to fruition, that day may never come," Corban said quietly, staring at the cup in his hands.

"What do you mean?"

"As I stated earlier, the Dimishuans of Hili have officially extended friendship to your Prince. As you are passionately loyal to Vannisarian, we will support his interests as well," Ferinar answered. He did nothing to mask the dark tone in his voice. "By removing the King's threat to the Prince. By expediting his ascension to the throne."

Kir's heart skipped a beat and her mouthful of tea almost christened Corban across the fire. "You mean to assassinate Soventine?"

"It is the only way," Corban said heavily. "The King plans to harm the Prince, Kiriana."

The statement took her by surprise. She had thought that information to be exclusive to but a few outside of the royal party. "How did you know about that?"

"We have connections in High Empyrea Palace." Ferinar opened the nearby case to reveal a stack of document scrolls. "Servants give eyes to the very walls. We have procured copies of orders to the slaves who maintain the Holy chamber. You'll want to note one specifically, concerning the handling of a particular weapon." Ferinar smiled humorlessly and continued. "We know that the King wants Vannisarian delivered alive, and that he is planning an evil use of the Prince. The Chaos Bringer is not the hand of abolition or positive change, as Farning would have us believe. The prophecy is wrapped in a sinister veil."

The blood fled from Kir's face as she read the commands the King had issued. They involved the care of Binding manacles, specific cleaning rituals for a stone slab and a cautionary memo regarding the handling of a particular magic-imbued dagger. Every memo head contained the same notation: *In preparation for the moonless night.* And every scroll was marked with Soventine's royal seal.

"A slab and dagger. Binding manacles. It is evident that the Prince will not survive the ritual. You are the Prince's Guardian. In helping us, you help him. By removing Soventine, the Chaos Bringer will not be born in Vannisarian, and he will be spared the torture and death inlaid into the execution of this prophetic ritual. Is it not your duty to save him from his father's warped scheme?" Corban finished.

There was no doubt in Kir's mind as to Soventine's intentions. Too many clues were indicting the King in some major plot against Vann. Farraday's handling of their escort. Ashkorai's assertions. And now this damning evidence. Kir could not have imagined why Soventine would want to harm his only remaining heir, but it was plain as print that he intended to invoke the prophecy, and Vann would not survive it.

A path was laid bare before her now, and, no matter how distasteful, Kir must walk it. Even if it might make her a traitor to the Crown she had sworn to protect. She wasn't Soventine's Guardian, after all. If the King's removal was the ultimate answer to saving Vann, then she would fulfill her duties as Guardian to one, and betrayer to the other.

*Betrayer.* She swallowed down the gravity of the word and steeled her feet to their new course.

The two men stared, awaiting a response.

It didn't take long for her to come to a decision. They were right—she was the only one who could provide them with the training and guidance they needed. She could not expect to fill the role of assassin, but she could provide the means for it to occur.

"Very well. If it saves lives. If it saves His Majesty. I'll do what I can on both fronts."

Ferinar announced Kir to the assembled group of militia members, who greeted her with boisterous applause, and a few shrill whistles. She judged the number in the range of two hundred bodies, though Ferinar had assured her that it was a mere fraction of the group. While they could never risk meeting all at once for the suspicions it would raise, the number of committed members was in the neighborhood of eighteen hundred.

The militia, codenamed Tree Vipers, was made up mostly of Libertines. It was becoming clear that there was some division between the Natives, who had never known the cold metal of a slave collar, and the Libertines, who had tasted it all too sharply.

Ferinar had explained that most of the assembly lived in villages around Hili, traveling to the encampment as their time permitted. Some of the militiamen were permanent residents, but the large majority were members of the surrounding communities. The group of Ulivall's soldiers that had joined the growing militia served as squad leaders, but their duties to the regular army took precedence over this operation, and so, they were not entirely reliable.

Kir issued a few words of greeting to the Tree Vipers and

saluted them. While she was not entirely comfortable with speechifying, she was not untrained in it.

"By Nomah's honor. I stand before you today as one of you, not only in the attire of my body, but in the passion of my heart. You are all my brothers now. We will laugh and cry together, sweat and bleed together," Kir affirmed with a fiery demeanor. Then, she cracked a lopsided grin. "Well, let's try to avoid the bleeding part."

Ripples of laughter undulated through the ranks.

"I've been asked by your leadership to give you aid, and I have to admit, I've struggled with this. In the short amount of time I have left in Hili, there is very little training I can actually offer you. My party will be departing in less than two weeks, which is no time at all. But I can leave you with something better than weapons training. Something you already have at your disposal."

Kir wasn't one to pat herself on the back, but she had to admit, her idea climbed up the ladder toward genius. Sitting in the tent an hour before, she, Corban and Ferinar had commenced to strategizing. When she heard a sectional outside the tent playing an energetic percussion on the drums, the idea smacked her like a malcraven's claw to the gut.

"My Master Kozias was a real disagreeable bastard. The worst *kadda tekano* south of Mercaria."

More chuckles. That was good. She was establishing a rapport with the audience.

"But he taught me something that I've used in every battle and every moment of my life since," Kir continued. "'Worm Food,' he said to me, 'A rock is a spade is a plate is a bludgeon to bash that bastard's head in. In other words, use what you got.' And as much as I hated his sorry *neeyah*, he was absolutely right.

"You don't have fancy weapons, many of you can't cast Elementals worth a damn, and your numbers are puny in the eyes of the Crown. But you have other attributes. Your insignificance in the eyes of those you've served becomes an advantage. Your culture, your language and your clan bonds become an advantage. I have a plan to utilize all of these elements against the people that choose to overlook your strengths. And it will come to fruition right under the noses of your oppressors."

One of the young men in the front row raised a hand in query. "But how can a people in bondage fight without weapons?"

"That's where Master Kozias' philosophy comes in. You use what you have. Swords don't make the warrior. Brains do," Kir answered. "Anything can be a weapon. Cooks can use their pots of boiling water. Farmers can use their scythes and shovels. Hell, even sticks can gouge out eyeballs. With some training, every one of you can easily take out a sentry."

"How can we teach slaves to fight without anyone knowing?"

another piped up.

"The beauty of the Dimishuan situation is that every slave hold has established routines that have endured the ages. We can use those routines to mask our true intentions. I've spent enough time amongst the slaves in the Karmine household to know your customs. Every night, our servants engaged in traditional dances, which I, myself, often took part in as a child. It was the foundation for my forms, which I practice every morning. The dances of your people gave birth to my own fighting style, and I can teach you. If incorporated into the nightly dances in the slave holds, it can be practiced right under the Master's nose, and he will be none the wiser.

"Slaves pretty much run households, so they're privy to schedules, estate layouts and all the inner workings that keep a manor running. Therefore, it won't be hard to coordinate a revolt, once sufficient training and planning have been established. Doors can be locked at just the right time. Security guards, foremen and masters can be drugged. This will not only save Dimishuan lives, but those of the Alakuwai, as well. There is no need for unnecessary bloodshed. There will still be fighting, but best to minimize hand-to-hand combat wherever possible."

One large man stepped forward. "With all due respect, Saiya Kunnai, this is a lofty vision. I'm a warrior in the regular army, and even at my size, I could not see myself capable of fighting an armed and armored man if I were without weapon or magic."

Kir pulled her shortsword from its sheath without a word. The man stepped back in alarm. Kir flipped the hilt around and offered the blade to the bewildered Viper.

"I'm half your size, but even unarmed, I can take you in three moves, using neither magic nor weapon. Attack me."

The man stared at her, then threw a glance to Ferinar. The counselor nodded curtly in permission.

As the militiaman lunged, brandishing the sword before him, Kir swiftly rolled aside and scooped a handful of dirt, throwing it in the man's face as she arose. He stumbled backward a step, trying to clear his vision and Kir skipped in beside him. Her hand moved to the leather lacing that bound her hair in a ponytail. She pulled the cord free and wrapped it around the man's neck as she swept his feet from under him. He hit the ground hard, the sword never posing a real threat. As an added demonstration, Kir thrust her palm downward, as if to strike him squarely in the back of the neck. She stopped just short of contact, pausing for dramatic effect.

There was a moment of stunned silence. Then, suddenly, the Vipers roared more like drunken kaiyo than snakes.

"And *that*, brothers, is what the miserable *kadda* meant!" Kir exclaimed over the laudation.

She offered her hand to the prone man, who stared up at her in disbelief. He accepted and came to his feet, shaking his head in wonder as he returned her sword.

"I stand corrected," he admitted, bowing his head in submission and returning to the crowd.

"How do we spread the training? Via the Underground?" someone called.

"No. We need to disseminate this information directly," Kir said, rebinding her ponytail. "I will provide the training. Your people will pass on the knowledge to the slaves. This means we'll need volunteers to filter back into bondage. That's the only drawback to my plan. If we include a few volunteers in His Majesty's entourage, I can work with them every evening during the journey to Empyrea. One or two will return here and continue teaching your militia. We can arrange for the capture and sale of the others by slave traders. When the volunteers are sold, they can pass the knowledge on to other estates, and hopefully, the training will spread like a wildfire. When I arrive in High Empyrea, I will do what I can from within the palace walls, but the rest of the kingdom will be up to you."

One warrior stepped forward. "I volunteer."

Two more men strode forth boldly, followed by several others, all issuing their committal. In minutes, twenty-two men and five women stood before Kir, all offering themselves for sacrifice to the returns of bondage.

Kir was taken aback. She had honestly expected this to be the hardest part of the sale. "Huh. I'll be rigged and keelhauled."

## -36-
## Of Wine and Water

*They say too much drink spoils the mind. I say drink anyway. You can't spoil what's already rotten.* - Master Kozias

Kir leaned forward on the bench, propping her elbows on her knees. Although her head was swimming and she had practically stepped off the Fer Waidan twice, she could not have been any happier.

Following her rousing speech to Ferinar's militia, Kir had commenced training the cohort. The instruction had taken several hours, and Kir had been pleased to see how quickly the men picked up on the battle techniques when worked into their dance.

The late afternoon had found Kir sharing drinks with her newfound disciples. The encampment gave itself to carousing, complete with food, music and an unending supply of rice wine. Kir had entirely enjoyed the company of the Vipers, and she traded wild stories and wilder jokes with them to solidify a camaraderie.

The men idolized Kir and their attentions were on the edge of unnerving. But as the wine kept flowing, Kir's inhibitions kept shriveling away. She had found herself entirely comfortable, and half-seas over, by the end of the afternoon. Kir bid the encampment a good evening and was escorted to the longboat by several of the warriors. When they had arrived in Hilihar, Kir asked to be delivered to the Fer Waidan.

A swarm had offered to accompany her, but Kir turned them all down and shooed them away. She wanted time to process the events of the day, and that would be next to impossible with people doting all over her. Besides, in her present state, she did not want to say anything she would later regret. The wine had relaxed her just a bit too much for her liking. She was still in control of herself, but only barely.

The Fer Waidan was bathed in the beauty of ages, and petals of cherry blossoms trickled down with every breath of wind. Kir inhaled deeply and sighed in contentment.

She tried to reflect on the militia and her plans. On Corban's heartfelt petition of clanship. On the instant worshipers that seemed ready to die at her word. On Ferinar's subsequent proclamation of loyalty. But try as she might, Kir could not settle her mind. It was too difficult to focus, for the beauty of the area and the wine that had tickled her senses.

"Kiri? What are you doing here?"

Kir startled and practically fell forward as her elbows slid off her knees. She hauled herself apeak and turned on the bench. "Stick?"

Vann was walking toward her on the path. His face was alive with some expression that Kir could not interpret at the moment. Scilio strolled to his rear, hands clasped behind his back.

"I didn't expect to see you here," Vann commented when he reached the bench deck.

"Well, I didn't expect to see me here, either." Kir shrugged, then realized the awkwardness of the statement and amended, "I mean, I wasn't planning on coming here. Just thought it would be nice to enjoy the Fer Waidan without a sword in my hand."

Vann smiled. "I actually had something to talk to you about. So, while we're here..." He motioned toward the path meaningfully.

Kir cocked her head, trying to make sense out of the gesture. Finally, she understood. "Oh. You wanna go for a walk?" It struck her that she shouldn't venture too far, lest she tumble right into the water on her sloshed legs. "Sure. But the view's kinda nice here, so maybe we could sit for a while."

Vann turned to Scilio. "Since Kiri's here, you may as well skip off, Toma. You've been on duty all afternoon. Besides, I think Daleara might be waiting for you back at the pavilion," he said, projecting some sort of hidden meaning in his tone.

Scilio placed a hand on his heart and winked at Vann. "Oh, I'm positive she is. Enjoy your evening, Majesty. I shall endeavor to do the same." With that, he pranced away.

"Daleara?" Kir asked. "What about Lili?"

Vann made a comical face. "Ah, well. You know Toma. He has a taste for variety."

"And Lili's okay with this?"

Vann's hand combed through his buttery mane and he coughed back a chuckle. "She said that no one person can lay claim to a Shunatar."

"As if he needs permission to wench-hop," Kir snorted. "So what did you want to talk to me about?"

Vann cracked a lopsided smile. "Nothing in particular. It just seemed weird being on the Path of Lovers with Toma. People might talk."

Kir laughed. An image popped into her head of Vann and Scilio, holding hands and skipping merrily along the planks with stars and hearts surrounding them. She shook it away and cursed the wine's effects on her good senses.

The gravity of the situation pulled her back to the ground. "Yeah, Stick, but now you're with a *woman* on the Fer Waidan. And *me*, of all people. That might be even worse."

Vann moved in alongside the bench and thrust his hands into his pockets. He cast his gaze over the lotus garden beyond the deck. "That's a rumor I don't mind so much."

That was sword-thrust forthright for mealy-mouthed Vann. Kir raised a scrutinizing eyebrow. "Have you been drinking?"

"No," Vann protested, then corrected himself. "Well, yes, of sorts. I just finished meeting with Elder Trenen and some dignitaries and they passed around a Veracity Chalice. I suppose I'll be under its effects for a while yet."

"Oh. Well, alrighty then."

Vann stood on the deck for a few awkward moments, studying the waterscape in silence. He threw a glance Kir's way every now and again. Finally, he asked, "Do you mind if I join you?"

Kir slid over to allow him room. "Sorry. I shoulda offered."

Vann sat next to her and a few more tense moments passed. The petal from a cherry blossom floated lackadaisically on the breeze and landed on the back of Vann's hand.

"That's something. Here it is late summer and they're still in bloom," Kir commented, plucking the petal from Vann's skin and rolling it between her fingers. "Wonder how they managed that?"

"The cherry trees?" Vann looked to the floating garden. "I believe the Hilians use Natural magics to keep them in bloom year-round. It's quite amazing, isn't it?"

"It surely is." Kir agreed. "I'm ashamed to say that I haven't paid mind to pretty things in the past few years. But it's easy to get caught up in the beauty here. The whole of this place is an ocean of sublime."

Vann leaned toward her like a whisper of air had nudged him. "The beauty here is undeniable, but it holds not a candle to yours."

Kir shamefully turned her head away at the stinging compliment and unconsciously covered the thin scar on her neck. Vann's hand closed around hers and he pulled it away.

His fingers traced the length of the scar, and when he reached her chest, he covered her heart with an open palm. "Any path that leads to your heart is beautiful, Kiri."

The Inferno lamps flickered light in Vann's eyes. Kir found herself lost in them for a frozen moment that might have been seconds or eternity. Vann tucked some stray bangs behind Kir's ear and his fingers tenderly caressed her cheek.

Kir clenched her jaw. A nagging sensation warned her to alarm. She was on the Fer Waidan with the most gentle and handsome creature she'd ever known, who embodied every perfection she could imagine, but had believed nonextant, in a man. She had consumed entirely too much wine and was at risk of losing her sense of propriety. The situation was too precarious. She should remove herself from it, before the Fer Waidan led her down a pathway too slippery to reascend.

"Well, how's about that walk?" Kir asked sheepishly, pulling away quickly.

"If you insist. However, you were certainly right about the view here," Vann smiled warmly. He stood and stretched, never removing his eyes from her.

Kir rose from the bench and took a step, but her balance teetered. Her foot caught on the uneven edge of a plank and she tripped right into Vann. He caught her firmly in his arms.

Her cheeks ran the sanguine gamut and Kir tried to pull away, but something held her solidly against Vann's chest. His hands. When she lifted her head, Kir found Vann gazing at her with a look that scared her to her core.

She started to speak, to spout any gibberish that would break the enchantment, but just as Kir opened her mouth, Vann leaned forward and kissed her softly.

## -37-
## Betrayer's Passion

*If you cannot be honest with yourself, look to your wine glass, for it is a much better mirror than the one on your vanity.* - Master Kozias

Kir wanted to scream. She wanted to run. She wanted to push him away. But instead, she felt the tension evaporate. She melted into Vann's embrace and savored the smell of him, the taste of him, the feel of him.

Vann's hand found the leather lacing of her ponytail and he pulled it loose, freeing Kir's hair to cascade down her shoulders. As if orchestrated by the Gods, a sudden breeze caught her mane and the loose folds of her pants, waving them gently. The cherry blossoms drifted like snow on the wind and mingled with her hair. Kir found herself unable to escape the moment, and to her surprise, she didn't want to.

Her mind began playing back all of the crystalline points that had captured her in the past months. The gentle touch of Vann's soft hands. The support he had shown her in the darkest times, and the smiles he had issued in the lightest. His quiet strength and boyish innocence. His strong and steadfast image—her talisman. It was like a flurry of radiant color, these memories. And, even through the muddled haze of her intoxicated brain, it was suddenly as clear as a winter morning. All of the feelings that had been confounding and harassing her in the past weeks—Kir understood now.

She was in love with him.

For a hesitant moment in the realization, Kir pulled her lips back. She studied Vann's face, a breath away. Then, Vann swept her in, opening his mind and heart through his natural Psychonics. Vann was giving Kir his deepest self, holding back nothing. Without saying a word, he told Kir everything he felt for her, encompassed in the palpable power of his bare emotion. As they melted together, Kir couldn't distinguish where she ended and he began.

*What's your greatest desire?* She could almost hear the question that Vann had asked her in Southport, all those months ago. Her response had been noncommittal, as she had no good reply back then. But now, Kir knew exactly the nature of her greatest desire.

"Can I change my answer?" she mumbled.

Vann looked puzzled. "Hmm?"

"Never mind," Kir said, pulling him to her own lips.

A series of possibilities raced before her. In the past three years, Kir had not dreamed of hoping for a future. Suddenly a raw, desperate hunger clawed from the lining of her soul. The only role she had seen for herself was Assassin, but now, Kir realized that her heart had been blindly guiding her down the path of Friend. Protector. Sister. Lover.

*Betrayer.*

Kir blinked and pushed away abruptly at the unbidden, painful accusation. She could see in Vann's enraptured face that the flash had not emanated from him. Instead, it came from within. From that nagging little conscience that reminded her who she really was.

"Kiri? What's wrong?" Vann asked, seeming to sense the sudden apprehension in Kir's demeanor.

Kir righted herself and pulled back from his embrace. "Nothing. It's nothing," she issued quickly, stumbling backward.

As Vann stepped toward her, Kir's instability toppled her sense of the upright. She felt her world tumbling as her foot met with the brief open air beyond the deck. Her arms windmilled frantically, but alas, she could not fly. Kir grabbed for Vann's arm, but it was too late for dry salvation. She unceremoniously deposited herself into the crisp waters of Lake Hili, dragging the hapless prince in behind her. Splashing and sputtering, they grabbed for the deck planks.

The refreshment seemed to sober them both. Kir banged her head softly against the wood, muttering a few choice Dimishuan curses.

"Have you been drinking?" Vann scolded.

Kir allowed a guilty groan.

"Vann?! Kir?!" Scilio shouted as he barreled toward them with a Dimishuan woman on his heels. He was shirtless and shoeless, and his unbuttoned pants clung precariously around his waist. The woman—an attendant from the festival—appeared to be wearing nothing but Scilio's tabard.

"Toma! Where did you come from?" Vann sputtered.

"Daleara and I were sharing a quiet moment nearby. Do you require assistance?"

"We're fine," Kir grumbled. "Just decided to go for an evening swim."

Scilio moaned theatrically. "It was pure poetry, inspired by Alokien himself. The breezy moonlit backdrop. The looks. The touches. The embrace. The passionate fire of your lips pressed together. Then the entire masterpiece was ruined with that ungainly plunge!"

Vann shook his head and laughed silently, but Kir was aghast. "You were *watching*?"

Scilio and Daleara exchanged sly glances.

"Yes," Scilio answered, then considered his obvious condition. "Well, intermittently."

Kir held up her hands in denial. She sank under the waterline and bobbed momentarily, before grasping the planks. "I take no responsibility for my actions. I'm almighty liquored up and as such have departed from my right mind. It was the wine done the talking."

Scilio chortled. "And the wine did the kissing, as well?"

Kir was utterly awash in embarrassment. She partially submerged her face below the waterline again, closing her eyes. If she couldn't see the problem, maybe it would go away.

Vann hopped up to sit on the edge of the deck, and he offered Kir a hand.

"No thanks, Majesty," she mumbled. "I think I'm just gonna stay here and drown now."

"Come on, Kiri. Is it so terrible to be seen in the arms of a handsome prince?" Vann joked lightly.

Scilio hemmed. "Perhaps the fair maiden is concerned with the way water affects Dimishuan fabrics? What with all that clingy transparency..."

Vann stood up quickly. "Oh. Of course. Perhaps we should... umm... retire for the evening?"

Daleara pulled Scilio's tabard over her head and placed it on the deck near the edge, leaving her glistening golden flesh completely bare.

"I won't be needing this, anyway, Saiya Kunnai," she stated. "Good evening."

Daleara spun on her heel and sashayed away, turning her head briefly to invite Scilio's attendance with a suggestive batting of her eyes.

Scilio sighed like a lovesick school girl. "Have I mentioned how I *so* appreciate the Dimishuan take on modesty?" He raised his chin an inch and strode purposefully after Daleara, leaving Kir and Vann alone.

Vann offered his hand once more, and Kir accepted it this time. When she was secure on the deck, she snatched up Scilio's tabard and threw it over her head.

"Well, that qualifies as the single most embarrassing moment of my life," Kir huffed.

Vann chuckled. "Am I so unseemly an escort?"

"No. But I am." With that, Kir hurried toward the Kion, giving Vann neither the time, nor the ability to respond.

## -38-
## Dragons and Wildcats

*A copper-bottomed cup of truth holds more weight than an iron pot of lies.* - Master Kozias

Kir's footfalls fell silently on the smooth planks as she patrolled the forward deck of the Kion. The moons were shining brightly and all was quiet. She had come to relish these midnight moments on duty in the last week, as the days were booked full with scheduled meetings, tours, presentations and, of course, her secretive training sessions with the Tree Vipers. The evening quiet was comfortable.

She didn't have to try very hard to avoid Vann. The constant stream of people surrounding them required Kir to remain in Guardian mode. The bustle kept Vann occupied, and it kept them from being alone together.

The only unencumbered moments were quickly dashed by Kir. She would scoot away to the militia encampment. Escape was the only way to circumvent Vann's attempts at conversation.

Vann knew that Kir was avoiding him—she could read the inquiry every time he looked at her. She hadn't yet built up the pluck and grit to tell him what she knew to be the inevitable truth: they could not be together.

The realization she had made on the Fer Waidan, that her heart was entirely given to Vann, had shaken Kir at her center and forced her to evaluate the entire situation. Her conclusions felt like a wasp sting over an ant bite. Although Kir could not deny her deeply rooted feelings for Vann, there was no conceivable way that such a union could work. The reasons were numbered as the stars in the sky.

First in her mind, Vann deserved much more than she could

give him. She had been broken and used, then cast out like a worn shoe into the street. There was little comfort a worn shoe could provide to the finder. It was understandable that Vann would have grown attached to her, for their shared travail. But he had not seen what wonders awaited him in High Empyrea. He knew nothing of the beautiful courtesans who would be presented for his consideration. Of their plump beauty and powdered skin.

To boot, Kir's reputation in the court was akin to the proverbial kaiyo-plop in the punch bowl. As a convicted felon and Crown-hater, she would never be accepted in the eyes of the people who gave monarchies power. The future King had to think first of his kingdom. Allying himself with a nobody—worse than a nobody, a disinherited criminal—could be divisive enough to encourage a coup. It could lead to chaos...

And there was Kir's new role of Betrayer to the Crown. Vann was not aware of her involvement with Ferinar's militia, but if he ever learned that she was in league with people who planned to assassinate the King... What would Vann think of her, then? She would be executed for such an association, but the thought of Vann hating her was abundantly worse than the possibility of beheading.

Kir was not right for Vann. He must find someone who embodied the perfection of a nation. A beautiful puppet with a family, a dowry and the political backing of the court. Kir could offer Vann none of these things. She was scarred and skinny, willful, without family or holdings, despised, and would not be seen as fit to polish the shoes of the nobility.

This love simply could not be.

"I was hoping I'd find you here," Vann's voice roused Kir from her thoughts.

"Your Majesty. I thought you were abed."

"I couldn't sleep. We need to talk."

Kir cleared her throat. "If you'll excuse me, Majesty, I'm on duty. Talk is distracting..."

Vann held his fingers to Kir's lips and shushed her. "You've been avoiding me for a week, Kiri. Since the Fer Waidan."

Kir grimaced and turned away. "I was stoutly pickled and sloshed that night. I don't really remember much of it..."

"If that were true, you wouldn't be avoiding me," Vann countered.

Kir bit her lip, fishing for responses. She snagged no answers and it was obvious that Vann was not about to let the subject drop. She would have to erect a bulwark against him. Otherwise, she would be powerless against his eyes. "Majesty, whatever you think occurred between us—it was a fallacy. We both were affected by substances that influence actions. My good senses were drenched, and as a consequence, I let things go far beyond what they should have. Please forget that it ever happened."

"Through the Psychonic window of my soul, I showed you, Kiri. I thought you understood how I feel about you. Perhaps it was the veracity potion that gave me the courage to tell you. But regardless of the potion..." Vann paused in consideration before amending, "...because of it, rather, I had no ability to lie to you that night. And now that I've laid bare those feelings, I can't pretend they don't exist."

"Then you'll just have to ignore them. I'm your Guardian. And this just cannot be," Kir forced, feeling the edges of her heart fraying with each word.

Vann was not swayed. He cupped Kir's face in his hand and gazed at her with those captivating eyes. "I never knew what heaven was, 'til I looked upon you here, and if heaven's half as beautiful, then death I'll never fear."

Kir pulled away. "Please. Stop."

Vann did not retreat. Instead, he stepped forward resolutely and gripped her shoulders firmly. "Kiri, I've never been an assertive man. I've spent so much of my life trying to run from people that I never really learned how to face them. The kid you met in the forest could never have been a King. But I'm learning my strength from your example. You've helped me to find confidence in who I am to be. I can't do this job without that fortitude.

"We've been on a whirlwind of a journey, Kiri. And somewhere along the way, I fell in love with you. You compliment my every fault. You bolster my every strength. I no longer need a veracity potion to assert my feelings. I'll take my leave to be bold."

Vann's lips pressed fire against hers with an electric wave that shivered the tiny hairs on her arms to attention. Her first instinct was to smack him and escape, but the seductive allure of Vann's aura held too strong a grip on her. She did not fight it, and allowed herself, instead, to drink him in.

After an enchanting moment in Vann's arms, that nagging conscience admonished her sharply. The memory of Xavien popped into her head, and she could hear his words: *Perhaps when you realize your love, you will understand what it is to lose it.*

That one piercing idea ripped Kir painfully out of the snare that was Vann's embrace. She disengaged and held her hand to his chest. "Your Majesty."

"Why the title? You hate formality," Vann commented dejectedly. He had lost his advantage, and he knew it.

"Because you've forgotten who you are. You've forgotten who *I* am," Kir replied. "When you've seen what your world will be, you'll realize that this is just a fantasy born of our circumstance. You deserve what that other life can give you. You're choosing a fallen apple from the dirt, when you've not yet looked up at the abundance on the tree. "

"But that I was a looking glass and you could see with my eyes and soul. You are so blind to your own beauty, Kiri. Not just out here..."

He brushed Kir's cheek with his fingers. "...but in here, as well." His hand fell to her chest, and he covered her heart. "I will spend every day of my life trying to open your eyes to my vision. There's nothing in High Empyrea I want that I don't already have right here."

"You don't know anything about me, Majesty. People that cling to me get hurt. You don't know what I did at Balinor."

"Malacar told me that you killed a lot of men. It was a terrible accident, but it's past."

"He didn't tell you everything."

"Then *you* tell me." Vann's gentle hand moved to Kir's temple to tuck a stray strand of bang behind her ear, but she slapped it away.

"You don't want to know."

He shook his head and tutted. "See? You're only using Balinor as an excuse. Nothing you did there could have been worse than killing all those soldiers. You've already been forgiven for that. By Malacar, and by me. You need no more pardon for your actions there."

Vann didn't know how wrong he was. Kir may have been pardoned for killing sixty men, but it was the death of only one that had condemned her most of all.

"Fine. You want to see Balinor? I'll show you what I did. Maybe then you'll understand what I *really* am!" Kir cried. She willed the memory of Balinor to the forefront of her mind. "You wanted it, Majesty. Here it is."

Kir pulled Vann into the Bonding. Into the roar of a black rain...

*She could have run. The forest behind her was dark and beckoning.*

*At least seventy-five men, trained soldiers all, stood before her on Balinor field. Kiriana could see Mirhana through the rain, shackled at the wrists, guarded behind one of the soldiers. She could not let them take Mir back to High Empyrea. Only death waited there. The soldiers would deliver Mirhana alive, but the execution in High Empyrea would be swift and unforgiving.*

*"Kiriana Karmine. You are hereby ordered to lay down your arms and surrender to His Majesty's Royal Army. Your punishment may be lenient if you come quietly," issued the Captain.*

*"I will not. Release the slave to me, or suffer the consequences," Kiriana called back in a strong voice that masked the trembling she felt to the pit of her stomach.*

*"You must not die for me, Kiriana," Mir called. "Let me go with them, and the King will spare you. I'll gladly trade my life for yours. Please, let me go. You have to live!"*

*"No!" Kiriana cried desperately. "You are my everything. I promised to protect you, Mir. And I will."*

*Lightning cracked the sky, and Kiriana had an idea...*

*She raised her hands, summoning her magic. Energy, congealing into a blue ball, grew large and strong. She rarely used Elementals, but she knew the basics. All they needed was a diversion.*

*They could make their escape if this worked.*

*Kiriana released the Blazer Bolt with tremendous force, willing it to cast directly above the cohort of troops, to stun and force them to dive for cover.*

*But something was wrong...*

*The electrical potential in the storm resonated with the Bolt and a massive charge of lightning shot down the shaft, furious and uncontrollable. It slammed into the troops with the devastating force of a massive Ruptor, rippling like a living wild creature through the ranks. Multiple voices screamed in agony as an eerie blue matrix of energy shook their bodies, rattling them like marionettes in the wind. Several unfortunate souls near the center of the blast, their bodies overloaded with the fury, exploded, sending a cascade of blood, bone fragments and gore in all directions.*

*Kiriana never knew what had sliced her flesh in the bloody gale, leaving a gaping trail from her jaw to her breast. Perhaps it was a bone fragment from the severed arm that had assaulted her. Perhaps it was a stray weapon blown free from the hand that grasped it. Or a splinter of wood, one of many that had pelted her like angry rain in the sanguine torrent. It didn't matter. She could hardly feel the scorching fire of the wound, anyway. Numbness and shock drowned out any pain.*

*Dozens of lucky ones died quickly, but many more moaned in pain, long after the rippling energy had dissipated into the mud. Cries of agony surrounded Kiriana, overshadowing the pattering of falling rain. The smell of burnt flesh and blood and gore filled her nostrils, and she raised her head. The dead lay around her in the mud, dozens of men, their eyes piercing. They stared at her, unblinking against the rain that fell on empty eyes. Her gaze fell to her blood-stained palms, held aloft. She screamed to the depths of her soul, cursing the rain. Cursing Tarnavarian. Cursing herself. She bellowed a long cry, halfway between terror and agony.*

*Kiriana stood, bathed in blood, staring in horror at the grizzly scene before her. Her eyes scanned the vicinity and fell to rest on a prostrate golden form, stark and contrasting against the crimson ground. She stumbled in a daze to Mirhana's side and pulled her friend into her arms. There was no breath, nor tremor. Only a shredded, lifeless shell.*

As Kir released the Bonding, Vann swayed. It took him a moment to surface from the wave of nausea that shimmied his knees.

"You see, Majesty? I killed her. I killed Mirhana. With my *own* hands. Everyone who loves me dies."

Vann shook away the sickness and replaced it with determination. "We all die, Kiri. But everyone who's loved you has truly lived. I'd die a thousand times to bring you to my arms, because that's where I'm alive. You cannot use Balinor to push me away. Mirhana's death was an accident, and you don't deserve the guilt of that burden."

"Dragons don't feel alive in the arms of wildcats. They kill each other from their differences," Kir muttered.

"No myth can turn my heart. All I know is that I love you," Vann said softly. "And your eyes say you feel the same about me."

If Balinor didn't faze him, there was only one thing that could. And while it hurt Kir to her core, she forced the words from her lips. "No. I love the Chaos Bringer."

## -39-
## Choices Made

*When faced with options, choose the one that provides the least pain, or the most gain. They rarely hold both.* - Master Kozias

Vann recoiled. "The Chaos Bringer?"

"Do you honestly think I could ever love *you*—the embodiment of the Crown—after all I've been through at its whim? Don't you understand? I live for the monarchy's *downfall*. Why else do you think I would have followed you? If the Chaos Bringer is the key to just such an end, I'll follow you to the basement of the Hells themselves!" Kir cried, forcing a false and wild smile. "Look to your prophecy. Maybe *I'm* your Betrayer. Maybe tomorrow this vambrace will be as black as Ashkorai's!" Kir held her armguard up and slapped it for effect, feeling the sting of the lumanere against her palm.

"That's impossible. I've already been marked by the Betrayer."

Kir turned toward the railing and cast her gaze across the waterscape. This conversation hurt more than any blazer whip or blade she'd ever tasted. "There are many kinds of marks, Majesty, and yours were already removed. Someone else will mark you in some way. And know this: betrayal, by its nature, must come from someone close to your heart."

Vann brooded silently on Kir's attack. He shook his head. "No. Whatever else you may be, Kiri, you are no betrayer. You want so badly to punish yourself for whatever sins you think you committed. But I know you. You can't convince me that you are anything but loyal, and pure, and wonderful."

Kir blew out a breath and waved in dismissal. "Fine. It's your time to waste. But I won't reciprocate. And once we get to High Empyrea, you'll see I was right all along."

She spun on her heel and hurried away, praying to the seven Gods that Vann didn't see the tears that spilled down her cheeks.

Three days melted away to Hilian attendance and Kir was only going through the motions of normalcy. It was a sort of playacting.

She'd never thought herself good at such thespianism, but maybe she'd picked up a fine point here and there from Scilio. As long as she could avoid Vann's piercing eyes, it was easier to keep the ruse up. Nobody seemed to notice the rift that she had plowed between them. Busy pretended normal, so Kir made sure to stay inundated with busyhood.

The Pavilion of Freedom was decorated for Kir's welcoming ceremony. Clad in the iridescent Hilian outfit that Ulivall had gifted her, Kir stood on the platform before the masses of clan patrons, ready to announce her decision. The ritualizing and speechifying had been run and done, and all that remained was Kir's proclamation.

Picking a clan association had been difficult. Kir had come to the realization that she could never escape politics, no matter how much wood or water surrounded her. Wherever there were people, there would be weaseling and coercion.

Corban and Ferinar had been trying to convince her that their clan was best, but they were hardly the only ones to make such a claim. They were, however, the most persistent and prevalent, since she spent so much time in their midst due to her training sessions. The militia was on the opposite political bank from Ulivall's more conservative army, putting Kir in an awkward position. Ulivall wanted peace with the Alakuwai, where Ferinar was open to hostilities. Ferinar had probably never seen real battle before—he spoke of war as something glorious and grand. Kir knew better.

She also knew that joining Corban and Ferinar's clan would solidify her allegiance with their cause, which she did not fully embrace. The King's assassination was necessary to Vann's safety, and that was the sole reason Kir had agreed to participate. Despite her hatred of the Crown and her urgent desire to protect Vann, there was something inherent in the plan that still felt wrong.

Kir had tried so very hard to escape politicking and games of intrigue, and yet, here she was, plunged right into the middle of the biggest game in Septauria. Her choice of clan had been largely influenced by maintaining neutrality. She would prepare for war with one side and strive for peace with the other.

Elder Trenen stepped forward. "What family have you chosen, Saiya Kunnai?"

Kir's eyes scanned the crowd, easily picking out Corban and Ferinar, who stood expectantly beside their clan patron. They were surrounded by many other Hilians, but it was their reaction that mattered most.

"I choose the clan of Grand Master Ulivall," Kir replied simply.

As she suspected, Corban and Ferinar balked and exchanged glances. They had thought her secured in their clutches. It did pain her to shun Corban's offer. He had long been, and still was, a treasured friend. For all that, though, Kir knew from her years in Governance Lessons that friendship and politics were the oil and water of society.

They mingled, but simply could not mix.

Ulivall stood rigidly beside the royal party, stuck in amber. The realization had not yet registered. Inagor cuffed Ulivall's shoulder in congratulations, and the Grand Master seemed to come out of his self-induced trance. He cocked his head momentarily, like a dog trying to comprehend its owner, then nodded and strode toward the stage. Kir wanted to laugh. He obviously had not anticipated this.

"My family is honored to welcome you, Saiya Kunnai," Ulivall stated. "I apologize for not having a prepared speech, but then, I have never been much of a wordsmith, anyway."

Ripples of chuckles undulated through the audience.

"When welcoming a new member, it is customary in our family, small though it may be, to present our clan emblem engraved upon a throwing knife. As I was unprepared, I will present you with my own, until yours can be commissioned." He handed Kir the small weapon hilt first. Her eyes strayed to the emblem etched upon the blade. "How ironic," she mused. The image was that of a sword, wrapped in blossoms of ithinar.

"You are not the only one who finds symbolism in warrior mythology," Ulivall provided. "And keep in mind, our clan has been called *Ithinar Steel* almost as long as you've been alive."

The pavilion gave itself to celebration, and Kir was thankful to be surrounded by people. It kept her away from Vann. He socialized politely at his table, but there was something missing in his demeanor. The joy plastered on his face was as pretended as the ease on hers.

"It was a lovely ceremony, Saiya Kunnai," Corban greeted, handing Kir a goblet of wine. Ferinar accompanied him, and both seemed eager to exchange pleasantries or otherwise.

This was the one moment she dreaded. Kir couldn't care less about Ferinar's feelings, but she never intended to hurt Corban.

"It was a tough decision, Corban. Please let me explain..."

He pulled Kir to his shoulder. "There is no need. As you know all too well, it is not in the name that family strings are tied."

"You are far shrewder than I credited you, Saiya Kunnai. It was a well-played move." The corners of Ferinar's eyes narrowed as he spoke. "Your decision really did not matter in the end. We have you anyway."

Whether it was the statement icing her veins or the wine trickling down her throat, Kir wasn't sure, but something made her shudder.

A ruckus erupted at the water's edge and all eyes turned to see a newcomer scramble from a longboat before it even touched the deck. He was a Dimishuan, but not a free one. The gleam of a slave collar was stark among all of the bare necks surrounding him. His hand grasped some long object that Kir could only assume was a weapon.

The stranger leapt to the pavilion and launched himself toward Vann.

## -40-
## Convictions

*It's better to be fast and wrong than slow and dead.* - Master Kozias

Kir's goblet shattered, dropped at the instant her hand drew her shortsword. She instinctively catapulted toward the assassin and tackled him from behind. As his chest thumped against the floor, Kir thrust her knee into his back. She yanked a fistful of hair to expose his throat and held the edge of her blade just above the collar.

"Don't even breath, *kadda*, or I'll punch your one-way ticket on the Soul Collector ferry line..." she hissed.

"No, wait! I'm a messenger..." the man wheezed.

"Guardian Ithinar!" a voice shouted from behind. Ulivall's steadying hand eased toward her sword. He ushered the blade away from the attacker's throat-bobber.

"Stand down," Ulivall spoke calmly in her ear. "This man is no threat."

Kir's gaze fell to the extended weapon... No. It was a scroll box. She relaxed her hold and backed off. Vann was standing safely behind a wall of Guardians, though he was watching with full-moon eyes over their shoulders.

The stranger rolled upright and rubbed his chest. "Not the welcoming I expected upon my homecoming," he scoffed.

Kir sheathed her sword tentatively as the man came to his feet with Ulivall's aid. Ripples of recognition and excitement hummed from the crowd. Ulivall welcomed the man home and pulled him into an uncharacteristic bear hug, complete with a deep laugh.

"I take it you're no attacker," Kir managed, trying to snuff the flame of fluster.

Ulivall's chest puffed like a rooster on the pride-march. "Saiya Kunnai, meet Copellian. Your brother."

"Brother?" Kir and Copellian voiced together.

"You are just in time for the feast," Ulivall told the newcomer, "to welcome your new sister into our clan."

"I thought the clan only had eleven members," Kir said, doing the math in her head. All were definitely accounted by her reckoning.

"I apologize. Copellian has been gone for so long, I did not include him in my tally," Ulivall said. "Today, my clan jumps from eleven to thirteen."

Copellian blanched. If his eyes could have shot daggers, Kir thought, she would be bleeding on the floor. She instantly grew a firm dislike for the cut of his jib.

"I can't enjoy frivolities, Ulivall. I am here on a very specific errand. I bear an urgent message for His Majesty, Prince Vannisarian."

Vann pushed between the Guardians. "I will accept your

message. But first, won't you join us? You look travel-weary."

Copellian genuflected deeply before Vann, then raised his head boldly. "Thank you for your consideration, Your Majesty. As much as I would invite rest, I cannot yet. I have already been delayed and the message I carry bears the utmost urgency."

"I will hear it, then," Vann replied.

"This summons is issued by decree of His Majesty, Soventine Ellesainia, King of Septauria." Copellian extended the scroll box with elegant ceremony that bespoke of his acquaintance with royal protocol.

When the seal would not break, Vann turned the scroll over in his hand, hunting for a latch.

"It is Blood-Bonded, Your Majesty," Copellian provided. "The seal is keyed to you alone."

"Ah!" Vann plucked a rose from the nearest table's centerpiece and pricked his finger. He rubbed a crimson droplet on the seal and it hissed with acceptance, then dissolved away.

Vann unfurled the parchment and his eyes zigzagged as he read. His face betrayed no emotion. Finally, he handed the scroll to his mother and stepped toward the onlookers.

"While we were scheduled to remain for another four days, it is with great regret that we must depart earlier than expected. We leave on the morrow. I thank the citizens of Hili for your hospitality and your offer of friendship, which I carry with me. Please continue to enjoy the festivities," Vann announced. He turned to the Guardians. "Please attend me in the kitchen lounge. I would ask for Copellian and Ulivall's attendance, as well."

They retreated to the lounge and Corban appeared with a tray of refreshments. He busied himself with service and cleaning tasks that were not entirely necessary. His intent to eavesdrop was as obvious as a corpse flower in a rose garden. *Hence, the reason Corban is a Master Chef and not a Master Spy,* Kir thought.

When the group was comfortable, Vann made his way to Kir. "I'm sorry I called you away from your celebration. This won't take long."

Kir held her tongue, but she nodded in acknowledgment.

"My father awaits us in Gander's Ferry in northern Aquiline," Vann announced. "He was coming to meet us personally, but he took ill and cannot travel. As the King cannot come to us, we were summoned to him. We make haste to Suncrest and ride a private air ferry over the Arshenholm Mountains. Two soldiers wait at the Hili border to escort our party."

"Why doesn't he send an army company to procure us?" Scilio asked.

"I believe I can answer that," Copellian said. "King Soventine was afraid that large numbers would attract attention. Also, they move too slowly. If we hurry, our small group will probably go unnoticed."

"*We*? You are not planning to stay here?" Ulivall asked,

seeming disheartened for the first time all day.

"I must return," Copellian replied. "I've made a promise to my beloved Melia de Karmine, which I can't fulfill if I stay."

"Melia?!" Corban choked out. "You know my daughter?"

"*Your* daughter? She told me her father was dead."

"Dear Gods, but what tangled webs are woven by the fates?" Corban breathed. "Please, tell me of my girl. Is she well?"

Copellian updated Corban and Kir listened raptly. He seemed hesitant as she spoke of his courtship, but Kir could see the sincerity behind his eyes. His love for Melia saturated his story like water in a rice field.

The sentiments of the heart strayed Kir's gaze involuntarily to Vann. He was ogling her too, and she quickly threw her eyeballs to the opposite wall.

When the briefing was concluded, Corban wrapped his arms around the young man. "I suppose I will be calling you 'son' someday soon."

"I'll bring her home to you, Corban. I swear it," Copellian said. Every word dripped conviction.

"Is there no other way to free her?" Ulivall asked. "Returning yourself to bondage guarantees nothing."

"I have a plan," Copellian said cockily. "I will not fail."

"I can help you with estate layout or whatever..." Kir offered.

"Don't know that I'll need it, but thanks anyway," he interjected darkly.

"I believe you'll want her help," Corban said. "But this is a subject for another time." He glanced warily at Ulivall, then nodded curtly to Kir in silent warning to let the matter drop. She blinked in understanding. Too much information might jeopardize the secrecy of their operation.

Kir felt Vann's eyes boring holes into her. She tightened the mental grip on her talisman to keep any stray feelings or notions from leaking out. It was not only the truth of her heart she had to lock away from his awareness. There were bigger matters she had to guard.

Copellian suddenly gasped and turned to Vann. "Forgive me, Majesty. I conspire to break the law, and have the audacity to do so in your very presence. I would do it behind your back, were there time."

Vann laughed heartily. "Carry on, Copellian. I will neither hinder, nor fault your efforts."

"Yes, bask in this happy group of lawbreakers," Scilio chortled, topping off Copellian's goblet. "You are right at home with us scoundrels and rogues in royal colors."

Palinora rose. "I will have Lili see to our arrangements so we can continue to enjoy Kiriana's special event. I recommend early retirement, as we have a long journey ahead."

"The volunteers for your entourage have been bleeding from

the woodwork, Majesty," Ulivall said. "I will send word that they are to be ready at daybreak." He turned to Copellian. "Your errand is done. Enjoy this feast while you can. We have only a few hours to squeeze in the happenings of two years."

"I'll need the Master Prophet to dissolve the magic in my collar before I go," Copellian said.

"I'll arrange it," Ulivall replied.

As the group shifted outside, the gravity of the situation tugged Kir's knees to wobbly at her inability to stop the whirlwind. It was like she was about to jump off a cliff, but only now was realizing the height. Second thoughts belayed her confidence, and the ropes of doubt dangled freely at the prospect of introducing Vann to his father, and his father to the Hilian assassins. Too much could go wrong, and any one of those muches could be disastrous.

Just before he escaped her, Kir pulled Vann aside. "Are you sure about this? Maybe we should stay here, just for a moonless night or two..."

"I know you're worried about my father, Kiri. Don't be," Vann said.

"It's my job to be," Kir reminded him. "Besides, there might be some information you don't have. Things that he's planning and you don't know the extent of the evil—"

"You told me yourself not to issue trust so readily. I'm taking your advice and not trusting Ashkorai. His assertions cannot influence my faith in my father."

"What if you saw more damning evidence than Ashkorai has given?"

"Then I'd still have a hard time believing it. The message my father sent was so warm and heartfelt, Kiri. Like he had scripted it with the inkwell of devotion. I know he is as thrilled for our reunion as I am. Whatever suspicions have been planted by my brother's murderer, I am washing them away in favor of my father."

She almost cracked loose with the truth, but there were stars twinkling in Vann's eyes, and nothing she could say would overcast them. All she could do was bob her head and bite her lip.

"You take too much on your shoulders, Kiri. I'll prove that to you someday. Let's enjoy the rest of your celebration. You dropped your glass before. I'll get you another." Vann tucked a stray bang behind her ear and slipped out the door.

Corban had been hanging back, waiting for opportunity. "Milady..." he said cautiously.

"Don't worry. His Majesty doesn't appear eager to see the truth, and I won't be the one to spill it. Copellian will want in with the Vipers. I'll fill him in tomorrow."

Corban pulled Kir to his shoulder. "I've lost one dear one, and my heart trembles with fear of losing another."

"Don't worry about Melia," Kir patted his back. "I'm sure

Copellian will bring her home."

"I wasn't talking about Melia. I have no gift for prophecy, but I have a terrible feeling about this parting."

Kir was about to make a flippant remark to make light of his worries, but Malacar's warning, that their journey to Empyrea would likely be rife with danger, came rushing back to her. Although Hili had allowed Kir to forget them, she could almost imagine her old game-mates, the Soul Collectors, sitting across the card table. That familiar sensation of imminent doom washed over her once more.

Damn Corban, for reminding her that the real world awaited them, outside this wonderful illusion of safety.

# Deceptions

\* \* \*

## -41-
## The Stowaway

*I ran away at a young age and joined a traveling minstrel show.*
*They worked me hard and paid me little, but I saw the sun rise*
*on a new world every day. I was overpaid.* - Master Kozias

The farewells had been issued and the royal caravan had
departed from the wetlands with the King's two soldiers and forty
Hilian volunteers in the escort, including Copellian. Twenty-seven of
the guards were militia volunteers, and an additional ten were from
Ulivall's cavalry. Counselor Gertraul would serve as ambassador. Lili
rounded out the party. She was only along for the twelve day trek to
Suncrest and would return to Hilihar with the cavalry upon the royals'
safe arrival at the ferry.

Kir's saddle creaked as her mare trotted alongside the royal
carriage. Ulivall had met them on the border with a squadron of
warhorses. Kir's bottom much preferred the soft leather of the saddle to
that hard, unforgiving plank atop the carriage.

The caravan made haste, and an uneventful day passed. Kir was
careful to limit her time in Vann's presence, choosing instead to keep a
safe distance. She was close enough to protect him, far enough to avoid
conversation. Their interaction was polite and formal, but Vann seemed
as awkward as Kir felt. He tracked her every move from his window.
She regretted having no ugly hat to hide under.

Inagor, good leader that he was, began Guardian training
sessions again, even in mid-horse-stride. Since their time would no
longer be hindered by guard duty, for the soldiers standing post, the
Guardians were free to work on team-building skills. They practiced
switching horses in motion, tossing objects between riders, and
mounted combat training. Kir was deft at the challenges but the men
proved just as handy.

The day was drawing to a close. They were tuckered from the
hard ride, so Inagor had suggested they try to access the Guardian
Bonding that evening, instead of sword practice.

Kir was excited about the prospect, but also wary. Vann would
be participating, and she would be forced to shield her layered secrets
from his mind. At the same time, the Bonding was so swaddling and
warm that Kir longed for it. The self-inflicted wounds to her heart
caused it to ache, and the only remedy was a desire Kir could never
sate. Thank the Gods for the constant distractions, as they kept her
mind occupied and off Vann.

The truth was, she just wanted to be held. She wanted the
comfort of a caring embrace that she had never really known before.
The Bonding was the closest thing she could get to that, without
throwing herself into Vann's arms and undoing all the sacrifices she

was making on his behalf.

"Pack it in," Inagor boomed across the convoy to halt them. He reined up and turned to Malacar. "Oversee the tents. I'll take fire brigade."

Malacar banged his fist to his chest and made for the supply wagon. As he began issuing orders, Kir set off on her familiar task. She had assumed the job of Horse Master for the royal party. It was her private little tribute to Mirhana, who had so loved the creatures, and had rubbed that affection onto Kir. The downside to the job was the working side-by-side with Copellian, who had taken the same role for the cavalry.

While he leaned on the brooding side, there was a burr under his saddle where Kir was concerned. She had tried to be friendly, even attempting to strike up conversation, but he had evaded all her efforts. Kir wasn't exactly sure why he disliked her so much. In the end, it was no sweat off her brow. They may be "adopted" siblings, but she would likely see little of him in the future, anyway.

As she collected the reins of the Guardian mounts, Malacar's voice boomed sharply in alert. "Guardians to arms!"

Kir sprang forward, horses forgotten. Scilio was already Shielding Vann and Palinora, so Kir pushed through the circle of armed soldiers standing between her and the supply wagon.

When she burst onto the scene, Malacar and Inagor were brandishing their Guardian swords toward the back of the wagon. Rather than joining them, Kir sprang to the buckboard and threw a Binding spell into the jumble of blankets that squirmed like a mackerel in a fish barrel.

Inagor jumped to the step as Kir held the Binding firm. When he threw aside the pile of blankets, a body lay huddled beneath. A child. Kir released the Binding as Inagor lifted the boy up by the shoulders.

"Well, well. A stowaway?" Inagor said. The tensions eased immediately when the soldiers realized there was no threat.

The moment Kir spied the child's face, she laughed. "Tad bit runty for a cloaker, ain't he?"

Dailan dropped from Inagor's grip. "Never been to High Empyrea before. Pickin's might be pretty good up there."

Kir almost choked when she spied the slave collar around the boy's previously naked neck. She was about to ask what in the wenchin furies he was doing in it, when one of the King's soldiers, Captain Jurian, approached. He eyeballed Dailan, then gruffly snatched his collar. "This is no place for a child. Have two of the volunteers return him."

Dailan opened his mouth to protest, but Kir interjected. "He can come along if he wants to. It's a free country."

"Pleasant dream there, but as you well know, there is nothing free about it," Lieutenant Trual, the other soldier, remarked.

"True enough. But this kid's under my employ, and he still owes me some tutoring. I'll thank you to release him to me."

Trual's face practically petrified to stone. "We didn't bring any nappies along, and we're not babysitters. Scrawny nippers will only slow our progress."

Dailan struggled against Jurian's iron grip, spewing Dimishuan curses that Kir hadn't learned yet. "Shove off! It ain't polite to manhandle a Guardian's slave, you know!"

Practically every jaw hit the dirt, and Dailan took the opportunity to stomp on Jurian's foot. The soldier did not release his grip, but it slackened and he turned Dailan's collar around to read the owner's inscription. He shoved the boy toward Kir. "I guess he is yours, after all. Keep him from underfoot."

Jurian and Trual pushed through the crowd and disappeared.

When they were gone, Kir grabbed Dailan by the shoulders and thumped him against the wagon's side. "Don't you even *talk* about being my slave," she growled. "This ain't a game, boy."

"Ain't it, now?" Dailan nodded to the congregation of Hilians that were watching. "I have just as much right to play as they do." He threatened Kir with an impish smile.

He knew. The sprat knew exactly what they were up to. Kir cursed herself for underestimating him. Of course, he would know. She had seen him scurrying out of holes during their entire stay in Hilihar. It was possible he was in Ferinar's employ. What better spy than a willful, intelligent child?

Dailan's words were something akin to blackmail. If he survived to adulthood, he would make an excellent politician, Kir thought with a scowl. The more Dailan's trap kept moving, the greater the risk of spilling secrets. She couldn't fault him for doing the exact same thing she would have done, were she in his shoes. Besides, there just might be a benefit to keeping him around. What better spy, indeed?

Kir let Dailan slide to the ground and he tugged at his collar to straighten it.

"It's your life, Dagnabber. But if you're gonna play my property, you best act the part and do exactly what I tell you. They don't take kindly to unruly slaves where we're going."

Dailan dipped low at the waist until his head practically touched the ground. "Yes, Master."

Kir shook her head and smiled, despite herself. She cuffed the boy on the back of the head. "Keh! And no more'a that. If you're gonna mock me, do it behind my back."

Vann slipped up behind Kir and bent slightly to bring himself to Dailan's level. "That collar is quite realistic. Did you make it yourself?"

"I'm no Creative, Majesty. I just found it cast-off and Master Prophet Farning helped me with the alterations. It's not real, 'cause the magic's already been killed in it. It's just so I look credible. My kind don't exactly walk around without 'em in Alakuwai-land."

Vann nodded in understanding.

"Show's over, people. We have a camp to erect." Inagor began barking orders and the entourage burst into activity.

Kir slapped her hand against Dailan's shoulder. "Later, I'll teach you the proper way to smash an instep. Right now, I have a job for you. Ever rubbed down a horse before?"

# -42-
# Bridging Gaps and Gaping Bridges

*A bridge can connect friends and bottleneck an
army. Be sure to know who waits on the other side
before forging ahead.* - Master Kozias

Every evening in the week that followed found the camp in the same routine and formation. The royal tents were erected in an inviting horseshoe, always open to the Hilians. The invitation had yet to be accepted. The Hilians erected their tents near enough to the royal party, but far enough to create a brief social chasm. Their arrangement was a closed space, ringed around their fire and dance circle.

Kir would excuse herself every night to the Hilian encampment for what amounted to a perfect cover. Her welcome into a Hilian clan meant that her participation in their culture would be expected. She twirled around the fire circle in gaiety and elegance alongside her Hilian co-conspirators, and the training was inlaid into the steps of the dance. They were practicing right under the nose of the royal party, and not a soul was the wiser. It lent credence to Kir's plan. It would be easy to accomplish the same on any slave-holding estate.

Dailan's assistance helped to complete the ruse. He was teaching her the Dimishuan language, so she made sure to demonstrate her growing proficiency at every opportunity, just for good measure.

Kir's "instant brother" had been anxious to join in the militia's cabal. It took no coaxing or persuasion to convince him, once Kir had divulged their plans. She thought Copellian might try to usurp her authority over the project, but every time he made a suspect move, Kir immediately stomped him back to his place. His disdain spread like a stain, but she had to be firm to maintain control so their group dynamic wouldn't dissolve into chaos.

Copellian never called Kir *Saiya Kunnai*, as his comrades did. It was just another subtle attempt to diminish her value. Of course, Copellian could call her *Dirt* for all she cared. His opinion didn't matter, in the end. How Melia could have fallen for such an arrogant wencher was beyond her.

The first break in the evening routine came from Vann. He summoned for Copellian and Kir's attendance at his circle. Kir wasn't privy to his reason, but they had concluded their practice early to honor the request. The Vipers were advanced enough now to continue training in Kir's absence.

When Kir and Copellian arrived at the royal fire circle, they found the Guardians jawboning over coffee cups. Malacar's fingers were busy folding paper thingies while Inagor put spit and vigor into a dagger's shine. Scilio was, as usual, gazing at his favorite view on Lili's person. Palinora was perched next to Vann, thumbing through his journal and appraising the latest sketches and writings.

"Your Majesty," Kir announced, "I bring Horse Master Copellian."

Vann rose and greeted them. "We have been on the road for days, yet I realized how little we know of you, Copellian. Please, join us tonight and let us become more acquainted. You are, after all, practically family." Vann's words were to Copellian, but his smile was aimed directly at Kir, and it was loaded with agenda.

Copellian almost betrayed a scowl at that notion. He nodded curtly and thanked Vann, then sat in the indicated space beside his reluctant sister.

Rounds of libations were brought by Lili, and more jawboning commenced. Kir and Copellian both stewed and bubbled quietly, the scant inches between them feeling like a roaring chasm.

Vann jawed along jovially with the more cordial attendees, but he kept glancing Kir's way. He seemed to pick up on the rift between her and the disagreeable Dimishuan, and finally, he asked, "So, what might you tell us about yourself, Copellian?"

Like a classroom full of shushed school children, the circle went silent.

"Don't suppose there's much to tell," Copellian began tersely. "I was a Libertine until two years ago when I was captured by slave traders on an errand to Havenlen. I was purchased by the royal house Ellesainia and serve as a Stable Master for the King."

"You mentioned ties to the Karmine household. Have you spent much time there?" Vann inquired. He threw another quick glance Kir's way.

She crossed her arms in disinterest.

"King Soventine frequents Duke Karmine's estate in pursuit of their shared hobby of hawking. As Stable Master, I was required to attend the royal horses on the hunt. The King fell ill last summer while on holiday there, and he was forced to remain bedridden for several months. I've spent more time in the Karmine stables than in High Empyrea, I think," Copellian provided with a mild grin. "Not that I minded. There were many things there to keep me occupied."

"Do tell us of fair Melia," Scilio cooed. "Vivid detail would not be unappreciated."

"Actually, I was referring to the horses," Copellian chuckled, the hard lines across his forehead finally easing away with the melting tension. "The Karmines have the finest stock I've ever seen. But yes, Melia, kept me occupied, too. She's an apprentice to the Stable Master."

"How terribly romantic," Scilio mused, producing his journal. "This could be the foundation for the next masterpiece of Septauria's grandest playwright. Might I hear more of your promise to the lovely maiden?"

"She wanted so badly to escape her bonds and live free, like the wild horses on the Cornian plains. I swore that I would see it happen. I don't care if I have to kill a hundred sentries. I will free her."

"You spoke of a plan," Malacar said. His eyes never strayed from Copellian, but his fingers continued in their expert speed, creasing and folding. "Might you divulge it?"

Copellian stared at Vann. It looked as though he were hesitant to talk about such lawlessness in the presence of the law's representative.

Vann raised his hand to signal peace. "I've already told you I will not interfere, my friend. In fact, I hope to take a legal route to the very same end."

Copellian still looked as apprehensive as a bunny down the badger hole, but he nodded anyway. "I plan to stage a revolt. Partially for the benefit of the household's slaves, but mostly as a diversion. If the eyes of the guards are elsewhere, I can slip Melia out on horseback."

Kir, for the first time, felt compelled to speak. To cover over her involvement in revolutionary schemes, she laughed in ridicule. "Keh! You planned to just waltz right in there and sweep her away like the wenchin hero in some ridiculous story? That's a weak plan. Revolt's already been tried and failed there. The sentries are certainly on high alert for such a repeat action."

"A revolt? At the Karmine estate? I highly doubt that," Copellian scoffed. "No such thing was spoken of and I talked to several of the Karmine slaves about just such a prospect. They were all for trying. If a revolt had already occurred, they'd have told me."

Kir's backbone went rigid.

"Do you not know how Melia's sister died?" Scilio asked cautiously.

"Of course," Copellian replied. "Jurnet died three years ago in an outbreak of the gingerpox. It wracked the household and claimed about twenty lives..." He stopped and his brow furrowed in confusion born of realization. "Melia said that's how her father died, too."

Kir swallowed down spit and consternation. What was going on? Had Corban been lying all along? Or was Copellian stringing them a line of bull for his own purposes?

"The mystery deepens," Scilio breathed. He almost looked excited at the prospect of more material for his bardly works.

"Calls to question the validity of your word," Kir muttered, more to herself, but the barb was heard.

"Are you accusing me of something, Guardian Ithinar?"

Copellian growled, swelling from his seat like a puff adder on the defensive.

Palinora served as the voice of reason and calm. "There must be more to this story than we know. Never fear, Copellian. You will have plenty of time to determine the facts, once you are with your beloved again. There was certainly some information that Melia was lacking, as her father still lives."

Copellian nodded and relaxed, but he did not remove his accusatory glare from Kir. She matched him stare for stare. He had raised Kir's ire such that had he made challenge, Kir would have gladly taken him to task. He was wanting for a proper whoopin'.

Vann interrupted their sparring of glares. "At any rate, Copellian, your noble heart intrigues me. I have the greatest respect for a man who would sacrifice anything for love."

"I hope I won't have to sacrifice at all. Call me selfish, but I want to live to share my freedom with her."

"If you intend to survive," Inagor said, "you must do this right. How do you plan to slip past the estate's defenses?"

"There is an unguarded pass near the eastern canyon. I'll have the horses waiting in the ravine and we can ride right through while the revolt is in full progress," Copellian answered.

"You don't want to go that way," Kir stated flatly. The hidden Blazer Barriers along the ravine walls were so trace that they were practically undetectable, but they were powerful enough to kill. Many a hapless bird or beast had been caught unawares in that pass. Only with the proper Barrier keys could one enter and exit untouched by the magic.

"What would you know of it?" Copellian barked.

"Keh! Apparently nuthin," Kir muttered. She wouldn't dole out aid where it wasn't wanted. "I'm taking watch." She scooped up her Guardian sword, shoved it into her belt and stalked away.

"You don't know who she is, do you, Copellian?" Malacar commented softly as Kir skirted the fire. "That's Duke Karmine's daughter."

"I didn't think the Karmines had a daughter," Copellian said.

"They don't," Kir called gruffly over her shoulder.

## -43-
## The Heart of a Dragon

*Sometimes the best remedy for a hurting heart is*
*a friend to talk to...* - Master Kozias

Vann waved as Copellian saluted in farewell and disappeared into the darkness beyond the fire. He had stayed in their circle long after Kir had stalked away, and somehow the man seemed different in the last hour. Unlike the stiff and cold character Copellian projected in Kir's presence, he was actually very friendly and congenial in her absence.

It was a puzzle, and Vann could not determine just what it was about Kir that bothered the man so. The two were spending a fair amount of time together, between Kir's duties to the horses and her nightly engagements in the Hilian encampment, so Vann would have expected them to be closer.

Vann's invitation to Copellian had been of multiple purpose. The first had failed miserably. There was no bridge built to close the distance between Kir and her "adopted" brother, as Vann had hoped to accomplish. But at least they had learned more about Copellian. That was a start.

The second reason was still bearing fruit. Vann was hoping Copellian would take his experience at the royal fire back to the other Hilians. He wanted them to understand that he was approachable, and not some object of reverence or fear.

The Hilian delegates, while hardworking and polite, seemed distant. It was evident in their tent positioning. It was evident in their humble respect. And it was never more evident as when they addressed him. Formal in the extreme, despite Vann's insistence on casualty.

It was an attitude to which he must become accustomed, Vann told himself, for he was no longer an ordinary man. His status and title would place him on a separate pedestal, socially inaccessible to those around him. It was difficult to stand there, allowing people to bow and subserviate to him, when he'd only inherited the title by birth and happenstance. He was no different than the whimsical actor he had been a few months before. Or was he? Even his Guardians were treating him more formally and separately than they had previously.

For the first time since his flight through the Hatchel forest, Vann felt alone.

After Palinora and Inagor bid the company a good night and slipped into their tent, Vann scooped up his journal. "I'm going to take a walk."

Scilio and Malacar nodded at each other surreptitiously. They seemed to have an unspoken arrangement.

"Very well, Majesty. Guardian Scilio will accompany you," Malacar said.

Vann eyed the two men. He could sense nothing amiss, so he nodded and set out toward the northern hillside. When he found a comfortable spot, he plopped down and withdrew his new set of color chalks. Maybe he could distract himself by sketching the moonlit landscape. Scilio sat beside him in unusual silence.

Vann stared at the blank page for some time, trying to access his Creatives. The only image he could produce on the canvas of his mind was Kir. The beauty of the valley seemed dull and pedestrian compared to hers. He sighed in defeat and replaced the chalks in their case.

"Well? I'm waiting," Scilio said.

"For what?"

Scilio's uncharacteristically serious demeanor faded and the Bardian rolled his eyes in a very Kir-like manner. "It has been over two weeks since your passionate confession on the Fer Waidan and you have not spoken one word of it, Vann! We've been busy, I'll grant you. But as your closest confidant and best friend, I thought you would have talked to me by now."

"I guess there's nothing to tell, Toma. After the Fer Waidan, we just undressed and went to bed." Vann gasped, realizing that his statement would undoubtedly have an alternate meaning to someone of Scilio's mindset. "I mean...that's not..." he stammered, trying to fix the unintentional double entendre.

Scilio laughed and threw an arm around Vann's shoulder. "I understood your original intention. And they say *I* have a dirty mind." He mussed Vann's hair and cuffed the back of his head playfully, like an older brother.

Vann shoved him away and smiled distractedly.

"But it is apparent, Vann," Scilio said seriously, "that something more *did* happen between you and our loveliest Guardian. That Kir is avoiding you is not a product of embarrassment at getting 'caught' in your arms."

"I don't think we share the same feelings, Toma. The more I try, the more she pulls away." He summarized the conversation on the Kion, then described Kir's memory of Balinor.

"She blossomed so much after divulging her torment in Tarnavarian's prison, so I believed that if she shared Balinor with me, it would bring us that much closer. I was hoping her trust might create a special bond between us, like the one she shares with Denian. Instead, she used Balinor to ward me off, to convince me that she hurts those who love her. That's what she *wanted* me to see, but what I saw was a frightened and desperate girl trying to protect the only friend she had left in the world. I honestly thought she felt the same as I do, but now I don't know."

"I have learned in our months with the fair Kiriana," Scilio said pensively, "that oft times, her mouth flies one way while her soul another. I may not have your gift of Psychonics, but Kir is an open book. There is no doubt in my mind that her heart is fighting a losing battle against her own will."

"I wish I could be so sure. She was clinging so desperately to the whole Chaos Bringer scenario."

"Because it's the only weapon in her arsenal that could hurt you," Scilio reasoned bluntly.

"If she cares for me, why would she *want* to hurt me? Why would she push me away?"

"She is a Guardian, and she is trying to protect you from yourself. Kir knows, full well, what it means to be a royal. Her rejection is the most damning proof of her feelings for you, Vann. If she cared nothing at all, she would not evade you every day. Instead, she is just trying to hold back the floodgate long enough."

"Long enough? What is she waiting for?" Vann asked, bewildered.

"For you to take a queen, face your future, and forget all about her."

Vann shook his head. "That makes no sense. If she really cares for me, she would never be fine leaving me to another woman."

"She would not be *fine* with it, but she would do it, anyway. Because she wants what's best for the one she loves the most," Scilio explained.

The social rules of the upper nobility made little sense to Vann, as he had never played in their arena before. Suddenly, the picture became clear. He understood now why Kir had chosen to reject him.

"What am I supposed to do?" Vann pleaded. "Are you saying I should just forget about her? Go about my life looking every day at the single thing my coffers cannot buy? The only desire my title cannot command?"

"Now, I didn't say that. That's what society would demand, and the inevitability to which Kir is submitting. But I am a bard. As such, I know that the most gallant of all tales are those in which the hero does not do as society wills." Scilio smiled confidently.

"Will you help me, Toma?"

"It is my happy duty to assist you in any way," Scilio bent at the waist theatrically. He added slyly, "Provided I maintain all rights to said story, upon its happy consummation."

Vann coughed. "Provided there are no *details* on said consummation."

"Your dirty mind at work again. I was referring to the *conclusory* definition of the term." Scilio winked and elbowed Vann playfully.

"I'm sure you were," Vann laughed.

## -44-
## The Heart of a Wildcat

*...and sometimes you simply need someone to hear through your silence.* - Master Kozias

Kir whirled in a series of high wheel-kicks, soundly pummeling her imaginary foe. She knew Malacar was standing there, just beyond the tree line, but she continued in her fighting forms, finishing the last few acrobatic moves before sinking into her conclusive bow.

She grabbed up her handkerchief and dabbed sweat beads from her forehead,then sat on a fallen log as Malacar approached.

"Did you come to pry my soul open?" Kir asked, unintentionally mimicking Malacar's words from the Kion.

"No. Your demons are your own," he returned, likely for the irony. "Just wanted to make sure you were alright."

"I'm fine," Kir said, shrugging nonchalantly.

Malacar offered a water bladder and she chugged deeply before handing it back. He sat beside her, and they listened to the chirping frogs.

Finally, Kir asked, "Did Vann send you?"

"No. He doesn't know I'm here."

"Oh," Kir said, for lack of anything better. "Well, if you're here about Copellian, don't worry. It's just a mutual dislike, that's all. We won't let it affect our duties."

"I'm not concerned about Copellian. You're quite adept at handling him."

More unbearable silence. Kir usually found peace in quiet moments with Malacar, but for some reason, it was different tonight. Although Malacar never opened his mouth, Kir wanted to say something. To appease him. To ensure him that his presence was not necessary. That she was entirely fine.

But she held her tongue and hung her head, unable to lie to her brother Guardian. She *did* want him there, and she was anything but fine. Malacar's steady confidence was a rock in the middle of quicksand.

It dawned on Kir, suddenly, that Malacar knew. Scilio, the wenchin quidnunc, had certainly told him of the events on the Fer Waidan. Her pathetic attempts to distance herself from Vann had probably made her feelings for him all the more obvious. She was nineteen and an accomplished warrior, and yet, still nothing more than a ridiculous lovesick girl.

Malacar did not speak. He did not belittle her for the unrealizable feelings she held for their prince. He did not commend her for pushing away at those feelings. He did not remind her that she was dutifully adhering to her lowly social station. As a fellow Guardian, he would have been in his right to say any of those things.

Instead, he pulled Kir toward him and wrapped an arm around her shoulder. She leaned into his brotherly embrace and let Malacar hold her. Thousands of frog songs passed the minutes in rhythmic chaos, nature's discordant choir.

After some time, Malacar's voice interrupted the chorus, sounding as out of place as a bull horn in a symphony. "What do you have against me, Kir?"

She blinked in astonishment. "Of all people, Denian, I have no quarrel with you."

"And yet, you've never bestowed an appellation upon me."

Kir blinked again. "Huh?"

"*Ponytail* and *Stick* have names of affection, but I don't. You jest and banter with them, but not with *me*. And so, I was wondering why," he answered simply.

Kir hadn't really thought about it. Malacar was...Malacar. He needed no nickname or term of affection to connect them, as they were already bound in blood. It would almost seem irreverent to sully their special bond with a jest. She couldn't bring herself to make light of the painful past they shared, and so, she had never considered him anything but *Malacar*. And she had never thought to tease him, for she held him in the highest regard.

"You don't need a nickname. We had Balinor," she replied softly.

He nodded, seeming to understand every nuance in those brief words. He touched his head to hers lightly.

Their percussive heartbeats marked time within the nocturnal music. For reasons Kir could not fathom, the tight strings of her heart seemed to loosen slightly.

When Malacar finally rose, he kissed Kir's forehead. "Whenever you need me." He started through the trees.

"Lunchbox," Kir said.

Malacar turned. "Come again?"

She smiled mischievously. "Well, you asked."

"Lunchbox?" He paused for a moment. "I suppose it could be worse."

As Malacar disappeared into the darkness, Kir heard his booming laughter thunder through the trees, and the frogs stilled their voices in alarm.

## -45-
## Soulwhispers

*A mother of the heart is as true as a*
*mother of the blood.* - Master Kozias

The journey was uneventful and Kir was relieved when they arrived safely at the ferry station in Suncrest. After parting company with the Lili and the Hili cavalry, they boarded the empty ferry, which promptly departed.

The group settled into their staterooms, took in a mid-morning meal, then engaged in a few rounds of cards before Dailan coerced them to the upper deck for the scenery.

The Guardians stood silently beside Kir as they observed the view from the railing. They were entranced by the kaleidoscope of color from the distant trees that hinted of early autumn's horizon. If it hadn't yet, the reality would hit them soon. At the end of the cable awaited the

King.

Kir was abundantly aware of the gravity of that notion. Once the week was out, they would be entering a whole new arena of danger. At least the face of *this* peril was known. If the Vipers' plan was successful, the threat would be short-lived.

It took scant minutes before Scilio's attention fell on a crew woman. Her interest was as clear as a ship in the offing, and she quickly lured the lecher away. Probably to the comfort and pleasure of her cabin's bunk. Kir rolled her eyes and grinned.

Malacar and Inagor grabbed up plates and helped themselves to a table of refreshments. Although they had just eaten brunch an hour before, Kir had no doubt their heaping mounds would be devoured in seconds.

Vann seemed enthralled. He glanced at Kir with contentment. The sight of his smile seemed more enchanting than all the horizons in the world and Kir found herself returning it. Instantly, she remembered herself and chomped down hard on her tongue. It worked, summarily wiping the joy off her face. She craned her neck over the railing to watch the hamlet fall gently away below them.

She was surprised that the air was uncomfortably hot, even so far above the ground. The ferry's decks were protected from the raging winds by Barriers, so there was no moving air to cool them. The view of the ground was obscured by the curve of the hull. Kir climbed to the middle rungs for better access and leaned precariously over the edge.

"Now, Kiriana," Palinora chided, "if you plummet to your demise, don't come crying to me."

Kir laughed. It sounded like something *she'd* say to Vann. "Yes, mother."

Palinora cocked her head at the jest. Kir almost saw smoke from the gears turning in her head.

"Would you come with me? I require your attendance."

Hopping down from the rail, Kir trailed her down the passageway toward the immaculate and luxurious royal stateroom. Palinora closed the door and paused.

Kir grit her teeth against the realization that Palinora might want to talk about matters of the heart. Namely Kir's. Unwilling to discuss such a tender topic, she considered throwing out an excuse and soundly retreating. After all, Master Kozias always used to say, *Just run away and regain your honor tomorrow.*

When Palinora turned around, Kir saw in the mirror of the Queen's visage an image of herself as a pathetic creature. Palinora stepped forward and wrapped her arms around Kir abruptly, pulling her into a motherly embrace.

Taken aback by such a personal gesture, Kir stood in shock for a moment. Finally, she reciprocated, returning the hug awkwardly. Palinora's fine golden curls smelled of lilac and rose water. Kir wanted to bury her nose in the fragrance, but held back from the childish notion.

"Has no one ever loved you, Kiriana? But that you were *my* daughter."

Kir thought she detected a trace of pain in Palinora's voice, though it might have been sympathy. She held the Queen tighter and whispered, "Tarnavarian may have grown up the privileged Prince, but Vann was the lucky one. But that you were *my* mother."

"Well, we are family now, Kiriana. You need not be ashamed to embrace me. You've known little enough affection in your life."

Palinora released her, then held her hand out for Kir's appraisal, indicating a petite silver ring, inlaid with a radiant light blue stone. "There were precious few relics I brought with me upon our flight from Empyrea, but this was one."

Kir admired the ring and caressed the gem's smooth crystalline surface with a finger. "It's beautiful. The stone reminds me of Vann."

"Perhaps because Vann is my soulwhisper."

"I'm not familiar with that expression," Kir said.

"The legend passed down with this ring from mother to daughter speaks of the soulwhisper. The ring's bearer is connected to someone she most wants to protect, through the magic and the mystery of the stone. Or so I hear. It is a legend, after all. I cannot explain how it works, but I truly believe it does. Sometimes, I feel like Vann is close to me when I wear the ring, even though he be half a world away. During our separation, I knew he was well. I felt as though the stone were assuring me of that fact."

Kir stared in awe. She had never heard of such protective magic, or such a legend, and her heart tickled at the romantic notion.

"My mother passed this ring to me, but I have no daughters, and I doubt it would look appropriate on Vann's finger," Palinora said. "There were complications during the delivery and after Vann was born, I was unable to have any more children. I always longed terribly for a little girl. You are the closest I have to a daughter, Kiriana, so I pass it to you."

Kir pulled her hand away timidly. "I can't accept this."

"You must. It has been offered, and it would be rude to refuse, according to nobility's standards," Palinora reminded her.

"And here I thought you were free of haughty noble notions," Kir smirked, mimicking Palinora's words from weeks before.

The Queen laughed, then her features fell into a more serious demeanor. "Vann is almost eighteen, he has Guardians, and he is about to accept his destiny. For too long I have sheltered him, and I suppose my release of this heirloom is my way of letting him go. Vann will always be my soulwhisper. But I no longer need a trinket to remind me of that. It is time for him to find *his own* soulwhisper. And you, yours."

"With the highest respect, Palinora, I don't think it's my place to accept so familiar a gift. You haven't known me all that long."

"You doubt the motherly depth of my feelings for you? I admit to some jealousy of Ulivall when you joined his clan, because he beat me to the honor. It may have only been weeks, but my heart claims years. Shall I show you?"

Kir opened her mouth to speak, but no words found their way to her voicebox. She had no idea what to say, and her mind fumbled for a million responses, only to come up empty.

"These are my most precious memories of our time together."

*Palinora took Kir's hands and pulled her effortlessly into a field of wavy Arshenholm grass, where Vann and Inagor were faced off in a spar before an audience of a remembered Kir and Palinora.*

*The Bonding Palinora called forth was different than before— she was actually standing next to Kir physically this time.*

*"Do you feel the emotion of my memory?"*

*Kir was awash in a sense of compassion, tinged with a hint of kinship and pride. "Clearly. Were you feeling those things for me?"*

*"That was our first connection. I saw something of myself in you, and I wanted nothing more than to fill the role that Eserillia should have. I've always had a soft spot for abandoned kittens..."* Palinora tittered.

*"Is that how I looked to you?"* Kir fought the urge to mew in jest.

*"Just wait until you have a child. Maternal instincts are the driving force of the world, you will learn."*

*Palinora's Psychonic memory shifted to an Arshenholm stream where Kir had tried to scrub away her shame. To Palinora's tent and a hair-brush bonding. On to Kir's confession in the healer's tent, where she touched Palinora's heartache and sympathy woven into the memory. The recollections, laden with Palinora's sincere emotions, continued to melt into each other, from moments shared under Palinora's fussing hands and hair-brush, to their talk in the Hilian bathhouse, to a laughter-filled market longboat, to the battle on the Fer Waidan. Each layer of Palinora's feelings grew stronger and richer with each memory. There was one that felt suspiciously like Kir's own desire to protect Vann, and she wondered if it was the "maternal instinct" that Palinora had alluded to. If so, it was a lot like the Guardian magic, Kir decided.*

*When the memory of Kir's Healing in the pavilion kitchen lounge unfolded, she was inundated with a sharp mound of fear, eroding from a wave of subsequent relief. These emotions were more muddled, like they had been stewing together in a big pot, and it was harder to pick out the individual threads. As a bandaged Kir drifted off to sleep in the memory, there was a definite flavor of love from Palinora, which shocked Kir's eyes to blinking. It was only then that she recognized the same feeling in her own gut.*

"I didn't realize you felt so strongly," Kir managed. "These

*Psychonic connections sure can bring people closer, can't they?"*

Palinora leaned toward Kir and wrinkled her nose with conspiracy. *"More than you can imagine. Psychonics can bond two people in tangible emotion in the course of their intimate nocturnal activities. Maybe someday you'll be lucky enough to experience it."*

Kir choked back a gasp and strangled a giggle. *It wasn't exactly a topic that mothers and daughters discussed lightly over tea. She marveled that it was the second time she had been reduced to wordlessness.*

The memory was about to move on to the next scene, when Kir caught another twinge from Palinora's deepest self. It was a powerful sensation of guilt, and Kir focused quickly on the scene to place its location...

*"Returning to the subject of secrets,"* Vann said, *"I've been thinking a lot today. There was information withheld from me over the years and I understand the desire to protect me from the world in its ugliest forms. However, I am making it officially known. Henceforth, I will tolerate no more secrets. From anyone."* He threw a meaningful look to Palinora and Inagor. *"If there are important revelations that have not yet been divulged, now is the time."*

*"Why did you feel guilty?"* Kir chanced. *It wasn't really her business, but the sensation was too strong to ignore.*

This time, it was Palinora that struggled for words. *"I should have concluded that memory before then..."* she finally said, and her jaw tightened. *The Psychonic memory dissolved away, but Palinora did not released the Bonding.*

*"You're keeping something from Vann. Is it bad? Is there more you know about his fate?"* Kir scraped up every ounce of grit from the lining of her soul to ask the question she dreaded.

*"Oh no, nothing so ominous,"* Palinora said quickly. *"This secret is guarded carefully for more selfish reasons than for Vann's protection."*

*"If it's none of my business, you can tell me and I'll ask no more. As long as Vann's safety isn't at issue, you don't have to satisfy my intrusive curiosity,"* Kir assured her. *She tramped on her own guilt for voicing the question in the first place.*

*"No. Mistrust festers from a tiny nick, and I want your full confidence in me. You know I have a secret. I will divulge it to you now, and someday when I have gathered my courage, I will tell Vann."*

*"Don't worry. I won't judge you. It's not like you marked his magics or anything..."* Kir said.

Palinora blanched, and Kir knew that she had hit a bullseye blindfolded.

*A minute and a year passed in dread tension.*

*"You marked him?"* Kir begged silently for a denial. *But all she got through the riggings of their emotional connection was a tsunami*

*of pain, guilt and heartbreak, lined with a gnawing bittersweet regret.*

Betrayer.

*This time, the pang was not Kir's own, but Palinora's.*

"Why?"

"The simplest answer? A life on the run. There was always danger of separation in an attack, and I knew I could always find him with the mark..."

"If it were that simple, you would have marked him years ago. That's not all there is to it."

"No. The harder truth is that Farning convinced me it was necessary. To..."

Kir didn't need a Psychonic link to recognize the raw pain grating Palinora's heart.

"...to set things in motion."

"To Vann's end as the Chaos Bringer?" Kir breathed.

"Not to his end. To his beginning. The Chaos Bringer isn't the end of times. It's the start of something better. We had to save the world from Tarnavarian's evil. Vann was the tool to such. Or, so I believed at the time."

"What do you believe now?"

"I don't know." A tear trailed Palinora's cheek. "All this happened scant hours before Tarnavarian's assassination. I never anticipated that events would not occur exactly as Farning had predicted. I fear I may have played a part in guiding us toward a self-fufilling prophecy. I wholeheartedly believed in Farning then, but now...I just don't know."

As Palinora covered her eyes to plug the breaking dam, Kir stood dumbly. Red shame, insecurity and fear painted the ebb of Palinora's soul. She seemed as vulnerable as a newborn kitten. She dissolved to sobs, so Kir pulled her forward and tried to cover her naked soul with the shield of her own body.

"Whatever fate Vann is heading toward, it would have happened with or without your interference. I tend to think Vann is stronger than you or I could ever influence. Vann will make the choice to follow his own path now, but you were the one to nudge him on the way. If you hadn't, I would have never met him, and my walk in this life would have been long since over by now. I'd have drowned in the bottom of a rum bottle, or met my end on an angry blade. In a roundabout way, you might have saved me. If your marking Vann is what led me to him, I don't think he'd count that as a betrayal," Kir soothed.

"Short of leaving Tarnavarian a young child, marking Vann was the hardest thing I've ever had to do," Palinora confessed into Kir's shoulder. The tears balled up and fell away from the fabric of the tabard. "To betray the one I love the most."

"For a long time, I believed I had betrayed Mirhana when I accidentally killed her. But in truth, we didn't sacrifice our beloveds. We were both trying to save them. We're the same, Palinora, in a manner of speaking. We're both Betrayers for love. It's not the same kind of betrayal, and we're not condemned for it," Kir said, hoping to find her own conviction in the words of assurance. "Vann's marks have been removed, and there is no more harm can come from them. So don't bear the burden of guilt anymore. You don't deserve it."

They held each other for a long time, exchanging torment, sheeting in their sails, and building a bond that Kir had only ever known in her dreams. When it came time to let go, Palinora wiped the streaks from her face and allowed the Bonding to dissipate.

"Now then. Will you be the daughter I never had?" She slipped the ring from her digit and reached for Kir's hand.

"I've never been more honored," Kir whispered.

When Palinora slid the soulwhisper onto her ring finger, Kir felt a pulse echo in her ears. The band, which had been slightly too large, adhered to Kir's size on its own accord, hugging her finger perfectly. The stone burst into a blinding radiance that drove the shadows from every corner and cranny. When the luminescence faded away, the stone was exactly the same color as before.

"It appears that your soulwhisper has something in common with mine," Palinora said slyly.

"How can you tell? It looks the same."

"My point exactly. It does, doesn't it?"

## -46-
## A Collage of Change

*I was once told that I risked my life at every wenching, because the next could be an assassin. That's why I make every wenching count.* - Master Kozias

Soreina sashayed along the passage to the forecastle, gyrating her hips in rhythmic, inviting motion. Just for assurance, she fingered the amulet which dangled at her cleavage. The magic in the device was steady, projecting its image like a dutiful slave. She had no need to worry for recognition. The alterlet made Soreina's hair appear blond, her eyes green and her features much softer than they were. While it did not change her, it did change what people thought they saw. The bending of light. The trick of the eye.

The lecherous ponytailed Guardian followed closely behind, gliding smoothly in her tracks. He was ridiculously charming and Soreina almost regretted the plan. He was a necessary casualty, but she suddenly wished for more time. Such a delightful toy as he was difficult to come by and deserved more attention than she could afford to give at the moment. Perhaps she could wrap him up for later enjoyment, once her mission was fulfilled.

When they arrived at her cabin...rather, the cabin of the servant Soreina had "relieved"... the Guardian slipped up from behind and eased a hand over hers at the knob. "Allow me, milady. No work shall you engage this day. For I aim to pleasure and pleasure alone."

Ooh. A true noble gentleman. In Soreina's experience, not all gentlemen were gentle, and not all noblemen were noble. The words were simply a facade used by highborn fools to impress lowborn fools. But this one was the genuine article. His intention was to pamper his lady, and he actually derived enjoyment from providing *her* delectation. Which made him that much more the fool.

Soreina normally preferred men with a rough edge, but this fop would satisfy her cravings on multiple levels. After which, he would serve as the bait to lure the hapless princeling to her snare.

The Guardian opened the door suavely and ushered her inside with all the bombast of a priest, laced with the intent of a sinner. She played the part of coy attendant just long enough for the latch to click shut on the door, then Soreina dropped the act instantly.

"Enough talk," she snapped, slamming the Guardian roughly against the wall.

He looked confused through the grin that materialized across his face. "But I have not yet said a word."

"Then don't start," Soreina growled wickedly. "Words will only distract from intensity."

This fop was far too sweet for her liking. A little rough foreplay was in order. Soreina began to peel his clothes away forcefully, article by article, to demonstrate her vehement desire for carnal passion in the extreme.

His confusion only lasted a moment before his purple eyes flashed with a fire that Soreina recognized all too well. She knew the Guardian could play her way, after all.

He grasped her shoulders firmly and spun her into the wall, just hard enough to make an impact that caught her breath. As her clothes melted away, Soreina hissed with delight.

This was why she enjoyed her job. The wonderful perks it included.

\* \* \*

Dailan's annoying little hand was clenched around Kir's tabard firmly, tugging her down the passageway. "Just wait 'til you see this, Saiya Kunnai!"

"It ain't my first boat ride, ya know," Kir chuckled, soothing the heat from her cheeks with a paper fan she'd found in the galley. They skirted a passel of crew—awful lot of staff for such a small party of passengers—and rounded a corner.

"But it's mine. I've never seen mountains rising up from under my butt before!"

"Don't kink your coil, Dagnabber. I'm coming. Now will you please cut your towline?"

His fingers were clamped and true, and despite Kir's command, he yanked as though her feet would match his urgency. Finally, Kir folded the fan briskly and whacked him over the head. He ducked and covered, scooting just out of reach, continuing to goad her forward.

When they arrived at the port bow's curving stair that led to the observation deck below the keel, Dailan flew down them, two steps at a time.

The observation deck was like that on any other ferry, extended below the massive belly of the craft for unobstructed views. But, unlike the other decks, Vann was here. And he was suspiciously alone.

"Would ya look at that? Mountains, sky, clouds... Well, I think I've seen my fill. See ya later," Dailan rattled off quickly. He gave Kir a shove toward Vann, then shot away.

It was clear as crystal, by the wink Vann threw to the boy before his flight, that this had been staged. Had the little rodent not scurried up the stairs so fast, Kir might have chased him with the fan.

"It's amazing how far a loran will go these days," Vann commented drolly, shoving his hands into his pockets.

"Thank the Gods you ain't planning to be a merchant, Majesty," Kir said as she moved to the railing. "'Cause no intelligent man would pay for something he's entitled to get for free."

"Dailan drives a hard bargain," Vann said. "And he's rather adept at blackmail."

Kir winced at the truth behind that statement. "So, you've lured me here for a reason, I assume. Might as well spill it."

"I wanted to show you something." Vann pointed to the Arshenholm mountains that were looming on the horizon. "That's the final hurdle, Kiri. When we set out months ago, our initial goal was to reach my father. I was just thinking, on the cusp of that reality, that you are the primary reason I made it. You brought me here, to this point, and I've never really thanked you for it. So, thank you."

Kir shrugged the gratitude off. "Don't think much on it, Majesty. It's just a job, after all."

"You haven't called me *Stick* in weeks."

It was a roundabout way for Vann to address her persistent formality. There was power in a name that went beyond just the word itself. Vann could feel that power, as surely as Kir had intended. She had successfully created a distance between them by the simple use of one name, and the withholding of another.

"You ain't a stick no more."

He looked like a hurt puppy, so pathetic that Kir felt sorry for the remark. Every wound she issued Vann was another cut to her own heart.

"You have your journal with you," she said, to change the mood. "Gonna draw the mountains?"

Vann opened the book. "I already did. But there's something missing." He held the page out for Kir's scrutiny. The full-color of the chalked sketch captured the grandeur of the distant peaks in vivid detail, but an empty spot, just before the railing and right of center was blank. "Every sketch I've done on this journey has been devoid of humans. It's occurred to me that a journey is only important for the people making it. So, I need someone in the sketch. Since my quest began with you, it's only fitting that you fill the void at its conclusion."

"You want me to pose for you?"

"Would you?"

A thousand possible refusals crossed Kir's mind, but none of them could withstand Vann's eyes, so she settled on, "Okay."

Vann retrieved his chalks from their case, which was lying open on a bench. Kir stood awkwardly in front of the railing, trying to decide on a posture. After a moment of positioning, Vann began his sketch.

He had only been working for ten minutes when Copellian stepped from the stairs. "Your Majesty, Queen Palinora summons you to the dining hall for lunch."

Kir held her breath in mortification at being caught posing for a drawing.

"Always interruptions," Vann sighed as he replaced the chalks in their case. He stuffed them with the journal into his sack on the bench, then turned to Kir at the rail. He stopped a touch away and too close for comfort, but he paused in her space like it was his to command.

Kir could feel his breath on her forehead. She looked past his arm to avoid the climb up to his eyes.

"Perhaps we can finish this later, Kiri," Vann practically whispered. There was a yearning on the air that seemed to speak without needing words. His hand extended like he wanted to touch her, but he seemed to remember Copellian's presence and pulled back.

"Of course, Majesty. It's part of the job, after all," Kir forced, trying to sweep away the footprints of embarrassment. "Go ahead. I'll be up directly."

"Part of the job? I don't know. I can't imagine drawing Malacar," Vann said wryly as he started for the stairs.

"That's 'cause you'd need two pages to fit Malacar. And that's without the mountains," Kir said.

Vann chuckled and started upward and onward. Copellian hung back patiently, waiting for her undivided attention.

When Vann disappeared up the stairs, Kir turned to him. "Report?"

Just as she spoke, Kir caught notice of Vann's sack that had been left behind on the bench. She hauled the strap to her shoulder to take up when Copellian was done jawboning.

He looked annoyed, but he waited until she had situated the sack comfortably before speaking. "There is a consensus among the Vipers that we should carry out the assassination as soon as we're in the King's presence. With him weakened and ill, poison will be quick and effective."

Kir growled under her breath. An antsy assassination was a careless assassination. While Kir would play no part in the actual deed, she had to discourage the militia from acting prematurely.

"No. You should carry on as planned. It will look too suspicious if he dies right after Vann's arrival. Believe me, there are scads of noble scavengers who would point fingers at the Crown Prince, or the Dimishuan people in general. Patience. Bide your time and act when the moment is right. He's not going to harm Vann right away. Give yourself time to cover your tracks and divert responsibility to the Keepers of Magic."

"But the longer His Majesty remains in the company of the King, the greater the risk. Soventine will be easy to access in Gander's Ferry. In Empyrea, he will be nearly unreachable," Copellian argued, his voice raising a heated decibel. "The King must be assassinated as quickly as possible!"

"Guard your tongue, soldier! We can't risk someone overhearing such a treasonous plot," Kir barked. "The last thing we need is for His Majesty to find out. He's been marked by his own mother, and his Guardian now completes the betrayal. If Vann knew how many people he loves and trusts were conspiring behind his back to evoke the Chaos Bringer and assassinate the King..."

A strangled gasp tried for breathing from the stairs.

Kir's head swiveled and her heart tumbled. Vann was standing on mid-step, staring. Wide eyed. Horrified.

*Betrayer.*

### -47-
### Fury of an Awakened Dragon

*If I have to choose, I'll take luck over talent any day.* - Master Kozias

A torrent of desperation washed over Kir, drowning out any hope of logic. Her mind fumbled for the words to convince Vann that she was in the right. That this was in the interest of his protection. But how in the Five Layers of Hell would she explain that? How did you tell someone that murder would prevent murder? How could she persuade Vann that she was not a betrayer, when in her heart, she couldn't even assure herself?

Vann said nothing. He stared with a dumbfounded expression

that intermingled with shocked disbelief.

Copellian hung his head, defeated. He was likely envisioning his own execution.

Kir, though, was less worried about herself than she was about Vann. There was no torture she could issue that would be more excruciating than that she had just leveled on him in her carelessness. As she stepped toward him, Vann backed away. His feet inched in a stumble up the stairs, like they were coated in molasses.

"Did I never know you at all?" he whispered.

"Majesty, please! This isn't what it sounds like," Kir insisted, knowing full well that it was. "Just listen to us and we'll tell you everything..." She threw a pleading glance to Copellian, but the guilt was painted all over his expression.

"When you spoke of the Betrayer, I thought you were being figurative. When you said not to trust you, I thought you were helping me learn independence. But you meant every word. What better place for an assassin, than to hide in plain sight?" Vann's breath sounded hollow in his chest. His color faded to putrid, like he was about to lose his stomach.

"This is for you, Majesty...*Vann*. Your father conspires to harm you. We have proof," Kir said firmly. She bounced up the steps in multiples and grabbed his arm. "I'm only doing my duty as Guardian. I'm trying to save your life! You *know* I can't harm you as your Guardian."

"You've already admitted there's a flaw in the magic. It didn't stop Ashkorai from killing my brother." Vann pulled from Kir's grasp. He seemed to fall into a whirlpool of his churning mind. "This was your plan, all along, wasn't it? You said it yourself. You've intended to bring down the monarchy from the outset. Am I next...? No, don't answer that. You speak lies and truths mingled to the same breath, and even dare to impugn your own Queen. *How dare you* make me love you?"

Kir shook her head, willing away tears of desperation. She couldn't show weakness. It would only serve to frame her guilt. "Please, Vann. Just hear me out. When I've said my piece, pass your judgments and take my head if you want it. It's about all I haven't given you yet."

Vann tensed like a cold branding iron had formed his bones. "I've heard enough," he seethed. He came about and bolted up the stairs.

The talisman, that cherished image that Kir had so treasured, seemed to fly on Vann's heels, leaving Kir as vulnerable as a chick on the forest floor. She grabbed ineffectually for the strands that seemed to slip right through her grasp.

Kir's knees went as mushy as sour mash. They kissed the deck as she was gripped with utter despair that she had not felt since Tarnavarian's death. Tears plopped on her clenched hands. She hadn't resigned herself to the gallows or headsman yet, but it would sure be a welcome end to the agony of ripping Vann's heart out with the truth.

A warm hand gripped her shoulder. Copellian was offering support. One condemned conspirator to another. Or perhaps, brother to sister?

"I will meet the Collectors by your side," he said softly.

Wrenching grief threatened to founder her in the undertow, and she almost missed the peril. Without the talisman to shield her mind, it was open to the sensation that had been blocked before—a tingling at the nape of her neck. Familiar. Alarming.

Mages.

Her guilt and heartbreak were instantly forgotten in the jolt of realization. Vann was in danger. Fighting petrification that threatened to bolt her knees to the floor, she managed to choke out warning to Copellian. She clasped his shirt to pull herself upright.

"They're here..."

\* \* \*

Vann raced along the passageways, unsure if he was going the right direction. The massive ferry was honeycombed with options. He was not entirely in control of his own motions or thoughts, and was floating beside himself in a state of shock. His mind was fuzzy against a blue-washed whirl that painted his awareness and his legs seemed to be moving of their own volition with one destination in mind. The dining hall. Where his mother, his safety, awaited.

But what would he do when he arrived? What could he say?

*The King must be assassinated as quickly as possible... If Vann knew how many people he loves and trusts were conspiring behind his back to evoke the Chaos Bringer and assassinate the King...*

Kir was a traitor. Betrayer. Just as she had claimed to be all along. And he had never listened. Kir always scolded him for trusting too much. For finding light in darkness. For believing in anyone but himself.

And she was right.

Vann wanted to scream, but his voice would not work. Only his legs kept him stumbling forward.

When he came to a familiar set of doors, he slammed them open, despite the strange sounds emanating from within. Clanging and shouting. It was a battle that raged, but was it only an echo of the tumultuous war in his heart?

When Vann blundered into the large hall, his mind took a moment to register the reality before him. Inagor and Malacar were engaged with several men in black cloaks. Magic flew. Swords clashed in metallic ringing.

Palinora was huddled against a bulkhead, Shielding herself and Dailan. The sight of the Queen in danger seemed to sober Vann, and his head cleared instantly.

"Mother!" he shouted, barreling toward her.

As a Keeper threw a Diminishing spell at Palinora's Shield, Vann slammed a Wind Wisp against the table between them. It leapt toward the attacker, knocking him soundly against a mirror on the opposite wall. The mage fell to the floor under a shower of glass that rained upon him.

Taking in the situation, Vann realized that the room was inundated with Keepers. Even if Kir and Scilio had been present, they would be overrun. Something inside Vann snapped at the powerful anger he had tried to withhold. There was no longer a reason to be politic... or merciful. He was simply overtaken with fury.

One Keeper launched at Vann, swiping his sword downward in a fatal arc. Rather than sidestep, Vann's hand intercepted the sword arm, catching it in mid-strike. Stopping it cold. The mage jolted at the force and screamed as Vann summarily shattered the forearm with a twist of his wrist. The attacker's scream was silenced with a backhand that snapped the man's neck. It barely occurred to Vann that these moves were Kir's very own technique, internalized. And yet, the inhuman strength and speed were his own.

He might have been horrified at his own savagery, but there was no time, nor reason, to care. Vann met several more Keepers with murderous intensity and equal brutality, leaving all of them broken at his feet.

A pulsing in his ears stopped his motion. For a moment, Vann would have sworn that he saw the image of a silver dragon on the backdrop of his mind's eye. He shook the hallucination away as a Blazer Bolt was unleashed toward him. Vann's Shield, raw and powerful, easily deflected the attack. There were too many mages and Vann was ready to end the battle. Without even thinking, he extended the Shield outward like a physical hand, sweeping the mages through the shattering windows and onto the outer deck.

Vann backed toward Palinora, who stood in stupefaction. "Are you okay, mother?"

The Queen nodded, but her voice seemed caught on her tongue.

Malacar and Inagor, having dispatched their own opponents, bolted toward Vann. They appeared as stunned as Palinora.

"Majesty, your eyes..." Malacar whispered in awe.

"What of my eyes?" Vann asked, taken aback.

Inagor plucked a jagged shard of mirror from the floor and held it up. Vann's knees almost buckled at the reflection. His eyes were aglow in azure flame.

## -48-
## View from the Spider's Web

*Sometimes it takes a push out the nest*
*to realize the gift of flight.* - Master Kozias

Soreina walked her long fingers up the length of the Guardian's arm, teasingly. He was everything she had hoped for, and she wanted for another round. Then, pleasure would give way to business which would, in its own way, be just as tantalizing.

She was just about to walk her fingers back down his chest and onward when the door burst open with abrupt force.

"Milady! It's begun!" a crewman shouted. That would be Four. He was always the twitchy one.

"I told you I was not to be disturbed," Soreina spat venomously.

The Guardian sat up, protectively shielding Soreina's nakedness from Four's eyes. "I say, man, have you no decency?"

Four danced nervously in place. "But milady," he insisted. "They're making their move. Now!"

Soreina wanted to scream her frustration to the Gods. This was exactly why she did not want the fool Keepers along. They had no ability to sense the pacing of the hunt, or the rhythm of the kill. There was an art to these things, which could not be rushed. And it was not as though the royal party had anywhere to go—all of the escape crafts had been disabled. There was plenty of time with which to act.

Reparations would be taken from Wardion, himself. This outrage would not go unpunished.

As events were already in motion, there was no need to keep up the ruse. Turning to the Guardian, who was attempting to cover her with a sheet, Soreina scowled. "I suppose our pleasure has reached its pinnacle, my pet. Get dressed."

The Guardian threw a dark glare at Four. "Might I remind you that the only passengers on this ferry are the royal party. The lady need not return to her usual occupation, as I have her engaged in alternate duties. Please inform your Captain that I have retained her services. He can charge her time to the King."

Soreina convulsed with mirthless laughter. "You still don't understand, do you, pet?" She grabbed the Guardian's ponytail and pulled him to her face. "I *am* the Captain."

\* \* \*

Wardion cursed the bogtrot brat who'd forced his hand. Had the little thief—Dailan, they had called him—not been rifling through crew quarters, he might not have stumbled upon the mage cloak in a duffel. And Wardion would not have been spurred to action.

Thank the Gods he happened by his suspiciously open hatch. He and his officers, brilliantly disguised as ship's company, had been conducting a brief update as they walked the crew passage in the forecastle. They had planned to move on the following morning, at Soreina's command. She had already dealt with the King's two Night Wind that had come aboard with the royals, so they would not interfere with her hostage presentation. The Keepers were merely a backup, in case force was needed.

When Wardion had poked his head into the room, Dailan startled and bolted for the nearest exit, with the cloak still in his hands. Wardion had not been fast enough to grab the nip as he scurried out the porthole like a rat.

Their cover was blown so, utilizing what little surprise he might still have, he made the premature order to attack.

Soreina would, no doubt, be furious. In the end, it didn't matter, as she would be meeting her own fate on the ferry with the princeling. But it was just one more thing to worry about. One more potential problem.

Wardion hated problems.

It was a problem that he now faced. He stood over the bodies of nearly twenty of his Keepers, many of whom were shredded and moaning on the deck outside the dining hall. His remaining thirty were engaged elsewhere with the Hilian entourage, and Wardion knew better than to face the prince alone. Vannisarian was unexpectedly stronger in his magics than Galvatine had led him to believe.

He needed to establish an upper hand. But how?

As though the Gods had heard his query, Soreina, cloaked in the phony image of her alterlet, appeared. She was clutching handfuls of hair from the severed heads of the two Night Wind. The heads swung casually as she walked. Two of her wretched henchmen followed behind, with the foppish Guardian held between them at knifepoint.

She looked as furious as Wardion had expected. "I'll have your jewels for this, fool," she hissed. Flicking Wardion aside as though he were a maggot upon her meat, Soreina threw the dining hall doors open and they thudded against the bulkhead.

Wardion began to follow the witch, but her henchman stopped him. "I wouldn't, if I were you," he warned. "Interfere with her fun and dying will be the least of your problems."

Wardion moved to the shattered window. He stepped over the writhing body of a brother Keeper and leaned forward to observe the inner dining hall as Soreina strode in purposefully. Fearlessly. As though twenty men did not lie in agony behind her.

Targeting the royal party across the room, Soreina spun the gruesome trophies over her head like a shepherd's rope-and-ball. She released the heads at her horrified audience and they rolled to a stop near the prince.

One of the henchman shoved the Guardian forward and Soreina grabbed him by the ponytail. She pulled him into the room and drove his knees to the floor. The Guardian's hands, bound behind his back, clenched as Soreina's long fingernails sunk into the flesh around his windpipe, trailing blood down his neck.

"He has a lovely throat. I'd hate to tear it out," Soreina warned. "If you do not wish for his head to join the others, you will surrender now."

The princeling's eyes—were they glowing?—widened, but not with fear. Wardion saw a wild fury behind them that he'd rarely glimpsed in any man.

"Surrender? For you to kill us all, anyway? I think not. Release my Guardian, assassin. I will warn you but once," the princeling commanded.

"Pity. And I was so hoping to take you home with me, pet," Soreina cooed to the Guardian as she tightened her grip fiercely. Should she flick her wrist, the Guardian would be worm food. This battle would be over quickly, and Wardion had no desire to observe the inside of a man's windpipe.

Being a creature of opportunity, Wardion immediately saw his. He turned his head and slipped away, unnoticed as the Guardian grunted in agony.

When he was safely beyond the sight of Soreina's henchman, Wardion fingered the broach clasp at his collar. One little order and it would be done. He would dispatch Soreina *and* the princeling in one fell swoop. Magic would prevail once more. Just as it had for untold ages, thanks to their Order. And now, thanks to *him*. He could almost imagine the tales of his feat that bards would sing in the years to come!

Wardion summoned his Keepers through their broaches and ascended the stairs. When he arrived on the upper deck, he made his way under the suspension grip.

The grip was a magical device of unimaginable scale, a work of pure genius. It served two purposes for an air ferry. The first was simply to anchor the massive ferry to the overheard cable. The second was to act as a conduit for the magic infused in the cable. The Blazer magic was fed through the grip to the craft below, powering its mobility and all magical systems within. If the grip failed, the ferry would arc to ground with earth-shattering force.

He was counting on it.

Wardion wanted to act now, to bring the massive craft down, but he was one man. It would require the strength of many, so he would wait.

It did not take long. In just minutes, twenty-two Keepers stood with him, gazing upward. On his mark, Diminishing spells slammed against the device. The purple energy that had encompassed the grip flickered. Crackled. And faltered.

It would take time. There would be enough magic inherent in

the grip to hold it for roughly twenty minutes. This fail-safe ensured that passengers could flee a failing craft via the escape vessels. Of course, that was under normal circumstances.

Wardion had made certain that this circumstance would be far from "normal."

Satisfied with the sabotage, he signaled through the broach once more. It was time to abandon the princeling and the witch to their fates.

It was a shame that he would not be able to assist his fallen comrades. If they were unconscious or too badly wounded to transport through their vortexes, they would die, as well. Their memories would be honored for all time in the annuls of history's heroes.

Taking one last, triumphant look around the deck of the doomed ferry, Wardion nodded, then disappeared into his cloak's gateway.

## -49-
## Ensnared

*No matter the lay of the field, be it for battle or love*
*(which are often one and the same), hold fast to your escape*
*plan and ensure the route is clear before the march.* - Master Kozias

Kir skirted several one-on-ones between militiaman and cloaker. The passages were alive with combat. While Kir normally would have delighted to barrel into the fray, she had only one objective: Vann. She barely noticed that the militiamen were holding their own. At least, there was more black than gold on the ground.

Copellian followed closely behind, blocking an occasional strike or casting. Jumping over a black cloak, Kir skid to a stop before a wall of Keepers that barred her way.

"Go protect the prince. I'll hold them off," Copellian said, saluting her for the first time.

"By Nomah's honor," she returned.

Kir came about and raced along the passageways, directing any unencumbered Hilian to Copellian's aid.

There were any number of places Vann might be, but the most likely would be his cabin. When a quick search revealed an empty stateroom, she tossed his sack to the bed and whirled away. She sprinted for the outer decks. Random searches were coming up empty, and she was growing more desperate with every stride.

"Where the hell are you, Stick?" she panted, glancing to the soulwhisper on her finger. The sky blue stone was glowing like it contained a churning, living flame. She hadn't the foggiest notion of when it had started, or what it meant.

"The mess hall," she breathed, frustrated that panic had stolen her wits. Vann had been summoned there, and she should have remembered. Her feet knew exactly where to go, but was there time? Precious minutes in her search had already ticked away.

Rounding a corner, Kir came upon a sparkling glass dome that dominated the entire upper-middle deck: the luxurious dining hall's skylight. Fortune had guided her to the perfect observation point. If Vann was in danger, she would be able to tell through the glass.

Leaning forward, she craned her neck and found him, standing protectively in front of Palinora and Dailan, with Malacar and Inagor at his sides. Scilio was unaccounted for.

Kir gasped when she finally spied the Bardian, almost directly under her. He had been obscured from her view by the massive floating chandelier. Scilio's throat was bleeding under the grip of a crewwoman—the same one he'd left with earlier. The intent was plain and Kir lost herself in the eruption of fury. Long fingernails dug into flesh; there was no time to think.

Kir threw an angry Wind Wisp at the dome and crashed through, riding the wild current downward with the shattering glass. Her Guardian sword was clutched in both hands, though she couldn't remember drawing it.

The crewwoman threw up her palms instinctively to protect her head from the cascade as Kir pummeled into her like a snarling ball of wet cat. Scilio, free from the bloody fingernails, rolled away. Malacar rushed in and sliced through his bonds, then ushered him back toward Palinora, who promptly began healing the puncture wounds.

With Scilio now safe, Kir tried to utilize the remaining element of surprise. She put away the wild rage, collected herself, adjusted her grip, then stepped toward the rising woman. Spinning inwardly, she rammed the hilt of her weapon into the opponent's chest, hoping to knock wind from lung. Rather than flesh, the hilt met with crystal. Kir hadn't noticed the amulet. It shattered as the woman slammed against the wall.

Instantly, the assassin's appearance began to change. Tanned skin paled. Rounded features lengthened. Blond hair faded to a silvery white and it seemed to grow the span of years in only a few seconds until it reached her ankles. It moved with an organic motion that Kir had only seen in living things. Was it...alive?

"I'll take the cost of that from your hide, wench," the woman spat with a tone that oozed poison.

"Milady Soreina!" a fidgety man called nervously from the hatch to the outer deck.

"Silence, Four," Soreina yelled, seeming to struggle as she rose. Then, moving with unexpected, scorpion-like speed, her hair pounced upon the Guardian sword, coiling up the length to Kir's arm. It gripped tightly, unaffected by the sharp blade. Stiffening with steely rigidity, the shaft of hair lifted Kir into the air, as though it were the arm of a giant. It threw her like a limp rag toward the royal party.

Kir had expected to slam mightily into them, breaking bones in the process. But instead, her impact was pillowed by familiar hands. Vann caught her, barely stepping back against a force that should have floored him.

When Kir looked up, her heart did a little tripsy dance inside her chest. Vann's eyes were ablaze with some other-worldly essence. He set Kir down without a word, his eyes fixed on Soreina. Fixed with flames that bled blue murder.

Soreina's hair puffed and writhed like a living web.

Vann stepped toward the inhuman thing, but Malacar held out a hand. "This is not your job, Majesty."

The Guardians, in unity, stepped before Vann, ready to face their adversary.

"Guardian Scilio," Kir said, eying the bruises around his throat. She shoved her shortsword at his chest. "Protect the Guarded."

Scilio nodded and ushered Palinora and Vann across the room, then Shielded.

The rift felt long and endless to Kir as she and the Guardians advanced through the broken tables and debris that littered the hall. Soreina waited, all smiles and venom.

At once, the silence in the room dissolved into discordant frenzy. Soreina's hair, separated into tentacle-like shafts, became multiple opponents for each Guardian. Had they been battling individually, Kir doubted that they would have stood a chance.

Malacar and Inagor dodged and sliced, but brute strength did little against the array. They were repeatedly entangled, and even as they severed a cord, another would assault them. Kir, with her dodgy speed and agility, fared better, but she couldn't get close enough to strike. After a woven-wall of hair shielded the witch from Kir's Fire Star, the mass unwound and an army of threads sprang forward, slicing razor-thin cuts across Kir's cheeks. Thin strands were easier to cut than cords, but they were abundantly more difficult to avoid.

It was apparent, after some time, that the Guardians were losing.

Inagor signaled for Kir to deliver another Fire Star. She cast the swirling flame, coaxing it to encompass her Guardian sword, and launched again toward Soreina. Inagor and Malacar circumvented the spidery woman's defense as she was forced to weave another wall of hair against the incoming flame assault.

Utilizing the opening, Inagor caught Soreina with a Blazer Wisp from behind. Some of the energy connected, but most crackled up the strands of hair, dissipating as it flowed. Soreina was thrown forward, wrapped in her own wild mane.

She recovered quickly. Throwing a network of hair at Inagor, she pinned him against the bulkhead and rushed in. She stopped, a breath away, and studied him. She sniffed his neck, then cocked her head slightly with a malicious grin.

"I know you..." her syrupy voice drizzled, "...Sanguinary Tide."

Inagor's eyes saucered in alarm. "You're kaiyo?"

"Half, to be precise. Your kind call us kaienze."

"There should be no more kaienze left," Inagor growled.

Soreina laughed wickedly. "You missed a few."

That must have meant something because Inagor's breathing intensified. "Guardians, abandon ship! Protect the Guarded at all costs! This creature is *my* opponent." He looked back to Soreina, who was crawling her spidery fingers up his chest. "I always rectify my mistakes."

Palinora cried out at the command. "No! Inagor, I won't leave you here."

Inagor smiled hauntingly. "I won't be long without you."

Catching Soreina off-guard, Inagor blasted the witch backwards with an Inferno Bolt. Not even her unnatural hair could withstand the scorching heat. It wilted and curled as it released him. Soreina's shiny, melted complexion oozed smoke from bubbled char, but that was all. Singed though she was, the flames had done the witch little more harm than melting off chunks of her pallored surface skin and flaming away her clothes. Most humans would have been stewed in such a conflagration. Even the paint on the bulkhead had peeled in the fury. Inagor's claims that Soreina was of kaiyo blood must bear truth, Kir thought.

Soreina rose, seething.

Inagor circled to place himself before the wounded thing. "Guardian Ithinar, in my absence, you are charged with the Queen's protection," he called back.

While he could not see the gesture, Kir saluted him anyway. "By Nomah's honor."

"Go!" Inagor commanded. "While you still can."

## -50-
## From the Mouths of Nabbers

*Keep your friends close. Your enemies closer.*
*And your flask closer still.* - Master Kozias

Malacar led the party toward the escape dinghies which, along with three slain mages, lined the edges of the lower decks. The vessels were small, only intended for thirty passengers. Wind Bolts, blasted downward in short bursts, would ease the dinghy's decent on brief cushions of air. It was a fancy way of falling, really.

In a brief moment of ironic nostalgia, Kir remembered doing the same thing, months ago in Findelore, with Vann clinging to her back for dear life. She only hoped that these craft did not impact quite so hard.

"This one is inoperable," Malacar reported, leaning over to examine the dead capacitor orb that should have been glowing. "Let's take the next."

A quick inspection of the subsequent four found the same results.

"This was designed from the start," Palinora said. A hint of fear seeped through her tremulous voice. "We were fated to this, the moment we stepped aboard."

"We're not sunk yet," Vann countered. "Soreina would need a way off the vessel. She will have a working dinghy waiting somewhere nearby."

"Majesties!" Copellian shouted, racing toward them with Dailan on his heels. "I'm sorry I was delayed. My brothers and I were occupied battling Keepers."

Dailan raised his hand for attention, but went ignored as Copellian continued. Kir wondered fleetingly when the little rodent had slipped away from the mess hall. She had been so preoccupied trying to squash the spider that she hadn't even noticed his exit.

"They suddenly ceased their aggressions and fled upward. To where, I do not know," Copellian reported.

"I saw..." Dailan interrupted, but Malacar waved him silent.

Copellian added, "The Vipers are searching for the Keepers, as we speak."

"Seems like the Keepers have been busy already," Malacar gestured to the escape boats. "The capacitors are depleted."

Dailan began jumping up and down, like rice popping on a hot griddle. "Hey! Listen to this!"

Kir almost put her paper fan to his head in exasperation. "Stow it, bilge rat! Wenchin nips..."

"But why would they have abruptly fled from battle?" Copellian asked. "It takes time to deplete a capacitor, so these vessels must have been tampered with beforehand."

Malacar nodded. "The Keepers must have another agenda..."

A loud and pointed string of profanity that would have even made Master Kozias blush gushered from Dailan's lips. Every jaw flopped and every head turned. They stared for a fraction of a second, trying to process the effusive blasphemy that had just escaped the tender lips of a child.

"Thank you!" Dailan shouted in the space of the silence.

Despite the literal and figurative gravity of their situation, Scilio's amused grin spread like a stain. "Might you have something to add, young poet?"

"You're all jawing questions whilst I gots your answers!" Dailan exclaimed.

Vann nodded permission. "Tell us what you know, Dailan."

"Just before Saiya Kunnai dropped into the mess hall, there was that wenchin cloaker standing out the window. Remember, Highness? The one I was telling you about before the cloakers attacked us. He's the same one I swiped the black robe from."

"I remember. What of him?" Palinora prodded.

"Well, he high-tailed it, so I followed him. I knew he was up to no good, cause why would he want to leave such a great fight? Turns out, he went to the upper deck and met the other cloakers there."

Kir grasped his shoulders firmly. "You done good, Dailan. Now, what happened?"

"You know that hangy-boxy thing? The one that connects this ship to the sparkly rope? Well, they cast something purple at it. Then, they sucked-gone into their black cloaks. I think what they done was something pretty bad, 'cause they was in an all-fired hurry to leave," Dailan finished.

There was a collective gasp.

"Oh dear," Scilio breathed, glancing at the row of disabled dinghies. "Does anyone, by chance, know how to fly?"

"Think people," Malacar urged. "How do we get the royals to safety? If the ferry is coming down, we have no time to waste."

Kir's heart was a rabbit and time was a turtle. They couldn't grow wings, and they couldn't jump. It took all her might and decency not to kick the closest mage's corpse in frustration at his part in this.

And then, it struck her. Replacing her panic with elation, Kir decided she just might kiss the corpse instead. She ripped the black cloak from lifeless arms and threw it around Vann's shoulders. "We can't fly, but we can sure-as-shootin' shadow-hop off this wenchin tub."

"Brilliant!" Palinora cheered.

Malacar and Copellian wasted no time in collecting the other two cloaks.

"Cope," Kir called, "Guard them in my stead." She started for the nearest passage.

"Wait. Where are you going?"

"I gotta round up Inagor and the Hilians. There are plenty enough cloaks, what with all these bloody wenchers lying around. And I gotta grab our dunnage. We'll meet you on the ground."

"No," Vann commanded firmly. "Guardian Arrelius entrusted you with the Queen's life. You will fulfill your duty to them. And to me."

"I didn't think you'd trust the Betrayer with the Queen's life," Kir said softly.

"We'll discuss the details of your treachery later, Guardian Ithinar," Vann replied coldly. "In the meantime, I will keep my friends close, and... well. You know the rest."

Kir swallowed down a hard lump of humiliation and spit, ignoring the looks of shock on every face. She began to protest, but Copellian grasped her shoulder.

"I will go, Saiya Kunnai," he said with a respect that he had never issued before. "My place is with my people, and you, yours."

She would have argued, but time wasn't a turtle anymore. "By Nomah's honor. Be careful, Cope."

"That's the last time you call me *Cope*," he said, but the words held no cold resentment.

"We'll argue that point when you come back safely," Kir returned.

"Count on it." With a nod and salute, Copellian disappeared around a bulkhead.

Turning attentions to the cloaks, the group partnered up under the fabric.

"How do we operate these devices?" Malacar asked.

\* \* \*

His brother Hilians had rallied to the upper deck, as was the pre-established meeting place in any shipboard emergency. Copellian issued a succinct briefing, then ordered the cohort to obtain the royal baggage before they shadow-hopped to the ground.

When they were off, Copellian made for the dining hall to assist Guardian Arrelius.

It was a hopeless scene he came upon.

Guardian Arrelius was bloody, his face swollen almost beyond recognition. His limbs were ensnared in the web of a half-naked woman's silvery mane. He was spread in painful extension, a torturous X against the charred bulkhead. He was weaponless, bleeding and defeated.

The witch looked little better, but despite her burns, bloody rivers, and a gouged eye socket, she had prevailed.

"Unhand him, Arcadian beast!" Copellian cried.

Soreina blinked through the undamaged eye. "Ah! Another pretty come to dance in my web?"

Guardian Arrelius turned his head weakly. "Stay away, Copellian! This creature is too strong."

Copellian knew his own talent and he would not be easily swayed. "She's a mere woman, and damaged, at that. I can take her."

The witch laughed with the bluster of a gale. "By all means, come forth and try, young blood."

Just before Copellian stepped beyond the threshold of the hatch, Guardian Arrelius flicked his wrist, casting a flaming vortex that encompassed the room. The swirling riptide of heat roared like a great tornado, forcing Copellian to retreat. He could see the two opponents through the maelstrom, facing off for their final deathstrike.

It was a battle that Copellian wished he had seen in its entirety. The two seemed connected by some powerful hatred that extended beyond the boundaries of time.

"Guardian!" Copellian shouted, "The ferry will not make it over the mountains. It will founder!"

"Then you'd best get off it, soldier!" Arrelius called back.

"I was sent to aid you!"

"Some strings can never be untangled, son. The past is the most convoluted knot of all, and I am spliced in its eternal clutches," Arrelius replied. "But bear witness that I have left this world a proud Guardian."

"What are you saying?" Copellian spat angrily. He had never known a Guardian to cowardly surrender to any fate. "Are you striking your colors?"

Despite the inflammation that stiffened his mouth, the Guardian was smiling bittersweetly. "I have not given up. I've lived my life for this moment. To die laughing."

Copellian wanted to reason with the man, but he could think of no words.

"Go while there's time," Arrelius commanded. "Tell my family that I laughed to the end."

The flames intensified, until Copellian could no longer see beyond the whirring energy. He cursed his own failure, and that he had never been given an opportunity to rescue. He certainly could have handled a single wench.

Copellian threw the odorous mage cloak around his shoulders and closed his eyes, willing himself groundward.

## -51-
## Addolorato

*Play for me, sad lumachord, and sing thy flame in blue and gray.*
*For never once have shed mine tears, as on this bitter, sorrowed day.*
- Excerpt from *Tears of Cerener*, A Poem by J. Kozias, Master Warrior

Kir's eyes shifted from the ferry to the horizon and back again. There was no sign. Inagor and Copellian didn't materialize. The ferry was precariously close to the mountains. If it fell now, it would collide with thunderous devastation in a craggy face.

The Hilians were gathered alongside the royal party, and there were no boundaries anymore. There was no rift or divide to distinguish race or class. There were only people there, sharing a common fear.

Every eye scanned the horizon for some hope, some trace evidence that their last two companions had made it. The Hilians had been lucky. They had only lost seven of their number to the Keepers. Sadly, one of the seven had been Counselor Gertraul, who had no fighting experience.

It might have comforted Kir to know that the militia's training had come to some good, but she couldn't find pride in the midst of the sickening tension than knotted her stomach.

When a distortion shaped the air, a stone's throw away, there were collective inhales and no releases.

Copellian unfolded from nothingness before them. He was alone.

Palinora, who had been clinging desperately to Vann, freed herself and rushed to Copellian's side. "Inagor? Is he not with you?"

Copellian, seemingly lost for words, merely shook his head.

"Then..." Palinora asked feebly, "...where is he?"

His throat bulged as Copellian swallowed. "He is... he is laughing."

Copellian came about and fixed his gaze on the ferry, probably to avoid Palinora's pleading eyes.

Even though the ferry was at least four leagues away, Kir shuddered at the ominous splintering that cracked the air. Massive sparks flew and metal screeched as the grip slipped from its umbilical.

The ferry began its descent toward the tree line on the nearest mountain, arcing in a fatal dive. Kir's voice caught in her throat. She cursed time in its cruel allargando, as it seemed to stretch in infinite agony to torment the horrified onlookers.

Vann wrapped his arms around Palinora's shoulders and tried to shift her away from the impending collision, but she stood firmly. Stoically. "Love demands that I see him through to the end."

Kir could not count the seconds. They were stolen away by the helplessness.

When the ferry hull slammed its mass against the stubborn wall of stone and dirt and tree, the air roared with protest. Kir was certain she felt the ground convulse in agony, too. A cloud bellowed from the insulted mountainside like the very heart of the earth was being ripped from its bosom.

Palinora made no sound. No cry. Her fingers tightened around a dog-eared scrap she had produced from her pouch. It looked to be an image capture, and Kir could discern Inagor's visage through the gaps. Vann was pressed close against Palinora's back, and his hands clenched her arms.

They stood in silent reverence and despair.

Kir had almost expected to feel something from the Guardian magic, but no glimmer or tremble crossed her vambrace. Did a Guardian know when a brother had perished? Inagor was not in Vann's direct circle of protectors, so perhaps they wouldn't feel the loss. After all, Kir had no inkling of connection to Soventine's Guardians.

But even if Inagor's loss was not recognized by her vambrace, Kir's heart felt it fully.

An hour was stretched to the perception of a year as the group sat in the embrace of grassy blades that held no more comfort than their name suggested. Words were absent, as though they feared their own sound. There was nothing passed around, but the exchange of warm grief and a flagon of warm grog.

Palinora's head rested on Vann's lap. She had reclined on her side, staring at a barely-visible purple trail that cut the sky in two. The barren cable that once been a path to the future was now their incompletion. Kir wanted so badly to shield away the horrible world from Palinora, and return the golden joy that had fallen against a mountainside. But when she had tried to offer her empty arms, Vann had issued a brusk dismissal.

"I can see to my own family, thank you," he'd snapped.

Vann's brilliant blue eyes no longer glowed. And they no longer held a smile for her. It hurt as much as Inagor's loss, and perhaps even more. Kir had believed Vann and the Guardians to be her new family. She even dared to believe that this adopted family would never abandon her. But Vann was letting her go, and he had every right. Yet again, Kir had given herself cause to be forsaken.

It punctured with the teeth of a thousand dragons, but Kir knew that Vann was hurting even more than she was. He had been dealt a double blow. He'd first lost his Guardian, and now, his father.

Vann's voice shattered the melancholy silence. "Yet another dies for me."

"Inagor always knew this day might come. As did I," Palinora said, sitting upright. "He chose this life. Just as he chose to laugh in the face of death."

Vann wiped at his eyes with the back of his hand. "That makes no sense at all," he muttered. "Laughing as you go out? Nobody will hear you."

"If I may, Majesty," Malacar offered, "To a warrior, it matters not who hears you. History will never know of every man who ever gave his life for a greater good. But the world moves for those sacrifices, whether they make a boom, or are never heard at all. We all walk upon the road carved by those who would roar defiance, and blaze the trail as they go out."

Vann nodded somberly.

Scilio seemed deeply moved by Malacar's soliloquy. "Never again shall I call you inarticulate. You are as deep as you are broad."

"A Guardian's heartbeat is not his own, dear one. He lives for the day that when his stops, his Guarded's will go on," Palinora said, brushing bangs from Vann's forehead gently.

"I know. But Inagor died for me. It just doesn't seem fair. He wasn't even my Guardian."

Kir saw an opportunity to shorten the rift she'd created with Vann in the past few weeks. "Don't think you're so special, Stick," she said lightly, trying to dissolve her mask of formality. Using the nickname Vann had so longed to hear again might just bridge the chasm. "Every one of us is beholden to Inagor. When it comes right down to it, he saved us all from that spidery wench's mandibles."

Kir mustered up a genuine smile, laced with heartache,

sympathy and hope. For a shining moment, she thought Vann might return it. But instead, his face was inexpressive stone.

The entire party turned their eyes to the mountain, and Kir wondered if they were registering the truth of Inagor's sacrifice.

Vann hugged Palinora to his chest, then rose. "I'm sorry, mother, but we must away. Lingering here will only invite danger. I will not allow Inagor's loss to be for naught."

Without preamble, a tenor rang out in mournful melody. Scilio was standing at attention, his fist clenched in tribute at his chest. The song was a common requiem, but Kir had never felt the agony of the words so clearly as she did at that moment. Malacar joined Scilio in the salute, followed by the Hilians.

Vann rose and approached, adding his mellow baritone to the haunting chorus. Kir had been able to suppress her tears all afternoon, but Vann had just pulled the plug on that dam. She walked away a safe distance, to avoid embarrassing herself.

It was several minutes before she regained her composure, but when Kir returned to the group, she realized she had not been alone.

There was not a single eye that remained dry.

# -52-
# The Love of Betrayers

*Every dead man gifts us with the realization*
*of our own mortality.* - Master Kozias

When the requiem concluded, Kir scooped up her saddlebags and tossed them over her shoulder. The group collected their dunnage and turned their heading northwest.

They had opted not to use the mage cloaks again. The mana expended on their use had been staggering and nobody was comfortable with their function to begin with. Since none of them had been to northern Aquiline, they didn't really know where they were going and couldn't visualize a location to hop to. Malacar had suggested if they tried to hop to Gander's Ferry (if it was even possible to go that far),they might end up in the middle of a mountain or somebody's wall, or half a league in the air. It was too risky to use a device without knowing the how-to.

Kir was happy to be rid of the vile cloak. Shadow-hopping to the ground had been bad enough, and even so brief a distance wrapped them in a creepy feeling during the hop. It was like being caught between one world and the next, or sucked into a void, and Kir wondered if the sensation was akin to dying. Copellian collected the cloaks for good measure and stuffed them into his duffel. They would walk, and everyone was the happier for it.

The mountain was too high and treacherous to scale, but the

Hili River ran through a significant pass. It was the closest and most direct road to northern Aquiline, which was bisected by the craggy belt.

Vann did not pause for interrogation, and Kir did not remind him to. She bore her guilt by treading on jagged eggshells in silence.

They had been walking for ten minutes when Copellian barked an alarm. "Guardian Malacar! We are followed."

Kir spun to see black corks bobbing over the wavy green valley. It took no imagination to recognize the pursuers.

"They're the Keepers from the ferry," Malacar reasoned. "Thirty, give or take. They must have shadow-hopped a league behind us."

"How come they're so slow?" Dailan asked.

"I dare chance a suggestion that the cowardice of cur has depleted its mana," Scilio answered. "The ferry's grip would certainly beg an exorbitant level to unknot so hardy a clench."

"They're still half-hour behind," Kir gauged. "We have a good head-start, but if we can see them—"

"—they can see us," Vann finished. His eyes blazed not with that fantastical glow, but with another kind of fire. "I'm sick of running. We finish this here."

Copellian genuflected submissively. "Majesty, we have wronged the Crown. I make no apology for it, but I ask that you allow us to atone for our conspiracy. Any contact you have with the Keepers is contact that might bring you harm. Despite what you may think, our intent was to prevent just such a tragedy. We of the Hili militia, acknowledge you as the one true sovereign in this kingdom. Allow us to show you the depth of our loyalty."

"No," Vann said. "Eighteen novice warriors against thirty trained Keepers is akin to suicide. Conspiracy or not, the waste of life is foolish. I will not have it."

"If you die here, Guardian Arrelius' sacrifice would have been in vain," Copellian reminded him.

That seemed to make a crater's impact, and Vann hesitated.

"Majesty, it is a sound observation. As your Guardian, my first duty is to protect you. This is the best means to that end. And, keep in mind, my authority can override yours, if your safety is in question," Malacar said apologetically.

"Very well," Vann sighed. "But I expect your imminent return, Copellian. After all, I still must decide your punishment."

Copellian genuflected again, and the Hilians joined him. "By your leave."

"Let's make haste while the Hilians buy us some time," Malacar ordered. "Dailan, you're with us."

"You better come back alive, Cope," Kir said. "If my neck's to know the block, I don't want to be alone."

She ignored the dark and quizzical looks that flashed between Malacar and Scilio.

"I told you not to call me that."

"We'll trade fists over it when you come back," Kir offered, clasping his arm.

"It is a challenge, then," Copellian almost smiled.

The Hilians turned on their heels and trotted southways, while the royal party headed north.

Before they were out of earshot, Copellian called boldly, "Prince Vannisarian! We are the free Dimishuans of Hili. Carry our sacrifice with you to Empyrea. And make them hear our voices! By Nomah's honor!"

Vann turned back briefly to salute Copellian, then spun and jogged northward once more.


No word was uttered, in relief, grief or otherwise, as the royal party hustled northwest along the base of the mountains. Thankfully, no one had inquired as to the nature of Kir's conspiracy, but every now and again, Scilio or Malacar would throw an inquisitive glance her way. The subject would undoubtedly come up sooner or later, but Kir hoped it was much the latter. She had to shape an explanation, and it must be the best speech she'd ever crafted. She wrestled with the wording to her defense as they walked.

Late afternoon shadow thought longingly of dusk when the heavy-hearted group came to a well-tended and cobbled road leading uphill to an establishment. The stone structure, nestled in a horseshoe ledge on the mountain's knees, looked large and impressive, but there was no movement on the grounds. The road was equally lonely. Up the path a way, a stone marker named the establishment as the *Arshenholm Manor: hot spring and luxury resort*. Situated just a hop-skip east of the mountain pass would certainly be a prime location for tourists and travelers from the heavily populated northern half of the island. The manor was stone and timber, with the stock and air of an old King unwilling to move from his comfortable throne. It had a glorious view of the valley below.

The party approached cautiously. As Scilio guarded the royals a safe distance away, Kir, Malacar and Dailan scouted the resort. It was a fruitless search. There was not a soul abustle in the vacant structure.

Kir found Malacar waiting for her in the lobby.

"Nuthin," she reported. "No blood. No signs of a struggle. The rooms still have personal dunnage, but it's like everyone just up and vanished."

Malacar's brow was creased with worry. "Something is amiss. The grounds are too well tended to have been deserted for long. What would drive an entire operation of this size away?"

Dailan shouted through a window, "Saiya Kunnai! I found something!"

Malacar and Kir sprang out the doors to the immaculately landscaped courtyard beyond. The only blemish to the pristine grounds was a long dirt scar against the verdant grass. It was about the height of a man, and as long as forty. Dailan was waist-deep in a hole at the very end of the mound, and he was bent over something. As Kir approached, she wrinkled her nose at the sickening odor of decay. The long mound was a grave, meant to bed the masses, Kir realized with a start.

With Malacar beside her and her sword brandished outward, Kir approached Dailan. Peering over the edge of the hole, she held her breath. A man lay on his side. His empty eyes stared at nothing.

Dailan was busy rifling through the corpse's pockets. "He's mostly clean, but this was in his hand." He tossed a scroll to Malacar, then returned to his plundering.

When Malacar unfurled the parchment, a magic-infused key fell out and bounced off Kir's boot. Dailan, his greedy little ears tuned to the clink of anything valuable, popped his head up and Kir swore that his red eyes turned as gold as his skin. His hand shot out and closed around the key. Kir ground her boot on his roachy fingers.

"Hey! Salvage rights," Dailan claimed, flapping his insulted hand to wind away the sting. "I found him, so the spoils should be mine."

"Keh! My boot says otherwise," Kir growled, snatching the key from the ground.

Malacar read the scroll silently, then handed it to Kir. "Brave man, that," he said, gesturing to the corpse. "Dailan, go collect the royal party. We shelter here tonight, as the danger is past. I will fulfill this man's last request."

Kir read the letter silently as Dailan scurried from the grave and through the lobby doors.

> *My humble regards to whomever might find this letter,*
>
> *I ask for your respects and assistance, in this, my final act. I, Cressiel Westerfold of White Tower, Havenlen, ventured here on holiday, and it is here I shall be summoned by the Soul Collectors. The patrons of this fine establishment are interred beside me, as this was the only kindness I could bestow upon them. Alas, I could not save them from the terrible family of Kaiyo that terrorized the Spring Manor. The beasts were more intelligent than the finest show dogs I've ever trained, and they seemed to communicate Psychonically. Their method of murder was not of physical means, but of Psychonic invasion. Not a drop of blood was spilled, yet, we are dead all the same. It took many of us, nobles and Psychonics, all, to fell these mighty creatures. In the end, only I remain, and not for long. With the last of my strength, I call upon the Terra magics to bed their earthly remains, and I pen this missive to you, unknown stranger, that you might show me the same kindness. My bed is dug, you need only cover me.*
>
> *I might trouble you for one last boon. Please return this key to Merisha, a resident of White Tower. Deliver my message, infused upon the key. I can promise no reward, save the soul-warming knowledge that you have*

*helped one in need.*

*With that, I go to the Gods, and perhaps to be reborn if they so deem me worthy. That I may repay you this kindness one day, if ever our souls meet on this earthly plane.*

*With warm regards,*

*Cressiel Westerfold*

Kir nodded and rerolled the scroll as Malacar cast a Terra Wisp to the surrounding soil. It churned and bubbled, covering the remainder of the grave. The scar of earth was seamless and whole, a great ochre snake of dirt through the soft grass. Malacar knelt and issued a quick warrior's prayer for the departed, then followed Kir to the lobby. She handed him the scroll and key, then leaned against the wall.

The invading silence of the cold stone room crept up on the hackles as they awaited the others. Kir wanted to brush it away, but she could think of nothing useful to say that would not expose her discomfort. Finally, Malacar killed the quietude for her.

"Kir, I need to know. What conspiracy has been alleged against you that would turn His Majesty's eyes cold?"

If only he had broached any topic but that. "There was a cabal, Denian. To keep Vann's hands clean, I dirtied my own willingly. I wasn't trying to betray him. I was trying to save him..."

The heavy lobby doors swung open in the middle of her sentence.

"So the assassin speaks at last," Vann said. His voice was laced with quinine. He strode in ahead of Palinora and Scilio. Dailan was not with them, and Kir assumed that he had scurried off to plunder unchecked.

"I would have thought the long walk here to be ample opportunity for confession. Instead, it only allowed for time to craft another lie," Vann scoffed.

"It's not a lie," Kir protested. "I swear by Nomah's honor, I was only trying to protect you."

"Assassin?" Malacar's back tensed.

"No. Not me. I was only training the Hilian secret militia. It was never meant to be *my* hand..."

"You connive to murder my father under my very nose, and you think it matters whose hand holds the blade?" Vann cried.

"Sometimes murder prevents murder. I *had* to be involved. It's my duty to guard you from every threat, and the militia has proof. Soventine wants to make you the Chaos Bringer, and it will be your end on a dagger when it comes. I tried to tell you, but you hold Soventine on a pedestal that I can't touch. Please believe me..." Kir pleaded.

"My father would *never* hurt me," Vann barked. "Everything he's done has only been to my benefit."

"Or to the coming of the moonless night," Kir corrected tentatively. "You trust too much and always have."

"You've proven that much to me now," Vann returned hotly.

If the blue flame had been dancing in his eyes like before, Kir was certain he would have staked and charred her with it. Vann prided himself in gentility and passivity, but he was walking beside himself on the passionate edge of aggression.

Palinora stepped between Vann and Kir. Her hands pressed against his tunic. "There is more to your father than any of us know, Vann. I have, myself, doubted my once held convictions where the prophecy was concerned. If there is, indeed, proof, as Kiriana has indicated, we should see it before you pass any judgment."

Vann paused for the heartbeat of eternity, and his logic seemed to be kicking his anger back into a hole. "I asked General Farraday once if my Guardians were not proof enough of my identity. He said that any smithy in his employ could fashion a false vambrace. How can I know that my enemies are not capable of the same regarding your proof?"

Kir's mind stumbled over the outstanding point. She fished around for responses that could answer, but before she could hook a winner, Vann interrupted her thought with another rising assault.

"And furthermore, you don't stop at plotting murder, but you impugn the character of the Queen with your nefarious calumny. My mother would *never* mark me as the betrayer!"

Kir opened her mouth to refute, but her voice caught on her tongue. She couldn't pull Palinora into the prison pit with her. Her flustered face and guilty delay must have been painting a shinier collar around her neck with every passing second.

"As always, Vann, there are various ways to see things when they are viewed at different angles," Palinora said carefully. "Do not condemn Kiriana for my mistakes. They are many, believe me. But whatever you heard her speak is likely the truth. I did mark you, and I set us upon this path. Kiriana did not impugn me. She was only bold enough to say what I was too much the coward to confess."

Vann stared at his mother incredulously for several wordless moments. When the implication finally wormed its way through the thick wall of disbelief, all the color fled from his cheeks. "*You* are the betrayer?"

"Please understand that my intentions were wrapped in a mother's love, Vann. I believed at the time that you, as the Chaos Bringer, would bring our salvation. Like Kiriana, my heart is bound to protect you, and to lift you up to a place you cannot reach on your own."

"No mother's love in any story I've read ever included betrayal. If I cannot trust my own mother, there is *no one* to whom I can bestow my faith. I am, as I have always been, utterly alone."

"You have never been alone, dear one. Inagor and I may have skirted the edge of truth for your happiness, but it was for that only. We have always loved you, and we have always believed that you are meant for greatness. It was in that conviction that I found the courage to set in motion the events that would bring you to your destiny. It was *because*

I love you that I betrayed you."

A rumble in the pit of his gut burst forth in a mirthless round of laughter that convulsed his shoulders. It was the scariest thing Kir had ever heard.

He finally found his voice in the lap of fury. "Is there *anyone* I've ever really known? Is there nothing that has not been fabricated for my delusion? Is there anyone in this world who is not bent on deceiving me?"

The hours-old stains down Palinora's cheeks refreshed their desperate paths. "I'm so sorry, Vann. I never meant to hurt you. When this passes, you will understand how much your family loves you." She reached toward him, but he brushed her aside.

"I have no more family left. I have naught but shadows of love and illusions of friendship." He turned on his heel and stalked toward the doors. "I abjure you both."

Palinora's hands covered her face. Kir pulled her forward and held tight, as much for her own comfort. Despite her steady grip and forced mask of stoicism, she trembled. They clutched each other, Betrayers in arms and shame.

Kir wasn't about to resign herself to the block yet. She clung to the fringes of hope in Vann's capacity for reason. When he heard the entire story and was free of the shock that had frenzied his awareness, he would understand.

Malacar stood stump-still, processing and digesting, and likely trying to determine where the facts were fitting in his rigid system of honor.

Scilio chanced to grab Vann's wrist. "Majesty, stow your seething fire for a moment..."

Vann shook him free, not even wasting the motion of looking back. "Are you going to deceive me, too?"

"You can be angry at the world tomorrow, but for this evening, we've enough of grief and separation," Scilio said with a soothing, yet steady air. "You are drained to the body and more to the soul. Let us rest and regain our senses. On the morrow, things that have been shrouded by fatigue will be exposed to a clearer mind."

Vann's shoulders sagged and his hands closed around the massive oak door. Kir thought he might snap it in two with his fury, but it seemed to seep away with Scilio's words. He nodded and trudged to a seat near the fireplace. His fingers laced at his forehead as he hunched over against the weight of mountains that seemed to press upon his back.

Scilio turned to Malacar. "This place should be jumping out of its skin with activity at this time of year. Yet it seems more mausoleum than mania. What ill has befallen this paradise abandoned?"

Malacar handed over Westerfold's scroll and key without a word. After Scilio finished reading the letter aloud, he pocketed the key and said, "Perhaps I would have been happier in my ignorance of such facts. At least we can take heart knowing that the danger is past."

An iron stillness gripped the room, and Kir could almost feel the drag of torrential agonies threatening to drown her. She wasn't the only one. Every head was hung in an exhaustion laced with loss and tension. Every eye was puffy and dark. Kir could almost feel the despair like it could be quartered and served on a cold platter.

"It's getting dark," Malacar said after a moment. "We should retire for the night. The exertions of the day have strained us all."

"There are large apartment suites down the east wing." Kir fought through the quivering of her voice. "Let's make them ours for now."

There was unanimous agreement, though none of it was verbal. The royal party dragged collective feet down the hallway toward the suites. None of them even paused to marvel at the magnificent paintings lining the passage.

It was as though they were ghosts, passing shadows merely haunting the halls in funereal procession.

## -53-
## Bone March

*The taste of regret is just as bad going down as*
*it is coming back up.* - Master Kozias

Vann never paused to admire the luxurious suite. It had two bedrooms and that was all that mattered. He couldn't care less about the posh grandeur that surrounded him. His mind was spinning too quickly in a whirlwind. He could not identify the individual emotions swirling in his core, as they were all entwined in knots. Had he not been so determined to master the physical manifestation in his gut, he might easily have vomited. He surely felt sick enough.

The men took the largest room. Malacar propped himself on watch at the door. Vann didn't have the energy to concern himself with Scilio and Dailans' sleeping arrangements. He chose the closest mattress and slipped under the heavy blankets, not even bothering to disrobe.

Kir and Palinora shared the smaller second bedroom, seeming connected in more than just their gender. They could weep and bleed a crimson river for all Vann cared. Their room was a world away, and he was well removed from them for the night.

It had taken every ounce of Vann's willpower not to abjure Kir's Guardianship, but it made more sense to keep her bound, for the very same reason he had conscripted her in the first place. She could not harm him while under the yoke of the vambrace.

Kir had claimed innocence, and deep down, a tiny thread of

belief was still wound around his heart. But how could he trust a vocal Crown-hater and a self-admitted betrayer?

There had been no time for a detailed interrogation. There were too many factors and questions yet to be answered. Too many enemies to sort. He was far beyond exhaustion and in no mental state to be making momentous decisions or conclusions.

He wanted to sit Kir and Palinora down and force them to divulge every dirty little secret. Every plot and plan. He would make time in the morning, under the calm of a collected determination. If he had to invade their minds with his own Psychonics, he would do it. He did not fancy himself a memory thief, but in this case, he would pry open their schemes. There was no way he could allow the planned assassination of the King to go unchecked. Or the conspiracy of the Betrayer to go unanswered. No matter whom the culprits may be.

Vann wanted to ponder more on the matter, but Scilio had suggested that his unrestrained anger was interfering with rationality, and he recognized the truth in the warning. Aside from the emotional toll he'd paid in triplicate this day, whatever unrealized magic he had tapped in the dining hall had drained him significantly.

He wondered about the magic, and the inherent strength in it. The rampageous azure flame had pulsed through his veins, aching for release. Could he have used it to save Inagor? Had he been too passive in allowing his Guardians to fight Soreina in his place? If he had been able to harness the power, to control it, perhaps Inagor would still be alive. He should have, at least, tried.

If Inagor were here, he would certainly have some guidance to share. There had never been a river that Inagor hadn't helped him ford. Vann's weary mind suddenly lost track of the jumbled madness and drown itself in the sorrow of Inagor's loss.

He had never entertained regrets, but his eyes glazed under the wealth of options he should have taken where Inagor was concerned. So often in his youth, Vann had chosen his boyish interests—his books, his art, his acting—over Inagor. When Inagor asked Vann to spar, to go fishing, even to fix a deck board with him, there was usually another, more interesting activity that Vann would choose instead. Growing up, he had little in common with his adopted father. Their relationship had always been pleasant, but they had few shared interests. If only he had chosen to walk Inagor's path, just one more time...

Vann's heart convulsed with loss of the other choices. The ones that he never made. Why, only now, did he realize his mistakes? That time would never come again.

He was no longer a confident, decisive prince. He was a vulnerable child, with no parental hand to soothe away the nightmares. He wished for Inagor. He wished for his mother. He wished for the Kir that blossomed under cherry-kissed moonlight. He wished for yesterday.

Vann buried his face into the wetness of his pillow. He was saved from the wracking sobs by the oblivion of sleep that claimed him quickly, and thankfully.

\* \* \*

Not even forest pixies could have induced Kir to sleep. Her gut churned like it was sorting kaiyo. Even though she was exhausted, her mind would not relax.

Kir propped herself against Palinora's headboard. She did not move the Queen's head from her lap for fear of awakening her. Instead, she stroked Palinora's golden hair and listened to the sepulchral silence.

Palinora's tears were still damp on Kir's sleeves. She had found her grip on composure in the face of Vann's dismissal, but once she had settled into bed and her hand met with the vacant pillow beside her, Palinora had melted into grief in Kir's arms. That empty spot would never again know warmth and repletion. It would be forever barren at Palinora's side.

Never had Kir wanted so much to comfort someone, and never had she been so pathetically unable to do so. All she could do was allow Palinora to cry herself to sleep. No word of comfort would suffice, so Kir only hoped that her arms could express what her words could not.

"I'll not be long without you," Palinora mumbled from the heart of her dreams.

Kir chomped on the inside of her cheek to forestall her own eyes from fountaining. It was easier to bear pain of the body than pain of the heart. Her mind toggled between all the mixed up heartaches and griefs and empathies and guilts.

She knew her own private hell was nothing compared to what Vann and Palinora were facing. The fact that she had contributed to their pain, that she had essentially torn their worlds apart in carelessness, stabbed Kir anew. The spearing ache was punctuated with every heartbreaking murmur from Palinora's lips.

It was the most ithinary night of Kir's life.

The sun had not peeked a shining yet when Kir heard Dailan's feet patter out the door. She let him go without a word. He was as much rodent as he was boy.

Sometime later, a heavy door slammed and glass shattered in the distance. Palinora's eyes flew open as Kir jumped up, pulling her Guardian sword from the scabbard.

"Ahhhhh!" Dailan's screech crescendoed as he flew down the hallway toward their suite. For such a well-heeled establishment, the noise-control left something to be desired, Kir thought with a grimace.

She threw the doors open as Dailan raced past her and dove into a ridiculously over-sized vase, useless but for its ornamentation. "What in the wenchin furies..."

Dailan peeked his head over the rim and pointed toward the door. "Bone march!"

"Keh!" Kir scoffed, rolling her eyes at the old Dimishuan wives' tale that was meant as a scare-tactic for misbehaving children. "Dead men can't spring to life, you *benai jekai*."

Malacar, awake and alert, joined Kir. "What's going on?"

"The rodent's sleepwalking in nightmares," Kir grumbled, sheathing her sword. The morning sun had not yet vanquished the melancholy darkness, so she lit several Inferno lamps.

"No!" Dailan squeaked. "They're here! It's the bone march. They've come to spirit me to hell for my thievin' ways!"

"Little felon's grown a conscience, has he?" Scilio yawned from the bedroom doorway, rubbing his eyes.

Kir grabbed Dailan's collar and tried to drag him from the expensive jar.

"Hey!" he protested. "Find your own hiding place!"

Kir wondered fleetingly where her paper fan was, when the eerie sound of scraping began to echo down the hallway beyond the door.

"What is that?" Vann asked over Scilio's shoulder.

Kir drew her sword again and poked her head into the hallway. The passage was dark and ominous.

Malacar tossed an Inferno to light the nearest hallway lamp, and the gleam of eyes penetrated the shadows at the far end of the passage.

"Avast! Who goes there?" Malacar boomed.

Skin-crawling whispers floated through the air from some unknown source. As the eyes grew closer, the outline of their owner became apparent. The figure moved with jerking motion, something like a marionette. His hands brandished a garden scythe before him.

When he received no answer from the man, Malacar called warning to Scilio. "Take the Guarded. Barricade yourselves!"

Malacar and Kir stood shoulder to shoulder in the hallway, ready to face the mute foe. When his image, dirty and gray, was close enough for recognition, Kir gasped. "Isn't that...?"

Malacar nodded. "Westerfold."

"But that's impossible."

"Perhaps not with the Forbiddens," Malacar returned, throwing Kir a wary glance. "Soreina's legacy goes on."

The Forbidden magics could do many unknown and unspeakable things, hence the reason they were forbidden. They went against every teaching of Order and, according to the priests, their usage had led to chaos and the razing of the First World. Soreina's animated hair was obviously a manifestation of some Forbidden spell. But wild moving hair was nothing compared to the reanimation of a corpse. Kir wasn't even sure it was possible.

"He's mine!" Malacar shouted, announcing his warrior's claim on the battle. He launched an attack toward the corpse and deftly plunged his Guardian sword through the dead man's ribcage. Save for jarring the figure, the assault made no impact.

The corpse raised its scythe, slowly, but with an intent that was plain to divorce Malacar's head from his shoulders. Just before the dull blade connected with his spine, Malacar ducked. He summarily lopped off the corpse's head, but the body was not felled. It made another clumsy swipe with its weapon as Malacar retreated to Kir's side.

"How do we bring it down?" Kir asked.

An eruption of chaos welled from inside the suite and Kir turned frantically.

"They're coming through the windows!" Scilio shouted.

"By Nomah's honor," Malacar whispered. "Not all of them..."

"A resort like this must accommodate a hundred or more during the busy summer season," Kir reasoned, quelling panic. "Wenchin furies..."

Malacar threw an Inferno Wisp at the oncoming corpse. The body stumbled as the skin melted from muscle.

"That's it, Malacar!" Kir cried. "Inferno will work."

"But it's still coming," Malacar pointed out.

"Another Inferno. Burn away everything. The bones can't hold themselves up without something to connect them."

Malacar launched a strong Inferno Wisp at the monstrosity and Kir bolstered it with a quick Wind Wisp. The fiery projection ignited two nearby paintings. The charred corpse kept walking against the flames until no tendon or sinew connected its knees. It stumbled into a pile of boney gore.

Kir turned to aid Vann, but he was already running toward her. "They've breached the bedroom!" he cried.

"Retreat!" Kir called. She grabbed Palinora's arm to guide her into the hallway.

Malacar led the party into the large open lobby. "We must find the architects of this nightmare."

"You called?" a voice sneered from the rafters.

### -54-
### Spindled Puppets

*Armies are merely marionettes. The puppet puts on an entertaining front, but in the end, it's just dangling wood. The real performer is the one who stands above and dances the strings.* - Master Kozias

Every eye turned upward to the two gaunt, pale men perched in the rafters. They looked little more alive than the corpses. Their fingers were outstretched like those of a puppetmaster, and it was clear that they were controlling the boneys that were slowly bleeding into the hallway toward them. How they accomplished such a feat was a mystery.

Scilio whipped an arrow from his quiver and Targeted one. Before it impacted the man's chest, the arrow stopped abruptly, seeming suspended in mid-air. Kir wondered if the Forbiddens could control time, as well, but it became clear at the instant the man moved his finger. The arrow snapped in two and fell to Scilio's feet, cleaved neatly by the thin thread that had bound it. The wencher was manipulating hairs in the same way that Soreina had done.

"They're not raising the dead," Kir realized aloud. "They're controlling the bodies with threads!"

Malacar moved his hand to cast, but his vambraced arm snagged to his side.

"We'll have none of that," one called with mocking good cheer.

Malacar grunted as a thin line of blood circled his wrist.

"Be a good puppet and die," the man cooed.

Kir moved to act as Malacar gasped in pain. She raised her Guardian sword to slice the thin cord from his wrist but an instant snag whipped the weapon from her grasp.

"Wencher!" Kir's hand instinctively fell to her shortsword.

The second man tsked and wiggled a finger. An immediate trail of crimson encircled Kir's arm below the elbow. More lines of red, around her ankles and neck, welled up. A chorus of cries bellowed as Kir fought to contain her own. They were all ensnared in the razor hairs, about to be ripped apart.

As the threads ringed Palinora's neck, she wasted no time. Her hands levitated at her chest. She gripped an imaginary thread and simulated pulling it as she stared the two men down.

Suddenly convulsing, the men mimicked the Queen's movements, drawing their hands apart as though pulling taffy.

Thin hairs must have been wrapped around their necks, as lines of blood welled like scarlet collars. With a sharp jerking motion, their arms snapped wide. Their heads fell, cut as cleanly as any blade Kir had ever seen. They entangled in an invisible web of hair below as a shower of blood rained upon the stone floor.

The razor-like tension on the threads that bound them immediately ceased and Malacar sliced at the air to be sure.

"Mother?" Vann probed.

"I regret that Soreina did not have the same weakness of mind. These two were rather easy to infiltrate," she said with chilling calm. "A suggestion was sufficient."

"You used Psychonics against them?" Scilio reasoned.

Palinora nodded. "There is no level to which I will not stoop when my son is in danger. I would slay the Gods for him."

Vann and Palinora seemed to hang up on each other. Vann

opened him mouth to say something, but he was interrupted by Dailan, who had appeared suddenly at Kir's side.

He tugged on her tabard. "Boneys are still marching!"

"The battle is not yet won," Malacar reported.

One of the lobby windows shattered and corpses began spilling into the room. They seemed tangled in their invisible strings and it would take them several minutes to separate.

"They're still being controlled. More of Soreina's disciples must be around somewhere," Kir observed. She retrieved her dislodged weapon.

"We'll deplete ourselves using Infernos against the individual puppets," Malacar said as the corpses in the hall drew closer. "It's like trying to kill an ant mound one ant at a time."

"Then a decisive strike to the mound is in order," Scilio said. "I can do an Inferno Ruptor if we can get them all into this space."

"Ruptor? You'll bring the roof down on our heads," Kir protested.

"Fear not. These ancient stone estates are feats of architecture. I'm sure the structure will hold. Nevertheless, I will be especially careful. And Malacar has already demonstrated his aptitude for Shielding against Ruptors." Scilio winked confidently.

"That stone fireplace is hardy," Malacar observed, indicating the round furnace in the center of the room. "Even if the roof caves, the hearth will hold."

"Proceed," Vann commanded.

The party tightened up and waited for the bone march to filter in.

Suddenly, a roaring wind sped in from the far hallway. Kir and Palinora, being smaller and lighter of frame than the men, were flung backward. Malacar held a fixed arm around Dailan, but the women tumbled across the floor, coming to rest at the opposite end of the lobby.

Dead men cast no magic, so the Wind Wisp had come as a surprise.

"Well, we know where one of the masters is..." Kir muttered.

She pulled Palinora to her feet, then cursed as a line of corpses were swept into the room by another gale. The jumble of "boneys" had cut them off from the men. Kir fought off several clumsy blades and makeshift clubs. Kir tried to cut a path, but there were too many. A wall of death separated them from Vann and the Guardians.

"Ithinar! Get the Queen into the room behind you. The plan's still a go. Cast a Barrier in the door frame for protection!" Malacar shouted from across the lobby.

"Kir, please protect my mother!" Vann pleaded.

She nodded compliance to Vann and Malacar, then ushered Palinora behind her with a wave of her hand. Kir grabbed the nearest boney by the tunic and swung the corpse around as a shield against an oncoming spear.

Palinora retreated into the closest room, an moderate sized office, and Kir backed toward her, ready to take on the next attacker. She fought off several more as they came through the doorway. Their attacks were lubberly and awkward.

When she had cleared a few more boneys, Kir began erecting a strong Barrier. It would take several seconds to solidify the strength of the casting, but a powerful Barrier was necessary against the terrifying force of a Ruptor. She had just finished crafting when Palinora screamed.

Kir spun to see a man coming through the open window, lunging toward the Queen.

### -55-
## Worthless Shield

*Dying is easy. Living—that's the real challenge.* - Master Kozias

Vann shifted his weight and dodged a poorly aimed chair leg, then removed the corpse's arms succinctly with well aimed lops.

The dead were pouring into the lobby now, swept in by threads and wind.

Scilio, kneeling at Vann's side, began coaxing his mana into a swirling ball of energy. When no more bodies entered the room, Malacar gave the signal for Scilio to proceed.

The Bardian muttered his incantation and cast his hands forward, allowing the glowing ball of energy to swirl toward the center of the room.

"Hold on to your hats and jewels!" Scilio yelled.

They ducked into the fireplace and braced themselves against the sooty cylinder walls as Malacar cast his strongest Shield before them.

Energy rushed forward from Scilio's casting, swirling into a mass and hesitating for a moment, before exploding in a fiery tide. The corpses made no sound as they were engulfed, the flesh and tissue disintegrating in the ravenous flame. Windows and doors were blown from their frames and Vann closed his eyes against the blinding white radiance beyond the Shield that Malacar strained to maintain.

When the flames subsided and only scorched bones remained, Malacar dropped the Shield and stepped cautiously into the smoking room. A tapestry snapped from its ancient home on the wall and puffed its farewell in ash and smolder on the floor. The once pretentious luxury of the room was nothing more than a charred memory.

"From the furnace into the fire," Scilio said, fanning his face against the lingering heat.

Dailan whooped and skipped across the floor to nudge a skull with his toe.

Vann wasted no time. Without waiting for accompaniment, he bolted toward the room into which Kir and his mother had retreated.

The Barrier in the doorway crackled and dissipated as he approached.

"Mother?" he called as he breached the doorway. "Mother, are you...?" The words died on Vann's lips at the sight before him.

Blinking back sudden fog, he shook his head, trying to make sense of what he was seeing. Kir was propped on her knees with Palinora's head in her lap. Her arms were folded around the delicate trimming of Palinora's ruff and her face was buried in golden curls. Neither body moved.

A dead man lay sprawled on the floor nearby. Vann registered his identity as that of Four, the nervous henchman who had accompanied Soreina in the dining hall. His chest had collapsed inward and a spear was lodged upright like it had sprouted from the bloody hole. He was one of the many pieces of a puzzle that didn't seem to fit together.

"Mother, answer me," Vann commanded.

The Queen did not stir. She did not look up or even tremble. She was as lifeless as the bones in the other room. Her safflower dress was offended with a vile crimson, and the liquid dripped, as though in slow motion, from the sequins of the bodice to the exquisite Mercarian rug below her.

When Kir forced her head up, her splattered and streaked face begged Vann for something he could not yet comprehend.

His legs would not work. His feet were one with the stone. He was a spectator to his own body.

Malacar was not so affected by shock. He rushed in to Palinora's side and closed a Healing spell over the scarlet lake in her chest. His head lolled immediately and he shook it.

Vann said something, but whatever his mouth uttered was foreign to his own ears.

"I'm sorry, Majesty. She's long gone," Malacar answered heavily.

A blue flame engulfed the backdrop of Vann's vision. If he loosed his grip, even slightly, the power would consume him. It took every bit of strength he had left to contain the roar that begged for release.

"They bested Four," a voice pelted from the window as two heads popped into view beyond the shattered panes. They were thin and lanky, and both had gaunt features. Their skin was pale, like they had never known the sunshine.

"It doesn't matter. The mind-witch is dead," the other man said. He pointed a finger at Vann. "Now we repay you for our mistress."

They launched themselves into the room.

Vann's hands never moved. His lips never parted. A blinding

blue flame erupted before him, swirling into a long and snake-like rope of energy. The truculent vortex wrapped around the assailants in a dizzying torrent, and when it ceased, all that was left were two pair of smoldering boots.

He wasn't sure whether to be horrified or thrilled at the abrupt annihilation. What hellfire had he unleashed? He was no longer confident in his own actions.

"Whoa, Majesty! Can you teach me to belch dragons?" Dailan, oblivious to the numb horror around him, whooped with joy.

"Dailan," Scilio pressed. "Belay your tongue, lad."

"But..."

"His Majesty needs some time. Do your part to scout the grounds. Make sure there are no more surprises."

A thoughtful look crossed Dailan's face as he registered the lay of the room, and Palinora's form. The previous amusement vanished. He nodded seriously and sped off on the assignment.

"By the Gods," Kir managed through staccato breaths. She studied the glowing blue stone in a petite ring that graced her finger. It was splattered in blood. "Is there no path I take that does not bring this ghastly color to taint my hands?"

It took only a blink for Vann to recognize the ring. It had belonged to his mother. He didn't know why it was on Kir's finger, but the blue fire pulsed rage in his head.

Betrayer.

He struggled to keep the fervid power contained, but the task was like trying to barrier a tsunami behind a floodgate. He was no longer manning his own helm.

"Do you now pilfer from those you have murdered?" Vann erupted.

His feet were free of their stony anchors, and they moved with their own stride and purpose. Vann didn't recall hauling Kir up, but he would always remember the impact of her back to the wall as he slammed her against it. The fire ached for repletion in Kir's blood. Only a veil of awareness was holding it back.

"Whose hand stole her breath? Was it yours, or that vile thing's on the floor?" he cast a sweeping motion backward toward Four's corpse.

Kir inhaled sharply, like he had nailed her lungs with the accusation. She choked out, "It was my fault..."

Malacar and Scilio were at his side instantly, and their restraining grips on his shoulder and arm seemed to snap whatever hold the blue dragon fire had on his mind. It vaporized as quickly as the men it had incinerated, and Vann could touch its presence no longer.

"Sheathe this raging inferno, Majesty," Malacar commanded, but gently.

"It's already done," Vann assured them. His voice sounded

small and distant to himself. "But I have to know. It's the only way I can chain this beast in me."

His hands still pinned Kir to the stone, and he focused his will like his arms were the cables to her soul. Free of the uncontrollable tempest, and guided by another, more powerful urgency, Vann called on the Bonding. He thrust deep into Kir's mind and propelled them back through the past. He had to know how his mother died. And most importantly, he had to know the truth.

*The gray-blue vision unfolded like a blossoming flower. Malacar and Scilio were linked through the Bonding with him as he delved back toward the cabal under a sub-rosa tea. He sorted through the hushed conniving and the hesitant acceptance of a forbidden plan. Through the training of a militia and the preparation of a murder. He saw the evidence in Ferinar's hand, as clearly as Soventine's seal that branded each document. He witnessed his mother's confession, too, over a tiny silver ring and a bond. His urgency compressed the time-elapsed moments into scant seconds, until he had all the information he needed. He'd accessed Kir's innocence, and he knew none of the moments had been fabricated or altered. He was seeing the purity of Kir's intentions through the unfiltered memories that lay as bare to him as a naked sea. Kir was no traitor, any more than his mother had meant him harm. The realization pierced him with a double-edged dagger of relief and guilt.*

*When he was satisfied, he jumped forward in time to the familiar inn. To a bloody room. To his mother's death. This memory, he allowed to progress in full. He needed to experience every detail of what had happened.*

*He could feel Kir's excitement twinged with a lust for the call of battle, but there was also a profound lingering guilt that overshadowed her eagerness. Intense grief. Heartache. Fear. Concern for Vann and the Guardians. The urge to protect Palinora.*

*Kir erected a strong Barrier in the doorway. She had just finished crafting when Palinora screamed. Kir spun to see a man coming through the open window, lunging toward the Queen. It was Four. Palinora stumbled backward to her knees. There was no time to cast or fight. Kir simply acted. She threw herself between Palinora and the assailant, catching the spear in her back. It ripped through her body and out the front, plunging into Palinora's chest. Kir stared in shock and disbelief down into sky blue eyes, as they emptied of the spark behind them.*

*Sudden rage, blinding and furious, propelled her upwards. As Four ripped the spear from Kir's back, she turned and shattered his arm. She gripped the spear point and drove the shaft backwards, thrusting the blunt pole into his chest. Her body registered no pain as Kir cried with blood lust, driving the spear over and over into the dying man. He splattered across her face, but the droplets left no trace on her perfect tabard. The roaring fury of the Ruptor beyond the*

*Barriered doorway echoed the scream in Kir's heart.*

*When Four's last breath escaped his lips and his body went flaccid, Kir stumbled toward Palinora, praying aloud for the strength to heal her. To save her. Kir's hands closed around the wound, but there was no life to be saved. The Queen had passed from the earthly plane the moment the spear had pierced her heart. She was already with the Gods.*

*Kir pulled the lifeless body into her arms and closed empty eyes with gentle fingers. She cradled Palinora, sobbing into golden hair. Lilac and rose water drowned away the sweaty, metallic tang that tainted the room, and Kir never wanted to surface.*

*Vann's disembodied voice called through the haze, "Mother? Mother are you...?"*

When Vann released the Bonding and they slid themselves from the recesses of Kir's memories, his eyes trailed down to the red life that dripped rhythmically from Kir's pant hem to boot, collecting in a dark pool on the floor.

"It was all my fault. Even as a shield, I'm worthless," Kir struggled to finish. Her head pitched and her knees buckled.

Vann's pinning hands became bracing supports as she slipped into his arms.

Stunned disbelief melted into a river of desperation as Malacar tugged Kir's tabard up. Vann cried out at the grisly wound that had punctured through her side, just below her ribcage. They lowered her to the cold stone and Vann cradled her helplessly.

"There's an infirmary down the north wing," Malacar commanded and Scilio bounded out the door.

"I was so wrong, Kiri," Vann whispered into her ear. "Please, don't you leave me, too."

He pressed his fingers into the wounds, feeling the life force slipping through them with every heartbeat.

"Inside out. That's the way to heal, inside out..." Vann chanted. Remembering every detail of Bertrand's lesson, he found his focus through the panic and steadied his quivering stomach.

Malacar joined the incantation. Vann was thankful for the strength to bolster his own energies, though he knew it would take much more mana and experience than they collectively possessed to heal this mortal wound.

Vann opened his mind to Malacar through the Guardian Bonding. In tangent, they began working frantically to keep Kir's heart beating, to stop the bleeding, and to save what little life was left in her body.

\* \* \*

*Kir's fevered dreams came as a desultory quilt patchwork, a jumble of memories and unlived realities knitted together in ragged, uneven edges. So confusing were the transitions that she could not tell where memory deviated from fantasy. Time had no meaning in this churning chaos. A day or a century may have passed, she had no idea.*

*The chaos condensed into a waterless lake that lapped around her, and she was drifting with the ebbing tide. Perhaps it was a dream, but it seemed real enough to her awareness. Kir felt as though she were being pulled somehow, and she knew in her heart that it was the inevitable beyond, where the Soul Collectors waited. She should have fought it. Should have thrust out her hand to grasp for any hold on her life. But it was a failed life that she had mucked up enough. So complete was the wreckage, there was little Kir could do to salvage the remains of what she was leaving behind.*

*And so, she let the current take her.*

*Vann would scold her for not kicking her feet. Or, he would have, were she not a traitor. Part of her wished that she had succumbed to the malcraven from the beginning. The drifting would have been so much easier if she'd never known Vann and the Guardians. They were wenchin rocks in the current, confounding and irritating. Just when Kir was about to move past them, something snared her painfully.*

*"You would serve me better by choosing to live for me, instead."*

*Damn, that Stick. Why'd he have to entangle her in that trap? He'd gone and grabbed her by the heartstrings.*

*It was a snare she could not fight. Her futile attempts to detach were smothered by a warm blanket of...*blanket. A real one. Downy and soft and heavy. Much more luxurious than anything she owned.

A gentle hand caressed her cheek, but it could not chase away the excruciating spear of flame that wracked her body as consciousness kissed reality.

Kir cried out and strangled a whimper.

A cool hand pressed against her forehead. Soothing. Comforting.

Kir trembled uncontrollably. This wasn't how it should happen. She had never envisioned comfort in the end. Nobody to hold or reassure her.

"Fight, Kiriana," a voice urged. "Live for me."

It was Prince Tarnavarian's voice—his pleasant baritone was unmistakable. But that didn't make sense either. He would be the last person in the world who would encourage her. Besides, he was dead, wasn't he? And she was supposed to be, too. Kir remembered Palinora, and the spear, and her life force ebbing away. So was she dead, then? It was all too confusing.

*You would serve me better by choosing to live for me, instead.*

"I've got you, Kiri," Tarnavarian whispered tenderly in her ear. "I won't let go."

Suddenly, Kir understood. She recognized the voice too late as she began sliding back into darkness.

"Vann?" Kir called, but if he answered, she never heard him.

# Valoria

\* \* \*

## -56-
## Repentance

*Shake out the main and cut the anchors of regrets.*
*There is a smooth and inviting horizon ahead.*
*Don't let your drag hold you back from it.* - Master Kozias

Kir lay awake for several minutes before trying for a look around. Her head was swimming and she didn't trust her sense of balance. When her eyeballs walked across the walls, they tripped up on an ugly painting of a hawk that looked more like a carrion bird. It stared at her with hungry, beady eyes like it was wanting her for a snack.

The bedding was soft and cushioned but a bunched sheet poked up from underneath, pressing uncomfortably against her ribs. Kir shifted and gasped at the malcraven claws that impaled every fiber in her body.

"Look who the Soul Collectors spat back!" Scilio dropped his journal and jumped up from his seat near the door, with a grin that split his face in two.

He helped her upright, then lifted a cup of water to her mouth. She coughed and sputtered, but accepted more gratefully. When she'd had her fill, Kir nodded.

Scilio slapped his knee and laughed, then roped her into a hug that liked to squeeze her juices out. His enthusiasm tickled her smiley-bones, but he was cutting off her air.

"Umm, Ponytail...? Ahh caaan't breaathe!"

"Oh, apologies." He released her quickly and eased her back against the stack of pillows.

"I guess you won't have to sing my eulogy just yet, Master Bardian." Her voice sounded toady and dry.

Scilio's grin dissolved. He sank into the chair beside the bed. "Came close though. You gave us a scare to span the ages. We didn't think you'd last the first night. Or the second, for that matter." His speech pattern was unusually informal.

" The second? How long was I out?"

"Five days," he said, guardedly. He looked unsure of himself, as if there was more he wanted to tell her. "You've been in and out since yesterday, but your fever didn't break until this morning. We kept you soaking in potions and soporifics, so you probably don't remember much. The latest dose must be wearing off."

"Is Vann...?" Kir began, but she couldn't bring herself to finish.

Scilio smiled softly and brushed a strand of hair from her face. "He's fine, if fine is hopelessly beside himself. His guilty conscience has taxed my abilities in a best-friend capacity. He's been quite the handful."

"I gave him enough reason to be a handful and more. He doesn't deserve to be paining at my expense," Kir sighed. "I hope he found whatever he was looking for in my memories, because I don't know how else to explain myself."

"He did. That's why he is so bound in self-reproach. Don't condemn yourself in his words of anger. He wasn't himself that night, and he's spoken to that knowledge plainly. Every moment since has been to his torment in the fear that he might never have the chance to retract the accusations and beg your forgiveness.

"Vann never left your side, Kir. Not until this morning when Malacar practically dragged him outside for some fresh air. They wouldn't have left if they'd expected you to awaken so soon. Vann's sitting with his mother right now."

"His mother—?!" Kir gasped. For a brief moment she grasped a glimmer of hope.

Scilio nodded sadly. "We buried her in the garden. We knew you'd have wanted to be there, but..."

Kir's heart sank. There it was. Palinora was dead. It had all been real. She squeezed her eyes shut and bit back bitter tears, but they fell anyway.

Scilio pulled her to his chest. His posh tunic was soft against her cheek. He stroked her hair as she wept against his shoulder.

"I thought maybe it was just a horrible nightmare," Kir whispered when she finally regained control.

"I know. We've all been wishing the same," Scilio replied gently. "But the dawn is driving the nightmare away, now that you are on the mend."

When he eased her back against the pillows again, a sparkly gleam flashed in the light from the bedside table. She craned her neck to spy the gaudy piece of jewelry, a hunk of gold and gems that screamed of pretension and priss. It was the kind of monstrosity that noble women wore when they wanted to be noticed, or wanted to drown themselves by weight of an anchor.

"Yours?" Kir rummaged up a cackle. "It would look divine on that peacocky slender neck."

"Yours, actually. A gift from our accomplished young pirate. I'm certain he has more booty stashed away, but he wanted to show his depth of affection for the Saiya Kunnai," Scilio chuckled. "Be gracious when he presents it. You have no idea how difficult it was for him to part with it."

"His eyes glitter more than his golden skin."

"I must admit that Dailan's natural propensities have been a boon in our time of need. He's quite the scrounger, and a decent scout. For many hours in our depleted exhaustion, he stood guard in our stead," Scilio said.

"He's a good kid, but I didn't say it."

She cleared her throat and wiped her face dry. After a moment of decision, she took a deep breath and gathered her strength. Her Guardian sword had been graciously tucked under the mound of pillows and Kir closed her fingers around the sheathe.

Gripping the bedpost, she planted her bare feet on the rug. The wavy world tipped her sideways, but Scilio belayed gravity's harsh introduction to the floor.

"Just where, pray-tell, do you think you're going?" Renewed worry strained his voice. "Malacar will have my hide if I allow you to traipse around in your condition."

"It's okay. I have to do this."

"But, Kir..." Scilio protested.

"I'll tell him I hit you."

Scilio raised an eyebrow and stared at her incredulously.

"I'll tell him I Stunned you?" she tried.

"Kir," he scolded.

Unwilling to surrender, she stood her ground and raised her hand to bluff a casting.

Scilio stood there for a moment before chuckling and shaking his head. "You're incorrigible. If you must go, at least let me offer my back. The garden is no short jaunt to the other side of the estate. And you had better take care not to dislodge my masterful embroidery."

"Huh?"

"Stitchery, of course. Upon their depletion, I utilized my brilliant Creatives and finished closing your wounds where Vann and Denian left off. Mother always said I was the greatest Needle Master in Mercaria."

Kir grimaced. "You refrained from floral patterns, I hope."

"Floral patterns? How dare you suggest such a design! No, I stitched epic poetry upon your lovely canvas."

Kir fought the urge to tug her bandages away, just to be sure he was joking.

Scilio suddenly folded his arms around her. "Don't ever scare me like that again, Kir. I don't think my heart could withstand it."

Something wet plopped on her arm. Kir's fingers brushed against the dampness staining Scilio's cheeks. "Are those for me?"

"Ah, well. You've always accused me of being a softie. Perhaps I am proving you correct." He wiped away the evidence with his sleeve. "Shall we away?"

"What about Denian?"

"I can handle him. He's dealt with your stubborn streak before, and knows I am no match."

Scilio knelt and bent forward, easing her onto his back. Kir wrapped her arms around boney shoulders and lay her head on his back wearily as he started for the door. She ignored the jarring pain of his every step, focusing on the artwork that lined the passage.

A few hallways and a jolting staircase later, Scilio carried her out a door into the radiance of a mid-morning sun. It was so bright, Kir had to shield her eyes. The expansive gardens stretched farther than she could see, but Scilio's feet knew their way in the maze. The came upon a sun-splashed garth, ringed in every kind of flower that was ever conceived in yellow. A delicate mound of white stones, marked only by an embossed royal crest on the top, graced the center of the circle. Vann was seated on the ground, cross-legged before it. His blue tunic seemed out of place in this yellow world.

As she slipped from Scilio's back, Kir was suddenly plagued with a kaiyo stomp-dance in her gut. She needed closure. She needed to face up to Vann and commit her farewells to Palinora. But now that Vann and the grave lay before her, she was abandoned by her courage.

Malacar appeared from the shadow of a yellow rose bush where he had been guarding. Kir was ready for the admonition, but he didn't break the solemn calm. Instead, he pulled her close and displayed his relief and affection in his usual silent way. When he released, he nodded approval and slipped an arm around her waist. Scilio did likewise on the opposite side. They led her slowly and carefully across the grassy center toward Vann. A few yards away, Kir misstepped and gasped, unable to bite it back.

Vann's head rotated. Fatigue painted dark circles under his eyes, but it made their sparkle stand out even brighter. "Kiri!"

He rose and raced to her side, scooping her into his own support. An unspoken communication in the steady pressure of his arms said more than any apology could ever hint at. "What are you doing out here? You shouldn't be up."

Kir waved him off. "I'm fine."

Clearly not convinced, Vann led her to the foot of the mound and eased her to the soft grass as Malacar and Scilio fell back to nearby benches. The grass bedded her Guardian sword in its cushion.

Kir took in the peace of the clearing and the finality of the stone grave. She knew Vann eyed her, likely scrutinizing her health, but she didn't meet his gaze. The grass tickled her toes, so she fixed on them instead. It was such an insignificant thing, but after being tickled on the toes by death, she realized just how much she appreciated such a mundane sensation.

"You really shouldn't have come out here," Vann chided, finally.

"I know," Kir sighed. She had drained herself to empty and it probably showed.

"Kiri, about the things I said, and the accusations I... I was completely wrong. Something was fueling my rage and I couldn't staunch it. You're not..."

She shushed him. "I know that, too."

Vann nodded, seemingly grateful that she didn't make him fumble for the right words of apology. It was unspoken, but his intention was clear. Kir needed nothing more from him.

His pained expression never eased. There was more confession caught on his tongue.

"What is it?"

"I entered your mind without your permission. I infiltrated your memories with my Psychonics so I could see the complete truth. Later, when we were losing you, I did it again. This time, to anchor you to me. I couldn't sit back and let you slip away. Regardless of my intentions, entering your mind was a violation, and I beg your forgiveness. I know Tarnavarian has done the same, and I know how it hurt you. I don't ever intend to become what my brother was..."

She was thrilled that Vann had restored his faith in her through the Psychonic connection, and touched, if not troubled, that he would risk his own life to save hers. She had heard stories of Psychonic healers having died while inside the mind of a patient at the instant of death. If her heart had stopped while Vann was linked to her Psychonically, he might have died, too.

Kir was about to berate him for such a foolhardy act when his eyes glazed over, and it appeared to be more than a function of fatigue. She decided against scolding him. She would save that for another time.

"You don't have to ask forgiveness for that, Vann. If, in the end you don't hate me, it was worth having you poking around in there. And you're *nothing* like your brother."

"I don't know about that..." Vann said. "I did something horrible. Something that I gave no thought to at the time, and only now am I registering the magnitude of the deed."

Kir's brow furrowed as she tried to place the event that troubled him. He was pure, benevolent, virtuous Vann—how could *he* have done something horrible? In his veins pulsed the blood of dragons which made him a Guardian to the world in his own right, and it was inconceivable that Vann could have... It struck her then. The dragon. She was sure she had seen a dragon encased in his terrifying blue flame. That flame had killed—no, that was too mild a word—it had obliterated two of Soreina's men in its Ruptor of fury, and it had emanated from Vann.

"They had it coming, Vann. Don't feel bad for them." She spoke the words intended to comfort him, but in her mind, Kir knew full well that Vann had unleashed some manner of hellfire. It scared her to her core.

"I know they deserved justice, and I'm not sorry they're dead," Vann corrected. "I just... this power. It's not magic or nature. I don't know what it is. If anger can manifest as fire, that's as close as I can describe it. I'm not even sure I can control it. It just erupted. From some monstrous cavern in my soul that I didn't know existed. I fear that cavern more than all the Keepers in the world. I've known this power twice, and both times, I felt as though I were losing myself, my humanity, to it. The world almost disappeared to its fiery haze and I couldn't hear over its roar." His eyes were haunted. "And worst of all,

I'm afraid I liked it."

Kir swallowed a lump of nothing, trying to keep the terror from registering on her face. He needed her support, without adding her fears to the weight of his own.

"You're stronger than you think. I'm sure there's nothing you can't contain. I mean, you've managed to bear with me all this time," Kir smiled, bumping his shoulder lightly.

Vann attempted to return her smile, but his head hung. "What of next time? What if I lose myself to this voracious beast? I could hurt someone I love. I could destroy..."

"That won't happen. 'Cause if you can't hear over the roar, just listen for me. I can shout almighty loud when I have to."

Vann didn't respond, but he nodded and exhaled a long, forced breath. He wrapped his arm around Kir's shoulder. She leaned against his chest to relieve the burden of the injured back muscles that were straining to keep her upright. There was a warmth in Vann's touch that was more than fraternal.

"I've been talking to her all morning," he said, and it sounded like a confession.

"Talking to her?"

"Mother. To her grave. It's illogical, and I don't understand why I'm compelled to converse with the dead. Especially since she will never answer back."

"We don't talk to the dead for the dead, Vann," Kir said. "We talk to the dead for the living."

His gaze was fixed on the mound that folded its stone embrace around his mother's body. Vann's grief at the loss of his parents had probably been delayed, as he'd been so preoccupied with Kir's healing. But now, nothing lay between Vann and his sorrow but the smooth white stones that encompassed the Queen.

His chest began to shake with anguish. Kir folded herself around him. Vann had buttressed Kir on more than one occasion. This time, it was her turn. As he wept in her arms, she found no shame in matching him, tear for tear. It was not only in loss, but in the regret of what her pathetic shield's failure had cost them.

After several minutes, they unwound their tangled hearts and brushed tears from each others' cheeks.

"Palinora wouldn't want us to linger on sorrow," Kir said, with a conviction she didn't feel. "If the Gods are just, she's with Inagor somewhere. That's right where she'd want to be. We should be happy for her."

Vann nodded, though Kir knew he wasn't feeling *happy* by any meaning of the word. He felt as selfish for his parents as she did.

Kir glanced at the sun, her steady sky calendar. If they had been laid up for five days, it was high time to press on. "We need to be weighing anchor soon. Since Cope and the militia never caught up, it's safe to assume that we've lost them. We don't have a backup plan for your father, and I think you saw the evidence of his intentions in my head. We can hole up in Hili until he kicks it."

"We can't leave. Not yet. You're too weak to travel. You still need at least a week of healing before you're anywhere *near* ready to be up and about. In ideal circumstances, a Master Healer would probably have you in bed for a month."

"We don't have a month. We may not even have a day, Stick. The cloakers could materialize on our doorstep at any moment," Kir reminded him.

"If they do, we'll cross that bridge when we arrive. There's no way you can make this trek in your condition. Even a week is rushing it. We'll wait that long, and longer if necessary. Besides, Denian and I need to regain our energy, too. What wasn't depleted from the battle was drained in your healing."

The repressed sense of failure that Kir had been trying to quell came bubbling to the surface of her heart and she pulled away. "You shouldn't have bothered. You both risked entirely too much by draining your mana on me. It was a foolish waste of energy, Vann. You should have let me die."

Vann's brow creased. "I will never consider saving your life foolish, Kiri. Or a waste of *anything*. I can't just—"

"Yes you can," Kir interrupted. "And you must. Your most important job is to live. To take your throne. What if another enemy had come along while you were depleted? I'm not worth the risk. Malacar and Scilio, at least, can protect you. But—" Kir hesitated. The well that should have been emptied dry renewed itself fresh and threatened to spill down her cheeks. She hung her head. "But I can't protect anyone. I've proven that time and again. I'm not worthy of your Guardianship."

Kir picked up her Guardian sword from the grass and placed it in Vann's hands. "The wenchin Oath won't allow me to remove myself. So, please release me from your service, Your Majesty. I can no longer serve as your Guardian."

Vann's features softened and he brushed a few stray locks of hair from Kir's face, lifting her chin so her eyes met his own. "Kiri, you have nothing to be ashamed of. You nearly gave your life protecting the Queen. And Mirhana. You did not fail them."

Kir studied him, trying to comprehend. His logic made no sense. Of course she had failed. They were dead. There was no greater failure than hers.

"You gave both of them what they most desired. For the Queen, you gave her the daughter she always wanted. Isn't this proof enough?" He lifted her hand and touched the cool, inert stone on the soulwhisper.

"As for Mirhana, her greatest desire was for you to survive. So far, you've been true to Mirhana in that respect, too. So, you didn't really fail them at all, Kiri. As long as you keep living and guarding the soulwhisper, you fulfill both of their greatest wishes."

Vann placed the Guardian sword back in Kir's hands and closed her reluctant fingers around the sheath. "I do not release you from my service, Guardian Ithinar. I'm afraid you're stuck with me. For a while longer, anyway. If not for my sake, for my mother and Mirhana. I honor them both in retaining you. I hope you'll resolve to continue in honoring their wishes, too."

It was a slippery way to dodge the main issue, but Kir was suddenly too hazy to fool with deep thinking. She nodded, happy to have a support beam in Vann's perception. *How great his power of the Psychonic magics must be*, she thought, *for him to interpret things in such a way, even if it was all-powerful sneaky and twisty*. In all her heart, Kir knew that Vann was destined to be a great King.

"Besides," he added with a smile, raising his voice just a fraction of a decibel, "if you weren't around, I'd starve to death."

Scilio sighed dramatically. "I'm not *that* bad a cook." He turned to Malacar for reassurance. "I'm not, am I?"

Malacar rose from his bench. "Yes, you are."

"But, you always lick the pots clean," Scilio argued.

"That's because I'm hungrier than you are bad," Malacar replied. "I'm sorry Majesty, but we should return to the room. Kir needs her beauty sleep."

Vann helped Kir to her feet. The moment she wavered, he scooped her up. She rested her head on a sturdy shoulder and allowed sleep to claim her.

**-57-**
# Another White Flower

*Love is a flame and we are the moths. Sometimes we circle too close and get burned. But does anyone ask the moth if it was worth it?* - Master Kozias

It was a rare occurrence for Kir to enjoy such a heavenly dream. She was accustomed to sleep-memories and nightmares, which jousted any good dreams right out of the arena of her mind. So, this one was a luxury.

It was made up not of images, but of sensations and emotions, interlaced into an embrace of warmth that Kir was aware of long before she opened her dreaming eyes. She was oddly disconnected from her body, but the floating sensation did nothing to diminish the aroma. Flora, firewood and musk. She nestled into the warmth, inhaling the aromas, her favorites. They reminded her of freedom. Of the open road and the wild beauty of a woodland forest.

Kir knew exactly where she was. She needed no image, for she would know the feel of Vann's arms anywhere. She was snuggled against him, her head resting in the crook of his shoulder. It was too comfortable to move and she didn't want to spoil the dream, but she couldn't resist looking at Vann, tracing every inch of his porcelain skin with her eyes. Even in fantasy, he was as perfect as he was in the flesh. He no longer had the boyish visage of months before, when she'd found him in the Hatchel. Somewhere along the journey, he had matured from a gangly youth to the image of a prince, right before her eyes.

It didn't seem fair, somehow, for one person to hold such a monopoly on perfection, and not only by physical standards. Vann represented everything that a man should be. Kir could think of no other who embodied a soul as pure. Surely, Vann's very being had been handcrafted by the Gods themselves. It made sense. The royal bloodline was said to be that of the Gods.

Was Kir held in the arms of the heavens?

She reached out to touch the slumbering God's face. She didn't want to wake him, but Kir felt like she had some semblance of control over her own dream so she willed him to keep sleeping. Her fingers brushed his indefectible cheek, tracing the outline of his silhouette. Vann stirred only slightly, a contented sigh breaking his soft lips apart as he turned his head into her hand.

It seemed a contrived invitation. While dreams often made no sense, her mind knew exactly where it was leading her in this one. She wanted to kiss him, to answer that unspoken summons. Had she been awake, she would have resisted. She couldn't allow Vann to see how much she had fallen for him. But this was a dream. He would never know.

Kir craned her neck and stretched to reach him. It was no use— her lips grazed his jaw but were well removed from his mouth. Vann's hand curled unconsciously around her arm, locking her against his side. She squirmed, but his grip was rigid.

She wanted to growl. Even her happy dreams toyed with her.

Kir rolled inward to prop on her elbow and close the impossible space between their lips. The moment she turned, her side was ablaze and she cried out, more from surprise than from pain.

Vann's eyes flew open and he sat up abruptly. "Kiri?!"

Wenchin furies, but this wasn't how her dream was supposed to play out. Kir squeezed her eyes shut and tried to undo her mistake. If she willed the dream in reverse, she could start over and...

"Hang on, sweetheart. Denian's bringing you something," Vann soothed. He slipped his hands under Kir's shoulders and slid her upright, easing her against the headboard. He held her hand firmly with a grip that was utterly strong. And real.

Kir opened one eye and glared at him. "It's not a dream, is it?"

"A dream? No, you're not dreaming."

"Oh. Then, why am I floating?" Kir asked, acutely aware that the disconnected dreamy sensation hadn't diminished.

242 · *H. Jane Harrington*

Vann watched anxiously as Malacar fiddled with supplies over a crowded table that didn't belong in a bedroom. "It's probably a side effect. The potion we're giving you is the strongest they had in the infirmary."

"I don't need anything," Kir argued. "I'm fine, really. High tolerance for pain, remember?"

"Humor me."

When he was done, Malacar hurried to Kir's side with a small cup, filled to the brim with a transparent greenish liquid. The mattress gave as he sat on the edge and lifted the cup to Kir's lips. The smell assaulted her immediately and she winced. "Ugh. I hope it doesn't taste as bad as it smells."

Vann chuckled. "It does. But you're tough. I think you can handle it."

Kir shook her head and threw the blanket off her legs. "I don't need it. See? I'm absolutely—"

"Stubborn," Malacar finished. He pressed her down with his free hand. "Come on, Kir. If you don't take it, I can always knock you out. You know I can do it, too." He held up his fist and mimicked a swing to her jaw.

Kir sighed. She didn't need any potions to mask her pain, but then, she wasn't about to tell them why she had *really* cried out. That she was attempting to kiss the handsome prince who held her in a dream. "Fine. If it makes you feel better."

"We're trying to make *you* feel better," Vann responded, pulling the blanket back over her legs.

"How do you know what it tastes like, anyway?" Kir asked. She sipped at the edge of the cup and crossed her eyes for dramatic effect.

"I had to get it in you somehow." Vann blushed and bit his lip, gauging her reaction.

It took a minute for the implication to register in Kir's mind. "Couldn't you have used a cup?"

"We tried that," Vann admitted sheepishly, yet there was a hint of mischief in his expression. "It kept trickling out. I liked my method better. Not a drop spilled."

"Well, better you than the wench-machine," Kir shrugged, feigning indifference. Part of her wished Vann could have used the same method this time. His lips pressed against hers would have distracted her from the horrific flavor. It would have made flowers from manure of this vile task.

Sipping at the foul concoction was only prolonging the discomfort, so Kir swiped the cup from Malacar's hand and knocked it back swiftly in one gulp.

Malacar seemed satisfied. He rose and started out the doorway to the parlor beyond. "I'm relieving Scilio on watch. Behave yourself, Kir. You set your healing back two days with your little jaunt yesterday and I don't want you to exert yourself. If you give His Majesty any trouble, the offer is still in effect." He held his fist aloft again, grinning, then slipped out the door.

"I think he expects me to be difficult," Kir mumbled.

"Of course," Vann laughed. "It's you."

Kir threw him an insulted look. "When have I ever been difficult?"

"Oh, I can think of a few times. Remember Southport? You grumbled every time I even offered you a cup of water. You're not the best patient, Kiri."

Kir smirked, remembering the week she was laid up in Southport. How much had changed since then! "I'm a fine patient. Just hate being roped and hogtied, that's all."

"Then prove it. Let me do something for you."

"What?" Kir raised a wary eyebrow.

Vann sat up on his knees and stretched across Kir, his fingers fumbling with odds and ends on the nightstand table. His hand returned clutching a familiar wooden box. She bit her lip and turned her eyes away as he clicked the latch and opened the lid.

"No," Kir said, but it came out as more of a squeak.

Vann picked up the silver brush from Palinora's case and rubbed his fingers along the fine swirled etchings. "Please? You didn't object while you were sleeping. I could always ask Malacar to come back and..." Vann held up his fist jokingly.

It wasn't the act that Kir feared, but the intimacy it invited. Her heart was already tuned to Vann's at an alarming frequency, and just talking with him seemed to perfect that harmonic chord. She could think of no good reason to argue against him, though. "Whatever makes you happy. If it helps improve the scenery around here..."

Vann chided her with his eyes. He placed the soft brush at the top of her head and began sweeping it gently down the lengths of her chestnut mane. He might as well have been massaging her entire body, as Kir could feel herself getting more drowsy with every stroke.

To keep from falling asleep, she grumbled a few half-hearted complaints in Dimishuan. She didn't know their exact translations, but it didn't matter. Their purpose was clear.

"What's wrong? You don't enjoy this?" Vann asked, drawing the brush down at her temple.

Of course she did! It was the sweetest thing anyone had ever done for her, but she couldn't tell him that. "It's just not right, that's all. For a prince to be catering to someone else. Should be the other way around. I've been telling you to *be the people*, but you're just too damned close to the people, Stick. Monarchs should never know the bottom of the world."

"How can a ruler know what's best for his people unless he lives as one?"

Kir considered the statement. "So, you think holding my hand when I'm injured will make you a better ruler?"

"No. But I hope it will make me a better person."

"You can't improve upon perfection," Kir said honestly. The moment the words left her mouth, she cursed herself. It was too affectionate an observation, and she didn't want to invite Vann any closer than he already was. She doubted her strength to push him away.

And yet, to Kir's surprise, she *wanted* him to pamper her. Something in her heart tickled at the thought of him holding her hand and fussing over her. No one had ever cared for her in that way. Not her parents. Certainly not Tarnavarian. Vann was the first person who saw something in Kir worth loving.

Vann stopped brushing and was silent for a long moment. He stared at a vase of flowers on the bedside table. "Sans the red speckles, ithinar would only be another white flower. A specimen is only perfect when it is whole."

Kir understood his words entirely. In Vann's eyes, she was the speckles to his ithinar. She completed his imperfect flower, like he had done for her. "A King doesn't need a Guardian to make him whole, Vann."

"No. There's only one thing that makes me whole." Vann stared at his hands. He glanced at Kir's, folded across the blanket, and he seemed to hesitate, as though he were toying with a notion. His jaw clenched suddenly. "I was so scared, Kiri. The thought of never being whole again... of losing..." his voice cracked.

The conversation was getting dangerous, and Kir could not escape. Her mind was still suspended just a breath away from her body; she was trapped at Vann's mercy. Instinctively, she wanted to lash out like a cornered wildcat, but something held her back. She couldn't bring herself to hurt him, as she had before. Instead, she could turn the subject away from herself. Kir snatched up the brush and returned it to the case.

"It'll be hard, Vann. But Palinora is gone forever. You'll have to be whole without her."

Vann's eyes glazed. He looked away, seeming embarrassed at himself. "I wasn't talking about..." He hesitated, and Palinora's name seemed to die on his lips. His eyes registered the bed across the room. The undisturbed blankets that remained empty, save the ghost of a memory.

Kir felt Vann's underlying depression multiply tenfold. She needed no Psychonics to feel it radiating from him, powerful and potent. He'd lost his parents and his trust in the King all at once, and there had been little room for closure in any of it. As always, he had been hiding his insecurities behind a smile, and Kir understood that a moment of release before a grave would not mend so deep a fractured spirit. He was just as wounded as she was. Breaking of the heart was much harder to heal than breaking of the body. Vann was in dire need of bandaging.

*What would Master Kozias do?*

Kir searched her memory for any hint of advice that might prove useful in this situation. Nothing was springing to mind that didn't involve wenching, drinking or running.

Okay, from a tactical standpoint, then. The best strategy here was a diversion. In this case, a lot of them. Only one thing seemed to distract Vann from his depression, and that was Kir. Distancing herself from him didn't seem so important anymore. Not when he was hurting so much. Not when he needed her.

Kir knew what she must do. She would use what she had, just as she had taught the Vipers. Even an infirmity could be used as a tool. All she had to do was play it up a bit.

She slipped her hand over Vann's and squeezed it gently. "I'm a little thirsty. That potion's left an aftertaste worse than Scilio's swill." She sat up and stretched toward the water pitcher that was well out of her reach, waiting for Vann to intercede.

He sprang upward, sorrow forgotten, and pushed Kir back. "No you don't! Let me."

She bit her lip to suppress a grin. He was so easy to manipulate.

## -58-
## A Kingly Gift

*The best gift anyone ever gave me was the permission to be myself.* - Master Kozias

Kir stretched her arms high and tested her muscles, deeply breathing in the fresh air that teased through the open window. Every bitty iota of her being protested, but she forced the matter anyway, as much for show as for function.

"Morning," Malacar greeted, handing Kir a bowl of soupy rice porridge. "Or afternoon, if you want to be technical."

She thanked him with more gusto than her appetite demonstrated. He frowned as she picked at it.

"It's not Scilio's handiwork. It's quite safe," Malacar prodded.

"I heard that," Scilio muttered. He threw in his hand as Vann claimed the pot of empty potion bottles and herb packages.

The medicines, bandages and sundries that had littered the table had been pushed aside for the game. In the three days since she had awoken, it was the first time Vann had diverted his attention, and Kir was glad he was finally starting to resume some of the old habits. Until this morning, he hadn't left her side, hovering like a dragonfly over a lilypad.

It was wrong to exploit his gullibility, but her ploy had worked, keeping Vann's mind off depressing subjects and focused on her. All it took was a small wince or fluttering of her eyelashes to spur him to action. He would grasp her hand supportively and soothe her with his calming voice. He did everything possible to ensure her comfort, even singing her to sleep. It would have been terribly romantic, were she somebody else. Somebody beautiful and noble and whole. Somebody meant for him.

It was true that she wanted to keep Vann from sliding into the pit of despair, but Kir also allowed his indulgence for another, more self-serving reason. It would be the last time Vann would be able to devote his entire attention to her without an audience. She was selfish for these last few days as the center of Vann's world, before he returned to the formality of his royal position.

"Guardian Scilio, fetch Dailan from his guard post on the roof. It seems Guardian Ithinar requires his service in the spoon-feeding capacity," Malacar stated, with more than a little mirth in the suggestion.

As Kir grumbled and shoveled an unwelcome bite into her maw, Vann jumped up. "No need. I'm right here."

Kir rolled her eyes and fought the urge to fling the bland gunk at both their targets. "I'm eating, already. And you can stow that smug grin, you clinquant... fustian..." She stared down the chortling bard, stumbling through her dwindling repertoire of descriptives.

"Is that the best you can do? One would think after three days of staring at the ceiling, you would have mustered a better arsenal than you're launching," Scilio said slyly. "You saturnine skulldugger."

Kir scowled. "My nouns have run aground. Letch."

Vann plopped himself at Kir's bedside and nudged the bowl to remind her of its presence. "Things are starting to sound more normal around here. A week ago, I didn't think I'd ever hear this banter again."

There was a canyon-wide smile in the words that covered over the darkness behind the truth in them. Kir wasn't quite sure how Vann had managed to snag her away from the greedy grasp of the Soul Collectors, or how they had scraped up enough mana to heal even a nicked finger. That Snakey blue fire had drained Vann dry, and neither he, nor Malacar, boasted more than rudimentary Healing knowledge between them. Kir wondered if it was simply the emotion of the moment that was driving them. People had been known to do amazing things under the most dire of duress.

The makeshift Healing duo had expressed their hems and haws over their own work. They decided to have Kir seen by a Master Healer as soon as they could find one, to undo any mistakes they might have made. She hoped it was sooner than later, although she wouldn't dare express that thought aloud and renew the worry that was finally beginning to fade in their eyes.

When Vann's back was turned, Scilio waved to Kir and gestured to the door. She blinked acknowledgment. They needed Vann out of the room for some sneaky surreption, and it was her cue to implement the haphazard plan.

"A week ago, you were more branch than stick, but I think the stick might be trying for a comeback," Kir commented, pinching Vann's bicep. "Here. This will put some meat on those bones." She handed over her bowl. "When you're done, I think a round of sparring is in order. It's been a while, and you're out of practice."

Vann sniffed the spoon and tasted the gruel, then dunked it back for a heaping serving. "You don't get off that easy. You're not much more than a slip, yourself. Let's see about putting some meat on *your* bones." He wagged the spoon before Kir's mouth like a mother trying to coax her infant to open. "Unbatten that hatch, Guardian Ithinar."

"If you would be so kind, Lunchbox," Kir begged, "I can't get any decent repose with the doting dragonfly hovering overhead. Would you take him up to spar? He needs to pour himself over something other than my welfare, for once this week."

"Only if you promise to get that bowl emptied," Malacar said.

"On my honor as a Guardian. It'll be licked clean upon your return. Have fun whacking each other."

"We may be gone a while. I want to rotate the horses on stand-by and His Majesty can help me rub them down," Malacar reported. There was no way to access the skiff bay for the Lock Barrier that lacked a key, but the manor's stables and open pastures were loaded with stock. Malacar had been keeping six horses saddled, packed and ready every day, just in case a quick escape was in order.

"Send Dailan down, would you?" Kir said. "I have a job for him."

Malacar acknowledged and threw in a quick wink. He knew his role was to keep Vann away for a spell, and he wouldn't fail.

Vann handed Kir the bowl and tousled her bangs, then scooped up his sword from its post near the door. "If you need me, I won't be far."

"I thought he would never leave," Kir sighed as the latch clicked behind him.

"It is simply impossible to plan a birthday celebration when the celebree is hopelessly stuck to the planner. I was about to suggest a jaunt to the gardens, but your idea was even better. He needs an outlet for his penned energies," Scilio said.

It was Vann's eighteenth birthday, but they had all been conveniently forgetful of that fact in his presence. Kir wondered if Vann was even aware of the date, himself. If they had been in High Empyrea, it would have been a lively week of shindiggery. The entire country would have ceased routine to pickle its liver in grog at the toast of its future King. The inn was a far cry from royal ballrooms, but the Guardians would celebrate anyway. They decided to surprise him with a party. Or, as much of a party as could be considered with three Guardians and a young boy.

Kir hadn't the slightest clue what gift to offer. She thought about writing a poem or some such gushy-mush, but she wasn't much of a wordsmith to begin with, and there wasn't a moment that Vann wasn't in view. She would just have to think of some other gift for him. What tribute she could find that would be fitting for a prince, Kir couldn't fathom, though, and she was now out of time.

Dailan scurried into the room. "You called?"

Kir handed over her porridge bowl. "Lunch. Hope you're hungry."

"Needs salt," Dailan appraised, but he devoured the bowl in seconds anyway.

"Now that we schemers are ready to scheme..." Scilio began. He produced a sack from under Kir's bed. It was loaded with decorations and prism glass that Dailan had ransacked from different rooms. "Shall we hold the joyous festival in this room, or in the parlor?"

"The parlor, pleeeease," Kir urged. "I'm tired of staring at the same dull walls and the same hungry vulture that looks to want my liver for a pate'. There's more natural light in there, anyway. It will make those prisms sing their rainbows out."

"The plumed scavenger would likely go for your kidneys or eyeballs first," Scilio corrected with all the sly of a fox. "With regards to the parlor, I agree. I'll go place my magic touch." He plopped a sack of potatoes on the bed and offered over a small knife. He directed Kir to peeling and Dailan to fireplace duty, then slipped out to the parlor for his gussy-work.

While Dailan set the stock pot to boiling in the hearth, Kir rummaged through her brain to come up with a tribute worthy of eighteen and royalty. She was left short.

Scilio returned dancing at his self-admired genius. "The room has been kissed by my touch. All we lack now is the food."

He cozied up next to Kir on the bed to aid with potato duty. She was about to knock his history of culinary execution, but thought better of it. His knife was peeling away some of her own chore, and she welcomed the help.

"What are you giving Vann?" Kir asked as they worked.

"There's only one gift I own worthy of a Prince," Scilio replied suavely. He wiped his hand and produced a collection of small magi-captures from a pouch on his belt. The color-framed edges of the pictures were dog-earred and ragged. He caressed them adoringly and handed them over. "These are my precious beauties. Which do you think he would fancy the most?"

They were captures of women, posed in dramatic flair, and sunny-side-up, every one. The back of each capture listed information about the lady. Things like their favorite foods, hobbies, and even their pets' names.

Dailan popped his head over Scilio's shoulder. His eyes widened in awe.

"You want to give Vann...the *Crown Prince*...a nekkid-lady

picture?" Kir choked.

Scilio turned his nose up in offense. "Why not?" he asked in unison with a delighted Dailan.

"Oh, I can see it now, adorning the Kingly mantle. It would be a super conversation piece for King Vannisarian's noble courtesans," Kir cackled.

"Royal though he may be, Vann is still a man. What man would not fancy a Berndian Beauty of his very own?"

"A Berndian Beauty?"

"Oh, come now! You've never heard of the Berndian Beauties of Cuttis Corner?"

Kir stared dumbly.

"They're only the most beautiful and talented women in the whole of Septauria. They can perform magics upon a man that put the whores of noble Empyrea to shame, let me tell you! They can render a man speechless, powerless and trapped in fantasy for nights on end."

"Mmmm, sounds like buckets of fun," Kir said. "And you've experienced this, have you?"

Scilio paused. "Well, no. No, I haven't."

"Me neither," Dailan said wistfully.

Kir harrumphed.

"Many colleagues of the muse have sung passionately of the Berndian charms. I need no experience for validation," Scilio insisted.

"Seems to me that men who talk the most about wenching are the ones getting the least of it," Kir said.

"Can I see the others?" Dailan asked.

Scilio happily shared the captures, pointing out particular features he liked the best.

"Don't be polishing his eyeballs on such flash, Ponytail," Kir scolded.

"I seen lotsa naked women before," Dailan countered.

The Dimishuans were not encumbered with modesty, but Kir twisted a skeptical lip anyway.

"I have! I seen *you* a couple times."

"Keh! Name one."

"When they was dressing you for bed whilst you was ailing."

"Is that so?" Kir tried to hide her mortification with a false nonchalance.

"Yup. Guardian Scilio says he's never seen a more glorious, heaven-sculpted set of—"

Scilio's hand clasped over Dailan's mouth. "Ah, the child has such an imagination..."

"For your safety, I'm gonna pretend I didn't hear that," Kir said shortly.

"Now now, Kir, you look near apoplexy. Perhaps you should lie down..."

Dailan pulled out from under Scilio's hand. "What? I didn't spin you no yarns. You're always sayin' a cup of truth holds more weight than a pot of lies..."

Kir rolled her eyes to gloss it over. "Keh! Gimme them."

She snatched the stack and examined each capture in turn, finally settling on a gorgeous blond-haired woman with a hive of ringlet curls and plump breasts. Cerulean feathers adorned her hair, and she was surrounded by cornflower and foofaraw.

Kir presented the chosen capture. "This is the one he'd like. Blue's his color."

Scilio's expression fell. "But that's Emadella. She's my chosen, as well."

Kir shrugged and resumed her peeling.

Scilio muttered to himself for a moment, then he seemed to have come to a decision. "For certain?"

"Sure as sunlight." Kir couldn't help but notice that Emadella represented everything that she was not. Blond, beautiful, robust and plump with rosy cheeks and smooth, powdered skin. Unscarred skin.

*Emadella must live a wonderful, happy life*, Kir thought longingly. She wondered what the life of an Enchantment Whore must be like, with all its finery and glamor. *What an amazing existence...*

Kir shook her head, banishing the ludicrous thoughts from her mind. *Berndian Beauties must be able to enchant people through these captures*. If that were true, it was a brilliant marketing ploy on their part. What better way to entice a man and lure him to their charms than to sell enchanted captures?

"It's for my liege and best friend," Scilio reminded himself. "I'll do it for him."

"I'm sure Vann'll let you borrow her now and again," Kir offered.

He seemed to brighten at that idea, and the deck of Beauties slid back into the pouch. "So, what about you, Kir? What mark of affection shall you bequeath on our treasured prince?"

"I don't know," she admitted. "I was hoping you might have some ideas, but..." She considered the letch's notion of a proper gift and began to have second thoughts.

"I got stashes," Dailan offered. "The dunnage in this joint was ripe for the picking. If you want for it, I'll fish up a prime little fancy you can give him, Saiya Kunnai."

"Thanks, but I think it needs to be something a little more special than plundered trinkets."

"I can think of one beauteous bounty a woman can bestow upon her doting dragonfly..." Scilio bobbed his eyebrows.

"Gods, but you think with the wrong brain!" Kir flicked a potato peel at his face to wipe away his expression, but it fell short. "Why are we still talking about naked women?"

"I said no such thing. Who has the dirty mind here?"

*Something special*, Kir thought. *What gift, in all the world, could be worthy of Vann?*

## -59-
## Birthdays

*Choose your name with care, for they will etch
it upon your tombstone.* - Master Kozias

Scilio had done a dandy job in hanging up an atmosphere. The parlor didn't look like a ballroom, but it was ball enough for their purposes. Kir couldn't help but marvel at the rainbows splayed on every wall. She leaned back on her settee cushion and followed the dance of light from the prisms.

Dailan slammed the heavy suite doors and bounded across the room like a scurrying mouse. "He's coming!"

As Scilio vanquished the Inferno lamps, Dailan clench-closed the draperies to stifle the natural sun from the room. He hid behind Kir's settee and bobbed like a cork.

Teetering on the edge of excitement at their measly little surprise, Kir suddenly felt a twinge of regret. It was nothing on the scale of what Vann deserved, and they were two settings short of the table that should have been. She stowed the unhappy thought away so it wouldn't cast a shadow or hint a frown.

When the latch shifted and the hinge squeaked open, the door framed a familiar silhouette. Scilio launched a quick Inferno to the lamp and the blaze accompanied the chorus of exclamations.

Vann's quick hand fell instinctively to his sword hilt, and he stepped back into a defensive stance. A paper lantern fell from its shoddily-tied string over the door, and Vann's blade made no hesitation in cleaving it twain.

Dailan's belated flutey-horn bleated a pathetic little note of cheer.

Scilio stared dumbly for a moment. "There shall be no gifting of puppies in our disagreeable group, I suppose."

When Vann blinked away the defense and registered the occasion, he sheathed his sword and slapped his forehead. "Leave it to me to ruin a perfectly staged surprise."

The good-natured rounds made their way through the room in boisterous jolly. Dailan flooded the room with sunlight and dancing rainbows when the drapes slid apart. Malacar slipped up from behind and offered Vann a glass of vintage Beckett.

"Really, this wasn't necessary," Vann told them, accepting the goblet humbly. "But I appreciate it, all the same. Honestly, I didn't even realize it was my birthday."

Scilio loaded Vann's bowl with stew and dunking bread, then

handed it over. Vann thanked him and brought it straight to Kir.

"Since you haven't eaten today..." he said, brandishing his spoon in front of her face. He slid next to her on the settee.

"My bowl was licked clean, just like I said it would be," Kir countered, but she slurped up the juicy broth all the same. It was leagues tastier than the rice slop.

"But who's tongue did the licking?" Malacar tutted, glancing at Dailan, who was already wrist-deep in the fruit bowl. "I know you too well, Kir. His Majesty always says that technicalities can make or break diplomacy."

"That's right," Kir said, taking a bite of mushy carrot from Vann's spoon. She shoveled a bite of meat into his mouth. He seemed perfectly content to share. "But I don't recall you specifying a named bowl-licker. I like technicalities when they work in my favor."

Malacar opened up the gift-giving moment with a parchment-wrapped square. "A warrior's heart demands a warrior's hobby. Here's to fair winds and cordial birthdays, Majesty."

Vann peeled away the packaging of colorful Hilian patterened papers.

"I'll teach you how to fold some simple designs later," Malacar said. "In the warrior class, we learn as young children how to manipulate objects from paper to focus our attentions. Executing perfect designs with no consciousness diverted from the surroundings makes for a honed warrior."

Kir had wondered why his fingers so enjoyed crafting their little trinkets, and it suddenly made a heap of sense. Malacar had always been dry up with his past, and to share a tidbit of it now made the day seem that much more intimate, in Kir's eyes.

Vann saluted his thanks and examined the papers proudly. "I've always wanted to learn how to shape a dragon like you can. I look forward to the lesson, Denian."

Scilio plopped next to Vann on the settee to offer over his own gift. He produced a handkerchief concealing the capture of Emadella and handed it over reluctantly.

"Take good care of her, Majesty," Scilio choked back a dramatic and phony tear. "I shall miss our time together, my darling."

Vann studied the capture, then poked Scilio in the ribs with his elbow. "You know her? Can you provide me an introduction?"

Scilio grinned devilishly. "If we ever get around to Cuttis Corner, I would be delighted to present you, my Liege."

Vann slapped Scilio on the back. "Thanks, Toma. It will look fantastic on my mantle someday... when I'm King."

"That's just what Kir said."

Dailan bounced from his perch on a chair back and scrambled upright before Vann. "I think *my* gift's the best," he reported proudly, handing Vann a stack of worn captures. Berndian Beauties.

As Vann fanned them for appraisal, Scilio's eyes narrowed.

"Wait a moment..." He ripped open his pouch frantically, searching through its contents. "You little freebooter..."

Scilio shot after Dailan, chasing him around the room to impart some manners on his backside. Dailan was always a step quicker, and Scilio finally admitted defeat, sinking into a chair beside Malacar to catch his breath.

Vann convulsed with laughter. "How generous of you, Dailan."

Scilio sighed despondently. "I don't suppose you'd be willing to share?"

Kir hung up in Vann's sparkling gaze but her ribcage objected to her own laughter. She put a damper on to preserve her tender innards. Seeing Vann cutting up was worth all the custards and Arcardian teas she'd ever pleasured across her lips.

"I suppose it's my turn." Kir set the bowl aside and threw the blanket off her legs. She wished she'd been outfitted in her tabard for its purpose, but it would have looked as out of place over her silky pale nightgown as a petticoat on a pig.

"I didn't really know what to give you. What do I have to offer the Crown that I haven't already given?" she began.

All the prior amusement fled away for the solemnity in the statement. The room went quiet, save the crackling of the fire in the hearth.

"When we first met, Your Majesty, I swore an oath to protect you without truly understanding what that meant. I gave you my word, but I didn't give you my loyalty. I was a Guardian in name, while in my heart you were just a means to an end. I had determined to die for you. Now, I only want to *live* for you. And so, this is the only gift I can bestow that can hold the depth of me."

Kir lowered herself gingerly to the floor at Vann's feet and bowed as submissively as her body would allow.

"I, Kiriana Ithinar, do swear to protect and serve, to offer up my body and soul to ensure the safety of my Lord, Crown Prince Vannisarian Ellesainia. This Oath I do take, offered freely and knowingly, as a Guardian of the Crown, until His Majesty releases me or the Gods welcome me into their deathly embrace," she recited, then added, "With all my heart."

"Kiri," Vann breathed. He stared at her profoundly.

"My heartbeat is no longer my own. I am your Guardian, Your Majesty. Not because I have to be. Because I *want* to be."

Vann eased her up and returned her to the settee. When Kir met his gaze, it was the countenance of command, of royalty, staring back at her. He was not Vann at this moment, she realized. He was Prince Vannisarian.

"Guardian Ithinar, what you give now honors me beyond measure," Vann stated. "You have always shown great courage in the face of danger and you have always stood before me, whether I asked you to or not. Nothing made you protect me on that first morning in the Hatchel, yet you were Guardian to me, even then. Your valor has been apparent, and your will steadfast.

"You claim to be an ithinary creature. Yet, there are four people in this very chamber who consider you family. You no longer require such a lonely name. This may be *my* birthday, but perhaps today *you* have been born anew. No longer will you be known as Ithinar. Henceforth, you shall be Kiriana Valoria."

Kir was overcome with sudden emotion and she smiled through unexplained tears that rolled down her cheeks. She had never been given so royal a gift. Not even when she had been betrothed to a royal. Vann sat beside her on the cushion and hugged her to his chest with a gentle, yet firm pressure that filled her with more warmth than the fire in the hearth could ever have wished to. Kir felt her talisman come rushing back like a swelling tide, filling in every jagged cranny of her defense with solidarity.

"Thank you," she whispered in his ear. "I didn't know honor could be gift-wrapped."

Malacar and Scilio both knelt and pulled her into their own impatient arms in turn.

"Happy re-birthday to you, Guardian Valoria," Scilio chimed.

"I'm honored to consider you a brother," Malacar told her.

"Brother?" Scilio piped. "If she qualifies as a brother, does she qualify to bathe with us?"

Kir cuffed the back of Scilio's head playfully. "Only in your dreams. On second thought, not even then."

Scilio and Malacar retreated merrily to their seats and began devouring their stew with greedy appetite.

Vann tugged Kir sideways into the crook of his shoulder. There was no place she would rather be than wrapped in his arms and Valoria's honor.

## -60-
## Fortuitous Encounter

*Don't be fooled by the innocence in puppy dog eyes. They wag their tails to our delight, but while we think they say, "I love you," what they really mean is "Feed me." - Master Kozias*

The black spiral unfolded around Keeper Mardas as he emerged from his cloak's vortex into shadow. He was one with the stone for a moment while his eyes skipped across the vacant lobby. It was a chamber that should have been bustling with comers and goers in this peak season. Patrons should have been traveling from suite to hot spring and back again. Instead, the room was strewn asunder, black with cinder and ash that left swirled ribbons painted across the walls and charred beams. By the debris field and char patterns, it looked like a work of magic. Perhaps a weak Inferno Ruptor.

It was a shame that such a fine chamber had come to ruin. Mardas had fond memories of the Arshenholm Manor. He'd brought his wife there on honeymoon twelve years before, so it held a special place of nostalgia in his heart. He'd not been able to afford the trip again, but his knowledge of the local area had lent him well to the scouting position he'd been assigned.

It was a vital role he was filling. There were many small mining towns along the Arshenholm, which made for many hiding places. The Keeper scouts had their work cut out for them. Mardas needed to find clues regarding the Chaos Bringer's whereabouts, and the manor had been high on the list of potential hideouts. The mages were limited in their shadow-hopping capacity, so if their force were to mobilize to a specific location, it must be the right one.

When he was confident that he was alone, he stepped out from the shadowed corner and removed his oval mask for a better look. The Luminas spell that was inlaid into the mask allowed the wearer to see clearly from the shadows, but Mardas wished there was some spell to make them more comfortable. Breathing stagnant air and sweat behind a wall of heavy mask was not to his appeal. Despite the benefit to seeing in the dark, he wished there was no need for the wretched thing. The order insisted that an icon of fear commanded respect, and he wasn't one to argue with ages of tradition.

Mardas slipped toward the west wing with the stealth of an owl. He poked his head into what had once been an office, but now looked to be the ghost of a battlefield. Broken furniture littered the floor and dark stains blackened the colorful patterns of what had been an expensive rug. How many died here, he wondered?

Mardas continued down the hall to the first disrobing room and he bent over to examine a bit of debris on the ground near the doorway. He still had no information to report, save the occurrence of a battle and the abandonment of the manor, so any clue would be welcome. The clinking of coins shattered the silence and Mardas' head shot up. On the other side of a bench, a dark head of hair bobbed and up popped a young Dimishuan slave. His fist was clenched around a gunny sack and his other hand was rooting through the pockets of a pair of trousers.

When the boy registered Mardas' presence, he jerked and froze. They stared at each other for a few moments, sharing their shock in company.

"Hello there," Mardas said finally, when he thought the boy might run. "It's okay. I won't harm you."

The boy's eyes flicked to the door and back.

"Are you alone?"

The boy tried for a nod.

"I have a son about your age. Do you like sweets?" Mardas

fished through his hip pouch for the Delfie Doodles he'd stashed the day before. "Here. These are my son's favorite. I bet you'd like them, too."

When the boy didn't move, Mardas approached the bench slowly. He needed some answers to take back to Keeper Wardion, and charred walls didn't say much. If he could get the boy to talk, his job might be over that much sooner and he could get on about his business.

"Do you live here?" Mardas placed the sack of sweets on the bench and backed away.

The boy shook his head cautiously and his hand inched toward the prize. He snatched it up and sniffed the candy, then popped one in his mouth.

"I'm only looking for information," Mardas said. "I just need to know what happened here, so I can report back to my superiors. My *own* masters, that is. Then, I can go home to my son and family. If you would help me, I would be most grateful."

The boy gnawed on the doodle thoughtfully. "I might could help."

"Thank you. This place is pretty creepy, don't you think? I'd just as soon put it behind me. I'm Nendel Mardas. What is your name?"

The boy hesitated for a moment, before answering, "Dailan."

"Where are you from, Dailan?"

"Here and there..." he said carefully. He bit his lip for a moment, then nodded his head like he had solidified his confidence. "Actually, I live with my master on the coast."

"Ah! Sandbridge, maybe?"

Dailan bobbed his head quickly. "That's it. Sandbridge."

Mardas smiled. "I'm from Suncrest. Where is your master now?"

"Well, he's not here..." Dailan said. "What I mean is, he's dead. I buried him in the back yonder."

"So there was a battle here? Tell me all you know, please."

"There was a battle. It was...big. With lots of....lots of kaiyo all around. They were real scary, so I hid. Everyone else got killed but me. And they're all buried in the back. So it's just me now. No one else."

Mardas inhaled sharply. "Everyone? That must have been terrible for you."

There had been rumors of kaiyo attacks becoming more frequent, and being so close to Arcadia meant that southern Aquiline was at the front line. That fact had limited the population growth in the southern half of the island, unlike the north that was booming with civilization. He didn't realize that the attacks were occurring so far inland, and it was a concern to a man with a wife and children. It was one reason he had taken up the family legacy and joined the Keepers of Magic. Just as his father had done, Mardas would gladly wear the cloak to protect his family, and the purity of magic. He only hoped he would not have to participate in an all-out kaiyo war. His father had not come home from Cerener Valley. He didn't want to leave his own son fatherless, as he had been.

"Dailan, did you see a young man with blond hair come here? He would have been with a beautiful noblewoman and three protectors. I need to know if he was here."

The boy blinked and narrowed his eyes like he was trying to locate the memory. "Oh yeah! I remember them folk!"

Mardas' heart did a dance in his chest. He was finally getting somewhere.

"Yup. They was here. Right before the battle, the man said he was a prince," Dailan reported.

"That is the very same person I am looking for. Where is he now?"

"Oh, he died. Him and the pretty blond lady that he said was the Queen. They're buried in the garden."

"They are dead? You are certain?"

"Sure. The prince's own Guardians buried them. I can show you..." Dailan started for the door and waved to invite Mardas along.

The boy moved so fast Mardas had to jog to keep up. They exited the manor and mazed through the garden pathways until they came to a white stone mound.

"This is it," he reported proudly.

Mardas approached the mound with reverence. The prince was to be the end of times, but he was still a man, and it was still a grave. It deserved respect. A royal seal lay across the top stones, and Mardas moved to brush his fingers over the embossing. A fuschia crackle bit his hand, and he snapped it back from the sting.

"A Lock Barrier to keep the grave from plunder," he noted aloud. "That is, indeed, the royal crest. You say they are both buried here? It looks to be a small grave for two."

Dailan bobbed his head. "They were mother and son, so they were put to rest arm in arm. A real tragic, beautiful thing, that."

"And what of the Guardians that did the burying?"

"They're dead too. By the kaiyo that came later. I can show you their graves," Dailan offered.

When they arrived at a long scar of earth in the courtyard, Dailan pointed. "That there is where the rest of the inn folks and the Guardians are."

Mardas nodded. "You're a brave lad, Dailan, taking a man's job like this. I'd better dig them up and see for myself. Where is the shovel you used?"

Dailan hesitated. "You can't. I mean, I don't remember where I buried them. There was an awful lot of people, you see, and I was beside myself with bawling. So, they could be anywhere in that big ditch of rotting corpses."

Mardas grimaced. It looked to be a long morning, and he didn't fancy defiling a grave. His superiors, however, would need facts and witness. "Well, I'd better get started."

"I wouldn't do that, if'n I was you," Dailan said quickly. "The stench is almighty powerful. It took me three days to quit from puking in all that nasty."

Mardas wrinkled his nose at the idea. "You're right. I'm a scout, not a grave robber."

Dailan displayed a large smile. "I guess you better be off then, mister. You don't want to keep your masters waiting."

"Too true. Since you aided me, let me return the favor. In a few hours, this manor will be alive with my colleagues. They will come here to secure the location and find the bodies of the Guardians for their proof. If I were you, I would make myself scarce, Dailan. I'm not saying they would bring you harm, but as you are masterless now, they would likely find a new home for you to serve. My advice? Head south to Hili. I've heard that escaped slaves can find a home there without the collar."

Dailan started and blinked. He was probably surprised that a free Alakuwai would give him such advice.

"I have no quarrel with the Hilians," Mardas explained. "While some would have the world believe they are barbarians, they've brought me good business. So long as they pose no threat to magic and Order, I don't have a problem with them."

Dailan shook his head slowly, steadily. "But...there's no time..."

"Don't worry. I'll buy you a little. I can't promise much, but two hours should get you a good head start to Hili. Be careful to avoid the Keeper army along the river. They're slowly moving north as they comb the valley for the prince. I wish you luck, son."

Dailan scurried out the door like a dragon was on his heels. Mardas chuckled and folded into his cloak's vortex.

He busied himself in his tent and let two hours tick by before he submitted his request for an audience. He hoped Dailan had utilized his time and was well on his way to a new life.

Grand Master Wardion wasted no time in summoning Mardas to the command tent, and he looked to be in a foul mood. He always looked that way, Mardas noted.

"What is the status of the Arshenholm Manor?" he asked impatiently.

"I think you will find my report most thrilling," Mardas answered. "I have evidence that the royal party has been defeated there."

Wardion's chair clattered against the floor as he jumped from it. "What? Tell me!"

"We will need a party of gravediggers to verify, but there was a massive kaiyo attack. The Prince, Queen and all three Guardians have perished. I witnessed the royal grave myself. The Guardians lie interred with the rest of the establishment's unfortunate patrons."

"And you know this how?"

"By statement of witness."

"Good. Bring him before me."

"He is no longer in our custody," Mardas said carefully. "But that doesn't matter, as we have the graves for proof."

Wardion's tight lips curled upward. It was the first time Mardas had ever seen the man smile, if it actually could qualify as such.

"Keeper Mardas, I know the southern Aquiline chapters of our order do not see much action, save the occasional kaiyo-slay, but you will learn that there are certain procedures to be followed. I would liked to have examined your witness myself. However, I will forgive your error in light of the wonderful news you bring," Wardion scolded, but it held no sharp edge.

"Yes, Grand Master. I apologize for my inexperience."

"So I can keep the records complete, who is this witness, and from where does he hail?" A journal fell open under Wardion's hand, and he chose a quill from his case.

"The boy's name is Dailan."

Wardion's head shot up. "I know that name..."

"I doubt very much that you would know this child. He is a slave. A Dimishuan boy, about eleven years old. His master was a patron at the manor and he was most helpful in showing me the graves." Mardas reported.

Wardion's nostrils flared. "That child is no mere slave. He is the royal party's pet rat, you imbecile."

"But that..." Madras stuttered. He fumbled for comprehension.

"The prince is alive," Wardion barked. "And now we know where."

Wardion flew out the tent flap and shouted mobilization orders to the men. Mardas would not be able to shadow-hop again, as his mana limit of two hops had been met for the day, so he watched as his colleagues disappeared into their vortexes and prayed that his mistake had not cost them the Chaos Bringer.

## -61-
## Saving the Last Dance

*Your enemy is the greatest mirror to
your own weakness.* - Master Kozias

Vann shifted in the saddle, feigning discomfort.

"You okay, Stick?" Kir asked wearily. Her back was molded to Vann's front and her head rested against his chest.

"Just need a break," Vann said, managing a false smile.

He didn't, really, but Kir did, whether she would admit it or not. Her eyes were sunken and dark, her cheeks awash in a pallor that Vann hadn't seen since her injury. It was far too soon to have forced her into the saddle, and Kir was suffering for their haste. Every bump and jolt from the horse's gait worked to unravel a hint of the healing.

"Royals and their uncallused butts," Kir muttered jokingly, but her tone only wished for the humor. She sounded completely spent.

"I think the horses could stand a rest, too," Malacar reported, throwing Vann a visual expression of his own concern.

"We just took a break a league back. The horses are fine. They haven't even worked up a sweat at this snail's pace you've set," Kir argued.

"Snail's pace? We crossed eight leagues in the first frantic two hours, and another three in the two hours since. I'd hardly call that slow when your horse carries a double burden," Malacar said as he dismounted. "Dailan's quick-thinking with the mage bought us some time. We can afford to take a breather."

Kir opened her mouth to argue, but Vann shushed her. "I'm hungry, Kiri. We won't stay long. Let's water the horses and grab some jerky, then we'll get back on the road."

Kir heaved a weighted sigh and threw her eyes toward the ground despondently. Vann didn't have to read her mind to know what she was thinking. She was frustrated with herself and felt that she was holding them back.

It had surprised Vann that Kir had welcomed his attentions in the days since she had awoken. He might have thought it was proof of how sick she was, but it seemed to be a function of something else. There was a bittersweet sorrow in her eyes. As though she were taking in a last meal or song, even though she had her entire life waiting ahead of her.

Vann had decided to withhold any talk of affection. He had wanted to shout that he loved her, to make it echo off every high ceiling in the manor. He'd wanted to pick a handful of the flowers from the garden and present them with a mushy poem that would flood her cheeks with color. He'd wanted to kiss her hand and share his every thought, his every heartbeat. She deserved that, and so much more.

Still, he had refrained. Kir had allowed Vann to *do* for her. To hold her, to sing to her, to profess his love in other, more obscure ways. He was afraid that any outward confessions on his part would only drive her away. If he wasn't careful, she might withdraw the space in which she had allowed him to take care of her.

As Dailan slid off his pony and scrambled to the riverbank to refill his canteen, Malacar tethered their reins. Vann helped Kir's leg over the saddle horn and she slid into Malacar's aid. He eased her against a tree trunk near the water and pressed a flagon into her hands.

"Thanks, Lunchbox," she murmured. It took only moments for her eyes to close.

Malacar lifted her tabard hem to ensure that her wound had not reopened. Satisfied, he joined Vann on the bank, out of Kir's immediate earshot.

In the haste of their retreat, they had decided to head north into the pass to Hafiss. It was a good long day's journey. There, they would hire a healer and a hideout. When Kir was well, they would slip downriver to Hili. That was the plan.

"She needs a healer soon, Denian. She doesn't complain, but the ride is agony. I can feel her getting weaker with every bounce of the horse's stride. I don't know if she can make it all the way to Hafiss."

Malacar's hands rested on his hips and he blew out a tense breath.

Clapping of hooves reverberated off the towering rocky walls that lined the pass. Malacar did not look up. "It's Scilio."

Vann wondered briefly how the big Guardian could identify the rider by the sound. Yet, in just seconds, Scilio bounded from his saddle and trotted toward them. He had been scouting ahead and Vann was surprised to see him back so soon.

"I fear something is amiss," Scilio reported with deep gravity.

From the corner of his eye, Vann noticed Kir open one of hers. "What did you see?"

"That's just it. I didn't. I didn't see anything. Not a single wagon or wanderer on this major route. As this is the only pass between the mountains, I fully expected bustling activity. And yet, not a soul journeys ahead or behind."

Vann's brow creased. "Perhaps an Empyrean blockade. By now the King knows that the ferry went down. I would expect the army to be on the move in our direction, to ascertain my whereabouts. The King will want to know if I survived."

"I don't believe it's the army," Malacar said pensively. "We would have seen scouts, at the very least."

"Kaiyo?" Scilio suggested.

"No. If there were a field of bodies from a kaiyo attack, we would see the carrion birds overhead," Malacar said.

Vann lowered his voice a decibel, aware that Kir was eavesdropping. "Still, if Hafiss is the closest town, it makes sense to press on. If we don't find a healer soon, Kir's life could be at stake."

"If you think a little saddle jaunt is gonna keel me over, think again," Kir said over Vann's shoulder, as though to demonstrate his underestimation. He startled and stepped forward.

"I didn't hear you approach."

"Neither did my Master Kozias. Good thing you're not drinking a brew."

Vann braced her against his side, unwilling to let her stubborn show of bravado sway him.

"It's pretty clear the cloakers are set to waylay us up the road. Let's backtrack and scale the ridgeline east along the mountains," Kir suggested.

"You have no time to do even that," a dainty voice called over

Kir's shoulder.

She spun and stepped back, drawing her shortsword with a speed to make lightning jealous. The exertion of that simple act etched strain across her face, but she held steady.

Vann and the Guardians tensed, hands falling to hilts at Xavien's voice.

"Well aren't you the stealthy weasel?" Kir sneered.

Xavien bowed with mocking grace. "Good thing *you* weren't drinking a brew, Princess."

All of Vann's fears came bubbling from the pit of his stomach at the thought of Kir facing Xavien now. He pushed the dread away and steeled his resolve. For once, he would protect *her*.

Vann and the Guardians moved forward in united motion to stand between Kir and her adversary. Over Xavien's shoulder, Dailan climbed onto a boulder. The boy's eyes widened in thrill for the pending battle.

"Oh dear. You certainly have a dedicated harem, Princess," Xavien said. "And here I merely came to pay my humble respects and return your token."

Kir stood motionless, glowering at Xavien with a promise of murder. Abruptly, her features softened and she casually sheathed her sword. She pushed between their bodily barricade. "Please stand down, gentlemen. He presents no harm today."

She was speaking more formally than usual in the presence of an enemy. In Kir's own words, her speech was intentionally rustic, derived from life at the bottom of the world, and such speech patterns were especially evident while she was engaged in battle. It was clear by her demeanor that she anticipated none here. Vann reluctantly sheathed his weapon and nodded to the Guardians to follow suit.

"For my first order of business, allow me to return that which you so graciously loaned upon our last parting," Xavien said. He flicked his wrist to the folds of his cloak and produced Malacar's Arcadian toothpick, which he smoothly handed over.

"Thanks. I was hoping you'd appreciate the gesture."

Xavien laughed deeply. "My right thigh enjoyed your kiss immensely. What a lovely reminder of your affections."

"How's your shoulder?" Kir quipped.

"How's your side?" Xavien shot back.

A lopsided grin broke Kir's measured expression. "It likes to see the light of day, apparently."

"On that matter, I have come to scold you," Xavien said grimly. "I thought I told you not to die. We have a dance to finish, and Gods forbid you allow my honor to be sullied on the blade of another."

"Do I look dead to you?"

Xavien appraised her from head to boot. "Fairly close, I'd say."

Kir scowled. "If you wish a dance, you should be more complimentary to your partner."

"I know you too well, Princess. You would have no respect for an obvious lie."

"Are you two gonna jaw each other to death, or are you gonna fight? We're burning daylight!" Dailan shouted from his perch.

"What a charming child. I've often heard that pets resemble their owners," Xavien smirked. "Fear not, lad. A fight you will have, soon enough. Though not with me. Which brings me to the secondary purpose of my visit."

"You spoke of having no time," Vann recalled. "Can you enlighten us?"

"You are surrounded by a barrier of Keepers. At the northern mouth of the pass lies an army, meant to stymie His Majesty's Aquilinian forces from coming to your aid. To the south, a contingent meant to block your retreat."

"We're trapped in this pass between two crushing waves of black?" Scilio summarized. "Then, we've naught but two options. Grow wings to fly or claws to dig, for I fear our blades to fight may be underwhelming."

"The only option I implore is the one that leads dear Kiriana straight to that Dimishuan healer brat. And that path is to the south," Xavien said.

"Hili is too far," Vann protested. "Even if we could evade the Keepers, she'd never make it."

"Who said anything about Hili? Bertrand sails up river with the Hilian army even as we speak," Xavien corrected. "But therein lies the problem. The Keepers know they come, and have set a magnificent trap with Forbiddens. If the Hilians are ambushed, the healer will be killed, too. I would advise you to turn south. Battles have been won on the timely turning of an eye, and His Majesty's sudden arrival would provide an instant diversion."

"I dare say the use of Forbiddens is anathema to the Keepers," Scilio argued. "Is not their entire platform built on the protection and purity of magic?"

"When the end is more important than the means, hypocrisy is but a mild inconvenience. I speak this from bitter experience—I'm standing here knee-deep in my own. Wardion will use Forbiddens to prevent their use by others. Or in this case, he'll use them to win, with the former justification qualifying his culpability."

Xavien was as trustworthy as a scorpion. It would make sense that he would lead them to a snare if it suited his purposes. Vann was about to voice the thought when Malacar beat him to it with a snarl.

"After your contemptible history of deception and torment, you expect us to believe you? We'd be walking His Majesty right into the enemy's jaws on your word."

Xavien shrugged. "Quite honestly, my interest in His Majesty's survival is only connected to his Guardian. Kiriana and I have an appointment that cannot be fulfilled if she is dead. By helping the Hilians, I help her, and thus, secure our future dance. Snare Grand Master Wardion's attentions however you wish, or don't—all I offer is the suggestion that such a tactic may very well work, and save the Hilian forces from an instant grave." He flashed a debonair smile under violet eyes, a match in color for Scilio's. Vann filed the curiosity away for future inquiry.

"I don't trust him," Malacar murmured through clenched teeth.

"I do," Kir said simply.

"If Kir backs him, then I will gamble the world on her word. And I won't let Ulivall walk right into a trap," Vann said resolutely. "We go south."

"Well then. It appears my work here is done," Xavien bowed gracefully, with less mockery in his manner than before. "I bid you fair winds, and future dances. Get well for me, Princess."

His cloak folded inward and he disappeared into its vortex.

The moment his hem vanished, Kir's false front faded away, taking with it the strength in her legs. Vann loaded her into the saddle and mounted behind.

"Are we truly to dangle you as bait, or can we devise some more intelligent means of creating a diversion, Vann?" Scilio asked as he adjusted his quiver and grabbed the reins.

"We'll figure it out when we get there. Right now, I'm more concerned about Kir," Vann said.

"I know you want to spare me a jouncing, but there's no room for coddling under a warning of Hilian blood splattering across the valley," Kir said firmly. "I have a high tolerance for pain and a low tolerance for cloakers. I can handle both, so don't hold back on my account. Ride hard, Vann."

Vann squeezed her forearm. "Hang in there for me."

Malacar tossed Dailan onto his own saddle.

"I can ride myself," Dailan snapped.

"That you can, but we fly like dragons now, and my sword can protect you better when you are close," Malacar explained as he mounted behind.

They kicked their horses to urgency and hoped they could close the distance in time to prevent a massacre.

## -62-
## A Festive Hilian Welcome

*To calculate your impact in the world, count how many will fight for you when trouble comes.* - Master Kozias

Ulivall closed the order scroll with a fast Lock Seal and added it to the message satchel. "That's the last. Now we wait to engage."

Copellian, seated behind Ulivall in the longboat, flipped the satchel flap shut. "I'll have eagles deliver them to the commanders when we make landfall."

"I only hope we're not too late," Ulivall said. He cast his sweeping gaze across the river ahead. The enemy was somewhere ahead, just beyond his line of sight.

He had never been more shocked than the evening, twelve past, that Copellian had burst into his shanty. Copellian had hastily recounted the story of the royal ferry and the death of Guardian Arrelius. Eight members of the Hilian entourage died in the valley fighting the mages that had trailed, and the royal party was left with no protection.

Ulivall prided himself in his levelheadedness, but he had to admit, it was difficult to remain calm. Inagor had been a close friend and the first Alakuwai to show him respect as a warrior. The loss would be hard to bear, though he had little time to grieve.

Copellian and the remaining nine warriors had chanced using mage cloaks to transport to the Hili border, rather than pursue the royal party in a wild kappa-chase. Copellian's report had spurred an emergency Circle session and there had been little debate. Elements of Hili's second division, in conjunction with Ferinar's no-longer secret militia, would pursue the royals up the river and give aid, while the remaining forces defended the Dimishuan homeland. They should have accompanied the royals to begin with but there was no time for regrets or recriminations now.

Ulivall had hoped that they would encounter the royal party somewhere between Hafiss and Gander's Ferry, but a messenger eagle from a scout had sent report of a large number of Keepers guarding the southern pass. There was only one thing they would be guarding, and that was a retreat. Which meant that Vannisarian was trapped between the mountains.

"They're still alive, Ulivall," Copellian said, seeming to read the stress in his demeanor. "Those Keepers wouldn't be there otherwise."

"I believe that," Ulivall agreed. "But I fear this path we take will lead to the demise of our people. I wholeheartedly wish to help our Prince. But our numbers are too few to take on the world."

"We don't have to go to war. The Circle did not approve of such an action. Only assistance. There is a difference," Copellian reminded him.

"Is there? By backing Vannisarian, perhaps we invite war from all sides. Ferinar has shown me the King's documents. He is trying to force my hand, and I fear he's right to do so. He calls me passive and cowardly. But his red eyes have never seen the red of blood."

Copellian was silent for a moment. "You are torn, between a peace you cannot have on your own and a prince who can give it to you."

Ulivall cocked his head. "Perhaps. But a war for our people will ultimately mean the end of us. If not as a people, then as a culture. There is no way Hili can remain closed to the world."

Copellian laughed. "I'll never understand how a softhearted peace-lover rose to power as the Grand Master of an army. But if you hadn't, perhaps Ferinar would have us sunk to the bottom of the lake by now."

"In the end, my desire to remain neutral and hidden from the world doesn't matter. Our fates were sealed the day Queen Palinora stepped aboard the Kion. I can't stand against a tide, so I will flow with it."

Copellian was about to speak, but Ulivall waved him silent. Something was different. The birds no longer chirped and there was a palpable stillness.

Eshuen, one of Ulivall's forward scouts, thundered toward them on horseback, ripping through the underbrush near the bank. He threw a hasty hand signal when he spotted Ulivall.

Just ahead, then.

Ulivall signaled silence, followed by the order to disembark. Copellian sprang to action the moment the boat hit the turf, passing the order scrolls to his austringers. It took only ten minutes for his well-trained troops to organize in absolute silence. Surely the mages knew they were coming, but they would come as ghosts on the wind, anyway.

Their formations looked scattered and disorganized to the untrained eye, a deliberate order in the appearance of chaos. Ulivall's men were woodland and wetland fighters, which required the ability to weave through obstacles during battle. When he was satisfied with the preparation, Ulivall signaled the march. Or run, was perhaps a better term.

As his men broke through the high grasses, four lines of Keepers, approximately two hundred or so and evenly spaced across the field, stood at the ready. Almost all had hands up in the preliminary forms of incantation. The Keepers were better known for their individual acts of terrorism, but their increasing organization as a military unit was becoming apparent.

There was a deafening silence in the minutes before his lead units, the Salamanders and Kingfishers, collided with the forward line of Keepers. Suddenly, defiant battle cries rolled across the field. The ring of steel, the shriek of magic, the scent of death wrapped in metallic salinity, all overtook Ulivall's senses. For the briefest of moments, he was lost in the sensation of battle. It was a thrill and a terror, all meshed together. He never lost his calm or the ability to lead, and yet, he still felt removed from his body somehow. It was as close to death, or perhaps true living, as he'd ever felt.

Ulivall fell back to a tactical position on a nearby hill and scanned the field. His numbers were much superior. The mages, however, had more magic at their disposal. And they were acting in unheard of unity. There was no question that the Hili cohort, two thousand strong, would prevail, but he feared their losses would be devastating before victory was at hand.

Twenty minutes into the battle, Ulivall began to breath easier. The Keepers had lost ground steadily, pushed back against the river's edge. The Hilian casualties were minimal by comparison. Ulivall was about to send eagles signaling for the final advance to finish the enemy off, when the mages cast a new and nasty surprise.

Almost in unison, they fell into the recesses of their cloaks and materialized a quarter-league behind the attacking Hilians. The Keepers, moving together, called a living wall of water from the river, upward like the hand of the sea. It swelled well over fifty feet high, and looked hungry enough to swallow the entire Hilian force. No spell to Ulivall's knowledge could summon so extraordinary a feat. It could only be a product of Forbiddens.

Ulivall signaled retreat, but he knew that it was too late. His men were about to meet their fates, and there was nothing he could do about it.

## -63-
## Showdown of Scales and Claws

*In every battle won, there was one brave soul who dared to challenge a God.* - Master Kozias

Kir Valoria felt a wrenching through the lining of her innards. It was not the jarring pain of the hole in her gut. It was a moment of pure dread at what she was about to witness.

They had ridden furiously southward at a four-beat gait, pushing the horses through their wind. Kir had insisted that she could bear the pace, but it had driven her endurance to the limit.

As they had crested a foothill, an impossible mountain of water raised its mighty torso over the Hilian unit at its base. The river that fed their home was about to drown them in a cascade of fury. From the quarter-league between them, the Hilians looked like ants under the foot of a God.

"Don't look, son," Malacar said.

Dailan squirmed out from behind Malacar's shielding hand, awe-struck and horrified, yet unable to look away.

"We didn't make it..." someone said.

Kir could not see Vann's expression, but she could feel his iron grip tighten around her waist. "Avast," he whispered, barely audible but for her proximity.

"Away," he said, this time louder.

Something resonated in Kir, through her vambrace or through Vann's contact, she couldn't tell. A cold flame, embers icy and burning, flared around her and she gasped at the consuming energy. She turned in the saddle and was assaulted by the piercing glow of Vann's flaming blue eyes.

"Vann?!" she screamed, terrified at the horribly beautiful torch that held her.

Vann bellowed a spine-chilling roar that set the foaming sorrel to a dead run.

Kir grabbed frantically for the horse's mane. Vann's arms were steel around her waist to keep her in the saddle, but her hands wanted for a good hold of their own.

The sorrel stumbled and Kir braced herself for the pitch and fall. The animal's chest never hit the grass. A cushion of blue flame pillowed the horse and Kir was certain that it was running in mid-air. The valley around them blurred away at an inconceivable speed as they closed the space in mere seconds. Malacar and Scilio were left ages behind.

Vann flew from the saddle, as sure as lightning, as light as a feather. His feet never touched the ground. The blue flames erupted forth to encase his entire being. It was the same appalling force that had reduced Soreina's henchmen to soot in an eyeblink. If Kir had thought it fearsome in the face of two foes, the Gods themselves must have been trembling as the corrupt power sped toward the plateauing water. It devoured the wave in a deafening roar, dispersing the towering aquaform into a rain shower. Another second later, the azure fury encased the stunned mages. They barely had time to scream.

Vann's head bowed and his arms raised, invoking the angry conflagration into its annihilating spiral. And it was clear this time. There was no mistaking the silvery dragon, long, winding and ferocious, that slithered amongst the tendrils of fire. The fire of the Gods.

Kir's jaw remained agape. Her body would not move. Never, not even in the rain of Balinor, had she been so utterly terrified.

The tender strands of grass, ablaze under icy flames, billowed smoke, and while the Keeper unit lay smoldering in its wake, the dragon still fumed. Vann no longer hovered in the tendrils of flame; his boots were planted firmly in the blood and river soaked soil. His furious eyes still aglow, he stood statuesque, unassailable. The Kion coiled its undulating spiral around Vann's space, like it owned him.

There was no recognition or remnant of compassion in Vann's face. He only knew death, and the thrill of its deliverance.

He was lost to the soul of the dragon.

Something felt very familiar about the scene. The nagging prodded the back of Kir's recollection to rummaging for a memory that she didn't even know the shape of. It felt like the sound of an old priest's voice. Something about the fires of the Gods, and a royal hand of justice.

It didn't matter. There was no time. The glowing blue stone in the soulwhisper spoke with words that Kir couldn't hear, and with an assurance that Kir couldn't bear. It said that Vann was slipping away. No human body could withstand such Godly power for long. It would deplete him as utterly as a desert soaked up a rain shower.

Fighting back consternation and panic, Kir focused on her vambrace, calling to Vann with the words that she was too terrified to produce aloud. Her vambrace was glowing, too, in some alien hue, and she was immediately repelled by an unrecognized barrier. Her voice would never reach him over the roar of the dragon in his head.

She slid from the saddle and advanced, numb to every sensation that clamored for her attention. If Vann registered that she was in danger, and if he was still in there, he might be able to rein in the snakey thing. She would make herself vulnerable. It was a risky gamble—one simple draconian whim would mean her obliteration. But if Vann could not contain the unleashed beast, he would be consumed by it. Living without Vann would be a fate worse than any death Kir could imagine. Vann could no longer hear her voice, so she *must* make him hear her soul.

"Valoria! No! Fall back!" Malacar cried desperately from somewhere worlds away.

Vann, immobile and fixed on a distant, otherwordly plane, did not respond as Kir approached. The dragon, growing more corporeal by the minute, turned its serpentine eyes toward Kir and appraised her with a look that seemed to laugh at her insignificance.

It belched a warning that would have curdled the pluck of the bravest warrior. Mythology claimed that dragons and wildcats were mortal enemies. Kir's wildcat heart would not be swayed by a trash-talking opponent. She had nothing to lose here—nothing but Vann.

Drawing her Guardian sword in outward defiance, Kir continued forward. "He is bound to me by the will of your heavenly masters. You will release his soul, Kion!"

As the dragon unwound its coil from the air around Vann and fixed its intentions on her, Kir half expected to see her life flash before her. Instead, she found herself back on the Kion deck, admiring a banner. She had felt a kinship with the Guardian facing down the dragon in the piece, but never had dreamed that she would be standing in his shoes. She briefly wondered if he had prevailed in *his* battle, and if there was even the slightest hint of hope that she might prevail in hers.

She wasn't the praying sort, since it had never done her much good in the past, but that nagging old priest's voice wouldn't leave her to die without his disapproving torment in her head. There was something more she was supposed to remember. Something from the temple, and all those boring childhood lectures. Was she supposed to be praying to the fires of the Gods...?

"The fires of the Gods," she recalled. "No mere mortal can tame the fires of the Gods..."

She tried for the rest of the verse. It was from the Book of Order, but the words escaped her. Trying to secure the remainder, a jumble of images tripped over her recollections. Pieces of myth and legend retold—from the Hilians and their Kion, and the old priests. They all told the story of fire... dragons... royal wielders of justice or something...

*In days of old, Kings held power over the dragons to protect Order. The day has long since passed that their glory is needed here... harbinger of justice and peace...*

The forgotten verse came to her suddenly, and she couldn't stop herself from voicing it aloud. "As man is a fragile being, born of divinity but mortal still, the royal avatar of justice was consumed by the power of the Kion and his soul rent asunder."

The dragons...the Kions...were emblazoned on the very pages of royal history. Their mark was on the royal seal, and branded onto Kir's shoulder blade. It was written into the ancient tales, and carved on royal chairs. It was on her tabard, embossed on her vambrace, and on her Guardian sword. The dragon was inlaid into every fiber of royalty because royalty represented the Godly hand in a very real sense. Kir had always thought the comparison was figurative, but she realized, in the face of the dragon before her, that the stories were not just figments of a Creative's mind.

It was said that the dragons were meant as a protection for the world, and a force to prevent the abuse of magic, like the Forbiddens. That's why the royal family was gifted the use of such unlimited magic. They were the hands meant to dish out justice. If the Forbiddens were the key to unlocking the fury of the Kion, it was no wonder that Vann's dragon had been loosed. The question was, how to rechain it.

"And the Gods created for him an equalizer, to balance him."

Kion-Eska. Dragon Guards. The Guardians.

It all came together in that realization. The true purpose of the Guardians was not to serve as royal bodyguards, but to serve as dragon guards, as the old name suggested. To protect the royal from his own weapon. They were the equalizers. The balance to the Godly power. They had the magic to contain what the royal avatar of justice could not. Vann was the wielder, his Guardians were the sheathe.

In the space of her last thought, the Kion struck. It rushed with a chilling heat that dried her eyeballs. In a vain attempt to shield, Kir thrust her glowing vambrace upward. Half expecting instant oblivion, she found validation when the Kion bounced back. The vambrace had repelled it.

Snakey shook his gourd out from the slap of vambrace and tilted to get a good scan on Kir from different angles.

Kir tightened her grip on the hilt of her Guardian sword. If she had repelled the Kion, perhaps she could fight it. When it launched again, she boldly thrust outward, bracing for the coming impact. The jarring of metal against energy threw sparks and almost wrenched the weapon from her grasp, so she dug her heels into the soil for leverage.

The Kion recoiled.

If she hadn't been about to plant her face in the dirt from exhaustion, Kir might have thrilled in this ludicrous combat. Her strength, however, was abandoning her, and she had only enough vitality left for a bluff. She threw a barrage of Dimishuan taunts and phrases with wild abandon, strung together with reckless laughter.

The Kion dipped his head like it understood. He seemed intrigued, and maybe even amused. He wreathed her, never dropping his eye lock. The two orbited, braced in a spiraling dance, neither backing off. Kir realized that she was behind Vann now, closing in on his flank.

Finally, she stopped, an arms-length away. The Kion stared her down, offering no submission to her challenge. He looked like he was calculating the ideal moment to strike again. He had seen through the bluff.

Kir's leadened arms could not even lift the sword one last time, so she thrust it into the scorched ground. She couldn't contain the ocean in a thimble, after all, and no weapon of steel could douse the flames of the heavens.

Lili had suggested that the Dimishuan language was the ancient tongue of the Gods. If there was any way to communicate with Snakey, that was the only way Kir could figure to do it.

"Put away your holy gauntlet, Kion," Kir commanded firmly in Dimishuan. "Your job is done. Now leave me to mine." She turned and grasped the folds of Vann's tunic, pressing her head into his back. "Stick, come back and chain your wenchin animal."

*Never turn your back to an enemy. You invite his eager blade.* Kir could hear Kozias' words clearly, though it seemed pathetically shallow advice now. When she dropped her eye lock with the beast, she had yielded to the inevitable. It was fine, this ending, Kir reminded herself. If she was to die, she could think of no better place than clutching her soulwhisper.

Kir's eyes were clenched tightly. An instant river of tears soaked into Vann's tunic, but she held firm, waiting for the Kion's final strike. It came suddenly, a roaring icy cyclone that pummeled her, stinging her exposed skin with blades of grass and flecks of dirt. Her fingers clutched tightly at the handfuls of fabric, but the winds did not rip her away from Vann, as she'd expected. Instead, the pressure created by the violent gyration pressed her firmly against him.

Kir Valoria grit her teeth, held her breath, and laughed at the end.

## -64-
## Rabbit Turned Dragon

*Wars are not won on the battlefield, but in the court.*
*Not with a warrior's calculating snarl, but with*
*a politician's conniving smile.* - Master Kozias

The winds abruptly ceased and the rigid wall of muscle that was Vann's back relaxed.

"Keep my animals chained, huh? Does that include you? Ambria Persimmons never made so worthwhile a suggestion." Vann's voice was droll-soaked and dripping.

Kir shuddered with relief. "You've already got me chained," she quipped, though her shaky voice was muffled against his shirt.

Vann turned and locked her securely in his arms. His eyes no longer glowed, and the dragon was gone.

"I heard you, Kiri," Vann said. "And you didn't even have to shout."

"Oh, I was too petrified to shout out loud, but my brain was screaming," Kir managed.

Vann's body shook, and when Kir glanced up, she realized he was laughing. "I always knew you were reckless, but facing down a dragon?"

"I had to give the name Valoria a test run, ya know?" Kir managed a weak chuckle. "That's a big assertion to live up to."

"Not for you," Vann said, wiping away a humored tear. His eyes were sunken and weary, even through his smile.

A murmur rippled through the scorched grasses, a prayer-like chant that raised the hair on Kir's arms. "Kion," it echoed, in pulsing repetition.

Vann and Kir turned their heads to see every Hilian prostrated before them, their foreheads touching the blackened soil in reverence. Kir had almost forgotten they were there during her little spar with Snakey.

When Ulivall broke through the crowd, he approached Vann reverently. "The Gods have spoken through your victory here, Your Majesty. I will boldly speak for my people, and the Hili army. Your will is ours. You have but to command, and we will obey. If the Gods have granted you their hand in the form of the Kion, allow us to be your tools."

Vann hesitated. He looked uncertain, or unnerved. "I would rather have friends than tools."

Ulivall raised a hand. "Then friends you have. The Circle shall hear of this, and I know they will back you. Even Ferinar, who has proclaimed loyalty in your absence, will be anxious to serve, I am certain. For we cannot deny the will of the Kion, of which you embody."

Malacar and Scilio had arrived and slipped up behind them at some point, and they placed steadying hands on Vann's shoulders to keep him upright. "Majesty, you look absolutely spent."

Vann sighed heavily. "A dragon is the heaviest weapon I've ever wielded."

Kir, still held tightly against Vann's chest, closed her eyes. She dared not step away, for fear of crumpling right to the ground. There was no longer a rigidity to her knees, no longer the energy to stand upright. Vann's arms were her backbone and her brace against the greedy pull of gravity. The voices around her grew hazy and distant, as though she were listening from underwater.

From a far away place, Kir could hear a deep and rhythmic chanting, undulations of names she knew.

Vannisarian. Kion. Saiya Kunnai.

And a new name that overshadowed them all.

Valoria.

* * *

"I do not think friends are so troublesome," Bertrand argued. He withdrew his mana from Kir's thorax and frowned.

"Of course they are. Friends are the most troublesome of all," Kir countered. She propped herself on her elbow and picked up her waiting cards. "That's how you know they're your friends. When they drive you crazy but you still want to be around them."

Bertrand looked bewildered. "I do not understand your logic." He retrieved his own hand and scrutinized each card individually with perplexed examination.

"Let us know if ever you do," Scilio put in merrily. His head was in Lili's lap and he was staring at her chest. "You will be the first."

Kir made a face at the Bardian, and Vann couldn't help but laugh.

She, Malacar and Dailan had been teaching Bertrand to play pebble-ante card games all evening, between their hourly healing sessions. After three days of Bertrand's attention, she was finally beginning to get her old feistiness back. Bertrand had assured them that Kir would be completely healed by the end of the week. When she was well, they could resume their journey downriver. Back to Vann's new home in Hili. Back to the obscurity of exile...

A nagging feeling prodded him. It seemed perfectly logical to return to safety. What was so inherently wrong with that?

Ulivall had wholeheartedly welcomed Vann's request for asylum in Hili. He had been extremely sympathetic, especially after learning of Palinora's death, and he seemed to have adopted a fatherly air. Perhaps Ulivall felt a parental responsibility to look after him in place of his parents. He seemed to have replaced their distant friendship with a relationship that hovered between paternal interest and reverent worship. He had been overly zealous and willing to jump at Vann's command, even offering the unquestioning support of the Hili army. It was everything Vann had hoped to achieve through diplomacy. It had only taken the unleashing of a dragon, he thought wryly.

Ulivall had also shown immense paternal compassion for Kir. He viewed her as a true daughter and Vann had never seen such pride in the man as when he presented Kir with her newly-forged throwing knife, emblazoned with the Ithinar Steel symbol. Every waking moment not dedicated to his troops was spent at her bedside. It was a gesture that Kir had never known from a parent until Palinora's affections, and she seemed truly touched by Ulivall's concern.

Kir's popularity amongst the Hilian soldiers had only exploded. It had taken two days, but when Vann had regained enough energy to walk, he had taken a stroll through the camp. He had not passed by a single warrior that did not gush like a schoolboy over the Saiya Kunnai. She had tamed the Kion, after all. If Kir had attracted devotees, Vann would be the first in line.

"Dagnabber's trying to snatch points away, Bertrand," Kir cautioned. "He's tricksier than a fox. Don't let him cheat you."

"How do I prevent him from doing so?"

"I'd whack him with a paper fan, but since we don't have one handy, you gotta talk trash to him," she said. "Keeps him on the wares so he knows you're watching him."

"Talk trash?" Bertrand threw a glance to the waste sack waiting for disposal by the tent flap. "How does that occur?"

"I dunno... just tell him creatively not to cheat."

"Very well. Do not cheat me creatively," Bertrand said pointedly to Dailan.

"Who needs to cheat with the likes of this lot?" Dailan cackled. "You all's dumber with a split stack of Queens than bricks is on a beach."

"Perhaps... but I know... where you keep your... pilfered accumulation... you deviant-louse-mite," Bertrand said, hovering upon each point. He tilted his head toward Kir for assurance. "Was that correct? I couldn't comprehend the entire phrasing. You were thinking it too quickly."

Kir had obviously tried to feed Bertrand a retort Psychonically. Her cheeks puffed and she couldn't restrain the chuckle. "Good try. We'll work on it."

Watching Kir facilitate an exchange between Dailan and Bertrand was fascinating from Vann's perspective. The two boys could not be more opposite in personality and social acumen, but through Kir, they had come to some semblance of an alliance. Vann suspected it was largely due to Dailan's appetite for acquisition in direct juxtaposition to Bertrand's ease of relinquishment. Rocks notwithstanding, the win was as rewarding to Dailan as any material gain. Regardless of who had the upper hand, they seemed to be enjoying themselves. Neither of the boys had experienced childhood in a normal regard, so the connection was good for both of them.

It didn't matter that they were so different, really. Kir and Vann had teetered on the opposite ends of a fulcrum, yet they were inching toward the balanced middle, too. There were no differences in the world too deep to be overcome by a bridge of commonality.

Vann propped his elbow against the pillow of his futon. His fingers moved quickly on the paper dragon he was folding as he watched Kir. Her hair was unbound, the way Vann liked it, and it spilled gently over her shoulders. Her cheeks were a healthy flush and her eyes radiant. Although she was still terribly thin, she looked healthier than she did even before her injury. She was beyond beautiful.

From her periphery, Kir noticed his gazing and asked, "Do you want to play?"

"No. I'm enjoying watching you."

"Yeah, I kinda noticed. It's creepy getting stared at. I'm glad *one* person—" she hooked at thumb at Bertrand, "—in this tent doesn't stare at me like you do. Not anymore, at least."

Vann's cheeks flushed and Bertrand began rocking on his haunches.

"Why is that, Bertrand? Why can't you look at people in the eye, unless you're healing them?" Kir asked with the bluntness of a spoon. She displayed her winning hand prominently in Dailan's face to goad him.

Bertrand continued to rock and his fingers flicked across his cards. "Peoples' eyes repel me. So I use other ways to see them."

Kir's fingers fumbled over her newly won rocks. She blinked a few times, the way she always did when she was processing some profound bit of knowledge. Then, she met Vann's gaze. "Other ways to see. I can understand that, kid."

Ulivall, with Copellian behind, poked his head through the tent flap. "May we enter?"

Malacar waved them in. "You're just in time. We were about to start another hand."

When Copellian sat next to Kir, she handed him the freshly shuffled deck. "Your deal, Cope."

He growled. "I told you..."

"I know, I know. We'll settle that score in the morning," Kir smirked. "*Cope.*"

"Kiriana Valoria," Vann scolded mildly, taking pride in the use of her new name. "Brothers and sisters shouldn't fight."

"That's what they do best," Kir returned. "Since you grew up unburdened with siblinghood, I wouldn't expect you to know that, but it's just the way the dragon roars." She sniggered at her own unintentional joke.

Vann shook his head. "At least wait a little longer. I want to enjoy a few days of your unblackened eyes. They've been so wreathed in shadow lately."

Bertrand shrugged. "Fear no marks of black and blue. My healing talents are above all."

Kir ignored him. She glowered at Vann, her features twisted in insult. "Keh! You actually think I'd let this flunkey land one on *me*? I was gonna grind his haughty jib into the dirt with one swing."

Copellian toggled between the two, then scowled. "I will not settle this tomorrow. When I beat you, I don't want people to say it was because I took advantage of an invalid."

"Invalid?!"

Ulivall's warm laughter filled the tent. "And here I was honestly worried that they wouldn't get along..."

The banter continued back and forth, and it was clear by Copellian's cool attitude that he held Kir in a slightly higher regard than in weeks prior. Though, he was incredibly smug with each winning hand he waved in front of her.

Vann wondered if the previous tension between them had been born of their grating similarities. Ships sailing parallel run the risk of colliding. The two instant siblings seemed to be sailing on common course, and fighting over the same wind in the process.

"Are you relieved, Your Majesty? Your fate has been postponed," Lili commented conversationally between hands. She had accompanied the army to offer attendance to Palinora but her duties were now to Vann's party, an assignment to which Scilio had made boisterous laudation.

Vann regarded the woman curiously. "What do you mean?"

"The moonless night. It is upon us. There is no possibility of the Chaos Bringer's birth on this cycle."

It all came together for Vann at that instant. The vision pummeled him like a cascading rock slide and his fingers dropped the nearly-finished paper dragon.

*Arms of emerald flame, driven as if by a living wind, snaked through the shanties and boathouses of Hilihar. The screams of Dimishuan children rent the billowing smoke, as the city crumbled into the poached lake, a water-kissed pyre. Amidst the writhing energy, two serpentine goldenrod eyes hunted, and there was laughter at the cataclysm...*

Vann pulled himself from the depths of his mind and his eyes shot upward, examining the canvas of the tent's ceiling, as though he could see the pending black night through it. He had been intended for his father's holy chamber this night. And that chamber, the gateway to chaos, was a world away. He had been spared his destiny for now. But...

"Vann? What's wrong?" Kir's alarmed voice shattered the smooth, cold surface of his fear. He inhaled sharply, only now aware that he had been holding his breath.

"The moonless night. If not for the Keepers, I would have been in that chamber right now," he breathed.

Kir and Malacar exchanged furtive glances.

"That's good, Vann. You're here with us, and not in your father's clutches," Kir soothed. "Now we can just wait in Hilihar for the Soul Collectors to drag his sorry *neeyah* to the basement of hell."

Vann blanched and he willed himself to breathe steadily. "That's just it. We can't wait. Because *he* won't."

Ulivall's brow fell. "He will come to claim you. Wherever you are."

Vann nodded. "If he's dying, he won't be able to wait. It's six months until the next moonless night, and that will probably be his last chance to carry out whatever foul deed he's planning. So he'll come, and he'll fight for me."

Vann picked up the tiny paper dragon and folded his gaze into it. The Kions were said to have been sleeping for centuries, as they were no longer needed in the world. It seemed that something had kicked them to wakefulness, and it was possible that the continued use of Forbidden magic in Vann's presence had been the spur in his Kion's side. If it had happened to Vann, it stood to reason that it had happened with his father, too.

"My overactive imagination hammered me with a grim vision. I saw my father's Kion laying waste to Hilihar. I think my mind was warning me of the possibility," Vann continued.

Scilio was lost in a pensive expression. "But Hili is protected by powerful defensive magics. He cannot just waltz in."

"Of course he can," Ulivall corrected. "If he accesses his Kion, that is. As a Shunatar, you should know this better than anyone."

Scilio's features hovered in puzzlement. "I'm afraid I am out of touch with my Shunatar ways..."

"Our barriers and protections only work against mankind. Creatures of the Gods, like Shunatars and the King's Kion, would be immune to our castings."

"Wait a minute," Scilio chimed, pointing a delighted finger at his own chest. "Creature of the Gods, you say?"

"Shunatars...Xavien! That's why he was able to move about undetected and undeterred in Hili," Vann realized aloud.

"Keeper Xavien is a Shunatar?" Ulivall seemed shocked. He threw a questioning glance at Kir.

"Damnation! I knew I was forgetting something. He has purple eyes like Scilio."

Scilio's chin raised a pride-laden inch. "Creature of the Gods..."

"That is useful information, and we will have to reconsider our security," Ulivall said. "But what concerns me more is the safety of the Hili people. I do not wish to see the King's Kion unbridled in our homewaters."

"You need not fear Soventine," Vann said, steeling the butterflies that were dancing in his stomach. "I'm not going back to Hili."

Every eye, save Bertrand's, widened in astonishment. There was utter silence.

Finally, Malacar spoke the question that surely weighed on every mind. "What is your plan, Majesty?"

"I will go to him."

An uproar of protest, chaotic and urgent, assaulted Vann, but he waved his hand for silence. "And I will introduce him to *my* Kion."

"You wage war with the King? With what army?" Kir asked.

"My own," Vann grinned mischievously. "I cannot win military loyalty while hiding in a swamp, and I cannot fight my father, even with the entire Hili army at my back. Instead, I will play the game my father's way. I will smile, I will scheme, and I will rip the royal carpet from under his wobbly legs."

Kir whistled in appreciation. "Wenchin furies, Stick. You're growing a wily side."

Ulivall nodded sagely. "You will dance the steps politic, wearing the mask of the filial son. The King will not harm you and you will have six months to put a plan in motion. Very impressive."

"But know this," Vann cautioned darkly, his eyes falling to rest on Kir. "And I want this message relayed to Ferinar and the Tree Vipers. When the time comes for the rebellion, I will suffer no other to dirty their hands with the King's foul blood. If my father is to fall before his time, it will be by my hand alone."

He handed Kir the completed paper dragon and solidified his confidence in her pride-laden smile.

For the first time in his fugitive life, Vann felt the wind changing direction. He would not run this time. There were a million impossible tasks before him. He must sweep aside the Keeper army that waited ahead. He must smile in the faces of the High Priest who would kill him and his father who would destroy him. He had to steal the loyalty of the royal military, sway the support of the court, and win the heart of the woman he loved. Under the very nose of his greatest enemy.

That wasn't so much to ask for.

The world had been tracking a vulnerable rabbit. But they were about to find a wildcat.

Or perhaps, a dragon.

# Epilogue

General Werther Farraday stood on the hilltop overlooking a black cloud. The Keeper army lay, three thousand strong, spread across the mouth of the great mountain pass, hugging either side of the river.

Farraday had been furious at his recent demotion. Aquiline, of all places! A dead island harboring nothing but ignorant miners, spoiled university whelps, and barbaric savages. Fort Krigdall was a filthy rat-trap. It was carved into the northern Arshenholm mountainside, stony, stark and cold. Farraday was a man of the city. He'd entertained aspirations for an appointment in High Empyrea, but these rock and limestone barracks were a far cry from cultured civilization. Noble-born men deserved noble-born privileges, not tomb-like caves.

The Gods, however, must have found irony in his situation, for they had turned his nightmare into a dream.

The terrorist group known as the Keepers of Magic had decided to wage a war, and Farraday was now sitting on the edge of history.

How ironic, that. He was about to protect the young nipper whose escape had led to his demotion. Personally handing the gift-wrapped princeling over to the King would have been sweet enough, but the boy also came with an additional bonus. That splendid Guardian wench would be a prize. He would take great delight in capturing her heart, or her body, whichever came first. She had welcomed the pursuit, verbally invited it, even.

Farraday was a man of the hunt, and he knew that she would not be easy prey. She was a Guardian, which would be a hurdle in itself, especially once the princeling was recognized to the world. Farraday had held Vannisarian's Guardians captive before, but he bore no legal ramifications to such an act, as the prince did not *officially* exist at the time. Once Vannisarian was announced and acknowledged, however, Farraday would have no choice but to follow the letter of the law where the Guardians were concerned.

It was an obstacle, but one which made the thrill even greater. He would steal the wench, right out from under the princeling's nose.

Farraday chuckled to himself. A Guardian wench—imagine that! She would look divine on his arm. And in his bed.

His musings were interrupted by a young, eager voice. "Your orders, sir."

The private handed a Blood-Bonded message scroll over and banged his fist against his chest.

Farraday slit his index finger against the crisp parchment edge and pressed his thumb south of the cut, coaxing a line of crimson to the surface. When the seal hissed open, Farraday scanned his orders in detail. He could not hide the smile that inched along his handsome visage.

"Private, send for my officers. The Keepers will shudder today. We're off to war."

When your father is a God,
don't let it go to your head.

**SHUNATAR'S FOLLY**
**Book Three of The Guardian Vambrace**

**www.guardianvambrace.com**

## About the Author

H. Jane Harrington is given to hermitship and flights of fancy. She is a science and history buff, an otaku, a scifi, fantasy and western aficionado, a student of Japanese culture and language, and a collector of general knowledge and outhouses. She lives in Birmingham, Alabama, with her husband, two children, basement-dwelling mother-in-law, and a small zoo. She is a champion of nerds and geeks everywhere.

She can be contacted at
hjaneharrington@guardianvambrace.com

\* \* \*

For more Guardian goodies, check out my website:

**www.guardianvambrace.com**

24019871R00165

Made in the USA
Charleston, SC
09 November 2013